P9-AFJ-457

ERNESTO'S GHOST

ERNESTO'S
GHOST

A Novel

Edward Gonzalez

Transaction Publishers
New Brunswick (U.S.A.) and London (U.K.)

Library of Congress Catalog Number: 2001054611
ISBN: 0-7658-0135-3
Printed in Canada

Library of Congress Cataloging-in-Publication Data

Gonzalez, Edward.
    Ernesto's ghost / Edward Gonzalez.
        p. cm.
        ISBN 0-7658-0135-3 (acid-free paper)
            1. Cuba—History—1959—Fiction. 2. Intelligence officers—Fiction.
3. Americans—Cuba—Fiction. 4. College teachers—Fiction. I. Title.

PS3607.O56 E76 2002
813' .54—dc21   2001054611

Contents

Acknowledgments

Over the course of writing this novel, I became indebted to Hal and Sue Dale, Ann Giacommeti, Jennifer Gonzalez, Rosalie Heacock Thompson, Beth Levin, Kathleen McDonnell, James Mulvenon, Norm Petersen, George Plinio Montalvan, Yolanda Porro, Luanne Rohrbach, David Ronfeldt, Michael Swaine, Tom Szayna, and Bruce Weiss. They read early drafts, made useful suggestions, and offered much appreciated encouragement. Additionally, Jennifer helped me compose a poem for the novel, while Bruce performed yeoman service by reading and commenting on the novel's many drafts. Irving Louis Horowitz deserves special mention for his wise counsel and support, and for his faith in my ability to write a work of fiction.

In the last of many rewrites, I benefited from the professional advice of Jonathan Estrin and the editorial efforts of Marian Branch. Marian not only helped me with my prose, but also noted other ways I could improve the novel. Anne Schneider of Transaction Publishers further rendered the novel more readable through her editorial contributions. Lastly, Kelly Schwartz, my proofreader, was invaluable in meticulously going through and polishing the finished product.

Edward Gonzalez
Malibu, California

Main Characters

Captain Joaquín Acosta, a State Security officer in the Ministry of Interior

Marina Alvarez, an escort in the Ministry of Foreign Relations

Lawton Armstrong, a senior CIA officer in the Directorate of Operations

Fidel Castro, Cuba's charismatic leader

Catalina Cruz, an escort in the Ministry of Foreign Relations

David Diamond, a California university professor conducting research in Cuba

Manuel Domínguez, a mid-level defector from the Ministry of Foreign Relations

Gustavo (Gustavito Durán), a homosexual Cuban poet

Sheila Frankel, an American expatriate and communist in Cuba

Rudy García, a CIA officer in the Directorate of Operations, responsible for Cuba

Isabela and Teresa, two sisters staying at the Hotel Habana Libre

Los muchachos, "the boys"—Chucho (Ramírez), Roberto, and Tomás

Lt. Colonel Antonio Martel, a Cuban army officer and friend of David Diamond

Cindy Mays, David Diamond's research assistant

Carlos Rafael Rodríguez, a member of the Politburo of the Cuban Communist Party

Carlos Salsamendi, a top aide to Carlos Rafael Rodríguez

Don Smith, a CIA analyst in the Directorate of Intelligence

Philip Taylor, a disillusioned Canadian socialist working in Cuba

Lieutenant José Torres, assistant to Captain Joaquín Acosta in the Villa Marista

Peter Vargas, a university professor acquainted with Diamond

Acronyms and Organizations

CDRs   Committees for the Defense of the Revolution, block organizations responsible for neighborhood surveillance in Cuba

DGI   General Directorate of Intelligence in the Ministry of Interior, charged with directing Cuba's foreign intelligence operations

ETA   The Basque terrorist organization

FAR   The Revolutionary Armed Forces of Cuba

MININT   Cuba's Ministry of Interior

MINREX   Cuba's Ministry of Foreign Relations

PCC   Communist Party of Cuba, established by Fidel Castro in 1965

PSP   Popular Socialist Party, Cuba's pre-1959 Moscow-oriented communist party

State Security   Part of Cuba's Ministry of Interior, responsible for ensuring internal security and rooting out conspiracies in and outside the government

Prologue

David awoke. For several seconds, he was unable to remember his whereabouts. He was cold. A skimpy blanket had scarcely provided warmth during the night. He was stiff from lying on his side, curled up on a hard cot. His head ached from too little sleep. The light overhead made him squint. Finally, with difficulty, he looked down at his wrist, only to find that his watch was missing. He had no idea what time it was; the lighted room had no windows. Turning onto his back, he stared at the stark, bright lightbulb screwed into the ceiling. Why had it been left on all night? And why was it in a protective steel cage as if he were in some kind of institution? Then the stench assaulted him, as it had when the guard had shoved him into the cell. His heart lurched when he remembered why he had been thrown into this hellhole.

He shuddered, recalling the awful dream—the nightmare—that had awaken him despite his fatigue. He had dreamed of Catalina. The green-eyed, black-haired beauty, Catalina. But the Catalina of his dream was not the spirited woman he had come to love with an intense passion that was missing from his previous relationships. This Catalina's eyes were hollow. Lifeless. She was haggard. Frightened. In the dream she seemed almost broken as she faced her interrogator from State Security in some brightly lit room in the Villa Marista.

Joaquín. Yes, the interrogator was Joaquín. He was hurling questions and accusations at her, demanding to know why she had fallen in love with the *norteamericano*. Catalina hadn't answered. Had her silence been prompted by prudence or doubts about whether she actually loved him? Or was it because of Ernesto? David hoped not. He would be unable to gain her love if she still couldn't let go of her beloved Ernesto. As the nightmare continued to unfold, Joaquín stepped up his incessant questioning.

"Didn't I warn you," he had screamed at her, *"that David Diamond was working for the CIA?"* Her eyes lowered, Catalina made no response. *"How could you betray Fidel and the revolution?"* he had demanded, but again she was silent. *"And how could you betray me and especially Ernesto?"* he had demanded in the incredulous, aggrieved voice of a jilted lover or cuckolded husband. She looked at him finally. He had struck a responsive chord.

"But I didn't betray you, Fidel, or the revolution," she had replied weakly. *"And don't you dare,"* she had added more forcefully, *"ac-*

cuse me of betraying Ernesto." Her eyes had flickered with anger for an instant, but then she lapsed into silence again, defeated. The nightmare had ended with her bowing her head to avoid the wrathful stare of her tormentor.

Now fully awake, David sat up, agitated. Hugging his knees tightly to his chest, he tried to calm himself; the nightmare had been so real, so foreboding. He feared for Catalina. For her future. He would be powerless if Joaquín decided to go after her. The State Security Captain already knew too much. "That bastard!" he exclaimed, knowing that he too would be facing him. How could he have been so careless? Why hadn't he done more to protect Catalina after he discovered Joaquín's suspicions about him and the CIA? "And damn you too, Rudy García," he cursed aloud, "for whatever game you and the CIA are playing with my life!"

He steadied himself. Despair could neither accomplish nor change anything. Losing his head over their predicament certainly wouldn't help Catalina or him. No. He had to get his mind off their plight. He had to get back to sleep. He would need a clear head if he was to save her and himself. He would need to outwit his interrogators, otherwise it would be the end for both of them. Of course, that was what Joaquín or whoever else from State Security was running the show was banking on—that he would be too worn down to defend himself, too confused to avoid incriminating her. Finally, in a desperate bid for sleep, he lay his head down on the cot, pulled up what passed for a blanket, and closed his eyes.

Still, his mind kept churning. Again and again he tried to refocus, first by reviewing in his head the latest scholarly book he had read, but the exercise didn't hold his attention for long. Nothing else worked either. Whatever imaginative trick he tried, his train of thought would invariably return to Catalina and the chain of events that had led to the Villa Marista.

Only seven months ago his life seemed to be coming together. He had thought of himself then as being more or less happily married. A junior professor, making a name for himself at the university, he was committed to Cuba, with plans to revisit the island to do research. Yes, he had everything going for him in the spring of 1974. Then his whole life began to change in ways that he never would have thought possible.

***

1

The True Believer

His posted office hours over, David Diamond ushered the last of his students out of his office and returned to his desk. The letter that he had been expecting from the Social Science Research Council had arrived earlier in the afternoon. It now lay before him on his desk. He read it once more. He had been awarded a grant to conduct field research in revolutionary Cuba—the only passion remaining in his life.

The letter served only as a momentary distraction as he soon began to brood once more over his wife's admission. Her words on that dismal Sunday morning more than six weeks earlier continued to haunt him. She had confessed an affair, with one of her law firm's senior partners, no less.

"For crying out loud," Julie had countered when he accused her of destroying their marriage by her infidelity. *"We're living in 1974, not 1954. Lots of married people nowadays have affairs. For all I know, you've been screwing some of your students just like when you were at Berkeley."*

Her reference to his earlier affairs had only made matters worse. Like so many of his contemporaries back then, he thought nothing of sleeping with his students. That had been part of the raucous Berkeley scene of the late 1960s and early 1970s when he was a teaching assistant. And being the defiant, radical student he was, he had fully expected to continue his philandering after he married and took up his assistant professor position at the University of Southern California. God knows, too, there was many a time in the two years that followed when he was sorely tempted by some of the coeds in his classes. They would openly flirt with him. But as a married professor, he held back, never crossing the line.

He was not acting simply out of prudence—from fear of the repercussions that would ensue were it discovered that he was having affairs with undergraduates. Nor was his restraint prompted by ethical considerations about abusing his position as a teacher. Unlike many of his former contemporaries at Berkeley, he had never traded grades for sex. No, the truth was that after he married he realized he didn't want to behave like his father, whom he blamed for his own unhappy childhood. He wanted his own children, once they were born, to be spared the kind of trauma he had experienced from his parents' constant quarreling over his father's many affairs. So, hoping for the loving, trusting marriage his parents never had, he stopped fooling around after he married Julie.

Until that awful Sunday, he had thought that Julie wanted the same thing from their marriage and was playing by the same rules as he. When she finally told him the truth, he found it difficult to deal with her infidelity. Two days later, he moved into a small, furnished studio apartment in the mid-Wilshire district not too far from campus. He immersed himself in his classes and departmental affairs as an antidote to his rage, jealousy, and sense of betrayal. He hit the bars at night. But nothing worked. The Gods had played a bitter joke on him: He had deliberately passed up several opportunities to go to bed with his female students, only to end up the cuckolded husband. And now, Cuba remained as the only thing in life he could still feel passionate about.

***

David took comfort in the way his career was taking off. When he had been hired as an assistant professor two years earlier, he feared that his outspoken support for the Cuban revolution would relegate him to the role of token radical on an otherwise conservative campus. But his fears had proven groundless. He became the department's most popular teacher, known for both his erudition and his irreverent style. Three articles in prestigious scholarly journals made him the department's rising star. Provided he finished his book, he and his closest colleagues were certain he would be promoted to tenure within two years.

That his long association with the New Left and his endorsement of the Cuban revolution had not hurt his academic career was testimony to his keen intellect. During two trips to Cuba in the late 1960s as a young freelance journalist, he had been swept up both intellectually and emotionally by Fidel Castro's charismatic rule, by the Cuban leader's commitment to social justice, and by his government's unyielding defiance of the United States. For David, revolutionary Cuba represented the antithesis to what he liked least about the American way of life—its crass materialism, corporate power, concentrated wealth, unbridled individualism, and imperial-like dominance of the Third World.

Though he later moderated his tone when he began writing more scholarly, less-impassioned papers and articles for academic audiences, David remained a strong supporter of Castro's policies. Cuba's "tropical communism," he would claim, was a unique social experiment that was "fundamentally different from the stultifying grayness of Soviet-style communism." David could be persuasive, too. Even his severest critics—and there were many—acknowledged that he pressed his arguments with rigor and a broad command of the facts. As a result, he had the attention not only of people on the Left, but also of more moderate observers of the Cuban revolution.

And now, in early April 1974, his hard work had paid off. The much-coveted grant from the Social Science Research Council would enable him to take the 1974–75 academic year off. If everything went according to schedule, he would carry out his field research in Cuba during late summer and fall, and finish his book on comparative socialist revolutions when he got back. Once published, the book would assure him of tenure in his department as well as outside job offers.

He sighed. Though he tried not to, he began thinking once more about Julie. He suspected she was probably up in San Francisco again, with her lover, *"working on a big legal case,"* as she used to tell him.

He tried smacking himself hard on the temples to rid his mind of such maddening thoughts. He had to get over his jealousy, this sense of betrayal, and once and for all get over his feelings about his wife. Cindy Mays, his research assistant, would soon be arriving for their 4:15 appointment. Through the department rumor mill, he had heard that she had recently broken off her engagement. He also knew word had spread among the faculty and graduate students that he and Julie had separated. He no longer needed to hold back from pursuing Cindy—or anybody else, for that matter.

His wife's affair might have shaken his confidence in his sexual prowess had she not often told him he was a good lover. And this was reinforced by the unusually high number of his female students who always seemed to find one pretext or another for visiting him during office hours. Standing six feet tall, he knew he cut a handsome figure: chiseled countenance, long, curly black hair, trim beard, inquisitive blue eyes. As for Cindy, he was hoping she found him more than intellectually stimulating and not too old at thirty-two.

"I've got a lot going for myself," he assured himself as he awaited Cindy's arrival. *"Besides, it's about time that I start living again."*

***

Sitting before his desk, Cindy Mays leaned forward to better show David her notes on the literature search she had finished for him. He could scarcely keep his attention focused on her crabbed, handwritten notes. His eyes repeatedly strayed to look her over. He noticed she had been in the sun since they last met. Her blonde hair was more sun-streaked than ever, and her small, slightly upturned nose was sunburned. Her forearms were a golden tan. In her tight jeans and rolled-up, blue denim shirt that showed off her well-proportioned figure, she looked sexier than ever. She was close enough for him to smell her subtle fragrance. He found it difficult to concentrate on her extensive notes.

"You know," he said finally after some twenty minutes of studious conversation, "I think we need more time to go over all this material in depth."

She looked up at him quizzically, a slight frown forming on her brow. She must have assumed he was about to ask her to return for another session.

"How about having dinner with me tonight, so we can continue this discussion?" he asked casually, in a more intimate tone of voice. She looked at him with surprise. "Besides," he added with a mischievous grin, "I need someone to help me celebrate my getting the grant."

"You got the SSRC grant?" she exclaimed.

"Yep," he replied, pleased by the genuine excitement in her voice. "Learned about it just this afternoon."

"That's terrific! Congratulations. Does that mean you'll be going to Cuba later this summer?"

"I'm keeping my fingers crossed, but I'm pretty sure Havana will give me the visa. Everything I've written about the revolution has been pretty positive." He paused, distracted by the tiny freckles on her nose. Until now, he hadn't noticed them before.

"Anyway, as I was saying," he continued with a renewed sense of assurance, "I really want to celebrate the occasion. And frankly, Cindy, I can't think of anyone else I would prefer inviting out to dinner. So how about it? Are you free tonight?"

She leaned back in her chair and regarded him with her large, inquiring blue eyes. He couldn't tell whether she was indifferent to his proposition or simply surprised by it. The fact that he couldn't made her all the more desirable.

Early on he had discovered that Cindy was like so many of her cohorts in the baby-boom generation: smart, self-absorbed, irreverent about authority, and fully convinced by their sheer numbers that they could define reality. He had always admired their hubris. He also liked boomers because most of them, he found from experience, had few hang-ups about sex. Julie had been that way. He was counting on Cindy being no different.

"I think dinner tonight sounds great," she answered, finally. "However, I'll only go on one condition," she added with a serious expression on her face.

"What's that?" He wondered if she was about to present him with some obstacle to their dinner date.

"That you take me with you to Cuba," she replied teasingly, her look now turning from mock seriousness to one of amusement.

"That's a great idea!"

"I think so, too," she responded in a playful voice. "I'm sure you could use a good research assistant. Right?"

"Absolutely. And believe me, you'd be great to have along. Christ! The Cuban men wouldn't be able to take their eyes off you. They love blondes."

"There, you see how valuable I could be," she agreed, flashing him a tantalizing smile. She was making it unbelievably easy for him. "I bet I could obtain access to lots of Cuban officials that you couldn't because you're a man," she went on coyly. "Maybe I could even meet Fidel," she added laughingly, her eyes bright with amusement at the thought.

"With your looks, Cindy, I'm certain just about anything is possible."

His eyes dropped to her throat and neckline, and the round, firm breasts pressing against her denim shirt. She was the quintessential Southern California girl—blonde, blue-eyed, tanned, and beautiful. In a word, she was a knockout. All of a sudden he felt as if he were back at Berkeley again, hustling girls.

"Anyway," he continued with mock seriousness, "I'll certainly give full consideration to taking you along as my research assistant." He paused to watch her expression. "So now that I've met your condition, we have to decide where to go for dinner."

"Well, make a suggestion," she said, "but don't pick too fancy a place. As you can see, I'm not exactly dressed up."

"You look fantastic," he said, giving her an appreciative glance. She didn't respond, but only looked at him again with the same tantalizing expression, making him wonder whether she was too accustomed to male compliments to acknowledge them, or simply amused by the fact that he was on the make.

"If you like Mexican food," he went on, "we could go over to El Cholo on Western Avenue. They serve killer margaritas and they have some really good specialties as well."

"Oh, I know El Cholo," she replied, enthusiastically. "I've been there lots of times. I mean, who hasn't?"

"Then it's O.K. with you?"

"Sure, El Cholo is one of my favorites."

"Good. So, should I pick you up at your place or meet you at the restaurant?" He was hoping she would ask him to pick her up where she lived.

"I've got to do a few things at the library," she replied after a moment's hesitation. "How about if I meet you at El Cholo around seven?"

"That's perfect," he answered cheerfully, hiding his disappointment.

He kept her a while longer so that they could finish going over some of her notes. He had no intention of spending the entire evening on business.

When at last she stood up to leave, she picked up her purse and notebook and walked toward the door of his office. David used the opportunity to take in the total look of her, the trim, yet sensuous, figure—the small waist, the rounded hips, the lithe legs that couldn't be entirely hidden by her jeans. She seemed to sense he was watching her because at the doorway, she turned and flashed him a warm, beckoning smile.

"See you in a bit," she said in a throaty voice, her blue eyes briefly meeting his. She waved good-bye.

David was elated. First, he had received news of the grant award from the SSRC and now Cindy Mays had agreed to have dinner with him. He smiled, thinking that a few of his colleagues would probably consider a date with Cindy an even bigger trophy than obtaining the grant. If he was reading her right, and he had every reason to believe he was, there was a better than even chance he would be in bed with her that night.

For a few moments he played with the fantasy of taking her along on the field trip as she had proposed, albeit in jest. Apart from the sex, she could make some of his work a lot easier and perhaps even help him gain entry to Cuban officials. But then he quickly dismissed the whole idea. The grant was barely sufficient to support him and he didn't have enough money of his own to cover her expenses. Still, if things worked out between them, they could have fun together in the few months before his departure for Havana. And then he would be back in Cuba, catching up with the changes on the island since his last visit, observing the work of Fidel's government firsthand, energized anew by the Cuban people and the revolution's many accomplishments.

Yes, things were finally starting to look up. No doubt about it. He was on a roll in both his personal and professional life. For the first time in weeks he ceased being consumed by thoughts about Julie and his failed marriage.

***

2

The Messenger

Manuel Domínguez was shivering. The room's air conditioning was on full blast. A thin little man, he suspected it had been turned up to weaken his will rather than to offset the heat and humidity of the July night. He had no idea where he was. He probably had been taken to another one of the safe houses the CIA kept outside Washington, D.C. Captain Joaquín Acosta, attached to State Security in Cuba's Ministry of Interior, had told him the Americans would not risk interrogating him at CIA Headquarters in Langley, Virginia. As a precaution, and as part of their standard operating procedure, they would take him elsewhere. If he was a double-agent, his presence at Headquarters could compromise their own agents.

Captain Acosta's directives had been right so far, Domínguez kept telling himself, struggling to recover his confidence. The week before, when he arrived in the United States, he had been taken to the first safe house, where two CIA officers had interrogated him for three days straight to ascertain whether he was a genuine defector. Then, earlier this evening, he had been put inside a windowless van and, with an escort seated beside him, whisked away to undergo a polygraph test, the one thing he dreaded most.

Captain Acosta had rehearsed him many times at the Villa Marista, the Ministry of Interior's notorious interrogation center, but the twenty- or twenty-five-minute trip to this second CIA safe house had unnerved him. Not only could he not see where the van was going, but the driver had carried out evasive maneuvers, turning abruptly onto side roads, or making quick U-turns to double back on the roads they were on, all of which made him physically ill. When they arrived at last at their destination, he was grateful.

The worst was yet to come. He was requested to undergo two nerve-racking rounds of questioning by the polygraph operator, answering "yes" or "no" to a battery of questions. But each time the operator had been obliged to interrupt the tests. Now, after the second round had been stopped, he could feel the drops of perspiration rolling down his armpits. His cold hands were clammy, too, despite the room's penetrating chill. He had been breathing too hard and doing everything Captain Acosta had warned him against when coaching him back in Havana.

The problem was that the redheaded, crew-cut CIA technician, who was seated behind the glass partition in the sparsely furnished room, was making him more nervous than he had ever been during his rehearsals with Acosta. Jerry, as the man called himself, had become increasingly irritated with him because of the way the testing was going.

"Come on, Manuel," Jerry suddenly exclaimed in an exasperated tone. "You're not cooperating!" He stopped himself abruptly. "You know," he went on a moment later in a calmer, more soothing voice, "this isn't going well at all. Like I told you before, I can't get a good reading when you breathe so hard. Now, please, try to breathe normally this time around. O.K.?"

Domínguez knew the lie-detector test was crucial if the Americans were finally to accept his bizarre story. A week earlier, he had sensed that his two CIA interrogators had not believed him or, worse yet, suspected he was a double-agent sent by the DGI—Cuba's General Directorate of Intelligence.

Six weeks earlier he would have thought it utterly preposterous if someone had told him he would become a defector. Long ago, he had come to accept who he was—an ordinary bureaucrat with no delusions about altering the course of history. Yet, for reasons he didn't understand, he had been chosen by Captain Acosta to deliver a message to the CIA. As he sat in the chair, quietly, attempting to control his rapid breathing, he recalled Acosta's final instructions:

"Mira, chico—*look here, buddy*—*it's really very simple. The only thing you have to do is tell the CIA everything. That's all. No lies, no fabrications, just the whole truth. That's the only message I want you to deliver. And once you convince yourself you're telling them everything you know, I guarantee you'll pass the polygraph test.*"

He took a deep breath, glanced down at the black rubber strap around his chest and the probes attached to his arms. He thought of making love to his wife, Margarita, and then, gulping another deep breath, stared ahead as Jerry began the test for the third time. Once he was through this ordeal, he reminded himself, he would be free to resume his role as an ordinary, insignificant person who would forever drop out of the public limelight.

***

As Domínguez had explained to his CIA interrogators, his story began in June 1974. He was a Second-Secretary in Cuba's Ministry of Foreign Relations, or MINREX, a post he had held for several years. With no illusions of rising much higher in the pecking order, he had been content with his career at MINREX and with the possibility of a future posting to one of Cuba's embassies. Then fate had intervened.

He had stayed late at his office one night, and as he passed by his superior's office upon leaving, he overheard the animated conversation of his boss and three other men. All four were "old communists"—former members of the defunct Popular Socialist Party, or PSP, the pre-1959 Cuban communist party that had slavishly aligned itself with Moscow before and after the revolution. The ex-PSP cadres had been cowed in the late 1960s because of the purge of some of their members by the Castro brothers in the so-called "microfaction" affair. But aided by Moscow, the old communists had staged a comeback after 1970, especially in the Foreign Ministry.

Normally, Domínguez would not have lingered outside his boss's office. However, his ears had pricked up when he heard him remark how Nixon's pending impeachment or resignation over Watergate could provide Cuba with the opportunity to normalize diplomatic relations with a less hostile Ford Administration. With normalization, his boss opined, Fidel would be less able to whip up nationalist support against the Yankees and the power of the *fidelistas* would wane. *"Once that happens,"* his boss continued, *"we real communists can expect to gain much greater influence. And then, Cuba will at last become like other communist states where the Party doesn't have to put up with the likes of a* caudillo *like Fidel."*

As Domínguez informed his CIA interrogators, he had never been a fanatical revolutionary. For that reason, he welcomed the prospect of restoring normal relations with Washington. It would ease Cuba's shortages of food and other necessities. And, contrary to what his boss had assumed would happen, he felt that renewed ties with the United States would prevent Cuba from further becoming like the Soviet Union and other Eastern bloc states. Having witnessed their gray conformity and depressed living standards firsthand two years earlier, he was repelled by what he had seen. Of course, he had never given voice to such subversive thoughts—except once: at a family reunion. After consuming too much beer and rum, he had lost all sense of discretion in a heated political argument with his cousin, Marina Alvarez.

"Look here, Marina," he had blurted out suddenly. *"I've seen conditions in the supposedly more advanced socialist states of the Soviet Union and Eastern Europe. And believe me, if that's what awaits us, then heaven help us because our future will be bleak indeed!"*

The instant he uttered those words he realized he had recklessly put his fate in the hands of Marina. Also employed by the Foreign Ministry, Marina was an *extremista*, an ardent supporter of the government. His only hope at the time was that family ties would prevent her from reporting him to State Security.

But now, back at the Foreign Ministry, he found himself in potentially greater jeopardy. One of the old communists had emerged from his boss's office just as he was slinking away from his listening post. Having been seen, he had no choice but to report what he had overheard to State Security. For all he knew, the man or one of the other old communists in the office could be an informer, in which case he himself would come under suspicion if he didn't report the conversation. Of course, he was sure the *fidelistas* in State Security would immediately suspect the old communists of hatching up another cabal against the government, reminiscent of the microfaction affair several years earlier.

***

The following day, Domínguez went directly to State Security in the Ministry of Interior, or MININT as it was usually called. Once there, he confided to his CIA interrogators, he met a tall officer by the name of Joaquín Acosta. Although Captain Acosta was *moreno*, or dark skinned, his fine, chiseled features made Domínguez suspect that he was not a mulatto but that he had been born to a white, upper-middle-class family. Since he appeared to be in his early thirties, Domínguez also presumed that he had joined Fidel's guerrilla force toward the end of the anti-Batista struggle while still in his teens. Having mentioned all this to his interrogators, Domínguez then continued with his story.

Exuding quiet confidence and authority, Acosta sat silently taking notes while Domínguez recounted the overheard conversation and gave the names of the old communists at the MINREX meeting. The Captain's first words were reassuring.

"First off, *compañero*," Acosta said, "let me compliment you on fulfilling your revolutionary duty. We will, of course, investigate this matter further to see whether there are more people involved beyond those you've identified."

"*Gracias, Capitán. Siempre estoy al servicio de la revolución.*"

"I am delighted to hear that you are ready to serve the revolution," Acosta replied with a hint of sarcasm. "As you see, Manuel—permit me to call you by your first name—we already have a small file on you."

Domínguez was startled. Seeing the brown MININT folder that Acosta had picked up, he immediately remembered his argument with his cousin Marina Alvarez. "*The damn bitch! She ratted on me after all!*" he thought. He became frightened. Even if he was not held for questioning, his career at the Foreign Ministry could be at risk.

"Don't alarm yourself," Acosta continued, reading Domínguez's tense expression. "We here at MININT realize that even a loyal revolutionary may sometimes become confused about the revolution, perhaps even question some of Fidel's policies. We realize that this is normal, *compañero.*"

Acosta paused to let the effect of his words sink in. A hint of a smile crossed his lips as he watched the nervous bureaucrat.

"In any event," the MININT Captain went on, "the government is stronger today than in the first decade of the revolution. Therefore, we can afford to be more tolerant. So relax, we wouldn't even consider imprisoning a Cuban for simply voicing an isolated criticism about the Soviet Union or socialism. I suspect that's what happened in your case, in the heat of your argument with your cousin a few weeks ago."

"Yes, *Capitán* Acosta, that's what happened exactly. Marina can be so . . . "

"On the other hand, Manuel," Captain Acosta broke in, assuming a more serious, official tone, "we all must remain vigilant in seeing that criticism does not turn into organized counterrevolutionary activity. That we cannot tolerate, especially when the imperialist monster is less than 150 kilometers from our shores."

"I fully understand, *Capitán,*" Domínguez replied shakily. "I entirely agree. It was a momentary weakness on my part. I tell you as a true patriot and revolutionary, I am prepared to do whatever you ask."

"Good," Acosta replied. "It is quite possible that you could be of some service to your government. I'll get back to you in a few days.

In the meantime, Manuel, don't tell anyone about any of this, not even your wife."

* * *

As he went on to relate to the two CIA officers, Captain Acosta phoned him five days later. He was to report to MININT headquarters at nine on Saturday morning. He had planned to spend the day with his wife, Margarita, but for all practical purposes he knew that most of Saturday would now be ruined. He lived far out, beyond the Miramar district. Just getting to and from the Ministry of Interior could take upward of a couple of hours, depending on bus connections. Besides, who knew how long he would be at MININT? Worse yet, there was a strong possibility that he would return home upset because of some unpleasant task that Acosta wanted him to perform, like spying and reporting on the activities of his ex-PSP colleagues at the Foreign Ministry.

He did not want to take a taxi to the Ministry of Interior. Perhaps he was being overly cautious as was his habit, but he worried that the taxi driver, possibly someone with whom he was acquainted, would wonder why he was going to MININT headquarters on a Saturday morning. No, despite the time and inconvenience, it was better to take buses. The last one would drop him off at the National Bus Station. From there it would be a short walk to the Ministry of Interior. Determined to give himself plenty of time, he left his home at seven o'clock in the morning.

The first bus was on schedule. The second, more than thirty minutes late, caused him to miss his third bus. After waiting nearly an hour, he decided he had no alternative. He would go the rest of the way by taxi—provided he could find one at this hour on a Saturday morning. Flagging down a cab just ten minutes later, he was about to tell the driver to drop him at the Teatro Nacional, but realized that it would be closed at that hour. Instead, he asked to be let off at the Biblioteca Nacional José Martí. Although the National Library was not as close to MININT headquarters as the Teatro Nacional, it would already be open.

Highly apprehensive, he was in no mood to talk with the driver—a mistake, he soon realized. The man kept glancing at him in the rearview mirror. He was certain that the driver had surmised his true destination. *"Things are starting out badly,"* he thought to himself.

Despite all his fretting, he arrived at the Ministry of Interior, an ordinary-looking eight-story building on the west side of the Plaza de la Revolución, with time to spare. But then a surly, uniformed sergeant kept him waiting at the front desk for several minutes. After initially ignoring him, the guard brusquely asked him the nature of his business. Finally cleared, he was escorted to an elevator and taken up to Acosta's outer office in State Security, arriving there precisely at nine as he had been instructed.

The MININT Captain kept him waiting for nearly fifteen minutes before summoning him into his office. After a brief exchange of pleasantries, Acosta wasted no time in getting to the point. Flustered by the mere fact he was again in MININT headquarters, Domínguez didn't understand what Acosta was telling him at first. Then he grew more and more agitated as Acosta's words began to sink in.

"But *Capitán*," he finally broke in. "I don't fully comprehend what it is that you are asking me to do."

"Let's start over again, *compañero*," Acosta replied condescendingly, amused by Domínguez's evident consternation. "It's really quite simple. We want you and your wife to defect. To be more precise, *we* will stage your defection. You and your wife will leave for Prague in ten days. I'll arrange your trip with your superiors at MINREX. I'll even see to it that your boss is the one to approve your vacation in a fraternal socialist country."

Pleased with the irony of his last remark, Acosta went on. "You'll spend a couple of weeks in Prague, then return to Cuba on a Czechoslovakian airline flight. But en route, you'll defect in Montreal. That's where all passengers must deplane while the plane is being refueled. After you're inside the terminal, you'll announce to Canadian officials that you are a Cuban diplomat and that you and your wife want asylum."

"But what if we're stopped by one of our agents or by some of the passengers from the plane?" Domínguez asked in a strained voice, his face paling with fright.

"You don't have to worry about that. One of our agents will be in the large international lounge after you deplane. He will have been instructed to become distracted for several seconds just as you approach immigration. That will give you and your wife enough time to dash over to the Canadian immigration official. And don't be concerned, the Canadian will immediately let you pass through the outside door. Of course, you will have to have your diplomatic passport in hand to prove your identity."

Acosta got up and walked over to a table on which there was a small electric coffee pot. He poured two *cafecitos*—demitasse-size cups of strong Cuban coffee with a mountain of sugar in each—and gave one to Domínguez, who by now was ashen-faced. Acosta returned to his desk and took a sip from his tiny cup.

"After the Royal Mounted Police interview you," Acosta resumed, "the Canadian government will hand you over to the Americans. You can expect to be interrogated by the CIA and, if you appear to be authentic, you'll then be given a lie-detector test. If they in the end believe your story, and I am going to make sure they do, you will be granted asylum as a bona fide Cuban defector. The CIA will also provide you with money to help you and your wife settle down somewhere."

Acosta stopped to take another sip of his *cafecito*. He gave Domínguez a casual glance before continuing. Domínguez was becoming even more agitated.

"By the way," he said nonchalantly, "the CIA will call on you later if they think you can be of further assistance to them. If so, they'll probably put you under contract and offer you a retainer to help you out financially. Feel free to get as much as you can from the *norteamericanos* and to cooperate with them to the best of your ability. You won't have to worry about any of our agents coming after you."

"I beg your pardon, *Capitán*," Domínguez exclaimed in a high-pitched voice, "but all this sounds preposterous. In the first place, I am a diplomat, not a spy. So the CIA will see through me right away. Besides, my wife and I can't suddenly abandon Cuba and our family and friends. We won't even have time to say good-bye . . . "

Swallowing the last of his coffee, Acosta interrupted him with an impatient wave of his hand. "Calm down, *hombre*," he ordered. "Finish your *cafecito* and try to get a hold of yourself."

"Look, Manuel," Acosta continued moments later, when he saw that Domínguez was doing his best to listen to him, "what you don't realize is that there will be *no* deception. Why? Because you will tell the CIA everything—and by that I mean everything!" He paused as Domínguez appeared more perplexed than ever. "Yes," he explained. "You'll tell them about what you overheard outside your boss's office, your visits to MININT headquarters, your talks with me, and so forth. In fact, you're even to relate to them everything that I've just told you concerning our plans for your defection."

Seeing the look of bewilderment on Domínguez's face, Acosta paused once more. "Of course," he continued with evident satisfaction, "the Americans won't know what to think. In the end, however, they'll believe you precisely because you won't be lying—something that will be confirmed by the lie-detector test they'll give you. And believe me, they take for granted the accuracy of their lie-detector machines."

The MININT Captain stopped as if to see whether his explanation had registered with the dumbfounded Domínguez. Seconds passed and then he leaned forward with his elbows on his desk and stared unblinkingly at Domínguez.

"As for your 'abandoning' the fatherland on such sudden notice," Acosta resumed in a harsh, admonishing voice, "let me remind you that you have nobody left here in Cuba. Your parents and those of your wife are dead. You also don't have any children. On the other hand, both you and your wife have sisters, brothers, and other relatives living either in Miami or New Jersey. I'm sure," he added scornfully, "they'll welcome you with open arms."

At the moment, Domínguez was too frightened to notice the contempt in Acosta's voice. He was also miserable. He was ruing the day he had stopped by his boss's door. "*Had I not done that,*" he kept telling himself, "*I wouldn't now be in this mess.*" His attention was suddenly drawn back to what the MININT Captain was saying.

"Let's be perfectly frank," Acosta was saying in a low, almost intimate voice. "You and I both know that your enthusiasm for the revolution is waning. All this means that you have nothing to lose and everything to gain by your defection to the United States."

Acosta stopped. He was waiting for Domínguez to agree with him or at least say something, but the small man before him remained speechless "*¡Coño!*" he shouted, deliberately allowing his exasperation to show. "For once in your life, show that you have *cojones* and do something for the revolution!"

Struggling to collect his wits, Domínguez tried to think through all the ramifications surrounding his planned defection. "*Acosta could be laying out some elaborate trap,*" he thought. "*In which case I would become a helpless pawn in a game that I don't understand. Or, even if he's on the level, something could go wrong with the plan. The Cuban agent at the airport might become confused and try to prevent our defection. Were that to happen, Margarita and I could get hurt—if not in Montreal, then in Havana if we're forced to return."*

But what else could he do? Prudent by nature, he knew it would be dangerous if not suicidal for him to refuse to cooperate. It was clear Acosta had received his superiors' backing for his wild scheme. At the very least, he would severely compromise himself and risk losing his MINREX position if he turned Acosta down.

"All right," he finally conceded with an air of resignation. "I'll do it, *Capitán* Acosta. But for God's sake, I beg you to make sure that everything goes off as you say it will."

"Don't worry, *compañero*," Acosta answered reassuringly. "Our people are real professionals. You can count on them doing their part. As for you, I'll personally coach you on how to behave with the Americans. And you can be assured I'll see to it that you pass the CIA's polygraph test."

Acosta paused for a moment and stood up. "There is one last thing," he said gravely, looking down at Domínguez. "It's absolutely imperative that you not disclose any of this to your wife. She must not know about the defection until just before you reach Montreal . . . "

"I beg your pardon, *Capitán* Acosta, but I just don't think I could do that to her . . . "

"Look here, Domínguez. Just think about it: If you tell her prematurely about your plans, she'd have too much time to fret about what might happen. She could even become paralyzed with fear. In either case, she'd upset you and spoil our plans."

Walking casually to his office window, Acosta gazed down to the street below. He then came back and stood before Domínguez.

"Now listen carefully. What I want you to do is to wait until twenty minutes before you land at the Mirabel Airport in Montreal. That's when you will tell your wife about the defection and explain to her exactly what she must do. At that point, she cannot hold you back and our man will be ready to facilitate your escape."

"I'll do exactly as you've ordered, *Capitán*."

"Good. Now if you'll wait, I'll have one of our drivers drop you off near your home. I'll also arrange to have a car pick you up and return you to your home when we set up future appointments. That should make things easier for you."

"*Mil gracias, Capitán*."

***

True to his word, Captain Acosta had a MININT car take him to his lessons. Except they were not conducted at headquarters. Domínguez had the fright of his life, he confessed to his CIA interrogators, the first time he was picked up. Instead of heading toward the central part of the city, the MININT car traveled southward on Avenida Rancho Boyeros, past the traffic circle, toward the Víbora district on the city's outskirts. He realized they were taking him to the Villa Marista, State Security's much feared interrogation and detention center. Sure enough, he soon saw the big old house with its large columns, sprawling yard, and tall iron fence so typical of the mansions belonging to a bygone era.

The villa had not always looked so foreboding. Before the revolution, it had been a seminary and a retreat run by the Marist brothers. Ironically, nearly a quarter of a century later, the Villa Marista continued to serve the same purpose—to ensure that Cubans kept the faith, except that now the new religion was Marxism-Leninism.

After being waved through by a MININT guard, the driver drove straight to the front door. Once inside the building, Domínguez felt his heart pounding. He had heard that interrogation sessions were conducted downstairs in the cellar, where he supposed the Marist brothers had once stored their food, wine, and other supplies, but where prisoners were now locked up. For an instant, he couldn't tell where he was being taken. Then, much to his relief, he was escorted up the circular stairway, to the second floor. They turned right and walked halfway down the hallway to an office. Acosta was waiting inside.

"Welcome to the Villa Marista, *compañero*," the Captain said in a voice that struck Domínguez as more business-like than friendly. "This is a better place than headquarters for your lessons on how to deal with your CIA interrogators, including how to convince their polygraph operator of your bona fides."

***

Domínguez had confided to his CIA interrogators that he didn't know how he managed to get through the next few weeks before he and Margarita finally found sanctuary in Canada. His three practice sessions at the Villa Marista with Acosta were draining. In the meantime, he could scarcely concentrate on his work at MINREX as the date of their scheduled departure from Havana approached. Then came the anxious days in Prague, which he couldn't enjoy, before their final undertaking, the long, tension-filled flight to Montreal. Compounding matters was his sense of guilt in lying to Margarita about their vacation and, worst of all, having to conceal the planned defection from her.

Completely ignorant of what lay ahead, Margarita was overjoyed when he told her they were going to Prague. Just to escape Havana was a welcome distraction: She was constantly complaining to him about its shabbiness and shortages, and all the other hardships they had to endure, all of which made their daily life so difficult. Then there were the mandatory political activities, which she detested, but in which she had to participate if she were to maintain her image as a committed revolutionary. She wore her *cara doble*—her double-face—convincingly enough to fool outsiders. But then, when they were alone, she didn't spare him her true feelings about life in Cuba.

Seven years younger than he, Margarita was short and vivacious, with the energy and spirit of most women half her age. She was also somewhat of a free spirit and far more independent-thinking than he ever dared be. Often he had to restrain her because he feared that she was about to throw caution to the wind in order to have a good time without thinking of the possible consequences.

Now her dreams had been fulfilled. Although they had been given but a meager travel allowance—unbeknownst to her, courtesy of State Security—she was ecstatic to be in Prague with its beautiful old buildings and fairy-tale-like charm. Not even Czechoslovakian communism, and all the massive, clumsy Soviet-inspired postwar construction, she had told him, could spoil the beauty of the Czech capital.

The trouble was that Domínguez had found that he couldn't hide his mounting anxiety from her. Worse, his high-strung, nervous behavior was spoiling their time together. As the day approached for their return trip to Cuba, he found that he could scarcely sleep, much less have sex. His seeming disinterest confused and hurt her; after several fruitless attempts, she gave up trying to get him interested in making love to her.

The day of their departure was the most nerve-racking of all. They arrived early at the Prague airport, only to learn an hour before their scheduled departure that their flight to Montreal would be delayed. Panic seized him when the delay stretched into several hours without any explanation from the inscrutable Czechoslovakian airport officials. With each passing hour, he feared the chances were growing that there would be a foul-up at the Canadian end of their journey. His worst fear was that a new Cuban security agent would go on shift at the Montreal airport without being properly instructed concerning their defection. *"Even MININT,"* he fretted to himself, *"has to be like any other bureaucracy where mix-ups can easily occur that can upset the best laid plans."*

Yet, once the Ilyushin was airborne, everything turned out as Acosta said it would. Precisely twenty minutes before touchdown at Mirabel Airport outside Montreal, he leaned over, took Margarita's hand, and quietly informed her of their prearranged defection. He saw her startled look, her eyes opening wide in momentary disbelief. But once she realized he was serious, she listened attentively to his instructions, trying to catch his whispered words above the roar of the Ilyushin's engines. Except for her purse and passport, he told her, she was to leave her belongings onboard the plane and walk with him to the international lounge in the terminal. She was to remain close beside him and await his signal.

As they entered the airport's international lounge with the other Cuban and East European passengers, he quickly spotted the MININT agent casually watching them at a distance of some thirty feet. A minute later, when he saw the agent turn away, he gave Margarita the signal, *"¡Ahora!"* Bolting the slow-moving line, they rushed toward the startled Canadian immigration officer seated by the exit door. Repeating in both French and English the phrases he had rehearsed with Acosta, and waving his diplomatic passport, he announced that they were defecting and requested the Canadian government's protection. Seconds later they were whisked through the lounge's exit door and into Canada's protective custody.

Three days later they were flown to Washington, then separated. A day later Domínguez began his interrogation with a stocky, muscular CIA officer in his early thirties. Though he called himself "Mr. Jones," the officer looked Latin and spoke good Spanish. He didn't appear to be of Mexican, Cuban, or Puerto Rican descent, however. Another, older CIA officer by the name of "Mr. Cooper" joined Jones on the second day of the interrogation. With gray hair, blue eyes, and fair skin Cooper was clearly an Anglo.

As Acosta had predicted, both men were clearly puzzled by his story and kept asking him questions to see if he would contradict himself. But his account evidently held up sufficiently for them to order a lie-detector test. Now, as the third round of questioning was about to begin, Domínguez knew that he had but one last opportunity to convince Jerry, and ultimately Jones and Cooper, of the veracity of his story.

*** *** ***

3

The Response

The next morning, Rudy García, the man who had called himself "Jones," raced up the steps under the concrete awning that spread itself eagle-like in front of the massive main building at CIA Headquarters. Once inside, he headed toward the steps at the opposite end of the immense marbled lobby where armed guards were checking the IDs of employees and routing visitors to an adjoining waiting room so that they could be escorted into the building.

Rudy flashed his ID card, jogged up the steps, and turned down the main corridor. Large windows along the corridor bathed the gray and white marbled floor with morning light from the inner courtyard. Don Smith, whom Domínguez knew as "Cooper," was already waiting for him outside the South Cafeteria. They wound their way further into the building before taking an elevator to an upstairs floor where the Latin American Division of the Operations Directorate was located. Rudy punched in the combination to open the door and escorted Don inside.

***

A member of the Agency's Clandestine Service, Rudy was head of the Cuba Branch of the Latin American Division within the Operations Directorate. He was responsible for monitoring Cuban intelligence operations in the United States, Canada, and Mexico, running the Agency's own operations on the island, and debriefing defectors like Domínguez to ascertain what Castro was planning next, and who was in, who was out in the Cuban government.

Although a Senior Analyst in the CIA's Directorate of Intelligence, DDI, Don Smith had but restricted access to the wing where the Directorate of Operations was located—and only then with an escort like Rudy—because the "spooks" in Operations didn't trust the analysts. The Agency's compartmentalized structure was designed to conceal the identity of its sources and maintain the security of its covert activities, both of which were run by the Directorate of Operations. But the system frequently excluded even senior intelligence analysts like Don from critical information, notwithstanding the fact he held code clearance. The division between the two Directorates even carried over into lunchtime: The spooks ate in the South Cafeteria of the CIA building; the analysts went to the North Cafeteria.

But Rudy seldom adhered to the Directorate of Operations' secretive, exclusive culture, especially now when he needed Don's knowledge and skills to help him unravel the Domínguez case. And there was no one better qualified than Don, a fifteen-year veteran of tracking Cuban developments and the anchor man in the Cuba Analytical Group within the Directorate of Intelligence.

"So," Rudy said, motioning to the analyst to remove his coat and take a chair in his small office, "you were saying earlier that you agree with Jerry on Domínguez."

"Absolutely," Don replied. "Domínguez is the genuine article and not just because he passed the polygraph test the third time around. No, major elements of his story also hold up. Besides, his tale is too bizarre to have been fabricated . . . "

"That's the same feeling I had."

"Yeah," Don went on, "but now the real problem is figuring out what Captain Joaquín Acosta and his boss in State Security, Major José Abrantes, have up their sleeves in orchestrating his defection. That's the $64 question."

"You're showing your age, Don," Rudy said, chuckling. "You mean the $64,000 question—the $64 question was when I was just a little kid." He grew silent for a moment. "Actually," he went on, "the bigger question is what Fidel is up to."

"Ah, let me guess," Don replied, giving Rudy a knowing look. "We're getting diplomatic feelers from the Cuban government through third channels that suggest it may have an interest in improving relations with us. Correct?"

"Sorry," Rudy responded sheepishly, "but I didn't know whether you had been kept in the dark on this one, too. O.K., so now you know there are big stakes involved if the Cuban overtures are genuine."

"Come on, Rudy," Don replied with a hint of sarcasm. "One doesn't have to be a Cuba analyst to know that if Castro is serious, if he's truly prepared to leave the Soviet fold, we could be on the verge of a major realignment in the Cold War."

"And that's why we've got to establish whether there's any connection between Domínguez and the Cuban diplomatic probes."

"Well," Don volunteered, "the conventional wisdom would have it that Fidel is ready to turn to the United States in order to escape the clutches of the Soviets."

"Yeah, but do you buy that?"

"Maybe, maybe not. There's no question that the 'Sovietization of the revolution' has been under way since Fidel bankrupted the economy with his 1970 sugar harvest debacle. Ever since, Moscow has been calling the shots and the *apparatchiks* from the old PSP have been moving in."

"Therefore, the *líder máximo* and his followers may be looking for a way out, right?"

"Correct. And since Fidel has always held tight control over matters of high policy, especially regarding the United States, we can assume that he approved the overtures before they were sent out through third channels . . . "

"But if that's the case," Rudy broke in, "how do you explain the Domínguez defection? I can't imagine that even Abrantes, though he's also Chief of Staff in MININT, would permit a subordinate like Acosta to initiate an operation that could sabotage Fidel's policy."

"Not if neither one of them knew anything about Fidel's feelers toward us," Don countered. "I think it's quite possible that even someone like Abrantes could be left out of the loop given the sensitivity of Fidel's overtures inside the regime."

"O.K.," Rudy said after pausing to mull over the analyst's theory. "But if that's the case, what are Acosta and Abrantes up to with Domínguez?"

"I would think the most likely explanation," Don answered, "is that they're trying to set up the old communists for a new purge by getting us to contact ex-PSP officials. They would be made to look like they were once again scheming against Fidel."

"O.K.," Rudy agreed. "I'll accept that as a plausible explanation for the Domínguez defection. But we still haven't resolved what's behind Havana's feelers—and that's a hell of a lot more important than whatever game Acosta and his boss may be playing."

***

As a thoughtful silence fell between them, Rudy walked to the large map of Cuba pinned on the opposite wall of his office. The analyst remained seated. Removing his glasses, he cleaned them with his handkerchief, and held them up to examine against the light before putting them back on. Then he turned his attention back to Rudy.

"You know," he said. "It's just possible that Fidel is playing more than one game by letting these overtures go forward. In other words, he could be covering himself by making several bets to see which one will give him the highest payoff."

"You're going to have to spell this one out for me," Rudy replied as he returned to his chair.

"All right, but bear with me. One hypothesis would be that he's really looking to us as a way to get out from under Soviet domination. Were he to do that, however, he'd lose the U.S. imperialist threat that he uses to whip up nationalist support. Just as important, he knows he wouldn't get very much from us—certainly nothing like the meal ticket he's enjoyed ever since he aligned himself with Moscow."

"Damn right," Rudy said, nodding in agreement.

"O.K. So that leaves an alternative hypothesis: Fidel's real aim is to somehow get reverse leverage on Moscow so as to increase the level of Soviet aid, yet regain much of the political independence that he enjoyed before 1970."

"Maybe that's what he wants, Don, but how in hell could he pull it off?"

"I'm not sure. I doubt he'd be able to get Moscow to up the ante by pretending he might return to the American fold. The Russians would be sure to see through his bluff, since everyone knows he could never get much from us."

"Exactly. So, what's left for him to do?" Rudy waited for Don to respond, but the analyst appeared stumped.

"I just don't know," Don finally admitted after a long pause. "I just don't know what it could be." Obviously perturbed, he added, "Except I've got a strong hunch Fidel is up to something. The problem is nothing is showing on my radar screen."

"I'm in a real bind, Don," Rudy confided quietly. "Kissinger has just asked for an assessment concerning the seriousness of the Cuban feelers, which means he may be considering some kind of deal with Havana. But first he wants to be certain that he's not going to be screwed by Fidel if he decides to enter into exploratory talks with the Cubans."

"In that case," Don replied quickly, "your only recourse is to get someone into Cuba soon, a person who has high-level contacts with the regime."

"I presume you don't mean someone like Senator Javits or Pell, do you? I'm sure they'll be going to Cuba anytime now, but as occurred with Cyrus Eaton earlier this year, Fidel will tell them what they want to hear and not what he intends to do."

"Of course. But that's not who I had in mind. I was thinking about possibly a foreign diplomat, someone who's posted to Havana and has a good feel for what's going on inside the regime."

"I've already thought of that. But you know the difficulties we've had in finding a good, reliable diplomatic source from a third country, somebody without an agenda. Besides, even with a cooperative Brit or Canadian, we'd never be certain whether or not he's feeding us information his government wants us to hear."

Don nodded in agreement. Rudy made a face and threw up his hands.

"I know this is a long shot," Don said finally. "But you might try recruiting an American academic who's going to Cuba. Someone in good standing with the regime, someone with strong left-wing credentials." He paused for a moment to measure Rudy's reaction. "And here's the tricky part, despite being on the Left, he'd have to be willing to cooperate with the U.S. Government and ask some discreet questions while he's in Havana."

"But, Don," Rudy protested, "wouldn't we be playing into Acosta's hands . . . ?"

"Only if your man starts talking to the old communists and even then I'm not sure it would matter much. I'll bet my shirt that Acosta's game has more to do with factional in-fighting than with his country's policy toward us."

"If you're right, then we don't have much to lose by trying to line up a cooperative academic," Rudy replied after a moment's reflection. "Yeah, it may be worth a shot. And it'll be easy enough to find out whether there are any academics who have applied for a Treasury license so they can go to Cuba."

***

Professor Peter Vargas stepped out of the cab at Wisconsin and N St., paid the driver, and waited for the traffic light to change. The muggy, midday August heat was oppressive in Georgetown, worse than back in Pittsburgh. He welcomed the rush of cold air that greeted him when he entered Martin's Tavern.

Vargas was early. Only two tables were occupied; Rudy García had not yet arrived. He chose an empty table in the back corner of the restaurant, which would give them privacy. Ever since Rudy's call the previous Friday, he was curious as to why the CIA officer had insisted on seeing him as soon as possible. Since he was coming to Washington to do research at the Library of Congress, they had agreed to meet for lunch the following Monday.

After ordering a cold beer, he scanned the *Washington Post*, the pages of which were filled with news about Watergate and President Nixon's impending impeachment or resignation. Nearly two weeks earlier, the Supreme Court had ruled by a vote of 8 to 0 that the President had to turn over the sixty-four tapes he had withheld from Special Prosecutor Judge John Sirica. Now, on August 5, one of the tapes was to be released to the public and rumor had it that the tape would show that Nixon had ordered the cover-up of the White House's involvement in the botched Watergate break-in back in July 1972.

"Sorry I'm late, Professor," Rudy García announced. "I really appreciate you meeting me on such short notice."

Vargas hadn't seen the CIA officer enter and jumped up to shake the shorter man's hand. Rudy's dark-complexioned square face, with its strong nose and jaw, hadn't changed a bit since their first meeting more than a year earlier at an academic-government conference on Cuba. His thick black hair—neatly cut in almost military fashion—was without a hint of gray. His stocky, muscular build was that of an athlete. His handshake was bone crushing.

"Well, I'm always ready to be of service to the U.S. Government," Vargas said as he and Rudy sat down. "Now, how can I help you?"

"I'll tell you in a minute. Let's decide first what we want for lunch, then I'll fill you in. But what I'll tell you is for your ears only; it's not to be repeated to anyone. Understood?"

"Completely," Vargas said, thinking that Rudy García was overplaying his role. Still, he remained extremely curious about what kind of sensitive information the CIA officer was going to reveal to him—and what his own role would be.

***

Rudy eyed the shapely waitress as she walked away from the table. He had ordered a hamburger with French fries and iced tea;

Vargas, a seafood salad and another beer. He had weighed in at exactly 180 pounds that morning, just where he wanted to be, so he felt he could indulge his appetite a bit. Besides, he planned to work out in the Agency's gym later that evening. He turned his attention to Vargas.

"Everybody in this town knows that, one way or another, President Nixon is finished," Rudy began. He waited several seconds before letting Vargas in on what few people in the rest of the country knew. "The Cubans also seem to have come to the same conclusion some time ago. We've been getting signals that Fidel may be prepared to enter into informal talks about normalizing relations after Ford is sworn in as President."

"Well, I'll be damned. I wouldn't have expected it."

"Yeah, but the signals are not entirely clear or unambiguous. The long and short of it is that we need someone in Havana to help us determine whether the Cuban feelers are genuine, or whether Fidel or someone else is jerking us around. We have our usual assets, but they're inadequate and we need to obtain as much information about Fidel's intentions as possible. That's where you come in."

"I'm not sure I can help you there," Vargas replied. "But go on. I'm intrigued."

"We believe that an American academic with solid leftist credentials, someone who'll be going to Cuba soon, and who has contacts inside the government, might be able to provide us with some useful information. That assumes, of course, that he or she would be willing to cooperate with us."

"Well, you and I know that person isn't me," Vargas said. "I've been on Havana's blacklist ever since I was last there and started writing things the regime didn't like."

Rudy nodded. "But you could do me a big favor by looking at this list of six academics. They've all been in Cuba and are planning to return there soon. In fact, they've already applied for Treasury licenses to spend dollars in Cuba."

***

Vargas scanned the names, universities, and fields of specialization on the list.

"On paper, at least, Professor David Diamond at USC is your man," he announced. "But, based on my encounters with him when I was at Berkeley for a couple of years, I'd be surprised if he agrees to cooperate with you."

"Why? Is he too much of a radical? Too committed to Cuba?"

"That's part of it," Vargas replied cautiously. "However, when I left Berkeley three years ago, Diamond was still in graduate school and a bit of a rabble-rouser at the time. From what I've heard recently, he's become a more serious scholar. In fact, I found his dissertation and some of his subsequent articles to be solid pieces of work, despite their quasi-Marxist perspective."

They stopped talking when the waitress brought lunch. Vargas asked for lemon for his seafood salad. Rudy spread mustard and ketchup on his hamburger. After the waitress had returned with the lemon wedges and left, Rudy resumed their discussion.

"So, if I understand you correctly, you're implying that Diamond isn't quite the ideologue he used to be."

"I think so," Vargas responded. "In any case, he's too much of a serious, independent thinker for the kind of mindless radicalism one sometimes sees on the Left."

"O.K. Anything else of importance I should know about him, whether it's political or personal?"

Vargas thought for a minute while he buttered a thick slice of bread and helped himself to more salad. "Well," he answered with a sly grin, "the scuttlebutt is that he's stopped screwing coeds since he got married and started teaching at USC."

"That's smart of him," Rudy chuckled. "Otherwise, I'd bet there'd be a lot of WASPs in San Marino, Pasadena, Newport Beach, and the likes, who'd be outraged if they heard that a radical professor, no less a Jewish one at that, was screwing their daughters at SC."

Vargas laughed as he gave Rudy a quizzical look. "Are you from L.A.?" he inquired.

"Hell, no! I'm an *Hispano*—an original New Mexican, born and raised near Santa Fe. My family goes all the way back to when the Spanish colonized the Southwest."

"Really?"

"You bet. In fact, my oldest brother still operates what's left of the old *rancho* that was established by the original Spanish land grant. Why'd you ask about L.A.?"

"Oh, that crack you made about San Marino, Pasadena, and so forth, made me think you were from L.A."

"That's pretty good guesswork. Actually, I played baseball at UCLA as an undergraduate. I might have gone into pro ball after college if I'd have been good enough." Wistful, Rudy paused to contemplate what might have been. "But I wasn't," he resumed abruptly. "So I decided on graduate work in Latin American Studies at UCLA before dropping out in 1965. I later joined the Agency. Anyway, I got to know all about the Trojans when I was a Bruin and L.A. was our town."

He stopped to take another bite of his hamburger, which he washed down with more iced tea. Vargas was still working on his salad.

"Let's get back to Diamond," Rudy said, finishing the last of his French fries. "Why don't you think he would work with us?"

"I'm sure he wouldn't cooperate with the CIA."

"O.K. But what if he thinks it's the State Department that's asking him to help bring about the normalization of relations between Cuba and the United States?"

"Well, he probably would find it tempting to play that role. But I think he'd still think twice about cooperating with the U.S. Government."

Rudy had taken out a small pad of paper and began to take notes.

"First of all," Vargas began, "he'd fear that the Cubans would find out and accuse him of being on a secret mission for the U.S. Government. Second, his standing with leftist circles in this country would be ruined if it ever came out that he had cooperated with you. And third . . . "

"Wait just a second," Rudy interrupted, giving Vargas the opportunity to finish his salad and gulp down the last of his beer. "We'd assure him that neither the Cuban government nor leftists in this country would ever find out that he had agreed to help us out. Besides, he wouldn't be a spy. We're only asking him to tell us if he hears anything about the Cuban government wanting to normalize relations."

"Except that I'm not sure Diamond himself wants to see a rapprochement between Havana and Washington," Vargas responded. "It's possible that he'd fear that the revolution would lose its purity if it stopped fighting American imperialism. Besides, there's one more consideration."

"What's that?"

"Most academics on the Left hate Kissinger not just because of Vietnam, but because he's also the architect and practitioner of realpolitik. His foreign policy is both immoral and amoral in their eyes. The fact that he's been pretty effective at his craft makes matters worse. So, if Diamond is like the rest of the Left, I doubt he'd cooperate if it means helping Kissinger."

"O.K.," Rudy affirmed after mulling over Vargas's comments. "You've made a pretty persuasive case as to why Diamond won't cooperate with us. But I'm an optimist. Maybe I can appeal to his ego or find some other way to bring him around."

They ordered coffee and made small talk until the waitress dropped off their bill. Rudy waved Vargas off. "The lunch is on the Company," he said, giving Vargas an appreciative nod.

***

Bob Watson ushered Rudy into his spacious office, "Make yourself comfortable, Rudy. While we're waiting for Lawton, I'll use the men's room."

Rudy seated himself in one of the two mahogany-colored leather arm chairs that were situated in front of Watson's meticulously clean desk. Watson had only recently taken over as Acting Chief of the Latin American Division in the Directorate of Operations. Noting the uncluttered desk, Rudy surmised that his boss still hadn't found much to do.

He cast an appreciative glance at the office's tall, rectangular windows, which from the outside looked like narrow, vertical slits of tinted glass along the seventh floor of the massive building. From the inside, however, they now offered him a sweeping vista of the rolling hills and woods surrounding the CIA complex. Gazing down at the leafy forest of willows and oaks below, he wondered whether he would ever rise high enough in the ranks to be assigned such an office. He doubted he would. He would continue to feel claustrophobic in his modest-sized inner office, which lacked even a single window to the outside world.

Headquarters had always been too large, too stuffy for his taste. The senior staff, who for the most part had entered the intelligence service during the first decade or so after the CIA had been established, were by and large Easterners in terms of family background and education. He could tell them right off by the well-tailored clothes, the tweedy sport coats, and rumpled summer poplins they wore— and, most of all, by their pipe smoking. He always considered their pipes an affectation: Either they were modeling themselves after Ivy League college professors or after the Agency's most famous Mandarins—Allen Dulles and his chief deputy, Richard Bissel, who would have succeeded Dulles as the Director of Intelligence had it not been for the Bay of Pigs.

For him, Headquarters' one saving grace was that it was located in the Virginia countryside. At the end of the day he could run several miles through the woods on the winding paths surrounding the complex. Still, hardly a day went by that he didn't miss the clean, dry mountain air he had so much taken for granted as a boy growing up in New Mexico. He would sometimes look at himself in the mirror and fear that if he remained holed up in Headquarters he would begin to lose his dark complexion. Then he would remind himself that he would always remain what his brothers and sisters in New Mexico teasingly called him—their "Oreo cookie" in Washington because he was brown on the outside, yet white on the inside.

He was irritated with Watson for having called in Lawton Armstrong to review his plan of enlisting Professor David Diamond's help. He suspected that Watson feared that any misstep could cost him his permanent appointment as Chief of the Latin American Division. Hence, Watson had turned to Armstrong, who had been a Cuba case officer earlier in his career. But Rudy suspected there was more to it than that. Like Watson, Armstrong had gone to Yale and was still part of the old boy network even though he'd been on the outs for years.

Still, Rudy had to concede that Armstrong had saved his career four years earlier, in 1970, by managing to clear him at the Agency's investigative hearing over the Managua incident. The hearing's surprise outcome hadn't helped Armstrong, however. He long had been disliked by many of his superiors because he had refused to be a team player before and after the Agency's disastrous operation at the Bay of Pigs in 1961. Yet, it was precisely Armstrong's whistle-blowing role—when he had put his career on the line—that had earned him the respect of younger intelligence officers like Rudy. Until 1961, in fact, Armstrong had been one of the Agency's rising stars.

* * *

With both a bachelor's and a master's degree in history from Yale, Lawton Armstrong had joined the CIA in 1949, and for the next twelve years had risen swiftly through its ranks. A son of a well-to-do lawyer and diplomat from Connecticut, he had the breeding, polish, and erudition, including fluency in both French and Spanish, that immediately led to his being courted by both the Agency's West European and Latin American Divisions. Armstrong chose Latin America. Soon he was posted to the region's hot spots—Peron's Argentina in 1950–51, then Guatemala until the ouster of its communist-leaning president, Jacobo Arbenz, in 1954, and finally Venezuela under Pérez Jiménez's military dictatorship in the late 1950s. For a while, too, he had been assigned to tracking the KGB's elusive spy master in Latin America, Aleksandr Alekseev.

Then came Cuba. In the fall of 1959, he was sent to Havana. The overtaxed CIA station chief needed a better handle on where the Cuban revolution was headed and Armstrong was the perfect intelligence officer for the job. Within weeks of his arrival Armstrong had established contact with disaffected revolutionaries who saw that Fidel, his brother, Raúl, and Che Guevara were now taking Cuba into the communist fold. His biggest breakthrough came when he was informed by his contacts of Fidel's secret meeting in October with the KGB's Alekseev who, unbeknownst to the CIA, had slipped into Havana earlier the previous summer as a TASS correspondent. From then on Armstrong's cables supplied Langley with further bits and pieces of evidence on additional meetings between Alekseev and the Castro brothers and Che. Finally, in mid-January 1960, he alerted Washington that Soviet Deputy Premier Anastas Mikoyan would arrive in Havana in early February. Mikoyan's visit, he warned, would most certainly lead to Cuba's de facto realignment with Moscow.

When events proved him right, Armstrong's credibility shot up in intelligence circles. But by then, Washington could only react to fast-breaking developments on the island. On March 17, 1960, President Dwight D. Eisenhower gave the go-ahead to the CIA to begin planning and organizing the island's liberation by Cuban exiles. Tasked with the mission of deposing Castro, the Agency became interested in Armstrong's reports only in so far as they bolstered the operation's chances of success, while ignoring his assessments of the Castro government's strengths. Finally, Armstrong was recalled to Langley in early January 1961, a week before President Eisenhower's decision to break diplomatic relations with the revolutionary government. The outgoing president's move paved the way for his successor, John F. Kennedy, to launch the Bay of Pigs invasion the following April. However, Armstrong was not brought into the group charged with planning the operation.

Headed by Richard Bissel, Deputy Director of Plans, the planning group believed that the exile force, which had received extensive training at a base in Guatemala, could establish a beachhead on the island, set up an anti-Castro government, and rally the majority of the Cuban people to its side. To the dismay of Bissel and other planners, however, newly elected President Kennedy ordered the invasion site changed late in the game, from Trinidad to the Bahía de Cochinos. The small city of Trinidad hugged the Escambray mountains where anti-Castro guerrilla forces were already operating. The less defensible Bahía de Cochinos lay some eighty miles from the sanctuary of the Escambray. Still, the CIA planners and operatives felt certain of success. The exiles' B-26 bombers would be able to destroy Castro's few combat aircraft and, if needed, the U.S. Navy would be standing by to provide vital air support to the invasion force at the Bahía de Cochinos.

When he and other outsiders were finally briefed on the impending invasion in early April, Armstrong argued strenuously against it. The small exile force would have to contend not only with the Cuban army but also with the people's militia. Even with U.S. air support, Armstrong maintained, the exiles would be vastly outnumbered. If cut off, they would be driven into the swamps surrounding the Bahía de Cochinos or back onto the narrow beaches and deep waters of the bay. At best, the fighting would be dragged out for a few weeks, with high casualties to both sides. Unless the United States was prepared to intervene militarily, he insisted, Castro's forces would almost certainly emerge victorious.

The operation was just as flawed politically, Armstrong continued, to the growing irritation of the invasion planners. The majority of the Cuban population was still enamored of the charismatic Castro and his reforms. Cuba's conversion to communism was not yet fully apparent to most Cubans, while the economy's deterioration had only just begun. The exile leadership, he added, was both too conservative, too compromised by its CIA connection to garner much popular support. Above all, he argued, nationalist-minded Cubans, including those concerned over where the revolution was headed, would rally to Castro's side to defend *la patria* against the Yankees.

Armstrong concluded with an admonition to those in attendance:

The Castro regime could not be toppled on the cheap. The only way to overthrow Castro, he advised, was for the United States to use its overwhelming force—attack with carrier-based planes and send in several Marine and Army divisions to destroy Castro's forces and then occupy the island.

Armstrong's negative critique was neither appreciated nor acted upon by the Bay of Pigs planners. While some of his warnings found echoes among State Department and Agency intelligence analysts attending the briefing, Armstrong's call for the use of massive air power and ground troops received no support. Also, his overbearing—at times, patronizing—attitude did little to win him converts. In the end, he was told to write down his dissenting views and recommendations in a memorandum to Bissel.

The Bay of Pigs fiasco that transpired two weeks later did little to help his standing in the Agency. Allen Dulles, Bissel, and Grayston Lynch, who had been with Brigade 2506 when it disembarked, along with most other senior Agency officials, insisted the operation had failed only because President Kennedy had lost his nerve. He had moved the landing site, canceled the second attack by the B-26 bombers manned by the Cuban exiles, and denied vital U.S. naval air support to Brigade 2506 after it had landed in the Bahía de Cochinos. As a result, Castro's obsolete air force was able to control the skies and attack amphibious crafts and the invasion forces on the ground. In their eyes, Armstrong had not been right. It was Kennedy who had removed or altered key components of the plan, thereby dooming the Brigade to certain defeat.

Later, Lyman B. Kirkpatrick, Inspector General of the CIA, wrote a scathing report of the operation, blaming—and to some, savaging—Dulles, Bissel, and other officials for faulty intelligence, poor planning, and a badly executed operation, among other things. Kirkpatrick's 150-page report was not made public; all but one of the twenty copies of the report were destroyed.

Those senior CIA officials who had read the report saw Armstrong's fingerprints on it and suspected that he had given Kirkpatrick a copy of his earlier memorandum to Bissel. In fact, Kirkpatrick's final report was far more critical than the one originally drafted by his staff. From then on, Armstrong's career would remain at a virtual standstill, with his enemies seeing to it that he was given routine slots in Washington or posted to the backwaters of

Latin America and the Caribbean. His personal life also unraveled in the meantime. Two marriages and the ensuing divorces devoured his inherited wealth. His drinking increased greatly nights after work, but most of all on the weekends when he went to his cottage and took his sailboat out on Chesapeake Bay.

***

When Bob Watson returned with Armstrong in tow, Rudy was shocked. The man's appearance had physically deteriorated since he last saw him. Bloated, Armstrong's pasty face was now covered by red splotches. From too much drinking? Too much sun? Both? His thinning, yellowish white hair was combed indifferently. His wrinkled seersucker suit was too tight across his spreading paunch. His old but expensive blue cotton shirt was frayed, the two Cartier gold cuff links adding an incongruous touch to his appearance. Armstrong appeared to be striving for the look of elegant decadence, but without much success.

"As I told you, Rudy," Watson said after the two men had greeted each other, "Lawton thought he could be of help to you. So now, tell us a bit more about your plans."

Rudy briefly summarized the Cuban government's feelers and the Domínguez defection. He gave a profile of Diamond, pointing out that his candidate of choice would be attending a conference in Washington in a week's time. As he finished, he caught Armstrong looking out the window, seemingly bored and disinterested.

"Well, Lawton," Watson asked, "do you still think Rudy's plan might work?"

Slowly Armstrong turned his attention to both men, his blue blood-shot eyes displaying a flicker of interest. "Overall," he announced, "I don't have any problems with the plan." Pausing, he fixed his eyes first on Rudy, then Watson, while Rudy waited for the other shoe to drop. "But I do have a problem with Diamond. The guy is literally out there in left field. As Rudy points out, however, we have no other alternative."

"If that's the case," Rudy said, still not certain whether Armstrong was committed to his plan, "can you help?"

"Actually, I believe I can. You see, I still have a few Cuban contacts left from the old days, people who were critical of the regime but never broke with it. A few have risen to moderately important positions in the government. And they still owe me."

Rudy was curious about these Cubans Armstrong was talking about, but since Bob Watson didn't press Armstrong to identify them, he remained silent.

" . . . I could call in my chits," Armstrong was saying. "I believe that at least one of my contacts could expedite Diamond's visa, as well as facilitate his access to higher officials once he's in. Of course, Bob, you'd have to authorize my contacting my Cuban *friends*."

"Christ, but excuse me," Rudy said, with a barely restrained edge to his voice. "If you've got those kinds of contacts, why in the hell do we need Diamond? Why don't you contact your *friends* directly for the information we need?"

"Rudy, you of all people should know that they wouldn't touch such a request with a ten-foot pole. They'd be much too scared of being implicated in a CIA plot. Or they'd immediately go to State Security just to protect themselves."

"O.K., but what makes you think they would risk expediting Diamond's visa request and opening a few doors for him?" Rudy asked.

"Simple. He has proven left-wing credentials, he supports Cuba, and he's part of the Jewish Mafia."

"Mafia?" Watson questioned, not comprehending.

"Bob, I'm not referring to *that* Mafia," Lawton replied with an air of amusement. "I only meant that Diamond is one of many Jewish academics and intellectuals able to go to Cuba in exchange for praising the Castro regime's revolutionary accomplishments. Of course, none of them say a word about Cuba having become a totalitarian state."

"People like that are by no means limited to Jewish academics," Rudy protested. "There are lots of non-Jewish intellectuals who are sympathetic to the regime. And personally," he went on, his voice rising, "as an *Hispano*, I don't like it when people are stereotyped on the basis of their religious or ethnic background."

"My, my, Rudy," Armstrong replied in a condescending voice. "I see that you're still the Boy Scout. But you misunderstand me. I wasn't attacking the Jewish people. I was merely observing that Jews are disproportionately represented among Castro sympathizers, many of whom teach at our most prestigious colleges and universities, including some in the Ivy League."

"Look, none of this has anything to do with the issue before us. So let's get off the subject," Rudy said, by now fed up with Armstrong's rant.

"You're right," Watson agreed, seeing an opportunity to steer the conversation back to the proposed plan. "Rudy, you've got my approval. I'll draw up memos for both you and Lawton this afternoon. When did you say Diamond was coming to Washington?"

"He's giving a presentation at a symposium on Cuba next Thursday. It's an all-day affair sponsored by the Smithsonian's Wilson Center. I'll try to make contact there and see if we can meet somewhere else. I know I'll have to treat him gingerly."

"Even then, it may not be careful enough," Watson interjected. "What worries me most about this guy is not that he'll turn you down, but that he'll blow everything wide open by going to the press—or worse, by becoming a double-agent. Christ! If that happens, the Cubans will be feeding us cooked information and we won't even know it."

"Bob," Armstrong broke in, "despite what I said earlier, I don't think our professor is the kind who would go so far as to collaborate with Cuban intelligence. But I do agree that he could take it upon himself to denounce Rudy's plan to the press."

"Look. If he's too squirrelly I won't try to set up a follow-up meeting with him," Rudy responded. "But if he seems open and receptive enough, then I'll go ahead. You're just going to have to trust my judgment."

"You're absolutely right, Rudy," Watson declared. "So, unless someone has anything else to bring up, I think that about wraps everything up."

As the three of them stood up, Armstrong reminded Watson that he would need authorization to contact the Cubans. Turning to Rudy, he said, "And Rudy, I'll give you a call next week before Diamond arrives to tell you whether I've been able to set things up."

"Thanks. I appreciate your cooperation," Rudy replied. His cordiality, however, was anything but genuine. He realized that he really didn't like Armstrong. *"No matter what you did for me four years ago,"* he thought as he left Watson's office, *"you're not the Lawton Armstrong I once admired. Hell, no! You're really an arrogant, bigoted, son-of-a-bitch."*

***

4

Crossroads

Bound for Dulles International Airport from LAX, David Diamond settled into his seat, glad finally to be aboard the American Airlines flight. He was tired after a restless night's sleep, and a bit down as well. His three-month-long affair with Cindy Mays had ended abruptly the previous day. Just like that! She had broken up with him, ostensibly over his refusal to take her to Cuba with him, but the real reason, he suspected, was that she saw no reason to continue their relationship with him being away for the next few months.

"She's not the kind who'd stick around for a guy who's going to be gone for a while," he thought. *"No way. She's too much of a good-time girl. She'd be going out with other guys right away."*

He couldn't blame her, though. There was no reason for her to sacrifice herself for him. She'd have no dearth of suitors. Men were always looking at her, always on the make, including some of the junior professors in his department. He smiled to himself. He had been the envy of all but the department's stodgiest male faculty once word got out that he was dating her. And they would have been even more envious had they known that Cindy Mays was every bit as good in bed as she was to look at—something he discovered their very first night after dinner at El Cholo.

Because their attraction to one another was primarily physical, he had known from the start that their affair wouldn't last. But in the interim, she had been good for him. She had made him forget Julie. She had helped his bruised male ego—he was indeed a good lover. But their relationship had remained rather superficial, nonetheless. There just hadn't been enough chemistry between them for him—or her—to fall in love. Still, it was hard for him to put her out of his mind.

***

He used a good part of the five-hour flight to prepare his presentation for the Wilson Center's consortium on Cuba. Afterward, he took a nap before landing at Dulles. Hopping a shuttle, he arrived at the Dupont Circle Hotel shortly before seven in the evening. He showered, enjoyed a leisurely dinner with drinks and wine at a popular restaurant on Connecticut Avenue, and was back in the hotel to watch a few minutes of the eleven o'clock news before retiring. Despite his body still being on L.A. time, he fell asleep in minutes.

Arriving at the Smithsonian's Wilson Center at nine the next morning, he was refreshed and ready for the symposium. But when the first morning panel turned out to be rather pedestrian, he found himself daydreaming about Cindy, Julie, and the void in his life. The second panel on Cuba's planned economy offered a more stimulating diversion from his personal problems. When his turn came to take the podium in the first afternoon session, he was fully charged and focused.

Referring only now and then to his notes, he gave his presentation with a spontaneity and flair that most of the other, more formal speakers before him had lacked. In concise, bold strokes, he laid out his thesis concerning Cuba's potential for grass-roots democracy. The organs of the *Poder Popular* being proposed for Cuba's forthcoming socialist constitution, he argued, could provide vehicles for more political participation by ordinary Cubans in the administration and governance of their lives than had hitherto been the case. The People's Power experiment, he concluded, could lead to genuine socialist democracy on the island, thereby differentiating Cuba from the Soviet Union, Eastern Europe, and China.

His remarks provoked much debate during the Q&A period that followed. Those in the audience who shared his leftist perspective were enthused by his sympathetic, upbeat portrayal of Cuba. Others of more conservative persuasion expressed skepticism regarding his thesis or attacked it directly. Still, he couldn't help but be pleased by the reception to his presentation given the general sophistication of his audience.

The one discordant note of the day came later, in the foreign policy panel, when the question arose during the Q&A period as to whether Nixon's resignation would lead to better relations between the United States and Cuba. When the panelists generally agreed that it would, David countered by declaring that it really made no difference that Gerald Ford was now President:

" . . . Corporate interests and the military-industrial complex in the United States," he opined, "will not permit any accommodation with revolutionary Cuba. Why? Because the ruling elites in this country cannot allow the Cuban revolution to succeed since Cuba would then serve as an example to be emulated by the rest of Latin America. For that reason, President Ford, like Nixon and the three presidents before him, will not—indeed, cannot—hold out an olive branch to Fidel."

An elderly, distinguished-looking man in the audience had become visibly agitated upon hearing David's remarks. His full white mustache virtually bristled as he stood and announced his name, which meant nothing to David. Without further ado, he proceeded to tear into him.

Looking directly at David, the white-haired gentleman declared, "Young man, I take strong exception to what you just said. It may be good Marxist theory, but believe me it bears no resemblance to the real world. For three decades I've worked closely with the people you call 'elites' in both the private and public sector, and I can tell you this: If there's one thing they're absolutely convinced about, it's the superiority of our capitalist system . . . " David was about to rise to defend his viewpoint, but it was obvious that the old man was not about to yield the floor to him. "So, contrary to what you claim," the stranger continued, "they don't for a minute fear the example of the Cuban revolution. They know damn well that Cuba's socialist system wouldn't be economically viable without the Soviet Union. So you're dead wrong because it's not your precious Cuban example that concerns them. No, it's the fact that Moscow now has a beachhead in our own hemisphere."

David stood up. But before he could reply he was cut off by the moderator. Later, when the symposium ended, the old man pointedly ignored him before leaving the room. David could only present his rebuttal to those who came up to chat with him.

***

After most of the audience had left, a short, compact man, with dark complexion and Latin features, approached David. Thinking he was a Cuban exile, David readied himself for an angry exchange.

"Dr. Diamond," the stranger said. "I was rather intrigued by your insistence that the U.S. Government wouldn't be interested in any accommodation with Castro."

"Well, I'm glad my viewpoint was of some interest. The trouble is, I wasn't given a chance to defend my position."

"I'm aware of that," the stranger noted sympathetically. "Perhaps you and I can talk a bit more about the subject if you have time."

"Sure. What's on your mind?"

"Let me first introduce myself," the stranger replied. Reaching into his pocket, he handed David his business card. "I'm Rudy García. I'm with the Department of State."

Surprised, David glanced at the card, which identified García as a "Special Advisor" at the State Department.

"Well, this is the first time I've ever been approached by someone at State." Picking up his briefcase, he added, as much in a serious vein as in jest, "I guess that means that I should be extra careful not to do anything that could cast doubt on my radical image."

García smiled politely as they walked toward the exit door. Once outside, well out of earshot of the stragglers remaining in the conference room, he said, slipping into a low, confidential tone of voice, "Look, Dr. Diamond, it's really important that I talk to you. We could go somewhere right now if you have time, or we could meet later this evening or tomorrow. It'll take maybe twenty or thirty minutes at most."

"Can't we talk right now, right here?"

"I don't think that would be a good idea."

"Why?" David asked, alarm bells now ringing in his head.

"What I have to tell you is pretty sensitive. It has to do with Cuba."

"You don't say? Look, I'm sorry, Mr. García," David said, glancing again at the State Department card. "But I really don't think I should be talking to you. You see, I'm really counting on going to Cuba next month and I don't want anything to screw up my trip."

"I fully appreciate your concern, Dr. Diamond. And I assure you, the last thing the U.S. Government wants is for your trip to be canceled or compromised in any way."

"*That's bullshit,*" David thought. "*Besides, why in hell should the U.S. Government want me to go to Cuba? That's what I should be concerned about.*"

García glanced furtively over his shoulder to make sure no one could overhear them. "What I'm about to tell you is not to be repeated to anyone. Is that understood?"

"Yes, yes, but do hurry up! I've got an academic reputation to protect," David added pointedly. "I don't like all this conspiratorial stuff."

"Of course," García replied reassuringly. "I understand your position. On the other hand, I think what I have to say will come as a complete surprise to you, given what you said inside about the United States being unwilling to reach out to Castro."

Pausing, García glanced once more toward the few people still in the conference room to make certain they were out of earshot. Then, returning his attention to David, a slight, nearly imperceptible smile played on his lips.

"You see, Dr. Diamond, we want you to go to Havana precisely because you may be the person who could help us decide whether we should try to normalize relations with the Cuban government . . . "

"I don't believe it!" David broke in.

"You can believe what you want, Dr. Diamond," García replied calmly. "But if you want to learn more, then tell me where and when we can meet privately. You could be doing both the United States and Cuba a great service."

David leaned back against the wall for a moment, trying to read García. His instincts told him to walk away from the State Department man—if, in fact, he was from State. But despite what he had said earlier, he was curious about what might be going on between Washington and Havana. Did the State Department want him to serve as a conduit to the Castro government? Perhaps they wanted him to relay a signal from Washington. He had to admit he was intrigued.

"O.K. I'll meet you tomorrow. But it's got to be in the morning sometime as I'm scheduled to leave from Dulles in the afternoon."

"I'm at your disposal. Do you want to meet at a restaurant for coffee . . . ?"

"No, I don't like that idea," David replied quickly. They could be overheard or their conversation taped inside a restaurant. Besides, he wanted to be able to break off the meeting easily in case García tried to involve him in something he wanted no part of. It had to be a place where they would be anonymous and not easily overheard.

"How about Washington Circle?" he suggested. "There we would be inconspicuous. I could meet you, say, at eleven o'clock on the New Hampshire side."

García looked at him, a quizzical expression on his face, but quickly agreed to the rendezvous site. "Washington Circle will be fine, Dr. Diamond. I'll see you there at eleven sharp."

* * *

Rudy arrived at his office in CIA Headquarters just after seven in the morning, allowing himself plenty of time to catch up on his classified cables and a mountain of paperwork before his appointment with Diamond. He checked his phone messages. Lawton Armstrong had left word the previous afternoon that he would call back first thing in the morning. Still, when the secure phone rang, he was surprised to hear Armstrong's cheerful voice on the other end of the line. The man did not strike him as an early riser.

"Rudy, Lawton here," Armstrong announced grandly with his affected Groton or Yale accent—Rudy didn't know or care which—that had always reminded him of William Buckley. "Glad I caught you, old boy. Sorry I wasn't able to get back to you until yesterday afternoon. Were you able to make contact?"

"Yeah, I met Diamond yesterday. I was able to set up a meeting with him for later this morning. That's why I'm in this early. Come to think of it, you're in awfully early yourself."

"Actually, Rudy, I'm calling from 'The Farm.' Drove down to Camp Peary day before yesterday to lecture our trainees about espionage and being a case officer and all the other things that we in Operations are involved in. So, since I could call from here on a secure line, I thought I'd bring you up-to-date. But first, my boy, tell me, how did it go yesterday with our good professor?"

"It was touch-and-go for a while," Rudy replied. "But I should know after eleven today whether or not he'll cooperate with us. Anyway, what's up at your end?"

"I was finally able to see my Cuban contact in New York and get everything arranged. But it took some doing, let me tell you. At first, my man wanted no part of the deal. So I had to really lean on him. I normally don't like to do that, you know. It's not my style."

"Not your style, my ass," Rudy thought.

"Anyway, I had to remind him that I knew he had done some things in the past that he didn't want Fidel or anyone else in his government to know about. After that, he came around. He'll help expedite the visa for sure. He'll also try to open some doors to higher-ups once Diamond is in Havana, though he didn't want to make any hard-and-fast promises."

"Christ, are you sure your man can be trusted?" Rudy asked, reflecting on what Lawton had just told him. "How do you know he won't go running to State Security and reveal what you want him to do?"

"Rudy, my boy, trust me. My guy knows that if he doesn't play ball, I'll expose him. After that, he'd lose his cushy post at Cuba's embassy to the U.N. Then he'd be returned post haste to Cuba where he'd either get shot or get sent to the *Combinado del Este* or some other prison. So, my friend, you can rest easy."

"I hope you're right. We can't afford any screw-ups. Diamond is already skittish enough as it is."

"There won't be a problem, I assure you. By the way, where are you meeting him?"

"He proposed that we meet on the New Hampshire side of Washington Circle at eleven. He seems to think that if we were to take a walk there we could mix with other people and that way be less conspicuous. I wasn't about to argue with him."

After a moment of silence on Lawton's end, Rudy could hear him chuckling. "What's so funny?" he asked, a bit annoyed.

"I can't help it, Rudy. I think Diamond has seen too many English espionage films—you know the scene where an elegant, well-dressed Mandarin from MI5 is strolling through Hyde Park with his accomplice, plotting against the Ruskies or their bureaucratic rivals."

"You could be right," Rudy replied, not in the least amused by Lawton's attempt at humor. "Anyway, I've got to get to work. Thanks for your help."

"I'll be back at Headquarters late this afternoon. If I can be of further assistance don't hesitate to call on me. Good luck!"

***

David arrived at Washington Circle several minutes early for their scheduled appointment. He wanted to make certain that Rudy García came alone, that they were not being watched. He took up a position near the 23rd Street corner, which gave him a commanding view of the large, circular walkway, along with most of the trees and benches inside the circle's perimeter. Everything looked normal. He waited. The sweltering heat was becoming oppressive. He hoped García wouldn't be late.

At last he saw García bounding across onto the traffic circle from New Hampshire Avenue. He waited another minute to determine whether anyone was observing García before he crossed over onto the circular sidewalk. He couldn't help but smile to himself at the figure approaching him: Attired in a tan poplin suit, pale blue button-down shirt, and striped blue and gold tie, García looked like he didn't belong in Washington, much less in the State Department. He had a swagger about him that reminded David of the way athletes walked. "*Yes,*" he said, smiling to himself. "*The guy looks a lot more like a jock who belongs on the playing field than a prim FSO from State.*"

"Good to see you, Dr. Diamond," García said as he extended a hand in greeting. "It's going to be one scorcher of a day."

For a moment, David hesitated. Then he shook the outstretched hand with its firm grip, but released it quickly.

"I can't wait to get back to L.A. tonight," David remarked. "This heat and humidity are just awful. Maybe you Washingtonians are accustomed to it, but I just wilt in this kind of climate. Same thing happens to me in Cuba, except that at least in Havana there's a sea breeze."

"We could go inside somewhere else if you like."

"No, I prefer to stay outdoors. If it becomes too hot, we can maybe find some shade under those trees."

As they began walking, David again glanced, checking for any signs of surveillance. Once assured, he decided not to waste any more time.

"Mr. García, since it's already hot as hell, let's get right down to the reason why you were so insistent on having this meeting. What does my trip to Cuba have to do with whether or not the U.S. normalizes relations with Fidel's government?"

"Professor Diamond, I'm going to level with you as much as I can." García stopped momentarily to remove his coat and sling it over his shoulder. His shirt was already clinging to his muscular torso and arms from perspiration. David removed his blazer as well.

"Of course, you realize there are some things I can't tell you because they are classified and very sensitive," García continued as they resumed walking.

"O.K., except I doubt they're all that sensitive."

"All right, but I have to remind you again that whatever I tell you is not to be repeated. O.K.?"

"Right, right, I agree," David answered impatiently.

"Good. In a nutshell, we've received some overtures and signals, directly from Havana or through third channels, indicating that the

Castro government may—and here I must underscore *may*—be interested in normalizing relations with us." García paused to let the disclosure sink in. "The problem," he continued, "is that the signals are contradictory. As a result, we're not at all sure we can take Havana's gestures seriously."

"So, why don't you just test Havana's intentions by talking to the Cubans directly? Egads, I don't see what harm can come of that."

"I should think that as a political scientist you of all people should know that it's not quite that simple."

"What you mean is that there are certain U.S. Government circles that are not interested in exploring whether there's a basis for normalizing relations with Cuba," David shot back. "Am I right?"

"No, you're wrong again, *Professor*," García replied pointedly. "The fact of the matter is that neither the President nor the Secretary of State is going to risk his political capital, and the prestige and reputation of the United States Government, by entering a dark alley with Castro."

"Oh, please, spare me the melodrama!"

"Hey, it may not be poli sci jargon," García said with a sarcastic ring to his voice. "But the analogy is appropriate. Ford and Kissinger don't want to be blindsided or mugged if they authorize talks with Cuba."

"You've got it reversed, Mr. García," David retorted, as they rounded the halfway mark on the southwest side of Washington Circle. "It's little Cuba that has been mugged countless times by the U.S. simply because its people want to build socialism."

He stopped abruptly and he turned to face García. The latter seemed resigned to letting him sound off.

"And I mean literally mugged by the government you work for, Mr. García, starting with the Bay of Pigs, and the assassination plots against Fidel that we're beginning to learn about. Add to that the economic embargo that we've had in place over the past twelve years. Christ! It's no wonder that Havana is sending out confusing signals."

"Look, Professor Diamond, I'm not here to debate our policy toward Cuba, much less do I want to defend every cockamamie thing we've tried against Castro." García was obviously frustrated by the turn the conversation had taken. "Look," he went on in a softer, more conciliatory voice, "I'm just here to ask for your help."

They had resumed walking but David stopped again.

"O.K.," he said, turning to García. "What is it that you want me to do?"

But García didn't respond immediately. He regarded David with uncertainty, as if wondering suddenly if he should confide in him. He began to walk again. "All right," he finally announced. "Here's what we want you to do: While you're in Cuba, just keep your eyes and ears open for anything that may have a bearing on the Castro government's intentions toward the United States." Quick to note David's expression of alarm, he went on. "It's not what you think. Look, we're only interested in what government and Party people may tell you about relations with the United States. And, of course, we'd very much like to learn about any scuttlebutt you come across concerning what top Cuban leaders may be saying to each other about their policy toward the United States. That's all."

"And then . . . ?"

"Then, when you get back to the United States, we'll debrief you. That's all there is to it. Oh, one more thing: If you agree to help, we might be able to expedite your visa from the Foreign Ministry. Maybe we can even help you obtain some high-level interviews."

"Wait a minute!" David exclaimed, coming to an abrupt halt. The full implication of Garcia's proposition had now sunk in. "What you're really asking," he declared as he turned to face García, "is for me to be a spy!"

"No, not at all. We are only asking you to help your own country—and Cuba as well—by simply reporting what you hear, so that then *your* government can better assess Castro's intentions."

Now convinced that García was from the CIA, David berated himself as they began to walk again. *What a damned fool I've been. I should have asked for proper identification, rather than accept just a State Department business card . . .* "

"You're from the CIA, aren't you?" he blurted out, once more coming to a halt. "I know you are! Damn it, show me your State Department identification!"

With a gleam in his eyes, García reached inside his inside coat pocket and pulled out his State Department ID card with his photograph on it. David was disappointed. It would have been far easier for him to break off this meeting if García hadn't been able to produce an ID card.

"Maybe the guy is on the level. Maybe I've exaggerated what he wants me to do when I'm in Cuba." After a moment of further reflec-

tion, *"No. I just can't afford to take that kind of risk."*

"Look," David said, more calmly, "I came here prepared to cooperate with you if it was a matter of my conveying a conciliatory
message to the Cubans."

"I'm happy to hear that," García jumped in, evidently seeing an
opening. "And who knows, the Cubans just might ask you to convey a message back to us."

"I doubt that's going to happen," David replied. "In the meantime, what you're asking me to do comes awful close to spying, no
matter what you say. And frankly, I don't want to get involved."

An awkward silence followed. David wanted to end the meeting.

"Look, Professor Diamond," García shot back. "I fully appreciate
your concern. But you've got it all wrong. We're not asking you to
spy. Please believe me. We're only asking you to be alert to information that could help us get a better fix on what the Cubans are up to."

The muscles in García's jaw twitched as he awaited a response.
David only shook his head in disagreement. Suddenly, García moved
closer and grabbed David firmly by the right shoulder. David's first
impulse was to push García's hand away.

"Christ!" García exclaimed, his eyes boring in on the professor.
"Don't you realize how important this is? Hell, man! You could be a
pivotal player in helping the U.S. and Cuba overcome their hostili-
ties toward one another." He eased his grip. "And you know what?
That'd almost be like what Kissinger accomplished a few years back
when he secured the opening to China. Think about it!"

***

Despite the precautions he had taken, David had missed the man
in the brick building across the street from Washington Circle. Concealed by the dark shadows of the second-story window, he was
armed with a 35-mm Nikon with a long telescopic lens. He had begun shooting his roll of film the moment David and Rudy García
shook hands. He kept shooting as the two of them rounded Washington Circle, frequently stopping, always engrossed in their conversation. Just before his film ran out, his last shots were of García
clutching David by the shoulder in a tense encounter on the K Street
side of the traffic circle.

***

5

Cuba Libre

Three weeks later, David stepped from the Cubana de Aviación turbo prop passenger plane onto the tarmac at the José Martí International Airport outside Havana. September had arrived, somewhat alleviating the oppressive heat of the summer. Still, coming from the coolness of Mexico City's high plateau, David was unprepared for the afternoon's enervating humidity and heat. He was perspiring heavily before he even reached the terminal building.

He had arrived in Cuba earlier than planned because his visa came through quicker than expected. In fact, when he telephoned the Cuban Consulate in Mexico City, he learned to his astonishment not only that his visa application had been approved for a sixty-day visit but that it was already waiting for him at the Consulate. He was further informed—again to his surprise—that the Foreign Ministry would coordinate his visit and arrange his interviews in Cuba.

The days that followed were a blur. He was forced to wind up his personal and professional affairs in Los Angeles in a hurry in order not to lose more precious days out of his allotted visa period in Cuba. As it was, the earliest he was able to arrive in Havana was Thursday, September 12. In the meantime, before departing Los Angeles, he asked Julie to hold off filing for divorce until his return. He didn't attempt to contact Cindy.

***

David cleared Cuban customs without a hitch, exchanged a thousand dollars for an equivalent number of Cuban pesos, and was on his way to Havana in a taxi less than forty-five minutes after landing. The cab was a rusted 1955 Chevrolet, but it ran surprisingly well for its age. He thought it ironic that revolutionary Cuba was now offering testimony to the longevity of Detroit-made automobiles and trucks built back in the 1950s or even earlier. He reminded himself that Cuban ingenuity and improvisation was the key to having kept so many of these junks running.

He settled back into the cab's threadbare, soiled seat. The windows were rolled down to allow the fresh air to cool the car as it picked up speed. Looking outside, he could see that he was in Cuba all right. The billboards along the road displayed revolutionary slogans, heroic images of Che Guevara, and fragments of Fidel's speeches. The unmistakable scent of Cuba was also in the air—a soft, alluring, slightly sweet, tropical fragrance that brought back memories of his two previous visits to the island.

He had come away from those trips convinced that other Caribbean islands might have white beaches and glassy aquamarine waters equal to those of Varadero, but none he believed could match the variety and beauty of Cuba's scenery. In Pinar del Río at the west end of the island, he had seen prehistoric-looking lumps or *mogotes* rising from the earth. He had flown over countless mangrove swamps that clung to portions of the northern and southern coasts. He had traveled by car across the hot, flat plains of Camagüey in Central Cuba, where enormous cloud formations gathered in the afternoons. Further to the east, he had traveled by Jeep into the Escambray, whose mountains quickly enveloped him in cool air tinged with mist. Later, he had been taken by horseback into the even more rugged Sierra Maestra with its steep ravines, dense foliage, and narrow trails. There, he had seen where the Cuban *mambises* waged their major battles against the Spanish army in the War of Independence and where, over a half-century later, Fidel launched his guerrilla campaign to liberate Cuba from Batista's tyranny.

Now, as his cab neared the capital, the island's ubiquitous royal palms, standing tall and stately, seemed to welcome him back as if he were an old friend. He looked forward to Havana again, especially to La Habana Vieja, which was more than four centuries old. He had fond memories of strolling through the old section of the city, with its cathedral, colonial buildings and parks, and its famed picture-postcard Moro Castle—a fortress the Spaniards had built in the vain hope it would defend Havana's harbor against the marauding British navy. He expected that Havana would be more run-down than when he last saw it. But he was certain that Cuba's capital still possessed a history, an architecture, and a sense of romance unmatched by other, more glamorous modern cities like Miami.

He now understood the Cuban exiles' sense of longing for the island they had abandoned earlier but which lay so tantalizingly close to their sanctuary in Miami. The thought crossed his mind that he must be getting soft. He had never had much empathy for the *gusanos*, or worms, as the government and its supporters called them, a term by which he, too, referred disparagingly to the exiles.

He stopped his musings and turned his attention to the cab driver, a heavyset middle-aged man with a thick neck and closely cropped gray hair. His was a dying breed in Cuba's command economy—a small entrepreneur licensed by the government to use his privately owned car as a taxi.

"How are things today?" David asked in Spanish.

The cab driver looked at him in his rearview mirror for a moment before replying.

"Everything is fine," the cab driver responded in a guarded, non-committal fashion.

David wondered about him. He had once been told that taxi drivers in Eastern Europe, especially those stationed at the airport, were frequently government informers.

"I was here in 1968 and 1969," David went on, trying to gain a better sense of the man. "At that time all of Cuba was mobilized for the ten-million-ton harvest. Even though I was a visitor, I could see that those were difficult times."

"*Sí, fueron años muy duros.* Yes, they were hard years," the driver repeated. "But life has improved since then, especially recently." He fell silent.

"In what way?" David asked, trying to elicit a fuller explanation.

"Well, for one thing, there's more food and other goods in the stores, so life has become easier. And also more orderly. Yes, things are better now."

The driver scrutinized David intently in his rearview mirror. "So let me guess," he said after a moment. "You're an American, yes?"

"Yes, but how can you tell?"

"*Es muy sencillo*—it's very simple, *señor*. It's your accent and clothes. Of course, we don't get many Americans coming here nowadays. Therefore you stand out all the more, especially in contrast to all the Russians and East Europeans who are here."

"I'll bet you have more Russians and East Europeans than a few years back. Am I right?"

"*Sin duda.* Without a doubt. You can find them all over the place. A lot of them are in government agencies, state enterprises, and so forth, where they serve as technicians and advisors. Like I say, all over. But they usually keep to themselves. They're not like the Americans who used to come here before the revolution, to visit the gambling casinos, cabarets, and beaches—to enjoy *la dolce vita* as it's called in the Italian film."

Pausing, the driver again eyed David in the rearview mirror. "And why, *señor*," he asked, "have you come back to Cuba?"

"I'm a professor of political science and I'm writing a book that deals partly with the Cuban revolution." He let his words sink in while he watched the driver's reaction in the mirror. "Your government has given me permission to carry out some studies here so that I can finish the book. That's why I'm here."

"I see." The driver nodded and lapsed into thought. After a few moments, he said, unexpectedly, "Life is strange at times."

"In what way?" David asked, sensing that the driver had chosen his words carefully.

"Here you are," the man replied hesitantly. "An American professor, coming to study us as if we were some strange, exotic species. Yet, at the same time, hundreds of thousands of Cubans have emigrated to your country, which Fidel says is the imperialist enemy of Cuba and Latin America. Don't you consider that ironic?"

"You have a point there," David replied with a laugh as he positioned himself to better watch the man's expression in the rearview mirror. "But you see, as a student of revolution, I'm really interested in what's going on here. You must realize of course that your revolution has had an enormous impact not only on Cuba but also on Latin America and the rest of the world." He stopped for a moment, searching for the right words that might put the driver at ease. "As an academic," he added, "I'm trying to pursue what you might call 'objective truth' about the revolution, whether I like what I find or not."

"Ah, yes, *la verdad*," the driver replied, sarcasm creeping into his voice. "Frankly, I think that there are only a few in this country who, as you put it, are pursuing 'objective truth.' On the other hand, we have many who see themselves as the purveyors of *the* truth."

Suddenly aware that he had come close to crossing the line of what was politically permissible, the man fell silent. David waited to see if he could find a way out.

"Of course," the driver resumed a few moments later, selecting his words carefully, "you must understand I was not referring to

Fidel or the Party. No. Only to the bureaucrats and petty officials who sometimes think they are Fidel." He caught David's reassuring nod in the rearview mirror, but said no more.

It was clear that the driver had concluded David was a Castro sympathizer. David had once heard that some Cubans would hardly talk to visiting Americans or other foreigners because they presumed them to be revolutionary tourists who had been granted visas by the Cuban government. In David's case, he was all the more suspect as the government had also granted him permission to conduct political research.

David was convinced that the man was a *contrarevolucionario*. At the very least, he harbored anti-revolutionary sentiments. *"Che was right,"* David noted, *"to scorn petite bourgeois people like this guy. They're simply incapable of solidarity with the popular masses."* He knew their type from his last visit. In less guarded moments, a few Cubans had complained to him about the shortages of food and consumer goods, the constant mobilizations, and all the other personal sacrifices they had to put up with. When he had pointed out that they were forgetting the corruption, oppression, exploitation, and poverty that had been rampant in pre-1959 Cuba, they clammed up. The same thing was happening now.

David gave up on the driver and turned his attention to the pedestrians and city streets when they entered Havana. The city looked shabbier than he had expected. Buildings and houses were sadly dilapidated, streets were etched black from the soot belching from diesel-burning Soviet bloc buses. Many were rutted and full of potholes. There was no doubt that the capital was sorely in need of major renovation and repair.

The physical blight of Havana was different than the poverty he had encountered in Mexico City earlier in the week. *"At least here,"* he thought, *"the government's priorities are the people, not showy, material things."*

As they drove on, he saw that the city was bustling with greater activity and life than he remembered from his previous trips—a good sign. He even spotted some of the newer Chrysler cars the government had begun importing from Argentina. Whether Soviet aid or the higher prices that Cuba was fetching for its sugar were responsible, his cab driver had been right on at least one count: Life had improved a bit for most ordinary Cubans compared with conditions five years earlier. "La revolución cumple," he murmured. "*Yes. The revolution fulfills its obligation to the people.*"

***

The rusted Chevrolet wheezed to a stop before the twenty-one-story Habana Libre. Once a showy symbol of the 1950s Havana, the former Havana Hilton was now a shoddy, graceless relic of those glittering times. David would have preferred to stay at the Hotel Inglaterra, Havana's oldest, most charming hotel in the center of the city. But the official at the Cuban Consulate in Mexico City had informed him politely, yet firmly, that reservations had been made for him at the Habana Libre. The reason was purely bureaucratic, she had explained, since the Foreign Ministry found it easier to make arrangements with the Habana Libre for foreign visitors like himself. For a fleeting moment he wondered whether he had been assigned to the Habana Libre because he could be more easily monitored there. Quickly dismissing the thought, he chided himself on the paranoia his little meeting with Rudy García had aroused.

He paid the taxi driver and gave him a three peso tip, which the man quickly pocketed, fearful of being seen accepting a *propina.* Tips were officially frowned on as a remnant of the island's decadent capitalist past. A bellman took his two pieces of luggage, and he walked through the large glass doors into the Habana Libre.

The hotel's spacious lobby with its high ceiling was as he remembered it. Stuffed chairs and sofas and area rugs were scattered about on the hardwood floor. Clearly, the lobby had seen better days. Its carpets were threadbare, its sofas and chairs frayed, and its faded walls needed repainting. The hotel reminded him of a once-glamorous woman who had fallen on hard times and was now showing her age.

The desk clerk treated him with indifference, checking his passport against the hotel's reservation list before assigning him a room on the fourteenth floor. He paid for two weeks' stay with the Cuban pesos he had obtained at the airport. Another bellman, with the mannerisms and speech of a *guajiro*, a peasant from the countryside, took his luggage and room key and motioned him toward one of the stainless-steel elevators. The bellman joked and flirted with the female elevator operator as they rode up to his floor. David found his rural dialect and slang almost incomprehensible. As for the operator, he knew she was not there to run the elevator but to prevent unauthorized visits to hotel patrons' rooms by non-guests, whether for perfectly innocent purposes or sexual liaisons.

He couldn't complain about his room. It offered him a sweeping vista of the city below and the azure sea beyond. It was also clean, the bed comfortable enough, and the phone worked, as did the plumbing in his bathroom. The one item that did not function was the air-conditioning system. According to the bellman, air conditioning was absent in all the rooms because the U.S. blockade prevented Cuba from obtaining American-made parts. With a stupid grin, the man told David that his room had *natural air conditioning*. With that, he opened the glass door leading to the small balcony to let in a fresh, cooling sea breeze.

"You're right. I can see that there's a definite advantage to being on the fourteenth floor," David told the bellman, handing him a couple of pesos. "As long as the breeze keeps blowing and the elevators don't break down."

***

After unpacking he returned to the lobby, intent upon heading out to Havana's famous seawall, the Malecón, to do some sightseeing. As he was leaving, a familiar figure pushed through the glass door and rushed into the hotel lobby.

"Tino!" David cried out.

The man pulled up short, an incredulous look coming over his face upon recognizing the American.

"*¡No puede ser!* No, it can't be—not David Diamond after all these years!"

Tino Garzarolli, one of Italy's premier journalists on the Left, was shorter, paunchier, and a few years older than David, and strikingly good looking. In Cuba, he was frequently mistaken for an Italian movie star. He and David had met in 1969 on David's second visit to Cuba as a correspondent for *Ramparts* magazine. The two men had become kindred spirits immediately, each trying to outdo the other in romancing women, and sharing ideas for their respective feature stories on Cuba.

"I just arrived at the hotel less than an hour ago," David said. "But what are you doing back in Cuba? Have you been here long? We've got to talk."

"*Sin duda, amigo.*"

"How about having a beer, or maybe dinner tonight—that is, if you haven't already lined up some sexy Cuban lady or foreign journalist."

"My friend, I wish I could say that I had such a woman. But no, unfortunately, I'm prevented from seeing you now or this evening because of a *compromiso* I have. It's connected with a story I'm writing. How about tomorrow?"

"Sure. I'm completely . . . "

"No, wait! I have a much better idea. Are you free Saturday night? The Italian Embassy is giving a big reception. Lots of good food and drink. And I've been told that Fidel will make an appearance. How about joining me?"

"That sounds great! Even brought my blue blazer and tie for such an occasion. What time should we meet?"

"Meet me here in the lobby around eight. No use getting there too early, eh, my friend? That will also give us time to talk a bit."

"Terrific! I look forward to Saturday night, Tino."

***

David spent the next two hours in the vicinity of his hotel roaming the streets of the Vedado district. Darkening clouds in the southern sky hinted at rain later that evening, which gave promise to an approach of cool air. The more he walked, the more he noticed the run-down condition of apartment houses, stores, and office buildings, all unpainted and seemingly in disrepair for years. The primary reason for this neglect, he knew, was the government's policy of allocating more state resources to the countryside to the detriment of Havana and other cities. Only the hotels that catered to foreigners, along with a few government buildings, seemed to have received a modicum of attention.

But he quickly found that what the city lacked in fresh paint and upkeep was made up for by signs of revolutionary fervor and militancy. At one apartment house alone he came across two large banners hanging from a rusted iron fence surrounding the property. "*15 Años Del Triunfo De La Revolución*"—15 Years Since the Triumph of the Revolution—proclaimed one banner, while the other declared, "*¡COMANDANTE EN JEFE: ÓRDENE!*"—Commander-in-Chief: At Your Orders!

It was just such signs of palpable mass support for Fidel and the revolution, much of it orchestrated to be sure, that had so impressed him on his earlier visits, and now, once again, gave him renewed hope for Cuba's future. The very fact that police and soldiers were scarcely in evidence showed that the vast majority of the masses, including Cuba's youth, were behind the revolution. He could especially feel the vitality of the young people as they congregated on *La Rampa* or strolled along the Malecón, where the breaking waves crashed against the seawall, now and then dousing them with spray.

He was surprised, however, by the ubiquitous *colas* that congregated in front of the state-operated shops and markets. The queues appeared to be every bit as long as the ones he had seen on previous visits. People were still queuing up for hours to buy rationed items such as clothes, shoes, toilet paper, rice, meat, chicken, fruit and vegetables, and other food staples, provided they were in stock. Clearly, shortages continued to bedevil the life of ordinary Cubans. For this he had always placed the blame not on Cuba communism but on the U.S. embargo. Now, for the first time, he wasn't so sure.

In both his scholarly writings and lectures, David had long insisted that Cuba's brand of revolutionary communism was unique. In satisfying the basic needs of its people through free education and medical care, low-cost housing, and an equitable rationing system for food, clothing, and other essentials, Cuba was similar to the Soviet Union and other communist states. Yet, he concluded that Cuba differed fundamentally from those countries: whereas they were ruled by an aging, repressive *nomenklatura*, Cuba's leadership was still relatively young, Fidel's finger was always on the pulse of the people, and the revolution's leaders lived modestly, working tirelessly and enduring the same sacrifices as the popular masses.

As he neared the end of his two-hour tour of the city, however, David experienced the first of several disquieting thoughts. Perhaps Cuban communism wasn't quite as distinct as he had previously assumed. The expressions on the passing Cuban faces suggested that their lives were nearly as grim as those of the countless Russians and East Europeans he had seen in photographs and films. And Cubans queuing up in front of stores, most of the time stocked with shoddy goods and a limited number of food items, was the mirror image of what was occurring in other communist societies.

Most troubling for him as he stopped and peeked into store windows was the nature of the shortages, which was by no means confined to imported consumer goods. Missing were all the fresh fruits, vegetables, and tubers, along with chicken, pork, and beef, that had once been grown or raised in abundance on the island and that had been moderately priced prior to the revolution. As much as David hated to admit it, he began wondering whether Cuba's food shortages and rationing system were not due more to the collectivization of agriculture and the mismanagement and inefficiencies of the state-run economy than to the embargo. If this were true, then he felt that Cuba was headed down the same path as other communist states.

Returning to the Habana Libre, David realized he was experiencing his first gnawing doubts about what he as an American academic called the *exceptionalism* of Cuban communism. But his doubts existed solely on an intellectual plane; in no way did they dilute his passion for the Cuban revolution. Nor did they alter his conviction that socialism was a far more equitable system than capitalism— something he was sure would be confirmed once he saw more of Cuba, especially the rural parts of the island.

Nevertheless, it was now becoming clear to him that he had to tackle the issue of Cuban exceptionalism in the last chapter of his book. This meant he would have to conduct his interviews with Cuban officials in ways that would elicit answers about how they envisioned Cuba remaining distinct from other communist societies. But he would have to be careful with his line of questioning. He didn't want to be expelled from Cuba as were other European and American leftists who were viewed as too critical of the government's policies. No. He must frame his inquiries along lines of learning how Cuba proposed to perfect its distinctive style of revolutionary communism.

* * *

David remained in his room on Friday, his first full day in Havana, awaiting a return call from the Foreign Ministry regarding the scheduling of his interviews. Finally, at three o'clock in the afternoon, he was informed that someone from MINREX would contact him on Monday. He was disappointed. That meant he would lose at least another whole day of work before any appointments could be made.

His luck wasn't any better upon calling some of the academics and researchers whom he had met at the University of Havana and government institutes in 1969. They either weren't in, didn't return his calls, or asked him to call back the following week. A few didn't even remember him. He finally gave up, and went for a swim in the Habana Libre's pool. Still feeling edgy afterward he decided he had to get out of the hotel. He hurriedly showered, dressed, and went downstairs.

***

The cab from the hotel dropped David at the entrance to the Catedral de San Cristóbal in La Habana Vieja, where he was forced to view the nearly 200-year-old cathedral from the outside since it was closed. Disappointed, he began walking south, past colonial buildings whose history or function he didn't know, until he reached the Plaza de Armas. Royal palms graced the park; in the center stood the marble statue of Carlos Manuel de Céspedes, who had ignited Cuba's struggle for independence in 1868. He continued westward along Calle Obispo, frequently turning up side streets to admire the three-story neoclassical buildings, many with arches and columns and tall, shaded passageways. Finally, he reached the Capitolio Nacional. The forty-five-year-old capitol was modeled after the U.S. Capitol and stood as mute testimony to Washington's influence during the dictatorship of Gerardo Machado in the late 1920s and early 1930s.

He strolled up the Paseo de Martí, noting its faded opulence. Veering off once again into side streets, he passed numerous nineteenth-century buildings worn down by time, weather, and lack of maintenance. Sitting atop arched passageways, some stood three stories tall. Barbershops, beauty parlors, laundries, and small shops, all nationalized and state-run since 1968, usually occupied the ground floors. He could tell that the second and third floors were mostly occupied as apartments, with all the sheets, towels, and clothing drying on the iron railings of the narrow balconies.

The voices of residents, yelling or arguing loudly, were audible despite the din of blaring radios and TVs. The few cars and trucks navigating the narrow streets added to the racket as drivers honked their horns to clear pedestrians and children from their paths. The entire scene was filled with life, clamor, and excitement—so chaotic, he thought, and so typically Cuban.

As he strolled through La Habana Vieja he saw that the disrepair was even worse than that of the Vedado district, which he had witnessed the evening before. He wished it were not so. Muttering to himself, he shook his head in silent disapproval. *"Christ, the government should devote at least some resources to restoring Old Havana. It's a national treasure, part of Cuba's very soul!"*

Nevertheless, the narrow streets and the buildings, whose balconies and iron railings jutted out over the thread-like sidewalks below, still retained the charm of a bygone era. In his imagination he could almost visualize Old Havana as it must have been in the decades before the revolution. But the spell was soon broken. The diesel buses and heavily laden trucks imported from Spain and Eastern Europe, rambling loudly through the wider thoroughfares, belching black, sooty smoke, brought him back to the present.

* * *

Hot and sweaty from his long walk, David made his way back to the Parque Central, next to the Capitolio. Unlike the capitol building, the park dated back to the colonial period. Its old laurel trees formed a green canopy over the paths, benches, and flower beds within the park, offering welcome shade to hot, perspiring visitors.

Sitting down on one of the park benches, he watched children at play and made a mental note that they looked healthy and well-nourished—unlike so many of the children he had seen just days earlier in Mexico City. A simply dressed woman was seated nearby with a young boy, who was playing with a ball. He guessed the lad was seven or eight years old. When the youngster kicked the ball toward him, he stretched out his right foot and kicked it back, soccer style. Delighted, the boy caught the ball, then kicked it again in his direction. This time David couldn't reach the ball with his outstretched foot and had to get up to kick it back. Before the boy could return it, the woman called to him.

"Ven acá, niño," David heard her say. She spoke briefly to the child; a moment later he reluctantly approached David.

"¿Ud. es inglés o norteamericano?" the boy inquired shyly.

"Soy norteamericano. But why do you ask?"

"Well," the boy said, obviously embarrassed by what he was about to say. "My mother wants to know whether you have any American cigarettes. My father likes cigarettes, but he can only buy ones that are made here in Cuba."

"Tell your mother I'm sorry, but I don't smoke. Otherwise, I would be happy to give you some cigarettes for your father." He watched as the boy trotted back to his mother. He could tell she was disappointed.

"*Lo siento, señora,*" David called out to her, trying to make amends for being without cigarettes. "*Pero como le dije a su hijo, yo no fumo y por eso no tengo cigaros.*"

"It's all right, *señor,*" the woman replied.

He wanted to strike up a conversation with her, but she and the child quickly gathered their belongings and left. Watching them depart, he realized he was bothered by the boy having asked him for cigarettes. It was too much like begging. "*But at least the kids here don't have to beg for money or food like so many children in the rest of Latin America,*" he reminded himself.

Leaving the park, he passed several *colas* in front of stores. Some of the men and women he saw standing in the queues looked in a foul mood, probably because they expected the shop would run out of the meat, the right-size shoes, or whatever else they were hoping to buy. Yet many others appeared to be in good humor, using their long wait to chat and joke with acquaintances. He marveled at the Cubans' knack for adjusting to life's irritating inconveniences while still keeping their sense of humor. As he walked by one of the *colas*, a man evidently recognizing him as a foreigner, nodded in his direction to a companion next to him. David was tempted to stop but decided against trying to strike up a conversation. By now it was early evening, it was still hot, and he was feeling worn down.

***

Returning to the Habana Libre after seven, he immediately headed for the downstairs bar to cool off. He had been sitting at his table only a few minutes, enjoying a refreshing cold Cuban beer, when he noticed a plump, middle-aged woman studying him from across the room. He was certain he had met her before on one of his earlier trips, but he couldn't immediately recall the circumstances or her name. Then, as she turned away from him, he saw the black, dime-sized mole protruding from her neck, just below her jawbone. "*Oh, God!*" How could he forget her! It was Sheila Frankel.

Frankel was the last person he wanted to see that day—or any other day, for that matter. An American Communist, she was an expatriate who had been living in Cuba since 1962. She never failed to remind everyone listening that she had arrived just before the October missile crisis, as if that fact alone was enough to establish her as a committed revolutionary.

First employed as a translator by the Cuban government, Frankel went on to become an unabashed propagandist for her hosts, frequently talking on Radio Havana and writing feature articles for *Prensa Latina*, the Cuban news service. The less discriminating left-wing press in the United States and Canada sometimes published her articles as well. Besides paying her a modest stipend, the Cuban government made her life comfortable enough by providing her with a two-bedroom apartment in one of Vedado's once-fashionable neighborhoods. Now and then it also arranged trips for her to Mexico, England, or Canada. She would use those travel opportunities to purchase consumer products that were unavailable in Cuba, even in the special shops reserved for the *nomenklatura*, the diplomatic corps, and other foreigners residing in Havana.

David had met her twice before in 1969, by which time she was well connected with the government. Her privileged status, Tino Garzarolli had informed him, enabled her to find lovers among not only Cuban men but also a few Black Panthers and other American radicals then living in temporary or permanent exile in Havana. David was certain that they were not attracted to her because of her looks.

As a former member of the New Left, however, he despised her most of all for her mindless communist orthodoxy. Not only was she an ardent defender of the Soviet system, she also was an unrepentant Stalinist who dismissed all the revelations contained in Khrushchev's 1956 secret speech concerning the Soviet dictator's crimes. Having come to Cuba, she now served as the worst kind of political hack for the government. David had found her news stories so transparently propagandistic that he feared they did more harm than good to the Cuban revolution.

Quickly averting his gaze, he pretended not to recognize her. But to his dismay, she rose abruptly from her table and came over to him.

"You're David Diamond, aren't you?" she asked pointedly. "Maybe you don't recall, but we met some years ago at the offices of *Prensa Latina*. I'm Sheila Frankel."

"Oh, of course! Sheila Frankel, yes, I do remember you." He stood up and with a forced smile extended his hand. "Wow! You really have a good memory to remember me after all these years. Anyway, have a seat. What are you drinking?"

"I'm having scotch, thank you. Well, when did you arrive? And what are you doing these days? I haven't read anything you've written lately. Are you still in journalism?"

"No, not any more. Since we last met I went on to finish my Ph.D. at Berkeley. I'm now a political science professor at the University of Southern California."

"Oh, so you're a professor now at, uh . . . did you say the University of Southern California? Isn't that the school best known for its football teams?"

"Among other things," he replied coolly. "USC in recent years has been building a first-rate political science department. That's why I accepted their offer."

"*Touché*, David!" she replied with false gaiety. "But tell me, when did you arrive and what are you doing here? Maybe I could interview you for Radio Havana or *Prensa Latina*."

"Hmm, I don't think so. You see I've hardly had time to get my bearings since I arrived yesterday afternoon. Right now, my first priority is to complete my research here, which I must do if I'm to finish my book."

"You're writing a book on Cuba?"

"Well, not entirely on Cuba. It's more about socialist revolutions and how the Bolshevik, Chinese, and Cuban experiences had to deal with several major theoretical questions common to Marxist revolutions." Not wanting to elaborate any further, he paused, then added, "It's in that context that Cuba occupies part of the book as a detailed case study." He motioned to the waiter and ordered her scotch.

"How fascinating," she broke in, her glazed eyes betraying her disinterest. "Of course, I'm sure you realize that Cuba has many important lessons to offer the Third World. I've lived here for nearly twelve years, you know, having arrived just before the missile crisis, and I've witnessed enormous changes."

"Yes, I bet you have," he said, hoping to cut short her speechmaking, but she paid him no heed.

"Let me tell you, during the first years that I was here, Cuba's capitalist class still hadn't been entirely eliminated. But later, when the bourgeoisie was gone, the workers and peasants truly gained power because they controlled the means of production. Now they're assured of their basic necessities, like free health care and education. So you see, Cuba is in the vanguard of the world's revolutionary movement. You've got to show all this in your book, David."

He was growing irritated. Frankel was spouting the kind of Soviet-style agitprop expected from an old Stalinist. She really was an embarrassment to the Left.

"Look, Sheila," he said, doing his best to remain civil. "Like you, I support the revolution with all my heart. But as a scholar, I just can't ignore or overlook all the complexities and contradictions of the revolution. No, I have to show warts and all . . . "

"I know all that," she interrupted impatiently. "But my point is that you've got to inform your readers about the struggle of the Cuban people. You've got to tell them all about the accomplishments of the revolution!"

"And what I'm trying to tell you," David replied sharply, "is that I'm not about to force-fit my assumptions and preferences about the revolution into my research findings. No way! I'll reach my conclusions based on the evidence that I've compiled, whatever their political implications."

"Oh, David, you really are so naïve! It's all very well for you to take the high road and talk about your scholarly commitment, except that the conclusions you draw can hurt Cuba. Don't you realize that the revolution is fighting for its life against the United States? Against imperialism? Against fascism?" She stopped to catch her breath before taking another swallow from the glass of scotch the waiter had set before her. "Anything you say that's critical of Cuba in pursuit of so-called 'objective' truth, which we all know is simply a reflection of false bourgeois values, will be used against Cuba, against Fidel, by the enemies of the revolution!"

"Sheila," David retorted, having a hard time controlling his temper. "I will not alter or otherwise distort my findings because of their potential political ramifications. No way. I'll call it as I see it. Besides, I can't control how my research findings might be used."

"Yes, you can," she replied testily. "If you're sympathetic to the revolution, and obviously you must be, otherwise the Cuban government wouldn't have given you a visa, then you don't have the luxury of being neutral in the struggle with imperialism, with fascism. I don't care whether you are a professor, *you've got to take sides!*"

She was glowering at him, her pudgy face flushed with self-righteous indignation. She took a couple of more sips of scotch and waited for him to respond.

Their heated, increasingly loud argument had not gone unnoticed by other patrons in the bar. Although they had been arguing in English, David feared that much of what they had said was overheard and understood. In any case, he wanted to end their discussion— she was too dogmatic, too closed-minded, and her cant too infuriating for him to bear.

"Look," he said quietly, but with deliberate finality. "I'll draw my own conclusions about Cuba. But I can tell you this: As an academic, I didn't come here with the purpose of trashing Fidel or the revolution."

She let out a sigh. "O.K., Professor," she said, her voice tinged with sarcasm. "I guess that's the best you can do."

A prolonged, awkward silence followed. She gulped down the last of her scotch and studied the professor before her with renewed interest.

"How about you and I having dinner tonight?" she asked, her voice suddenly assuming a soft, husky tone.

"What?" he blurted out, scarcely able to conceal his surprise.

"I asked whether you wanted to have dinner with me tonight," she repeated, watching his reaction. "You could come over to my apartment, if you like. Or we could at least go to a better restaurant than what this place has to offer." With a smirk, she added, "Don't be scared. We won't have to talk politics. I promise. What do you say?"

"*Holy shit!*" he told himself. "*She's trying to pick me up!*"

"I'm sorry, Sheila," he replied, his eyes inadvertently fastening on the unsightly mole on her neck. "But I already have a commitment for tonight."

He knew immediately that she didn't believe him. She caught his look of disgust.

"What are you looking at?" she demanded.

"Nothing," he replied lamely.

"Go fuck yourself, you bastard!" she said loudly. "That is, if you can, you academic eunuch!"

With that she gathered herself up from the table, grabbed her purse, and stormed out of the bar.

The other patrons looked at her retreating figure and then at David. A sunburned, red-haired man at the bar, who appeared to be an American, grinned knowingly at him. Embarrassed by the scene they had made, David hoped he had seen the last of Sheila Frankel.

***

Arriving late for their rendezvous the following evening, Tino introduced David to the tall, gangly young man who had followed him into the hotel lobby.

"I want you to meet Chucho," Tino said. "He and his friends can show you a good time. More importantly, they can talk intelligently about Cuba."

David guessed that Chucho was in his early twenties. He appeared amiable and quick witted. David liked the young Cuban immediately. Chucho promised he would bring his friends to the hotel the following night.

After Chucho had departed, Tino suggested they walk to the embassy.

"It will take us twenty minutes or so, but we have plenty of time. As I'm sure you remember, nobody here goes by *hora inglesa* except for the Cuban army. Besides, the walk will give us an opportunity to talk."

"Sounds good to me," David agreed, "just as long as we don't miss Fidel."

"Don't worry, my friend. I can assure you he'll keep all of us waiting."

As they proceeded along Calle 23, Tino explained that he had been in Cuba for nearly two months. He had arrived just before Fidel's speech on the 26th of July, the day commemorating the attack by the then twenty-five-year-old rebel leader and his followers on the Moncada Barracks twenty-one years earlier. His return to Havana was for the purpose of updating and revising his 1970 book on the Cuban revolution, which contained an exclusive interview of Fidel—a journalistic coup that he hadn't been able to replicate on this trip. Nevertheless, David knew the Italian had superb contacts in the government. As they walked, he soon began plying him with questions about the latest developments on the island.

"As you know," Tino said, responding to one of David's inquiries, "the whole governing process here has begun to be formalized along a less personalistic-type order."

"What is now being called the 'institutionalization of the revolution,'" David added.

"Precisely. The point is that Fidel is no longer running things *a la libre*—without restraints of any kind as he once did. His colossal failure in the 1970 harvest put an end to that. In addition, the army has pulled out of trying to run sectors of the economy; it's confining itself strictly to military affairs."

"So, who is running Cuba today?"

"Don't misunderstand me, David. Fidel is still very much in charge. And the army and MININT remain the government's two most important pillars. No, what I'm driving at is that the Cuban Communist Party, which Fidel all but ignored after its founding in 1965, is being groomed in Leninist fashion to become the leading organ in Cuba. The PCC, in other words, is to become like the communist parties in the Soviet Union and the rest of the socialist bloc."

"So, in effect, you're saying Cuba is becoming Sovietized?"

"On the surface, perhaps. But I think it would be more accurate to say that the *fidelismo* of old has been replaced by *fidelismo-comunismo*."

"You're right," David concurred. "That better portrays what's happening. However, even before I arrived here I heard that the Soviets have moved in on such a large scale that they are advising the Cubans on how to run just about everything."

"Yes, yes, that is largely correct, except that the Russians are using the old communists from the PSP as their surrogates. They're the ones reconstructing Cuba's governmental, state, and party structures along lines similar to those in the Soviet Union."

"Yes. I read where the old communist leader, Blas Roca, is now charged with drafting a new socialist constitution for Cuba."

"Exactly," Tino affirmed. "Other ex-PSP members are also in varying positions of authority throughout the government. But not in the Ministry of the Revolutionary Armed Forces or the Ministry of the Interior. They remain the exclusive strongholds of Fidel and Raúl, and the *veteranos* who fought with them in Sierra Maestra."

Tino paused in order for them to cross onto Paseo and turn in the direction of the embassy. "As I was saying," he resumed. "You won't find too many old communists in either the MINFAR or the MININT. As always, Fidel is too wary, too cunning, when it comes to any potential challenge to his power."

"So, will Cuba avoid becoming another Soviet satellite?" David asked, deliberately slowing down. "Or will it succumb because of its growing dependence on Moscow?"

"A good question, but it's too early to tell."

"Yes, of course, but make an educated guess. If anyone is capable of predicting Cuba's future, that person is you, Tino."

"Well, all right," Tino said with a smile, flattered by David's compliment. "My instincts tell me that Cuba will never become a satellite on the order of East Germany or Czechoslovakia. I say that not just because this island is six thousand miles away from the Soviet Union, or because the revolution has indigenous roots. No, I think the more important factor is that Fidel is a hero to his people, unlike the East European leaders."

"All that's true," David agreed. "But it's also clear that Cuba has now become more dependent on the Russians than was the case five or ten years ago. That could mean that Cuba will have no other alternative but to tow the party line emanating from Moscow."

"It would look that way," Tino said after a moment's reflection. "Except that I would never underestimate Fidel's resiliency and shrewdness. He still may be able to regain a degree of maneuverability—perhaps even a measure of independence—unknown to most of Eastern Europe."

"Which leads me to ask about something I heard in Washington. Do you think he might be ready to normalize relations with the U.S. in order to check the Soviets?"

"I think that's highly unlikely," Tino replied quickly, shaking his head. "Fidel is too much of a nationalist, too imbued with his sense of importance as the world's preeminent anti-imperialist figure, to turn to your country. No, I think that's wishful thinking on the part of whoever told you that in Washington."

"But, then, Tino, how's he going to maintain some degree of independence?"

"Believe me, I wish I knew. But I don't have the slightest idea of how he can pull the proverbial rabbit out of the hat, as you say in English. Unfortunately, that puts me in a real bind because I must return to Italy next week to finish my manuscript for the new edition."

"But why the hurry?"

"It's partly my fault," Tino sighed. "You see, the manuscript already is long overdue. Now my publisher is demanding that I submit it by the end of next month. I don't understand why, but he insists that the new edition must be out by early next year. Anyway, I have no choice in the matter."

To David's regret, they had to cut short their discussion. They were encountering too many people as they neared the Italian Embassy. He doubted he'd have another opportunity to talk to Tino before the Italian departed.

***

6

Encounters

The Italian Embassy reminded David of the fashionable homes
that were constructed in Havana during the boom years after World
War I, before the plunge in world sugar prices began devastating the
island's fragile economy in the late 1920s. Until then, the "dance of
the millions"—and with it, the massive infusion of American capital—had produced an opulent age during which the newly enriched
entrepreneurs and speculators built elegant homes. But once the
economy began to crumble, the houses proved far sturdier than the
island's social order. Only the dictatorship of Gerardo Machado
momentarily preserved the status quo. Then the 1933 revolution
erupted, bringing down the rickety structure, while ushering in the
first of many changes in Cuba's society and politics.

The reception was being held in the embassy's main salon. By the
time David and Tino arrived, it was already filled with some fifty or
more guests, who milled about or clustered together in small, animated groups. Tino introduced David to the Italian ambassador, and
then went off to make the rounds of his acquaintances. After accepting a glass of Pinot Grigio from a passing waiter and helping himself
to a slightly burnt piece of *bruschetta* from another, David began to
scan the crowd.

His eyes almost immediately met those of a dark-complexioned
man several feet away. The stranger was as tall as David, but leaner
and more muscular, with sharp, angular features, and his military
bearing and sense of authority made David wonder for a moment if
he was the embassy's military attaché. Except he wasn't in uniform
and he didn't look Italian. But it was clear to David that he was of
obvious interest to the stranger who was now making his way toward him.

* * *

"Let me introduce myself, Professor Diamond," the man said in
nearly flawless English that contained only a hint of a Cuban accent.
"I am Captain Joaquín Acosta. I am with State Security in the Ministry of Interior."

"Oh," replied David, a bit rattled. Quickly recovering and shaking the officer's outstretched hand, he said, "It's a pleasure to meet you, Captain Acosta. However, I'm somewhat perplexed. You know me by name, yet I don't think that we've met before."

"That's right, we haven't met until now. But I recognized you from your visa photograph, which is on file at MININT. Since I go over the daily reports on who's visiting our island, I am aware that you arrived a couple of days ago."

Acosta's explanation was not reassuring. On the contrary, David became concerned that the MININT officer from State Security seemed to be taking an unusual interest in him. Was it because of his meetings with Rudy García? *"No,"* he chided himself. *"That's really being too paranoid."* Still, he had better be on guard.

"It seems that everything I've heard about State Security is correct, Captain," he went on calmly, looking the MININT officer in the eye. "Yours must be a super-efficient organization to keep track of the likes of someone like me."

"But Professor Diamond," Acosta protested. "You're a distinguished visitor as far as we're concerned. You've been here on two previous occasions. Now you've returned to undertake research— this time on the *Poder Popular*. So, obviously, anyone investigating our politics, especially an American academic like yourself, is going to be of interest to us."

Acosta paused for a moment to weigh the effect of his words on David. "But don't be alarmed," he continued, a thin smile spreading his lips as he saw David's look of concern. "I haven't been following you. In fact, I had no idea you had been invited to the reception."

"It's purely by chance that I'm here," David replied, feeling somewhat relieved. "You see, I ran into an acquaintance of mine who had been invited to the reception, and he, in turn, brought me along."

"How fortunate for me, then," Acosta said. "Because now I have the opportunity to exchange views with an American scholar like yourself. By the way, do you mind if I call you David?"

"Oh, not at all. But can I call you by your first name, too?"

"By all means. If we all refer to the Commander-in-Chief of our armed forces, the First-Secretary of our Party, and the Prime Minister of our government as simply Fidel, then you should be able as well to call me Joaquín. We are not a formal people here in Cuba, David."

"Yes, I'm well aware of that," David nodded in agreement. He stopped a passing waiter to relieve him of another glass of wine and gestured to Joaquín to do the same. Shaking his head, the MININT Captain passed up the opportunity. David sized him up more carefully over the rim of his wine glass as he drank, but found his countenance virtually inscrutable.

"It occurs to me that as an American political scientist you might be interested in exchanging views with our own specialists in the Foreign Ministry and the Party," Joaquín said in a more serious vein, looking steadily at David. "Does that appeal to you?"

"Sure," David replied. "I'd like that very much as long as there's a free exchange of ideas between us and it's really a two-way street. I don't want to be the only one who's fielding questions."

"I understand," Joaquín responded with a knowing nod. "What kind of questions would you be asking of our people?"

"Well, I guess the most obvious one is whether your government thinks the prospects for restoring normal relations with Washington have improved now that Nixon is out of the picture."

"Yes, that's a most interesting question," Joaquín concurred, pausing to again fix his dark eyes on David. "But it's also somewhat of a sensitive policy question for us," he continued. "In any case, I'll have to first see whether our people can meet with you."

"I'm entirely at their disposal," David said agreeably.

"Good. Now, let's move over to that corner," Joaquín proposed with a nod of his head as he took David by the arm. "It's less crowded there so we can talk better. You see, I'm curious as to why you chose to study our *Poder Popular* experiment instead of, let's say, the successes the revolution has had in producing a more egalitarian society. My curiosity, by the way, is purely intellectual."

"I'm glad to hear that," David replied, laughing, as they took up their new position. "Anyway, let me assure you I have no intention of slighting the revolution in any way. It's just that I need to study the *Poder Popular* because of the book I'm writing on socialist revolutions. You see, it addresses the question of Cuba's potential for greater participatory democracy . . . "

"But our revolution already *is* democratic," Joaquín broke in. "We have a classless society where there aren't enormous income differentials since the state ensures that all the basic needs of the population are satisfied. That, my friend, is true socialist democracy, Cuban style."

David fell silent for a moment, wondering whether he should take issue with the Captain. Then, whether from the wine he was drinking or his years of intellectual combat, he couldn't resist taking him on.

"I entirely agree with you concerning the egalitarian dimensions of your revolution," David said. "But I'm not talking about social justice. I'm referring to *political* democracy. In my book, that's where people participate freely in choosing their leaders, in the making of policies that affect their lives—whether it's in the workplace, or in the community, or in the nation as a whole."

"That sounds like bourgeois democracy to me," Joaquín retorted.

"Well, you call it what you will. However, I believe that the kind of democracy I'm talking about is essential if socialist systems are to evolve beyond the stage of the dictatorship of the proletariat or, more accurately, the dictatorship of the Communist Party." Noting the trace of anger that flickered briefly in the MININT Captain's eyes, he paused momentarily before deciding to press his point. "So, Joaquín, I want to investigate whether the *Poder Popular* will grant people the power to freely choose their local leaders. I want to see whether those leaders, in turn, will be able to allocate resources to their local projects without interference from the Party. If it looks like the *Poder Popular* will do those things, then the prospects for Cuban democracy are good. But if it's negative on both counts, then I fear the *Poder Popular* will only come to resemble the local Soviets in the USSR."

"I must confess, that I don't know what form the *Poder Popular* experiment will ultimately take," Joaquín replied, after studying David for a moment. "But I doubt it will be either like the local Soviets or the kind of democracy you visualize. However, I can assure you it will take into account the level of political sophistication of the Cuban people. In the end, therefore, it will be genuinely democratic— unlike your system in which the two main parties don't represent the real interests of the American people."

***

Having stopped to help themselves to hors d'oeuvres, Joaquín now took a glass of wine. Aware that he had been treading on dangerous ground, David wished he could rid himself of the MININT officer. Just as he was about to manufacture an excuse to leave, Joaquín steered him into an adjoining room away from the packed main salon.

Joaquín began where he had left off moments earlier. "You know, the notion that you and other American progressives have about democracy really is of little relevance for a revolution like ours," he confided.

"And why is that?" David asked, mindful that his companion was determined to have the last word. Nevertheless, he was interested in hearing what Joaquín had to say.

"*Es muy sencillo*—it's quite simple," Joaquín began as if he were addressing a group of MININT cadets. "Do you think for one minute our revolution could have withstood the criminal aggression by the world's foremost imperialist power by relying on your so-called participatory democracy?" He continued, not waiting for David's answer. "Of course not. Fidel and a small vanguard of committed revolutionaries have always had to provide the impulse and guidance for the Cuban people to endure enormous sacrifices and to emerge victorious in their struggle against great odds. Otherwise, my learned friend, Cuba would have returned to the *status quo ante* long ago."

"Look, I don't deny the need for leadership, especially the role played by Fidel's charisma. But you also can't deny that communist systems rely on the Party's centralized command structure for ruling. So, as I said a moment ago, unless there is more democratic participation from below, such a system can degenerate into a permanent dictatorship under a political oligarchy. That's what's happened in the Soviet Union and Eastern Europe."

"I can assure you," Joaquín replied impatiently, "that Fidel will not permit such a thing to happen in Cuba. He and the Party will continue to be out in front, leading, but constantly in touch *con el pueblo*. And Fidel can do that better than anybody."

"Yes," David agreed, trying to find common ground between them. "There's no question that Fidel has a knack for feeling the pulse of the Cuban people. And he certainly enjoys overwhelming popular support. But what happens once Fidel is no longer here? Don't you see? At some point you're going to need to give the people the right to participate in your political process without the Party limiting their power or their choices."

"Ah, David, you're truly an idealist. Either that or we live on two entirely different planets when it comes to perceiving Cuba's reality."

"I can only tell you that in just two days' time I've already detected a different Cuban reality from the one I perceived in my earlier trips."

"Don't be too hasty, my friend," Joaquín replied with a half-smile. "Several years ago, a wise Russian intelligence officer gave me these words of advice which I'll pass on to you: 'Never assume that after your first, second, third, or even fourth visit to a foreign country you've come to know it. No, a foreign country is like an onion— you can keep peeling it, but there are still more layers of skin underneath the last one you've peeled.'"

***

When they returned to the main salon moments later, Joaquín's eyes came suddenly alive with a glow that surprised David. Glancing in the direction of Joaquín's gaze, he was startled to see Catalina Cruz standing less than ten paces away. She looked every bit as stunning as when he first set eyes on her six years earlier.

Catalina Cruz was as he remembered her: a green-eyed beauty, taller and more slender than most Cuban women, with long legs and straight, dark hair falling midway down her back. She was older now—in her late twenties, he guessed—and at the moment dressed not in jeans, as when he had last seen her, but in a cocktail dress. With its low-cut V-shaped halter-top, the short white dress accentuated her dusky skin and lustrous, raven-colored hair. Even in the crowded salon she radiated a beauty and sensuality that set her apart from all the other women at the reception. Unable to tear his eyes from her, he was smitten all over again.

"I see that you've discovered one of Cuba's most beautiful women," Joaquín observed, interrupting David's reverie.

David nodded slowly in agreement. "On that we're in complete agreement, Joaquín. In fact, I'd say Catalina Cruz is even more stunning than I remember."

"You know her?"

"Well, not exactly," David replied, reluctantly turning his attention back to Joaquín. "I first saw her when she gave a talk to the solidarity group I was with, mostly radical students like myself, thanking us for demonstrating our support for Cuba." He paused to steal a glance in her direction, but now there were too many people around her. "I think she was with the Union of Young Communists or perhaps she was representing the University Student Federation. Hell, I can't remember. Like other guys in our group, I wasn't hearing anything she said. I was just looking. *Lusting* would be more accurate," he added with a laugh.

"Yes, Catalina can do that to men. And if they don't react that way," Joaquín noted, partly in jest, "they must be *maricones*."

"When I came back the following year as a correspondent," David continued, ignoring Acosta's remark about gays, "I saw her again briefly. I think she was with the Foreign Ministry by then. In any case I'm sure she doesn't remember me."

"Well, come, I will reintroduce you."

Joaquín led David over to Catalina and the cluster of admirers who were surrounding her.

"Catalina," Joaquín said, as the men around her gave way. Speaking in Spanish, he continued, "I want to introduce you to someone who just recently arrived from the United States, Professor David Diamond. The two of you met back in 1968 and 1969, but he doesn't think you'd remember."

"Professor Diamond, how nice to have you back." She flashed a dazzling smile that nearly caused David's heart to skip a beat. "But I must confess you're right. I'm afraid I don't recall our meeting."

"Please, there's no need to apologize," David replied, his Spanish sounding more stilted than usual. "I'm sure you've met several thousand foreign visitors since I was last here. Besides, I was in a large group. So you couldn't possibly remember. But I, for one, am delighted that we meet again."

"And I, too, Professor Diamond."

"Please call me David." He was feeling more confident, even less clumsy in Spanish.

"Thank you, David, I will," she answered, her green eyes fastening on him. "Are you here to study our country?" she asked, giving him her full attention as she detached herself from the men clustered around her and moved into his space.

"Well, yes, for the next two months, I hope. I'm completing a book on socialist revolutions, in which Cuba gets star billing."

"Wonderful! I hope I will have the opportunity to learn more about it," she said, with genuine interest. "But I'm afraid that this isn't the time or the place for it. We'll have to wait for another occasion."

"I think you're right," David agreed. "I can only hope the opportunity presents itself soon."

"I do too," she responded warmly. "I don't know whether Joaquín told you, but in my job at MINREX I serve as a guide for foreign guests. On a few occasions I've been assigned to academic visitors from Western Europe." She hesitated for an instant, looking mischievously at David and then Joaquín. "But up to now," she continued in a flirtatious voice, "I haven't had the pleasure of escorting a young American professor like yourself."

"Well, I certainly look forward to being your first *norteamericano*," he replied with a smile, his heart quickening at her words.

"Yes, I think that might be fun for both of us. To tell you the truth, I'm tired of stodgy old foreign officials," she confided, lowering her voice and glancing at the people nearby to make sure no one would be offended. "Now, Joaquín, don't put on such a sour face!"

Catalina had caught Joaquín's look of disapproval, but David had already sensed that the MININT Captain did not approve of the overly friendly way she was behaving toward him. At the moment, however, Joaquín appeared embarrassed by her observation.

"Joaquín is always trying to protect me from you Yankees," Catalina laughed with delight at Joaquín's obvious discomfort.

"But he knows there is nothing to fear from me," David chimed in. "Right, Joaquín?"

"But of course," Joaquín replied coldly. "You and I know that you are a stalwart friend of the Cuban people and the revolution."

Hearing the cold sarcasm in Joaquín's voice, Catalina gave him a puzzled look, but the MININT officer's face masked whatever he was thinking. Suspecting that Joaquín was miffed by Catalina's flirtatious remarks, David decided to end their conversation.

"Well, Catalina, I really do hope we meet again," David announced, breaking the silence that had descended on the three of them. "Try to convince MINREX to assign you as my escort." With a quick glance at the Captain, he added recklessly as he would later come to realize, "And if we're lucky, it will be without Joaquín, here."

Her face lit up at the thought. "That would really be nice," she replied wistfully. "I'll see what I can arrange at the Foreign Ministry."

As they walked away, David felt Joaquín's hostility. He suspected that the MININT officer and Catalina were having an affair or had had one. "*Either that or Joaquín is in love with her but she's spurned him.*" Either way, he fully expected Joaquín to tell him to stay away from Catalina. The MININT Captain didn't strike him as the kind of man who would be shy about claiming the woman he loved.

"I'm sorry, David, but I have to see some of the other guests before I leave," Joaquín said curtly in English. "However," he added with a thin smile, "I'm sure we will have ample opportunities to renew our provocative discussion in the future."

***

Left alone, David milled about until he found a vantage point in the crowded room from where he could steal occasional glances at Catalina. Once, when she caught him staring at her, she had smiled and nodded ever so slightly in recognition. He was watching her again a few moments later when he heard a strange voice beside him.

"Catalina Cruz is a far sight better looking than Sheila Frankel, wouldn't you say?"

Turning, he was surprised to see the red-haired man from the Habana Libre bar, who had observed his argument with Frankel. From his accent, he sounded more American than British or European.

"Philip Taylor is my name," the stranger said, extending his right hand, while cradling a glass of red wine in his left.

"Glad to meet you. I'm David Diamond. And you're absolutely right; there's no comparison. Catalina is as beautiful as Frankel is ugly."

Taylor appeared to be in his early forties, but David couldn't really tell. His thinning reddish hair was streaked with gray. His face was fair, but craggy and weathered from age or too much sun. His rough hands were stained as if he were a workman or mechanic. And his ill-fitting sports coat with its narrow lapels had long been out of fashion and had seen better years. He definitely seemed out of place among the better dressed, more sophisticated European guests from the diplomatic corps.

"Well, Mr. Diamond," Taylor said, "I gather you're a recently arrived American visitor."

"Yes, you're right. I'm also probably something of an anomaly since I'm a political scientist doing field research here. This is my third visit, although it's been a few years since I was here last."

"Well, welcome back to Havana. Once the home of American gambling casinos and brothels, it's now the revolutionary capital of the world. Of course, I'm sure Frankel and Captain Acosta have fully filled you in on all that."

David laughed. "Except that at least Acosta didn't try to tell me what to write. But I'm curious. How do you know them both?"

"Well, even though I'm an engineer by profession, one gets to know lots of political people if you've been living here as a foreign guest as long as I have. I came here right after the Bay of Pigs."

"To do engineering work here?"

"Not only that. I'm a Canadian and a socialist, you see. So, I wanted to help tiny Cuba defend herself from the bully next door, which is how I viewed your country. Anyway, the Cuban government put me to work, so here I am."

"It must have been an exciting time, what with the missile crisis and all the political and social changes that occurred here during the 1960s."

"You betcha," Taylor responded, nodding his head in agreement, after which he drank some more of his wine. "However," he added sheepishly, "I have to confess that, except for the October crisis, I missed a lot of what was going on. I'm afraid I remained too focused on my engineering work."

"As a political scientist, I really find that hard to understand. Christ! There was so much history being made here. You could've been witness to it all."

"I know, I know," Taylor quickly conceded. "But I was an engineer and I wasn't all that interested in all the political stuff. But I've made up for it in recent years, though. Today I'm much more savvy politically." He stopped and looked at David for a moment. "That reminds me," he continued. "I need to give you a piece of advice."

"Oh, oh," David said. "I'll bet you're going to tell me that I shouldn't have gotten into an argument with Captain Acosta."

"Well, you're right—it would've been better had you avoided it. But that's not what I had in mind. No, I just wanted to tell you to be more careful in places like the Habana Libre bar." Taylor paused as he gently shook his head in silent reproach. "You see, I could hear a good deal of what you and Sheila Frankel were saying—and so could a lot of other people around me. Some of them probably have learned enough English to understand what you two were arguing about. And that could spell trouble, if you know what I mean."

David nodded in agreement. "Yes, I really got careless. But she had me riled up." As he set his empty glass on a nearby table, he looked anxiously at Taylor. "Oh, Christ, now you've got me worried."

"Well, don't be too upset. Most probably nothing will happen. And besides," Taylor added with a chuckle, "you've got Captain Acosta to protect you."

"Oh, sure. That would be like me asking the fox to protect the hen house."

Taylor laughed heartily.

***

After they each took fresh glasses of wine, David and Taylor ambled into an adjacent room where there were only a few other guests. David was determined to learn more about Taylor before he did any serious talking. He had no idea how trustworthy the Canadian was. His intuition told him that Taylor was what he appeared to be: a man without guile, a straight shooter. Nevertheless, he sensed a certain reticence on Taylor's part. Moreover, the very fact that Taylor had been living in Cuba for thirteen years suggested that he was in the government's good graces; at the very least, he knew how to survive politically.

"So, when were you last here, Professor Diamond?" Taylor inquired, as they took up positions flanking a huge potted palm.

"Oh, please, just call me David."

"All right, and I'm Philip. But please go on."

"I was here for short visits in 1968 and 1969. Each time I came away impressed by what Fidel and the government here were doing. Of course, those were rough years because of the ten-million-ton sugar harvest."

"I can personally testify to that," Philip said with a grunt. "You might be interested to know that I was very much involved in that harvest effort."

"Really?"

"Yep. As a mechanical engineer, I was dispatched to several of the *centrales* to help Cuban engineers complete the modernization and expansion of those sugar mills. That was Fidel's secret weapon, so to speak. They were to enable him to attain his goal of a super harvest in 1970 . . . "

"I know," David interjected. "I visited a *centrale* in 1969 to do a story on how the military had taken charge of the harvest preparations. Interviewed a Cuban army officer at some length. A great guy."

"Yeah. Well, I don't know what he told you," Philip replied. He stopped momentarily to allow a passing couple to get out of earshot before continuing in a lowered voice. "Even though I was no sugar expert, I could tell early on that hell would freeze over first before the ten-million-ton target was reached. I knew most of those mills wouldn't be ready. And those that would, wouldn't be capable of running at maximum capacity. I knew it already in '68."

"You knew it in 1968?" David asked incredulously.

"You betcha," Philip replied, looking around him to make sure no one else could hear him. "And not only did I know it then, but the Cuban engineers and technicians that I worked with knew it too."

"I never heard of that," David interjected.

"Not many people did," the red-haired Canadian went on in a barely audible voice. "The reason was, no one dared tell Fidel the bad news. You see, he had already sacked the Minister of Sugar for disagreeing with him over the harvest's feasibility. So millions of Cubans continued breaking their backs and enduring all kinds of hardships in order to try to achieve what many in the government already knew was impossible. What a waste . . . "

Philip didn't finish, but David caught his look of disapproval. He waited for him to continue, but Philip grew quiet.

"Sounds like what you experienced with the 1970 harvest turned out to be an epiphany for you," David finally remarked.

The Canadian gave him a puzzled look. "A what?"

"An epiphany. It means the beginning of one's awakening, sort of like a revelation that comes to you in a flash."

"I guess you could say that," Taylor answered hesitantly. Giving David an odd look, he added, "In any case, I've had much too much to drink. I don't think we should be holding this kind of deep discussion at a political reception. Agreed?"

"You're right. Let's talk about something else. So, tell me what you know about Catalina Cruz."

"Ah, hah," Taylor's eyes lit up as a knowing grin crossed his face. "You, too, have become infatuated with her, have you? Well, I'm afraid you're wasting your time."

"Why, is she married?"

"No, she's never been married, although I heard she once had a lover a few years back—a MININT officer, it was rumored."

"What happened?"

"It was all very hush-hush, but apparently he died abroad somewhere."

"Hmm. Well, how about now? Is she Joaquín's woman?"

"Hell, no. She's too independent and choosy to be his or anybody else's 'woman.' In fact, it's been said that she even turned Fidel down a number of years back when she was much younger. Wouldn't have anything to do with him."

"You've got to be kidding! What happened?"

"Well, the story goes that Fidel saw her at some meeting and was instantly attracted to her. Like he does with most women, including some well-known foreign actresses who've come here, he invited her to one of his private residences for an intimate dinner. Then he laid on the charm and tried to seduce her."

The Canadian stopped and suddenly expressed his need for more food and a refill of wine. He seemed to enjoy the drawing out of his story. David waited impatiently while his friend flagged down another waiter and disappeared. He returned from the main salon with a plate of fruit and hors d'oeuvres.

"But unlike most of the women he's gone to bed with and then discarded," Taylor resumed, a new wine glass in hand, "Catalina refused his advances. Told Fidel that she thought of him almost as a demigod—the father of the revolution, Cuba's great liberator, and all that. And if she became romantically involved with him, that image would be forever destroyed. He would be reduced to being a mere mortal among men."

"I'll be damned! She was already one smart young lady. But go on. How did Fidel react?"

"I've heard two different versions from people inside the government," Taylor replied with a shrug. "Some say he became extremely angry and had one of his famous temper tantrums. Others say, no, that he was quite cool and gracious and that he told her he respected her wishes. I think the latter version is probably closer to the truth because as far as I can tell, she hasn't suffered any adverse repercussions."

"Maybe Fidel respected her all the more for standing up to him and saying no."

"Could be." Philip's attention was diverted to the main salon. "But speaking of the devil, there's Fidel . . . !" There was a stir around them as everyone in the room crowded toward the doorway.

David turned toward the commotion at the entrance of the salon. Despite the crush of people, he could see the bearded face of the tall Cuban leader as he towered above the crowd. He started to move toward him.

"Don't you want to hear what Fidel has to say?" David called to Philip, who was hanging back, alone now in the empty room.

"You go on. I want to finish drinking my glass of wine in peace. Then I'll catch up with you. If he's in top form, we'll see some good theater."

***

Having succeeded in pushing his way through the crowded sa- lon, David found the Cuban leader chatting amiably with the Italian ambassador. He was at least two inches taller than David, and had put on a few more pounds since David had last seen him. His large torso seemed bulked up, perhaps from a bulletproof vest. He wore polished boots and his traditional olive green uniform, except that unlike military fatigues it was made of fine Italian wool and superbly tailored. David had often wondered how Fidel could stand to wear heavy uniforms. It was Tino who had explained that the Cuban leader's low metabolism enabled him to remain relatively comfort- able despite the island's hot, humid weather.

David noticed that Fidel's unruly beard, which was barely streaked with gray, hid his receding chin. Together with his large head, high- bridged nose, and high forehead inherited from his Galician father, the beard lent his countenance a Moses-like quality. Looking more closely, David noted that Fidel's face glistened from the oiliness of his skin. There were also fine little lines around his eyes, but his face was remarkably free of wrinkles. Though the years were beginning to leave their mark, it was obvious that Cuba's *líder máximo* was in robust good health for a man who had just turned forty-eight.

David recalled the first and only time he had seen Fidel at close quarters. It was a summer night in 1968 at a solidarity reception that was being held next to the swimming pool at the Hotel Riviera, once the hangout of gangster Meyer Lansky. The affair was for foreign visitors, mostly volunteer *macheteros* like himself who had come to cut sugarcane or do other agricultural work. Cuba's revolutionary leader had suddenly swooped in among the excited guests, radiating such a commanding, almost mythic, presence that when he departed, David had half expected him to stride miraculously across the water of the swimming pool. Now, as he stood among the throng of guests, David could see that Fidel still exuded the same aura of supreme confidence and authority that only men imbued with a historical mission and sense of destiny possessed.

He had never forgotten the Cuban leader's eyes. Though not large, they were intense and extraordinarily dark, almost obsidian in their color. They were penetrating eyes, capable of withering anyone, he had once been told, who incurred the *Comandante's* wrath. He was certain that few of Fidel's subordinates would ever dare conceal anything from him for fear he could see deep into their very souls. But now those same suspicious, commanding eyes were dancing with luminous charm. David could see that the *Comandante* was reveling in all the attention he was receiving.

David suddenly became all ears when he heard Tino ask Fidel whether diplomatic relations would be restored between Havana and Washington now that Ford had succeeded Nixon in the White House. Kissinger's foreign policy was based on realpolitik, Tino pointed out, and he had engineered Nixon's path-breaking trip to China in February 1972. Wasn't it now possible that the same turnabout could occur in U.S.–Cuban relations?

The Cuban leader eyed Tino for a moment and stroked his beard, teasing his audience as they waited with heightened anticipation. He was relishing the moment.

"An interesting question, Tino. One that I've considered several times these past weeks." The *líder máximo* paused and looked around at his listeners to see if he had produced the desired suspense. A mischievous gleam appeared in his eyes as his audience waited for him to continue.

For a moment, David wondered whether, without having to make inquiries of his own, Fidel was about to provide the information that Rudy García wanted him to obtain. *"Don't be a fool,"* he told himself. *"Fidel is too shrewd to telegraph his next move."*

"Of course," Fidel began softly, but in a voice that was steadily ascending, "you all know Cuba's principled position with regard to its struggle with the United States. Even though Washington broke off diplomatic relations thirteen years ago, even though Washington carried out armed aggression against us at the Bay of Pigs, even though Washington imposed the criminal blockade to destroy our economy and the will of the Cuban people, and even though Washington has tried, by numerous other means, to crush our revolution and even assassinate its leaders, we are still prepared to sit down with whatever administration is in office and negotiate in good faith!"

David could see that Fidel was getting wound up, his eyes fixing defiantly on those closest to him, as if daring anyone to contradict him. He was speaking the same way he did as when he addressed large audiences—pausing here and there for dramatic effect, turning his head and adopting a pensive look, raising his right index finger to his forehead as if searching for the right phrase, then arching his eyebrows and letting his voice fall almost to an intimate, confiding whisper before it rose again to emphasize a point. As David knew from experience, Fidel's voice conveyed so much conviction that his listeners often simply surrendered to the seductive power of his words.

"But I shouldn't have to remind you," Fidel was saying, his voice now rising to a crescendo, his eyebrows shooting upward. "There is one essential condition that must be met by the American government before we can talk. Whether it's Ford, Kissinger, or anybody else, the Americans must treat us as equals. That means they must respect our dignity, our sovereignty, our independence! That is the *sine qua non* we rightly insist on if there are going to be talks between the two countries! Otherwise, we are prepared to do without relations with the United States until the next millennium and beyond! We will never compromise our principles! We will never compromise with imperialism!"

Pleased with himself, the Cuban leader studied his audience for a moment, his dark eyes surveying those around him. One of his aides took advantage of the pause to hand him a glass of wine that was more vibrant, cherry-like in color than the red wine Philip Taylor had been drinking. David guessed it was Campari.

"Now, as to your question, Tino," Fidel said, giving the Italian a knowing look. "I must tell you that I'm not entirely in agreement with its premise. Yes, Kissinger is an intelligent man, a learned man, a man who has written about and practiced realpolitik. So, to some extent, we should expect that Kissinger will be more practical and less dogmatic in his attitude toward Cuba."

Again Fidel paused, this time to savor his drink. Along with others, David could tell that the Cuban leader was about to launch his verbal counteroffensive. He caught Tino's eye; the Italian nodded, a slight, knowing smile forming on his lips.

"On the other hand," the *Comandante* continued, "Marxism-Leninism teaches us that personalities do not control the history of mankind nor the behavior of an imperialist power such as the United States. In no way can they, because there are powerful economic forces that determine the behavior of the United States toward the Third World, toward Latin America, toward Cuba." He paused to let his words sink in, his eyes now unusually large and fearsome, before moving in for the kill. "That means that even were Kissinger to have the best of intentions toward Cuba, the multinationals and other powerful economic interests in the United States, along with the CIA, the Pentagon, and all the Cold War hawks, would never permit him to reach a *modus vivendi* with Cuba. It's as simple as that!"

Curiously, David had expressed exactly the same argument a month earlier at the Smithsonian symposium. But that was before he had learned of the Cuban probes regarding a possible rapprochement. Was Fidel now being deliberately disingenuous? Or had Havana's secret overtures fallen on deaf ears with the Ford Administration? David didn't know. Yet at least a month ago judging from Rudy García's attempt to have him ferret out information while he was in Havana, the U.S. Government seemed to be considering doing what Fidel had just claimed Washington would never do.

Deep into his own thoughts, he was only dimly aware that Fidel was now responding to another question. When finally he turned his attention back to the discussion, he felt the men around him moving. They were allowing someone to pass through to where he was standing. Catalina Cruz was suddenly at David's side.

***

When Fidel stopped to field another question, Catalina quickly called to him, "*Comandante.*"

"Ah, Catalina. What a pleasure!" Fidel exclaimed, affecting a broad smile. "Gentlemen, for those of you who don't know her, let me introduce Catalina Cruz. Not only is she one of Cuba's most beautiful women as you can plainly see. She also possesses an exemplary, revolutionary spirit!"

"*¡Oye, Fidel, como siempre, eres demasiado galante!*"

Her words—"as always, Fidel, you're too gallant"—sounded playful. But was there a hidden sub-text to them—a reproach to Fidel perhaps for his having tried to seduce her when she was still a young, innocent virgin? David had no way of telling, but he thought the Cuban leader's eyes flickered with suspicion for an instant. "*Either that,*" David thought, "*or he wants like hell to get into her pants but knows that he can't even get to first base with her.*"

"Fidel," Catalina continued in a confident voice, "beside me here is Professor David Diamond from the United States. He's visiting Cuba for the third time to do research for his book. I thought perhaps he might want to ask you a question."

"But of course! *Bienvenido*, Professor Diamond. I welcome you back to the island Christopher Columbus rightly called 'the pearl of the Antilles'—the island that today stands as an inspiration to revolutionaries throughout the world."

David was completely taken by surprise. He saw an ever-so-slight impish smile on Catalina's lips, but it was the mischievous gleam in her green eyes that gave her away. She was meaning to test him against Fidel, to see whether he could rise to the occasion, of that he was sure.

"Thank you, Mr. Prime Minister."

"We don't stand on formalities, Diamond. Call me Fidel as everyone does. Now, what is your question? Is it related to your research here in Cuba?"

"No, Fidel, I prefer not to bore you and the other guests with a question that is largely of interest to academics like myself," David replied, wracking his brain for something to ask that would be provocative, yet not upset the Cuban leader. At last he thought he had it, but he knew he would have to be careful how he framed the question.

"What I would really like to ask is . . . " He paused, groping for the right words in his not-too-polished Spanish. " . . . is, uh, a hypothetical question. Nevertheless, it has great historical significance for all of us on the Left who so admire the Cuban revolution. Now, I fully agree with what you said earlier about the forces behind my country's policy toward Cuba . . . " David could see that, having finished his Campari, the Cuban leader was becoming impatient. He hurried to finish the question.

" . . . But let us suppose, again, hypothetically, that the United States had been more accommodating toward the Cuban revolution in 1959 and 1960. Would that have changed the course of the revolution and prevented Cuba's turn to the Soviet Union?"

A hush fell over the large circle of guests. David's hypothetical question cut to the core of the historical controversy surrounding the revolution's sudden embrace of communism and the Soviet bloc. Washington's critics, David among them, maintained that the U.S. policy of hostility had pushed Fidel into the arms of the Soviet Union. Fidel's opponents, on the other hand, charged that he had concealed his Marxist agenda and all-consuming power ambitions from the Cuban people, after which he had cleverly manipulated the Eisenhower Administration into adopting hostile policies which made it appear that he had no choice but to turn to Moscow.

Tino and the other guests waited expectantly for Fidel's reply. David could almost see the wheels turning as the Cuban leader composed his answer. Bowing his head slightly, Fidel rested his chin on his fingertips that were now formed in an inverted V, tent-like. He finally looked up.

"Let me ask you something first, Diamond," he began, seemingly stalling for more time. "What will you do if I answer your hypothetical question? Because that's all it is, completely hypothetical. In 1959, Washington was incapable of treating Cuba as an equal, as an independent and sovereign nation, because it had long been accustomed to treating our fatherland as if it were some insignificant banana republic. No, from the beginning, imperialism simply could not reconcile itself to a revolution like ours."

David saw Philip Taylor elbowing his way through the crowd. *"We're all going to be disappointed my friend,"* David said to himself, *"because Fidel is starting to grandstand all over again."*

But the Cuban leader was already reading the boredom stealing over the faces of some of his listeners. With a sly look, he abruptly dropped the rhetoric.

"So, Diamond, what will you do if I answer you? Once you're back in the United States, will you write up my comments and rush into print with an exclusive article for some popular American magazine?"

"No, uh . . . I wasn't planning on doing anything like that," David stammered, caught off guard by the question. "Absolutely not, Fidel . . . "

"And why not?" Fidel inquired in mock seriousness, his eyebrows suddenly shooting up. "Lee Lockwood did it after he followed me around Cuba a few years back. He ended up with a big feature story in *Playboy* and, if my memory serves me correctly, I was even on the magazine's cover! Imagine that! My face displaced all those Playgirls, or whatever they are called, from *Playboy's* cover. Because of that, I probably antagonized many of your countrymen who would otherwise be sympathetic to the revolution!"

A titter of laughter rippled through the audience. Fidel, in turn, was clearly delighted with his little joke. David was now thoroughly uncomfortable; he was not accustomed to being someone else's foil.

"Now, Diamond, what I want to know is whether you can guarantee that you can do the same as Lockwood. Yes, I would like to be in *Playboy* again! How about it?"

"I'm sorry, Fidel, but I can't offer you that guarantee. You see, I don't write for *Playboy*. Besides, I'm an academic, not a journalist."

"Ah, ah! I was afraid you would say that. The problem, you see, is that your hypothetical question concerns one of the most critical moments in the first years of the revolution. Therefore, my reply to it deserves the widest possible audience in the United States, Latin America, Europe, and the Third World. However, I'm afraid that an article by you in some obscure academic journal would never, never reach such an audience!"

"I see your point, Fidel." David conceded, crestfallen. "I'm sorry."

"Don't look so downcast, Diamond!" Fidel exclaimed. "You will only have to wait until I write my memoirs twenty or twenty-five years from now to have your answer!"

Catalina and the others roared with laughter. Trying mightily to be the good sport, David joined in the fun. Fidel waited for quiet before resuming.

"Now, honored guests," he announced. "I must take my leave, because, as always, the work of the revolution never ends." With a scarcely concealed look of triumph at Catalina, he turned around and, with his aides in front and behind him, strode out of the salon.

"*Se escapó,*" Catalina said, as she turned to David. "Did you see how he escaped without answering your question, yet he did it with grace and humor. Sometimes, he can be an absolute political genius."

"You're right there," David sighed, shaking his head. "The only trouble was that it was at my expense."

"Don't take it personally," Catalina said, trying to cheer him. "You asked a very interesting question. The problem was that you were up against a master, who seldom if ever allows himself to be cornered. Believe me, you're not the first to fail in trying to pin him down. Anyway, *Profesor*, I'll see what the Foreign Ministry has in store for you. Who knows, maybe we'll see each other again soon."

"I sure hope so, Catalina," David replied, brightening at the thought he might soon be seeing her again. "*Mientras tanto, espero que todo vaya bien contigo*—meanwhile, I hope all goes well with you."

As he watched her disappear into the crowd, Philip Taylor approached him.

"Well, my friend," the Canadian said, his blues twinkling merrily. "What did I tell you? Fidel was in high form tonight. He put on a good show, didn't he? Really danced around your question, and it was a good one at that. But in the end, you were left empty-handed."

"Yes, and with egg on my face."

***

Half an hour later, having lost sight of Tino, David hitched a ride back to his hotel in Philip Taylor's rusted 1958 Ford sedan. To his surprise, the car ran surprisingly well. Actually, he was less concerned about the car than about Philip, who had had far too much wine to be driving. But despite it being a Saturday night, there was little traffic on the streets. They arrived at the Habana Libre without incident shortly before midnight.

"I've got to go into the countryside on a couple of job assignments over the next week or so," Philip said, as David was about to get out of the car. "But when I get back, I'd like to have you over at my house for dinner. My wife knows how to cook some really terrific Cuban dishes that you can't find in hotels and restaurants nowadays. I've also stashed away a box of fine Cuban cigars and a bottle of *Añejo* rum." In a conspiring tone, he added, "So, after dinner, we can drink and have a serious discussion while smoking fine cigars."

"Thanks, Philip. I don't know yet what my schedule will be like over the next week or two, but count me in. Dinner and cigars at your place sounds great."

***

7

Conflicts

David was in the hotel lobby when Chucho arrived Sunday evening with his two friends, Tomás and Roberto. All three were in their early twenties. None gave their last names when they introduced themselves.

Chucho, the more intellectual of the three, was an aspiring writer who worked as a copy editor in the state's major publishing house. Tomás held a low-level position in some government office. Roberto, the more reserved of the three, turned out to be a second-year medical student. The three youths—*los muchachos*, as David would call them—had been friends from their school days in Santa Clara. After military service and admittance to different universities, they had been reunited in Havana.

The four of them ambled down to the basement bar in the Habana Libre. After David bought a round of beers, the three *muchachos* began plying him with all sorts of questions about the latest American automobiles, consumer products, movies, Hollywood stars, and rock-and-roll songs. David didn't mind, though some of the questions were far-fetched or incredibly naïve, as when Roberto wanted to know whether the twist-off cap on Cokes not only opened but also chilled the bottles.

After another round of beers, Chucho suggested that Tomás get his father's automobile so that they could go out for a drive. The father, David would learn, was a Deputy Vice-Minister in some government ministry.

Half an hour later, the four of them were squeezed into a three-year-old Skoda from Czechoslovakia, with Tomás at the wheel. David soon lost his bearings once they reached the outskirts of Havana. After a ten-minute drive, Tomás pulled into a deserted field that was momentarily illuminated by the Skoda's headlights. It quickly vanished into the blackness of the night when the lights were switched off.

"We won't be bothered here," Tomás explained. David suspected that the Skoda, with its special government plates, would make sure of that.

***

"Oigan, muchachos," David exclaimed after having answered yet another battery of questions about the United States. *"Tienen que parar porque ahora es mi turno para hacer preguntas*—you have to stop because now it's my turn to ask questions." Despite the darkness, he could tell they were watching him intently, wondering what he would ask.

David began by telling them that since he had arrived he had noticed many changes for the better in Havana compared to his last trip, but that he was disappointed by the continued shortages of goods. He stopped to roll down the window to let out the smoke from Chucho's recently lighted cigarette; he was thankful that Tomás and Roberto didn't smoke.

"For instance," he continued. "I've hardly seen any fresh fruits and vegetables, or even tubers like *malanga* in the shops. And I've seen little in the way of meat, chicken, or fish. The only things that seem to be relatively plentiful are canned goods from Eastern Europe. Clothing and shoes are also pretty scarce everywhere I've gone. So, as far as I can tell, conditions of daily life have improved but not as much as I would have hoped. Now, I ask you, am I seeing things as they are? Are my impressions more or less correct?"

Accustomed now to the dark, David could see that his new friends were looking from one to the other, holding back to see who would go first. They suspected more sensitive questions were around the corner.

"I think I can speak for the three of us," Tomás said finally. "You're right about all the shortages. I haven't tasted a *lechoncito*, a suckling pig, since last December, and then it was only because my Dad had been given one by his boss. As for mangoes, tomatoes, avocados, and other fresh fruit, forget it! And you mentioned clothing. Well, let me tell you: The lousy shoes that we're importing here from other socialist countries don't even last a year! *"¿No es cierto?"* Tomás asked, turning to Chucho and Roberto in the back seat, who nodded in agreement.

"But not everything is bad these days," Tomás added. "There have been some improvements in our everyday lives. For example, we now have more free time to do things we want to do, like going to a movie or even a bar, which we couldn't do when you were last here. I think the biggest thing in this respect is that we're not subject to as many mobilizations as in the past, when we had to go out and cut cane or sow coffee. Sure, there's still *trabajo voluntario*, what the government facetiously calls voluntary work, but it's nothing like what it was a few years back. So, though life today is not a bed of roses, things have eased up a bit."

"I'm glad to hear that," David responded. "But what also interests me now as a political scientist is whether each of you thinks the *system* is at fault for these shortages and other economic problems? Or do you think that the fault lies with individuals working for the government?"

The safe answer, David knew, was to place the blame on individual officials. To assign blame to the system would signify disapproval of communism. He could feel the charged atmosphere in the car. A long silence followed.

"That's a very provocative question," Chucho commented from the back seat. "It's one that I've given a lot of thought, although I've never discussed it with either Roberto or Tomás." He drew leisurely on his cigarette and fell silent again.

"Hey, Chucho," Roberto exclaimed. "*Por Dios*, give us some air so we can breathe!"

"We had to have the revolution," Chucho resumed, as he obligingly cracked the window another couple of inches. "Because Batista's government was dictatorial and rotten to the core. It also exploited *el pueblo*. And it sold out the fatherland to the Americans, whether it was the Mafia, big corporations, or Washington. And believe me, all of what I'm telling you is something that we just didn't learn in school as kids. No, it's what our parents and aunts and uncles told us about as well. So, that's why the overwhelming majority of the Cuban people welcomed the revolution: It promised a new Cuba with democracy, social justice, and an honest, nationalist government. In fact, people were delirious in their support for Fidel and the revolution . . . "

"*Eso es cierto*," Tomás interrupted. "That's for sure."

"I, too, agree with Chucho," Roberto chimed in. "*Dice la verdad*— he's telling the truth."

"However," Chucho continued. "After a few years—and here I can only speak for myself—something began to happen to our cherished dream . . . " He stopped again to take a last drag from his cigarette. Rolling the window down, he tossed the smoldering butt into the night, and cranked the window most of the way closed. "It's painful for me to say this, but I've come to the conclusion that our dream will forever elude us. Why? Because the revolution took a bad turn years back."

"How so?" David asked.

"It's simple, *Profesor*. We began building so-called socialism with a system imported from the Soviet bloc, a communist system that is economically inefficient and politically oppressive, even totalitarian in its reach. Therefore, to get back to your original question, it won't make one iota of difference whether you change the people who are running things or not as long as the present system remains."

David was surprised. *"You certainly have got balls, that's for sure,"* he thought as he considered Chucho's answer. Not even the few malcontents he had encountered during his 1969 trip had ever voiced such a condemnation of the system. It disturbed him, too. He wondered whether Tomás and Roberto would counter with different, less negative viewpoints.

"You know what's so strange about this discussion?" Tomás asked suddenly. "Despite the fact that the three of us have been close friends since school we've never talked about the question you've just asked us."

"I'm happy to learn I've served some useful purpose," David said with a laugh. "But I interrupted you, Tomás. Please go on."

"Well, like Chucho, I'm also becoming increasingly disillusioned as I get older. But my disillusionment comes in part from listening to my Dad. You see, he constantly complains about all the problems he faces as a Deputy Vice-Minister. And, man, I tell you, those problems are not caused by people like my Dad—no way!"

"So you agree with Chucho that the system is at fault?"

"Absolutely," Tomás replied. "But let me make myself perfectly clear: That's my own opinion. It's certainly not my Dad's. If anyone is a firm believer in socialism, it's him. But not me. No, I think our system is only good for the bureaucracy. And you know why? It's because more bureaucrats and paperwork are always needed to correct the mistakes the government is always making."

"What mistakes, for instance?" David asked, though he was sure he knew the answer.

"O.K. Let's take the example of the Revolutionary Offensive which nationalized all the small shops and services back in 1968. The clerk at the laundry where I go once told me that clothes used to be washed,

pressed, and returned within three or four days before Fidel launched
the Offensive. Now, six years after the laundry was taken over by
the government, it still takes anywhere from two to three weeks for
my clothing to be returned because of all the paperwork. *¡Que
absurdo!*"

"Yes," Chucho added, "but let's not forget that it was Fidel himself who was behind the Revolutionary Offensive—and that was
only one of his many crazy policies."

For a long moment the darkness in the car was filled with utter
silence. All four were taken aback by Chucho's boldness in attacking Fidel.

"Fidel is unquestionably a great leader and an intelligent man,"
Chucho went on quickly, retreating to safer ground. "Nevertheless,
my point is that he has many serious deficiencies and limitations, as
do all men. So, you see, once again the system is to blame because
it gives Fidel and the people around him absolute power."

***

David felt a growing discomfort. These criticisms voiced by Tomás
and especially Chucho were reinforcing the nagging doubts he himself had been having about Cuba's prospects for a more open, democratic polity. But he still hadn't heard from Roberto. Perhaps the
most reticent of the three *muchachos* would surprise him with a spirited defense of the revolution.

"Well, what about it, Roberto?" David inquired, turning to the
silent figure in the back seat. "You've been pretty quiet so far. How
do you feel about all this?"

"I'm afraid I don't agree at all with Chucho and Tomás," Roberto
said, softly, hesitantly, as if unsure of what to expect from his companions. "Sure, I know we have problems. But I believe that most
are caused by the incompetence of individual officials, not by the
system itself." He paused, as if expecting a reaction from his listeners. When none came, he continued more forcefully. "We shouldn't
lose sight of the fact that Fidel's government is a tremendous improvement over what we had in the past. Under Batista and Prío, we
had both incompetent *and* corrupt governments." He waited as if
expecting Chucho and Tomás to concur. "Come on, *chicos*!" he
exclaimed, when they said nothing. "Don't you remember hearing

about government officials in those days? Those *cabrones* thought nothing of stealing hundreds of millions of pesos from the state treasury."

"You have to admit Roberto is right there," David observed, trying to give Roberto moral support.

"True enough," Tomás replied. "There's no question that Fidel, and most of the people in the government and Party, are honest, committed persons. They're trying to do the best for the fatherland. Jesus! My Dad is a perfect example."

"O.K.," Chucho conceded. "So we all agree that now under our Marxist-Leninist system we have more honest, well-meaning leaders."

"In addition to that," Roberto continued, mistaking Chucho's sarcastic remark for agreement, "the revolution has accomplished a great deal in so little time. That's why the revolution has the overwhelming support of the people. That's why they participate in the *Comités de Defensa*. That's why they're ready to defend the revolution in every neighborhood, in every locale around the island . . . "

"*¡Coño, chico!*" Chucho erupted. "*Estás diciendo mierda*—you're talking shit! You know as well as I do that a major reason most people belong to the *Comités* is because they don't want to be suspected of being counterrevolutionaries!"

"Well, I participate willingly," Roberto protested. "As do all the people I know, on account of what the revolution has accomplished."

"That may be true for you, Roberto, but Chucho is also right," Tomás broke in.

"Listen! You guys are forgetting what it was like for lots of people back in Santa Clara when we were kids," Roberto replied heatedly. "Today is different—poor people, ordinary people are receiving medical treatment as well as an education which would have been unheard of before the revolution. I, for one, am grateful for being able to attend medical school."

"Roberto, no one here disputes the revolution's many social achievements," Chucho said in an exasperated voice. "I certainly don't want to lose them. And there's no question that socialist Cuba is a good place if you're a kid, an old person, a poor worker, or a Negro or mulatto because now all your basic needs are taken care of. But how about all the rest of us who want to be creative, independent, or, heaven forbid, even prosperous? Or who just would like to breathe in freedom?" Stopping, he drew a deep breath and collected himself, then went on more calmly. "The issue, as I see it, is whether we've paid too high a political price for social justice. Just look at all the conformity and regimentation we must endure to achieve some measure of social justice."

"Chucho," Roberto interjected. "You know that all revolutions have their costs. At least here in Cuba we've been fortunate that they haven't been higher. You have to admit that."

"Of course things could be worse," the young man replied. "But that's hardly any consolation for the fact that Fidel has betrayed most of the noble, democratic ideals he so eloquently espoused before he came to power."

"*No, chico*," Roberto disagreed. "You're forgetting that Fidel couldn't comply with his promise regarding democracy because of the threat from the imperialists and counterrevolutionaries. But in the meantime he's made a revolution that has radically transformed Cuba without enormous bloodshed . . . "

"Roberto," Tomás broke in sharply. "Why don't you just answer the professor's question?"

"But that's precisely what I was doing!" Roberto retorted. "I was pointing out that the system is working as can be seen by the revolution's accomplishments."

"But again at what costs?" Chucho broke in angrily. "Look, instead of the democracy that Fidel promised, we now have the so-called dictatorship of the proletariat. But in reality, the workers, much less the *campesinos*, have no power. No, that belongs to the Party and especially Fidel. He's a communist *caudillo* who enjoys absolute power. And in that respect, Fidel's dictatorship is worse than Batista's."

"Chucho, *por Dios*," Tomás said. "This time you've gone too far."

"That's putting it mildly," Roberto added quickly, obviously glad to have finally found an ally in Tomás.

David, too, was glad that Chucho's comments had at last come under fire. But because Chucho was not a *Batistiano*, David wanted to learn the reasons for his audacious statement. For the moment, however, Chucho lit another cigarette and retreated to silence.

***

David turned in his seat to face the silent figure behind him. "I'm afraid I'm with Tomás and Roberto," he said. "I just can't agree with you that Fidel's dictatorship is worse than Batista's."

"No, I didn't say that!" Chucho protested, staring apprehensively at David, the whiteness of his eyes standing out in the darkness. "I only said that Fidel possesses absolute power as our *líder máximo*, which is something that Batista never had."

"O.K., I stand corrected. But I'm still curious as to why you said that. And believe me," David added, by way of reassurance, "I'll not repeat this discussion to anyone outside this car."

A strained silence followed. David could see the indecision in Chucho's eyes as he shifted his gaze to Roberto and Tomás, trying to fathom the three of them.

"All right," Chucho began slowly, drawing a deep breath. "I've already stuck my neck out, so I might as well go all the way." He paused to clear his throat. "What I was trying to point out is that, as a consequence of Fidel having absolute power, we've had to suffer all of his *locuras*—his crazy schemes. For instance, there's the Revolutionary Offensive, which in one fell swoop created the shortages and bottlenecks of the kind Tomás mentioned a. while ago with his laundry. After that came the ten-million-ton harvest, another one of Fidel's *locuras* . . . "

"But all that's past history," Roberto protested. "Times have changed. Now we're on the right path to perfecting socialism."

Chucho frowned. "Even if I could believe that, which I don't, I would still insist that in some aspects we're worse off than before the revolution. Just look at all the fear and distrust this government has instilled among the Cuban people . . . "

"It seems to me that there was a lot of that under Batista," David observed.

"Yes, that's true, *Profesor*. However, what you may not fully appreciate is that now we face more effective mechanisms of control and repression that do not simply reside in MININT. No, they also reside in all of us, making us parties to the continuation of the repression, tainting us, and turning us one against the other, even within families, and in the end corrupting us all."

Chucho's impassioned voice trailed off. He seemed unsure of how much it would be prudent for him to say. But when David asked him to elaborate, he didn't hesitate.

"Look," he explained. "We're all enrolled in the mass organizations and the *Comités* that are on every city block. That means that virtually all aspects of our lives are monitored and controlled not just by State Security, but by common citizens as well." He looked at Tomás for support. Finding none, he turned back to David again. "Do you understand? Do you see what I'm trying to say? We now fear our neighbors, our friends, even our brothers and sisters and cousins, because Cubans must spy and inform on one another. Look, sometimes I can't even type at night without some busybody from the *Comité* knocking on my door and asking what it is I'm writing."

"You're forgetting that the *Comités* are necessary to defend the revolution from its internal enemies as well as from imperialism," Roberto insisted.

"No," Chucho replied calmly. "What the government really fears is a free-thinking people. That's why it's created this totalitarian state we're in where ordinary citizens like ourselves police each other, inform on one another. Don't you see, Roberto?" he cried out. "Don't you see, Tomás? We've all become accomplices of the state, we've all become corrupted as human beings."

Roberto and Tomás remained absolutely still and silent. Insidious fear—or was it guilt?—had suddenly struck them.

"That's why we Cubans are unable to trust one another," Chucho resumed in a barely audible voice. "We all must wear our *caras dobles*—our double-faces and masks—to protect ourselves not just from the government but from each other." He reached forward to touch his friend's shoulder. "And that's why, Tomás, we've never had this kind of frank, political discussion among ourselves until tonight. *La desconfianza*, the mistrust, is too pervasive. It's even affected the three of us."

"I don't want to talk about this anymore!" Roberto exclaimed, bounding forward in his seat. "It's become a pointless argument."

In the long, strained silence that followed, David saw Chucho and Tomás exchange wary glances. Roberto seemed embarrassed by his outburst. After a minute or so, the tension subsided and *los muchachos* began talking about less controversial subjects.

Chucho's final observations had greatly troubled David, forcing him to rethink his assumptions regarding the extent of mutual trust among the Cuban people and the genuineness of their revolutionary commitment. His doubts about his theory of the exceptionalism of the Cuban revolution were now stronger than ever.

Thereafter, he and his three young acquaintances shied away from the subject of politics. Only later, on the eve of Roberto's departure for East Germany, would he learn why their political debate had ended so abruptly with Roberto's outburst—and why any further discussion of politics would remain off-limits during his subsequent outings with *los muchachos*.

***

The next day, David learned that the Foreign Ministry had assigned Marina Alvarez, not Catalina Cruz, as his coordinator and guide. His disappointment was compounded by the fact that she turned out to be more his shadow than a guide—and a thoroughly disagreeable one at that.

In the course of their days together, David learned that Marina Alvarez had married her one and only husband at the beginning of 1958, but before the year was out she was left a widow. Her young husband, who had become a guerrilla fighter in Fidel's rebel army, fell mortally wounded in one of the key battles for control of Las Villas province. She hadn't remarried even though for a woman in her late thirties she was not unattractive. She had a round face, a broad, slightly upturned nose, and large expressive brown eyes. Her figure also was close to what many Cuban men would consider ideal. No more than five feet four inches tall, she was well-endowed with large breasts, ample hips and thighs, and heavy but shapely legs.

After being in her company for several days, riding in one of the 1959 Cadillac sedans still used by MINREX for schlepping foreign guests around the island, David discovered the probable reasons why Marina hadn't remarried. Reason number one: She was totally devoid of a sense of humor. She saw nothing funny in the few jokes he told in a futile attempt to loosen her up. And his one or two efforts at flattery fell equally flat. And reason number two: Except perhaps for Sheila Frankel, she was the most narrow-minded, controlling woman he could remember.

Her politics went hand-in-hand with her controlling personality. She was the kind of person that Cubans referred to as an *extremista*— an ardent, rigid supporter of the government who saw everything in black and white. To David's irritation, she demanded complete, unquestioning compliance with whatever rules, regulations, and instructions the government had ordered. And as he discovered on their third day together, she would not tolerate his deviating from her instructions.

Marina had scheduled David for an appointment with the Assistant Coordinator of the Committees for the Defense of the Revolution. The CDRs, or *Comités* as they were commonly known, were the backbone of Cuba's extensive control and mobilization system. Manned by ordinary citizens, they were organized on a block basis and served as neighborhood watchdog committees. As such, they guarded against counterrevolutionary activities and ensured everyone's compliance with government directives—including turning out for Fidel's speeches and other mass rallies.

On this particular day, Marina, who was usually fairly punctual, failed to pick David up for their appointment at CDR headquarters. After waiting twenty minutes, David hailed a cab and went directly to CDR headquarters. There, he proceeded to interview the Assistant Coordinator concerning the role of CDRs in Cuba's future local government structure. He had been alone with the official, Mr. Rene Pérez, for a quarter of an hour when Marina angrily burst into Pérez's office, startling both men.

"What are you doing here?" she asked David with unmistakable fury in her voice.

"I'm talking with *Señor* Pérez. What's wrong with that?"

"I'll tell you what's wrong! You're supposed to wait for me and not go out interviewing people on your own, unless I tell you beforehand that you can!"

"*Para un momento, Marina, por favor.* Please stop a minute," David repeated, trying to reason with her. "Just think: What was I supposed to do? Miss my appointment because you were more than twenty minutes late?"

"Correct, *Profesor* Diamond!" she replied sharply. "It is my job to schedule your appointments and serve as your escort during interviews." She glared at him with eyes burning with anger. "We could've rescheduled the meeting with *Compañero* Pérez, if necessary," she continued. "So, from now on you will do things the Cuban way, the way my government wants them done, or you won't have any appointments!"

For an instant, David thought Marina Alvarez was putting on a show for the benefit of Mr. Pérez because of his position within the command structure of the CDRs. But seeing her smoldering eyes, and Mr. Pérez's apparent embarrassment at her outburst, he realized her anger was genuine.

"Very well, I understand what you're telling me," David announced with a sigh of resignation. He proceeded with the interview a while longer, but the strained atmosphere precluded a meaningful dialogue with Mr. Pérez.

It didn't take long for David to realize that Marina had disliked him from the start. His problem was that he was an American, a *norteamericano*. It didn't matter to her that his left-wing credentials had passed muster with her own government, which not only had granted him a visa but was also permitting him to conduct research on the politics of her country. No. The mere fact that he came from the United States made him suspect in her eyes. His occasional irreverent jokes touching on some of Cuba's problems didn't help matters. Like the incident over the restaurant's menus.

They had stopped for lunch at a restaurant outside Havana one hot afternoon. The timeworn, faded menus they were given still listed all the salads, soups, entrees, and desserts that were served back in 1959 or 1960—items that had not been available for years. On the flyleaf under *Especialidades del Día* were listed the only items being served that day: noodle soup and fish croquets. Jokingly referring to the title of the famous Cuban film on the revolution, David pointed to the old, soiled menu and said to Marina, *"Memorias del Subdesarrollo"*— *Memories of Underdevelopment.* Pursing her lips in unmistakable disapproval, she simply glared at him.

In the meantime, she made it a point to talk about her husband who had been killed by Batista's soldiers. The United States, she would remind David, had supplied Batista's men with their M-1 rifles and other weapons. She never would forgive the *norteamericanos* for that, she remarked to him pointedly. By then, however, David didn't care what she felt.

***

David was prepared to forgive Marina at the end of the second week, however, when she arranged an interview with Carlos Rafael Rodríguez. A member of the Politburo, the highest organ of the Communist Party of Cuba, Rodríguez was one of the few old communists who enjoyed Fidel's trust and respect. He was perhaps the only official who also was Fidel's intellectual equal. The regime's most urbane, cosmopolitan leader, he was content to play second fiddle to Fidel, always taking care to stay clear of the political machinations of his old comrades from the Popular Socialist Party. Fidel, in turn, found him useful as a sounding board for some of his ideas, as his point man in dealing with Moscow, and as his most effective spokesman with European and American intellectuals.

On that Friday evening, Marina made sure that they arrived at Communist Party Headquarters several minutes early. The massive, neo-Roman-style building that now housed the maze of Party offices had been constructed before the revolution. From the outside, in fact, the building looked like it could have been transplanted from Fascist Italy. As David and Marina tromped along the marble corridor with its high ceiling, he half-expected to see the ghost of Benito Mussolini, attired in cavalry pants and riding boots, strutting toward them.

Having arrived early, they were kept waiting fifteen minutes in the spartan anteroom adjoining Rodríguez's office before a wiry, clean-shaven man finally came out. David thought he looked vaguely familiar. Introducing himself as Carlos Salsamendi, personal advisor to Dr. Rodríguez, he told them they would be received in a few minutes. While they waited, Salsamendi conversed with David in heavily accented but good English. He had lived and worked in New York in the 1950s, he explained, adding with a grin that he had even served as a messenger boy on Wall Street. Finally, he escorted David and Marina into Rodríguez's private office.

Now well into middle age, Rodríguez was wearing a white embroidered *guayabera*. Worn outside the trousers, the loose-fitting shirt helped conceal his paunch. His trademark horn-rimmed glasses, together with his trimmed beard, made him look like the university professor he once was. He rose from his desk, shook hands with David, and nodded to Marina, who mumbled her name and an unintelligible greeting. He waved them to the small sofa, while he and Salsamendi took the two armchairs.

"Well, Professor Diamond, I understand that you have been here before and have now returned to study the democratic aspects of our revolution," Rodríguez said, cutting immediately to the purpose of David's visit.

"Yes, that's correct. I especially want to look at your experiment with the *Poder Popular.* I hope to use it as a case study of how socialist revolutions provide avenues for political participation by the masses."

"Ah, I see." As Fidel had done at the reception, Rodríguez paused to stroke his short, neatly trimmed gray beard. "That is an interesting issue for students of revolution. Of course, it's also an important one for socialist societies like ours. However," he added with a twinkle in his eye as he cast a sidelong glance at Salsamendi, "the topic doesn't strike me as having much sex appeal. Is that why you won't be publishing an article in *Playboy* magazine?"

For a split second, David didn't make the connection. Then he laughed. "How did you know about that? Don't tell me Fidel told you!"

"No, but Carlos here did. He was at the reception last Saturday night."

Now David remembered seeing Salsamendi among the guests at the Italian Embassy. "I thought I had asked a good question," he said. "But instead I really gave Fidel an opportunity to have some fun at my expense." With a slight smile, Salsamendi nodded in agreement.

David could tell that Marina hadn't the faintest notion what they were talking about. But she dared not ask for an explanation. She remained silent, a fixed smile on her face, pretending to know what was going on. She fixed her attention mainly on the Politburo member before her, ever ready to nod in agreement with whatever Rodríguez said.

"As you know, Dr. Rodríguez, Fidel promised to answer my question concerning the initial course of the revolution when he writes his memoirs," David commented, eager to get beyond pleasantries. "Therefore, I will confine my discussion with you to the role that you expect the Communist Party to play in the *Poder Popular* once it's introduced throughout the island as Cuba's form of local government."

"Very good, Professor Diamond. I appreciate you coming so quickly to the point. As Carlos, here, can attest, that is a particular trait that I admire in you Americans, one that we Cubans should try to emulate more. As a people, as I'm sure you're aware, we sometimes have the habit of talking too much. So I, too, will be as direct and concise as I possibly can."

Their discussion went on for another thirty minutes. David found that Rodríguez's position closely mirrored that of Captain Joaquín Acosta's, except that he was more subtle and seemingly less dogmatic. Still the Cuban leader was articulating the same line concerning the Communist Party's supremacy and vanguard role that he had found troubling when Acosta had earlier voiced it.

"But Professor Diamond," Rodríguez announced midway through their discussion. "Don't you see that we will give the popular masses precisely the kind of political participation you are asking for? People not only will be able to elect their local representatives every two years under the *Poder Popular*, but twice a year they also will be given the opportunity to ask them questions in an open forum concerning community issues. That way, local representatives will have to render accounts to the very people who elected them in the first place."

"I understand the procedures," David interjected, scarcely allowing Rodríguez to finish. "On the surface, of course, they appear democratic . . . "

"What do you mean, 'appear democratic'? They *are* democratic," Rodríguez insisted.

"Dr. Rodríguez, forgive me, but I don't want to get into a debate over, over . . . " Stumbling for words, David glanced quickly at Rodríguez's advisor. "How do you say the word 'semantics' in Spanish, Carlos?"

"The same as in English," Salsamendi replied. "*Semántica.*"

"Thanks. As I was saying, Dr. Rodríguez, I don't want to get into a debate over semantics. It's just that I can see critics of the *Poder Popular* arguing that the Communist Party will have the authority to decide who's eligible to run for election as a local representative, thus enabling it to reject those potential candidates it doesn't like." David hesitated. He could tell by the strained look on his face that Rodríguez was becoming irritated. But he decided to push forward a bit more, as he had done with Joaquín Acosta two weeks earlier. "Look, to be perfectly frank, those critics may have a valid point. You can't have democracy if the ruling party can ensure electoral outcomes beforehand."

"Professor Diamond, what you're saying may have currency in academic circles in your country. But it's purely a theoretical argument that's not rooted in Cuba's political reality," Rodríguez replied sharply.

David noted Salsamendi's scornful glance. Marina, too, was frowning in obvious disapproval. Rodríguez, meanwhile, had drawn himself up in his chair. He sized David up for a moment, evidently weighing which line of argumentation would carry the most weight with his American visitor.

"Professor Diamond, you must remember that we've had our revolution for only fifteen years," the communist leader went on to explain in a pedantic tone of voice. "During that short period of time, as Fidel has pointed out innumerable times, we are having to overcome centuries of underdevelopment. Despite our literacy campaign and our emphasis on education, most Cubans still have only a sixth- or seventh-grade education. Therefore, I ask you, a professor of political science, how can you expect our people to govern themselves without guidance from the Party? Without supervision and coordination by the Party?"

David realized it would be imprudent of him to answer. In any case, the Cuban leader didn't wait for him to respond.

"If you remove the Party's hardworking, conscientious cadres from various levels of society, we'll have not only administrative chaos," Rodríguez continued, now fully animated. "We'll have troublemakers and counterrevolutionaries trying to take over in order to undo everything the revolution has accomplished." He paused momentarily, looking squarely at David. "And believe me, we will *never* permit such a thing to happen—not after so many people have suffered and died defending the revolution," he said emphatically.

David was dismayed. This was not some captain from MININT talking. This was one of Cuba's top leaders speaking. What Rodríguez said reflected what Fidel and others in the Politburo intended to do with the *Poder Popular*. Clearly, David's hopes for greater participatory democracy under the *Poder Popular* had been completely unfounded.

"I believe I fully understand your position, Dr. Rodríguez," David said in a resigned voice. "And I promise that I'll give it a fair hearing in my book."

Rodríguez settled back in his chair, a look of satisfaction on his face.

Still determined to salvage something positive from the meeting, David said, "But if I may, I wonder if I could ask you about something else that has nothing to do with the *Poder Popular*."

"By all means," Rodríguez responded, stealing a glance at his watch, "as long as it doesn't require too elaborate an answer on my part. I have another meeting shortly."

"Thank you. I'll be brief. You see, I've been thinking about what Fidel said the other night concerning the possibility that may now exist for improved relations between your country and mine." He hesitated for a moment when he saw Rodríguez frown, but continued, feeling he had nothing to lose by proceeding. "Of course, Fidel was right in emphasizing that there are conservative, aggressive circles in the United States that want to destroy the Cuban revolution. Still, it occurs to me that it could be in Cuba's interest to send out diplomatic feelers to the Ford Administration. After all, Kissinger is an intelligent man and Cuba might have everything to gain by testing the waters, so to speak."

Marina cast him a disapproving look for having brought up a new, obviously delicate subject, one that had not been on David's agenda. But he didn't expect to have another opportunity like this to learn whether there was any truth to what Rudy García had told him.

Exchanging a knowing glance with Salsamendi, Rodríguez replied with a half-smile, "Professor Diamond, you seem to have a penchant for asking questions about complicated matters. Unfortunately, in the short time we have left, I'm afraid I can't give you the detailed answer your question deserves. But let me just say that what Fidel said the other night reflects not only the reality of the situation in your country but also the position of my government." The meeting was over.

Rodríguez, however, didn't appear upset by David, because he gave precise instructions to Marina Alvarez regarding David's fact-finding itinerary. David was to tour Matanzas province, where the *Poder Popular* experiment was being conducted, and he was to be given full access to whomever or whatever he wanted to see. Meanwhile, Salsamendi would alert local party officials that an American professor would be visiting the province. They were to make sure he was well treated.

Leaving the meeting, David was too disheartened to feel elated that doors were finally being officially opened to him. It had become abundantly clear to him that he would have to shelve his theory about the *Poder Popular's* democratic potential. He wondered what further disappointments were in store for him.

***

The weekend brought welcome relief from Marina's hovering presence. David again arranged to meet Chucho, Tomás, and Roberto in the Habana Libre's bar on Saturday night. When they arrived, they immediately invited him to a private party being given by a friend of Tomás. David ordered beers from room service to complement those that Tomás had already stashed away in the trunk of his father's car. Some forty minutes later the four of them slipped from the hotel, with David carrying four bottles of cold beer in his briefcase.

There were more than a dozen people at the party, all crammed into the small living and dining room of a modest, dilapidated apartment in the Marianao district of Havana. The place had been spruced up for the occasion with freshly cut flowers and a faded but elegant brocade tablecloth that must have been in someone's family long before the revolution. As far as David could tell, most of the guests were in their twenties, a few in their early thirties. *Los muchachos* made it a point to introduce him to everyone.

After nearly an hour of fruitless chitchatting, David realized that he was getting the cold shoulder from all of the guests. Each would converse with him for a minute or two, then, invariably, turn to someone else or find another reason to break off the conversation. He was puzzled by their behavior until Chucho took him aside.

"David, I think you've alarmed our host and his guests," Chucho confided.

"It sure seems that way. They're avoiding me like the plague. I can't understand, I haven't said or done anything that was inappropriate."

"I know, I know. It's your appearance that has alarmed them."

"My appearance?" He looked quickly down at his sport shirt and jeans.

"Your beard. It's your beard. Because you are a *barbudo*, they assume you are a *fidelista* sympathizer from the United States."

"Just because of my beard? That's absolutely ludicrous!"

"Yes, well, it's not only your beard," the young man confided. "It's also because you're an American professor and the government has granted you a visa. For these people, that all adds up to you being a supporter of the government. So, they don't want to say anything in front of you."

Feeling like some kind of pariah, David quietly drank his beer while Chucho, Tomás, and Roberto took the host and several guests aside, trying to reassure them that David could be trusted. To no avail. After a while, the four of them left and found a neighborhood bar where they could have a drink without disturbing anyone.

***

David finally returned to his hotel room after one o'clock in the morning. Despite the lateness of the hour and the beer he had consumed, he had trouble falling asleep. The conversations of the past two weeks with Captain Acosta, *los muchachos,* and Carlos Rafael Rodríguez kept eating at him, and he was further bothered by the reception he had received at the party. As much as he hated to admit it, he was beginning to think that his vision of Cuba had been rather naïve. His theories had been wrong on several counts; he would have to redraft much of his book manuscript.

After finally falling into a troubled sleep, he was awakened a short time later by the insistent ringing of the telephone. He looked at his watch as he groped for the phone and saw that it was well past two a.m.

"*¿Oiga?*" he heard himself asking in a hoarse, gravely voice.

"*¿Profesor Diamond?*" the operator asked. "*Un momento, por favor.*"

"Is that you, David?" For a split second he failed to connect the feminine voice. She wasn't supposed to be with him in Cuba. His heart lurched as he recognized Julie's voice. That the lilting sound of his wife's voice after more than five months of separation could stir him was a surprise.

"Yes, Julie, it's me. Is something wrong? It's nearly two-thirty in the morning."

"I'm sorry. I did try to call you earlier, but you weren't in. Are you all right?"

"Sure. It's Saturday night and I was out with some young guys I've met. But why are you calling? Is something wrong?"

"No, nothing is wrong." He could hear crackling over the telephone line during long pauses in their conversation. He couldn't tell whether it was a poor connection or because his phone was being tapped.

"I guess I just felt like talking to you," she explained, her voice strained and wistful.

"Well, go ahead," he replied, not knowing what to expect. "I'm listening."

"David, I just want to . . . to say," she stammered as she struggled, obviously to find the right words. "That I'm sorry for what happened, for how things turned out." She stopped, as if waiting for his reaction.

With a reluctant sigh, he said, "I'm sorry too, Julie. Real sorry." Then he fell silent.

"I didn't mean to hurt you, David. I really didn't," she said awkwardly. "It just happened. Before I knew it, I just started to fall for Matt and . . . "

"Don't Julie. Please, let's not go over this again." He felt as if she had torn open an old wound.

"I'm sorry." Another silence. "I hope you can forgive me someday," she resumed with a softness in her voice he hadn't heard for ages. "You know, I hope we can still be friends. Despite what you may think, I still care for you. I really do."

The memories and emotions he had suppressed suddenly gripped his throat, making it difficult to swallow. He was unable to reply. Despite her contrite tone and his own confusion, her infidelity still rankled him—and always would.

"I've got to be honest with you," he said, recovering from his momentary lapse into nostalgia. "Maybe the day will come when I can forgive you for what you did. Then we can be friends, I guess. But right now it's too fresh in my memory. I just can't forget."

He hung up and sank back into bed. Sadness, along with a gnawing sense of betrayal, was welling up inside of him. It would soon be Sunday in Los Angeles—and on Sunday mornings, he and Julie would sleep in late and make love before having brunch and reading the *Los Angeles Times*. His heart ached. Suddenly, he felt very much alone and adrift in Havana.

***

8

The Pursuer

Captain Joaquín Acosta ordered Sergeant Oscar Montoya to fetch a car from MININT's pool of automobiles for his appointments at the Ministry of Foreign Affairs. As was often the case on Monday mornings, he spent time catching up on developments over the weekend and planned his work schedule for the next few days. This would be a particularly busy week. Two American Senators were expected to arrive on Saturday to explore the possibility of the United States and Cuba resuming diplomatic relations.

The first thing he had to do at the Foreign Ministry was to ensure that the proper arrangements for their short stay and their meeting with Fidel were being made as planned. He also had to check on the visas for the gaggle of American reporters who would be covering their visit. Next he would talk to Marina Alvarez about Professor David Diamond. Afterward, if she was in, he would pay a visit to Catalina Cruz.

Joaquín had requested the car fifteen minutes earlier than usual, wanting the extra time to mull over recent events before the pressures of the week became too hectic. Unaware that his boss wanted a leisurely trip to the Foreign Ministry, however, Montoya began driving at his usual fast clip.

"*Chico*, slow down!" Joaquín commanded. "I don't have to be there until ten. Take your time getting there." Montoya, having learned to recognize his boss's moods and whims over the years, took a more circuitous route to MINREX, remaining silent during the remainder of the drive.

***

Not privy to the highest policymaking circles of the Party and government, Joaquín had only just learned about the game Fidel was playing with the *norteamericanos*. Using various channels, the *líder máximo* had quietly sent discrete feelers to Washington during the summer, hinting at the possibility of normalizing relations. Now, a Republican and a Democratic senator were coming to Cuba, supposedly on their own, but Joaquín suspected that the wily Kissinger was secretly behind their visit.

In the meantime, he felt fortunate that Fidel's overtures fit perfectly with his own scheme to snare the old communists in a trap. As he had planned, the CIA had sent someone to Havana to gain information on what Fidel might be up to. And that man, he knew for certain, was David Diamond.

"*Yes,*" he mused, "*the CIA's Rudy García fell for the Manuel Domínguez defection as we expected. Now, he's sent us Diamond. But if our plan is to succeed, I'll have to catch the professor consorting with the old communists. So let's see what kind of questions he asked Carlos Rafael last week.*"

In the meantime, Joaquín found it hard to believe that Fidel was actually contemplating an accommodation with the *norteamericanos* as a way of countering Moscow's growing hold over Cuba. The Empire was too close, too powerful, too threatening for it to play that kind of balancing role. Moreover, the Cuban government's defiance of the Yankees constituted the very essence of the revolution. In any case, Fidel was too much of an intransigent nationalist to submit Cuba once again to Washington's domination.

"Coño," he asked himself, puzzled by the riddle of the *Comandante's* latest gambit. "*What's he trying to accomplish by approaching Washington?*"

Joaquín greatly respected Fidel's strategic brilliance and tactical skills in the international arena. Save for the blunder that had led to the missile crisis, he had seen the *Comandante* time and again outwit four American presidents, none of whom were Fidel's equal. Only Kissinger could match Fidel intellectually. But the American Secretary of State was hobbled by Washington's bureaucracy and an obstreperous Congress. Joaquín had often remarked to Catalina and Ernesto, the only confidante he had ever had in MININT, that if Fidel had been in command of a larger country with more resources, the *norteamericanos* would really be in trouble.

The popular description of Fidel as *el caballo*, he had also told them, had turned into a prophetic metaphor for the revolution. Once Fidel had literally seized the reins of government by taking the bit in his mouth, the revolution had taken off at a full gallop. The Cuban people were in for a wild ride. Most held on for dear life. But others began jumping off as the revolution gained speed, becoming more radicalized as property was seized, while daily life became more difficult and tumultuous. Some of the disaffected, particularly the

Americanized bourgeoisie, chose exile abroad. Still others on the island became bitter, internal émigrés. Yet nothing slowed Fidel. On the contrary, he forced the revolution to race onward, eliminating racial discrimination, private property, and the bourgeoisie in the process, creating a more just, egalitarian society—and, above all else, liberating Cuba from Yankee domination.

"Cuba had not gained true independence in 1898, when the Spanish yoke was finally broken," he used to lecture his MININT cadets. *"On the contrary, the Yankees replaced the Spaniards as our masters—sending in the Marines, and ruling through their plenipotentiaries, their New York banks and big business interests, and their Cuban puppets. Not until the triumph of the revolution in 1959 were we Cubans able to reclaim our independence, sovereignty, and dignity, thanks to Fidel."*

At the same time, however, Joaquín remained ambivalent toward Cuba's fraternal ally, the Soviet Union, whose support had been essential to maintaining the Yankees at bay.

On the one hand, he admired the Soviet Union's military strength and scientific achievements, particularly in space. *"Who can fail to recall that when Sputnik was successfully launched into the heavens in 1957,"* he was fond of saying, *"all that the North Americans could do that year was introduce a new line of cars—the failed Edsel!"* As a professional, too, he held the KGB in high regard, considering it superior to the CIA, which relied too much on technology. The KGB was more effective because it more skillfully employed its human assets—KGB spies, communist sympathizers, and double-agents who spied for reasons of greed or blackmail—to steal secrets from the imperialists.

On the other hand, he had been dismayed by the conditions he found during a long training session in the Soviet Union: deplorable housing, shortages of even the most basic consumer goods, and somber, ill-clothed Russians everywhere. He concluded that, after more than five decades of building socialism in their march toward communism, the Soviets had only plenty of bread, potatoes and vodka to show for their effort. The Russian people were not all that much better off than the people in underdeveloped Cuba. In fact, he recalled smiling to himself when he first read the dossier on Manuel Domínguez in which he learned that Marina Alvarez had denounced her cousin for saying that he had seen Cuba's future in the Soviet Union and had been repelled by it.

A member of the Communist Party since its formal unveiling in 1965, Joaquín had always been more of a nationalist than a Marxist-Leninist. His trip to the Soviet Union had served only to strengthen his doubts about communism. What worried him now was that Cuba seemed headed down the same path as the Soviets. Fidel's colossal failure with the ten-million-ton harvest had left Moscow—and its minions in the PSP—in a position to take control. He wasn't at all sure this time around that Fidel would be able to fend off the Soviets and regain the maneuvering room he had once enjoyed.

Fidel's intelligence and near photographic memory, Joaquín had noticed, invariably made him an instant expert on almost any sub-ject—sometimes with disastrous results, particularly in domestic policy. Here, his immense pride and self-confidence frequently led him to overestimate his intellectual capacity, to confuse quick study with knowledge and experience. That Fidel was surrounded by sy-cophants—*comemierdas*, or shit-eaters, as Joaquín was wont to call them—compounded the problem because few within his inner circle dared rein him in. Indeed, Joaquín remembered what happened when he once saw Raúl argue with his brother, and later when Ramiro Valdés, at the time Minister of Interior, also had the temerity to dis-agree with Fidel over a policy matter. "*Fueron aplastados*"—they were squashed, he had related to Ernesto and Catalina.

At first, Joaquín was puzzled by what seemed a contradiction in Fidel. Many of his worst blunders were in agriculture, yet he had lived much of his boyhood on his father's large farm in Oriente prov-ince. Fidel's grandiose harvest drive had been sheer folly, as had been his decision to collectivize most of agriculture. And he had further compounded the food problem by offering such low prices to what remained of the small private farmers that they had no in-centive to produce or sell crops—and every reason to consume the crops themselves. Joaquín had finally concluded that Fidel had never really farmed himself. He simply had been the son of a rich farmer, who had sent his son away to boarding schools and then to the Uni-versity of Havana to study law.

"*If only Fidel would confine himself to foreign affairs and not meddle in economics and agrarian matters,*" Joaquín would com-plain to himself. "*That way Cuba would be much better off—and we at MININT would have less of an internal security problem.*"

He never voiced these criticisms to anyone except Ernesto and

Catalina, who were both as committed as he to the revolution. The three of them would often engage in long, at times heated, political discussions, freely venting their thoughts and concerns about the revolution. Their trust in one another was absolute, unshakable. He missed those talks now that Ernesto was no longer with them.

***

Ernesto had been like a younger brother. Joaquín had taken an instant liking to him when they first met at the Ministry of Interior, soon becoming the young man's patron and mentor. To his credit, to make it on his own, without Joaquín's help, Ernesto had later moved out of State Security and into MININT's foreign operations. He had been good, too. So good that he was considered for Che's Bolivian expedition. But Che had finally decided against him on grounds that Ernesto was still too green, too inexperienced. That decision had spared Ernesto's life for a couple of years; he would have been killed in Bolivia in 1967, along with Che and the rest of his men. But the prolongation of Ernesto's life, Joaquín always thought with bitterness, had scarcely been worth it. The death he would suffer two years later was an even worse horror.

How his heart still ached, even now after nearly five years, whenever he thought of the dying Ernesto. Captured while fighting with the Sandinistas in Nicaragua, he had been brutally tortured by Somoza's National Guard before his life finally was mercifully extinguished. Unlike the loss of other comrades who had been on clandestine internationalist missions for the Ministry of Interior, Ernesto's death had inflicted a terrible wound on his own body and soul. Only then had Joaquín realized the high human price exacted by Cuba's policy of solidarity with guerrilla movements in Latin America and elsewhere.

Almost as painful was the chasm that had opened between Catalina and him following Ernesto's death. He could still recall that day when the terrible news arrived. While consoling her, he had tried to rein in his own anguish. She had cried with abandonment—wailing with the grief that only the death of one's child or loved one can unleash—and then attacked him for not preventing Ernesto from going on such a dangerous mission. But she reserved most of her vitriol for Fidel.

"You know damn well," she had screamed at him without regard to the heresy she was committing, *"that Fidel is the one really responsible for Ernesto's death. He's so obsessed with fomenting revolutions and fighting imperialism that it doesn't matter to him whether it costs the life of men like Ernesto."* He recalled her vehemence, the look of accusation as she fixed fiery eyes on him, as if his position in MININT made him culpable as well. *"Their deaths don't matter because Fidel is intent on fulfilling his historic destiny. Yes, Joaquín, don't deny it. You know it as well as I do: He wants to go down in history as someone bigger than José Martí, bigger than Simón Bolívar—as the first Latin American that the Yankees and the whole world must reckon with."*

Joaquín had not replied to Catalina's apostasy that day, nor did he report it to State Security. Such an act on his part truly would have betrayed Ernesto. It would also have been contrary to his own code of ethics. But for months afterward it didn't seem important to her that he had laid his career on the line by shielding her. She repeatedly avoided him and refused to take his phone calls. He was certain that he had lost her as well as Ernesto, the only two people he had truly loved besides his mother. To his immense relief, after what seemed like an eternity, she had finally softened. She expressed her gratitude for what he had done. Soon they began seeing one another again. Once at her apartment, he had held her tightly after she had suddenly dissolved into tears, sobbing uncontrollably over the loss of her lover.

Joaquín ceased his musings. They were at the Foreign Ministry. He frowned at the sight of the old building whose neo-Baroque architecture always seemed to him to stand as an appropriate metaphor for the workings of Cuban diplomacy, both before and after the revolution. He directed Sergeant Montoya to wait for him in the vestibule after he had parked the car. He strode purposefully into MINREX's large marble foyer.

***

Joaquín was pleasantly surprised during his meeting with the young Foreign Ministry official. The man had made all the arrangements for the visit by the American senators, right down to the smallest details. He had doubled-checked and found nothing wanting. The proper arrangements for the American reporters had also been taken care of. *"For once,"* Joaquín thought. *"MINREX is doing something right."*

Although he was ten minutes early for his appointment with Marina Alvarez, he walked up to the second floor where she and Catalina had their offices. He approached the secretary, who was doing her best to ignore him while she finished putting up her hair in curlers. "Por Dios," he thought, *"what an uncouth habit Cuban women have gotten into."*

"Compañera," he said in a commanding voice, his patience having run out. "I have an appointment with Marina Alvarez. Please tell her I am here."

"Por parte de quién?" the woman asked, almost insolently, still not bothering to look directly at Joaquín as she continued to fiddle with the hair curlers. At last he realized that she had no idea who he was because he was wearing civilian clothes.

"I am Captain Joaquín Acosta from State Security," he announced, inwardly smiling at the startled look that crossed the woman's face. In an instant, she dropped the curlers and spun her swivel chair around to face him. "As I said, please inform *Compañera* Alvarez that I am here. Also, if she is in the building, please notify *Compañera* Catalina Cruz that I would like to stop by her office after I am through with *Compañera* Alvarez. Is all that understood, *compañera?"*

"Of course, *Capitán* Acosta!" the woman replied, wide-eyed. "I'm truly sorry for having been distracted a moment ago. Please forgive my discourtesy, *Capitán*. I'll tell Marina and Catalina that you are here."

"Good."

As the secretary rushed off, he spied Catalina exiting a meeting at the far end of the hallway. Engrossed in conversation with her companions, she did not notice him as he stood at a distance appreciating her beauty. Had their circumstances been different, he would have done everything in his power to possess her. Watching her walk away, he shook his head. No. One did not possess Catalina. One had to gain her love and respect for her to give freely of herself. Ernesto was able to do that. Joaquín had to admit that it was best that he was prevented from pursuing her. He would have been crestfallen had she rejected him, as she probably would have since he lacked many of the qualities that had caused her to fall passionately in love with Ernesto.

Conscious of the sound of hurrying footsteps behind him, Joaquín swung around to find Marina Alvarez scurrying up to him, flushed and breathless, with the secretary right behind her.

"I'm terribly sorry, *Capitán* Acosta. I didn't know you had arrived. I'm terribly sorry to have kept you waiting," she repeated, her dark eyes shooting barbs at the secretary.

"No need to apologize, *Compañera* Alvarez. Actually, I arrived early. So, if anyone is at fault, then it is I. Now, please, let's go to your office or somewhere where we can talk privately. This will only take half an hour at most."

"Come this way, *Capitán.*"

* * *

Marina Alvarez closed the door to her small office as Joaquín took the chair in front of her desk. He could see that she was apprehensive—a common reaction with people who were about to be interviewed by State Security.

"*Capitán* Acosta," she blurted out suddenly. "I guess you've come to ask me some questions about my cousin, no?"

"Your cousin?"

"Yes. Don't you want to talk to me about Manuel Domínguez?" Marina replied somewhat bewildered. "You know, he was Second-Secretary here at MINREX. Then he betrayed our fatherland by defecting a few months ago. In fact, I had earlier reported him to State Security . . . "

"Ah, yes, Manuel Domínguez," Joaquín said, cutting her off before she could finish. "Believe me, I'm quite familiar with his case."

The irony of the situation didn't escape him. Marina Alvarez assumed that he was there to question her about her cousin, the very man whose defection he had orchestrated earlier in the summer. Her assumption, of course, was logical, but incorrect.

He studied her for a moment. Though she had complied with her revolutionary duty by having informed on her cousin, he really didn't like her. He could tell she was the type of person who contributed to the mediocrity rampant in MINREX and other ministries—rigid, suspicious, scheming, not terribly bright, and self-serving as well.

"Don't concern yourself about your cousin," Joaquín said with a dismissing wave of his hand. "You see, he's but an insignificant

figure in the overall scheme of things. In fact, he's done our fatherland a favor by no longer being here. So just forget entirely about
Manuel Domínguez. The person I'm really interested in is the
norteamericano, Professor David Diamond."

"I knew it!" Marina exclaimed excitedly, a triumphant smile parting her full lips. "I just knew it! I could tell that he's no friend of the
revolution. Is he spying for the CIA?"

"*Compañera* Alvarez, I ask the questions here! Furthermore, don't
jump to conclusions." Seeing her recoil, he continued in a more soothing, confidential voice. "Now, tell me why you think Professor Diamond is no friend of the revolution? Did he say anything or do something against our government?"

She hesitated for several moments, obviously wracking her
memory.

"No, he hasn't gone that far, at least not when I've been escorting
him. He knows I'm too committed a revolutionary to put up with
any outright counterrevolutionary talk from him." She paused as if
overcome by emotion. "You see, *Capitán* Acosta, I lost my husband
in Fidel's final guerrilla offensive, just before the triumph of the revolution. Since then, the revolution has become my whole life."

"I know you're a conscientious, dedicated revolutionary, Marina."
He saw her beam. "But now, please tell me, what makes you suspect
that Diamond is working for the CIA? Is it something he's said or done?"

Marina looked nonplussed. "Again, *Capitán*, it's not so much what
he says exactly. It's his attitude. It's how he behaves. For example,
there have been times when he's been uncooperative as when he
took it upon himself to go directly to CDR headquarters without me.
Then he began interviewing Comrade Rene Pérez before I got there.
Believe me, I gave him a scolding he'll never forget."

"Anything else that arouses your suspicion about his true intentions?"

"Well, he never accepts what I tell him. He's always skeptical,
argumentative, sometimes even disrespectful of the revolution. He
seems to enjoy making fun of some of our problems." She paused to
see whether Joaquín was finding her observations useful. "As a
norteamericano, he should consider himself fortunate to be our guest
and not behave the way he does. *¿No es cierto?* Isn't that right,
Capitán Acosta?"

"Of course. Part of his problem most likely is that he's an American professor who enjoys being argumentative and skeptical just for

the sake of sounding intellectual."

Joaquín studied the woman for a moment. He had to get her to focus directly on what most concerned him.

"Now, listen carefully to what I'm about to ask you, Marina," he said, as if wishing to take her into his confidence. "Of the interviews that Professor Diamond has had so far, the one that interests me the most is the one he held with Comrade Carlos Rafael Rodríguez. So I want you to tell me exactly what they discussed."

She was staring at him wide-eyed. He could tell she feared he was trying to find out whether Carlos Rafael, a member of the Politburo, had committed some kind of indiscretion with Diamond. Frightened and confused, she couldn't respond.

"*Compañera*, don't misunderstand me," he said, hoping to put her at ease. "It's all very simple. I only want to know what subjects Diamond brought up in his talk with Comrade Rodríguez last week. That's all. I would ask Comrade Rodríguez directly, but I prefer not to bother him with this trifling issue when he has so much important work to do. So, don't be alarmed. Collect your thoughts. We have plenty of time," he added in a disarming voice. "Just try to remember as best you can what Diamond wanted to talk about."

Marina gave a deep sigh of relief.

"Thank you. Now I understand what you're asking. But you should know that Comrade Salsamendi was also present, so you may want to check with him, too, about the questions Diamond asked."

"Good, I'm glad to know he was there. If necessary, I can get further clarification from him if any questions still remain when we've finished. In the meantime, please, go on." He assumed a nonchalant manner. "*Like hell I'll go to Salsamendi about this!*" he thought. "*That's all I need is for Carlos Rafael and his old communist pals to get wind of what I'm up to.*" He waited for Marina's response.

"Yes, well, let me see," she began, making a point of looking thoughtful. "Yes, there was lots of general talk, mostly about the *Poder Popular* and the kind of elections that were being considered. Yes, I remember it quite clearly because Diamond was almost insolent with Comrade Rodríguez, disagreeing with him about our democracy and the role of the Party. I found his behavior disrespectful. But Comrade Rodríguez was very firm in maintaining the correctness of our approach . . . "

"I'm sure that Comrade Rodríguez was more than Diamond's intellectual match," Joaquín broke in. "Now think, besides the *Poder*

Popular, what else did they talk about? For instance, did Diamond ask about Cuba normalizing relations with Washington?"

"Why, yes," Marina responded brightly, eager now to please. "Yes, at the end of the meeting he suddenly asked Comrade Rodríguez about whether it would not be in Cuba's best interests to approach the American government—specifically Kissinger—about normalizing relations now that Ford is President."

"And how did Comrade Rodríguez reply?" Joaquín asked in a casual tone that concealed his interest.

"He simply said there wasn't enough time to go into a detailed answer. He then stated that Fidel's response to that question a couple of weeks earlier contained everything that needed to be said on the subject. That was all there was to it."

"Are you sure, Marina? Neither one said anything more on the subject? Take as much time as you need."

"I don't need more time, *Capitán* Acosta. Nothing more was said about foreign policy questions. As I said earlier, most of the time was spent on the *Poder Popular*, to the point that I began to find the discussion far too academic for my taste."

"You are certain?"

"Absolutely! For God's sake, *Capitán* Acosta, I'm not so old that my memory is failing me. But if you doubt me, consult Comrade Salsamendi. I'm sure he'll tell you the same thing."

"All right, Marina, I believe you."

***

Joaquín was disappointed. As he had fully expected, David Diamond had used the interview with Carlos Rafael Rodríguez to sound him out about Havana's secret overtures to Washington. A ranking member of the Politburo with historic ties to the defunct PSP, Carlos Rafael was a logical choice for Diamond. But according to Marina, the wily old communist had refused to be drawn out. Joaquín knew what that meant: He still lacked the evidence he needed to show Fidel that the old communists were conspiring with an American professor working for the CIA.

Joaquín recalled what his mentor, Major José Abrantes, had told him a few days earlier when they were discussing Diamond. *"You baited the hook with the defection of Manuel Domínguez last July,"* Abrantes said. *"And now the CIA has taken the bait by sending us this American professor. So, he's your fish. You can play him any way you want, so long as you make sure he doesn't implicate just himself. He's got to implicate the old communists as well."*

Some things about the *norteamericano* weren't adding up, however. The report from the Cuban intelligence agent in Washington showed conclusively that Diamond was involved with the CIA's Rudy García. Yet for a spy, Diamond seemed to be taking his time in ferreting out information about Cuba's overtures to Washington. Instead, his inquiries were almost exclusively about the *Poder Popular.* Moreover, everything about Diamond, from his recruitment by the CIA to his trip to Cuba, struck Joaquín as exceedingly amateurish.

Like most of his fellow counterintelligence colleagues in the Ministry of Interior, Joaquín was contemptuous of Langley's covert activities on the island. Only in 1959 and 1960, when Lawton Armstrong was stationed in Cuba, had the CIA presented a real threat to the government. But Armstrong had soon run afoul of his superiors, after which he ceased to be a player. In the meantime, the General Directorate of Intelligence had already begun to turn many of the Agency's Cuban spies into double-agents who fed their CIA handlers false information. The DGI had also succeeded in recruiting from among the droves of American leftists visiting the island scores of useful contacts and even agents who would become part of the DGI's network in the United States.

Without doubt, the CIA couldn't compare with the DGI. Still, Joaquín found the Diamond affair incredibly inept even for the CIA. *"Did the CIA want Diamond's cover blown?"* he wondered. *"Were they trying to create an international incident over Diamond so as to derail any possibility of talks between Havana and Washington?"* But judging from Rudy García's track record, Joaquín didn't think the CIA officer was capable of concocting such a devious, Machiavellian ploy. He remained perplexed as he approached the MINREX secretary.

"Oh, *Capitán* Acosta! *Compañera* Cruz said you could come to her office whenever you've finished with Marina. Her office is down the hall, fourth on the right."

* * *

"Why, *Capitán* Acosta," Catalina exclaimed in an unusually loud, friendly voice. "What a pleasant surprise! Please come in."

Her warm greeting, Joaquín suspected, was also for the benefit of the busybodies outside her office. They doubtlessly would be impressed by her being on friendly terms with an officer from State Security. Once again, he marveled at her ability to turn delicate situations to her personal advantage—as when years earlier she had deftly deflected Fidel's overtures, only to remain in his good graces.

Upon closing the door, Catalina kissed him affectionately on the cheek and then gestured for him to take the spare office chair. Returning to her seat behind her desk, her green eyes glowing, she smiled warmly at him. He could see she was genuinely pleased by his unexpected visit.

"You know, you're truly amazing," he exclaimed in admiration. "Here you are hard at work on Monday morning looking every bit as beautiful as the other night at the Italian Embassy."

"Joaquín. I didn't know you could be such a flatterer!" she replied laughingly, blushing slightly. "You should cultivate this talent more. You're bound to catch a woman that way. We all love compliments, you know. Even the revolution can't change that."

"I'm afraid I have little time to chase women these days, unless they're counterrevolutionaries." Seeing her frown, he instantly regretted his remark. She had been playful just a moment earlier, as she used to be when Ernesto was around, but now she was looking at him disapprovingly. He reproached himself for being so clumsy with the opposite sex.

"*Coño,* I shouldn't have said that," he said ruefully. "It's just that it's hard for me to forget that I'm a State Security officer. But I know now that I must learn to put my work aside on occasions like these when I'm in the company of a beautiful woman such as yourself."

She laughed, her face aglow once again. "Well, I have to admit that right now you've recovered nicely. But no more *piropos, por favor.* Two compliments are more than enough for one morning. Now, what brings you here to the Ministry?"

"I had to check on how MINREX is coming along with the arrangements for the visit of the two American senators. They're arriving Saturday. I also wanted to ask Marina Alvarez some questions about Professor David Diamond's interviews."

"Poor Professor Diamond," Catalina replied, making a face. "To be stuck with Marina as his MINREX guide. But why, may I ask, are you taking a special interest in our American friend?"

Shaking his head, Joaquín frowned. "You know I can't divulge information like that, *niña*. Just accept that I have my reasons."

"After all that we've been through, don't you think you can trust me to be discreet?"

"*¡Por Dios*, Catalina! You know it's not a matter of trust."

Pausing, he searched for a way to discourage her interest in the *norteamericano* without revealing anything. He was thankful that her MINREX office, with its thick walls and solid door, offered them the privacy he needed for what he could safely divulge. He recalled how Manuel Domínguez had overheard the conversation that had taken place in his boss's office that fateful evening only a few months past because the old communists had carelessly left the transom over the door open. But Catalina's was shut.

Confident that they were safe, he said, "Look, I can only tell you that despite his being on the Left, despite his apparent support for the revolution, our American friend may not be all that he seems. Even Marina has noted that he's too critical of some of the things our government has done."

"Well, what does she expect? He's a professor, after all. Anyway, you should know better than to believe everything Marina says." She searched his face for clues before going on. "Frankly, Joaquín, I really find it hard to believe that you can be suspicious of Professor Diamond. He doesn't strike me at all like the CIA type. He's too far to the Left. And besides, he's too *simpático*."

"*Niña*," he cried out indignantly. "I can't believe you could possibly find this *norteamericano* attractive! In any case, the very fact that I'm warning you to stay away from him should be enough for you to dismiss him out of your mind."

"Are you telling me this for personal reasons?" she asked calmly, but with a note of irritation. "Or are you acting in your official capacity as a State Security officer?"

"You shouldn't have to ask that," he responded reproachfully. "You know I will do everything possible to protect you from harm . . . " Realizing that he was starting to sound like the father she had come to despise, he stopped short. "I'm sorry," he said a moment later in a more conciliatory tone. "I should know better than to try to tell you how to run your life." Shaking his head, he let out a deep sigh. "It's just that I could tell that you were attracted to Diamond the moment I introduced you at the Italian Embassy. I haven't seen your face light up like that since Ernesto was alive . . . " His voice trailed off. She was looking at him strangely. *"If I'm not careful,"* he cautioned, *"this could end in an argument and she'll do exactly the opposite of what I want."*

"I'm only trying to tell you that it was painful for me to see the look you had at the reception wasted on someone like this *norteamericano,"* he confided. "So it hurts to think that you might fall in love with a man who in no way begins to measure up to Ernesto."

"Who said anything about falling in love? I only said that I found him attractive and charming, that's all."

She turned away as if she were mulling something over in her mind. He waited, not wanting to say anything that would instigate an argument. From experience, he knew they had already come perilously close to that flash point.

"And by the way," she said suddenly. "As a woman, don't I have the right to say that I find Diamond attractive just as a man would express his appreciation of a beautiful woman?"

"Of course you have that right," he agreed quickly. "You know perfectly well from all our years together that I've always believed women should have the same rights as men. I've never been into *machismo.*"

"I know you believe that intellectually, but sometimes you're overly protective."

"Perhaps. But I can't help it, *niña.* It's been four years since Ernesto died and I . . . " He paused momentarily, unsure whether to continue. ". . . And I imagine that by now you're ready to become romantically involved with someone."

"Can't you accept that as something perfectly normal for a woman in my situation?"

"Of course I can accept it. But why must it be with someone like Diamond? I mean, he's everything that Ernesto was not. You, of all people, must know that . . . "

"Joaquín, *por Dios!"* she broke in heatedly, her voice now rising. "Don't you think I know that he's not at all like Ernesto? Please give me some credit for knowing that I'll never again find another man like Ernesto."

Her voice and the fire in her eyes told Joaquín that he had gone too far. He wondered how he could mollify her. But suddenly, before he could say or do anything, she rose from her chair and came around the desk to stand in front of him.

"Poor Joaquín," she said gently, grasping his hands in hers, her expression softening. "I know how you have suffered with Ernesto's death. Your pain has been as unbearable as mine because the two of you were like brothers. And our pain has been all the greater because he was such an extraordinary person. As you used to say, he was in many ways a young Che, but without Che's ruthlessness." She paused to collect herself. "That's why he died at an even younger age than Che, without accomplishing anything. What a waste."

Joaquín saw the tears forming. She released his hands abruptly to dry her eyes with the back of her hand. She clenched her jaw to stop its trembling and looking toward the ceiling. He rose from his chair to comfort her, but she stepped away from him quickly. As had happened many times following Ernesto's death, he felt helpless.

"I'll be all right," she said finally. "I am getting much better at being able to think and talk about him without dissolving into tears. But it's still hard sometimes. Especially just now, because you reminded me of all the good times the three of us had together."

"I know," Joaquín concurred, relieved that they were back on safer ground. "I was thinking the same thing earlier this morning on the way here. Except for you, I've no one I can really talk to nowadays. Absolutely no one, *niña*! How I miss those discussions with Ernesto and you."

"I do too," she sighed, nodding her head. "But we have to let go of him, Joaquín. We've got to get on with our lives. At least I know I have to. I can't be like Marina Alvarez. Her life stopped sixteen years ago when her husband was killed." Pausing, she shook her head. "And let me tell you something: I won't allow myself to waste my life like that when I haven't even turned thirty. No, to do that would only compound the tragedy of Ernesto's death by adding another wasted life to it."

"You're right, you need to move on. But please, for your own sake, don't allow yourself to get caught up with Diamond."

"*¡Por Dios, Joaquín!*" she cried out angrily once again. "For Heaven's sake, I'm not some innocent school girl or virgin who needs protection. In case you haven't realized it yet, I'm a grown woman. So, *por favor*, permit me to enjoy whatever opportunities come my way, whether it's with Diamond or someone else. You know that I'll always cherish Ernesto's memory. But please realize that I must also begin to live again."

"Yes, Catalina," Joaquín said in a resigned voice. "But for your sake, just be careful, please."

"And in the meantime," he thought, "I'll begin playing the fish. I'll see to it that Diamond meets with some of the old communists at MINREX and then we'll see what he asks them. And I'll do everything I can to make damn sure that you, niña, don't have the opportunity to fall in love with him."

***

9

La Cara Doble

At the beginning of his third week, David met with three officials from the Foreign Ministry to discuss the prospects for more normalized relations between Havana and Washington. The surprise afternoon meeting had been arranged suddenly by Marina Alvarez, who hadn't bothered to inform him of it until late that same morning. Two of the officials turned out to be dogmatic communists—he presumed they once had belonged to the old PSP—and they conversed spiritedly about the United States, including what policies could be expected under Ford and Kissinger. But despite some discreet probing on David's part, there was no hint from the Cubans of any secret governmental overtures. *"The issue has got to be so sensitive that only Fidel and a few of his most trusted officials must know about them,"* David surmised. *"Either that, or Rudy Garciá is full of bull!"*

The following day, Marina informed him that their scheduled trip to Matanzas province, where the *Poder Popular* experiment was taking place, would have to be postponed until the middle of the following week. Rescheduling would take them well into October, the height of the hurricane season, which might cause still further delays. David resigned himself to writing off the next seven or eight days as essentially downtime, to be spent idly in Havana. What he didn't know, however, was that additional surprises were in store for him, beginning with Isabela.

***

It had begun quite innocently enough. On Wednesday afternoon, while leaving his hotel room, he encountered a teenage girl and a young woman in the hallway. They told him they had moved into a nearby room two days earlier and now they couldn't open their jammed balcony door to let in fresh air. Could he assist them? The hotel help, they complained, had ignored their calls. He thought it unusual for Cubans—especially two women—to be staying in a hotel normally reserved for foreigners. For a fleeting instant, he wondered whether he was being set up, but quickly dismissed the idea. Neither of the two looked like police agents or hookers.

Once in their room, it took him only seconds to muscle open the stuck sliding door. After thanking him profusely, they asked where he was from and were thrilled to learn that he was an American. Seeing their innocence, he relaxed and soon began asking them questions. He learned they were sisters who lived in the city of Cienfuegos; they were in Havana for only a few days so that the older sister, Isabela, could see a medical specialist and have some laboratory tests taken. The only reason they had been lucky enough to be staying at the Habana Libre, they said, was that the medical authorities had put them there. They were due to return to Cienfuegos on Friday if the lab results turned out negative. They were having such a good time they were hoping the results would be delayed so that they could stay at least until Saturday.

As he was about to leave their room, he toyed momentarily with the thought of inviting them both to dinner or perhaps a movie. Their feminine company would be a much welcome change from *los muchachos*. But he decided against it. Isabela really didn't appeal to him. She appeared to be in her mid-twenties, with a slender, flat figure, and a slightly pocked, melancholy face, made sadder by her dark, brooding eyes. Teresa, who was taller, had long, lustrous, dark hair and the makings of a real beauty. He guessed she was only seventeen at most. He wouldn't even dream of touching her.

***

The next day, shortly before six in the evening, he was startled by a sharp rap on his hotel door. He opened it to find Isabela and Teresa standing in the hallway, both looking ecstatic. The lab tests had turned out negative, Isabela informed him excitedly. She didn't reveal what illness she had been tested for, but all along he had assumed it was for some kind of cancer. Watching them, he found their childlike elation contagious.

"Listen, I have a proposal to make," he announced grandly. "I want to invite you both to have dinner with me tonight so that we can celebrate the wonderful news together. We could have dinner downstairs, say, about eight o'clock. What do you think?"

The sisters looked at each other and immediately accepted. Clearly thrilled by his invitation, they rushed back to their room to shower and change.

He was surprised by the transformation when he later knocked on their door. Teresa had put on lipstick; she looked grown up and luscious in her simple cotton print dress. Isabela, too, was dressed in what must have been her best outfit, a plain, navy rayon dress that was so soft and billowy it hid her thinness. Like her sister, she had applied lipstick and added some rouge to brighten her features. Her mood had noticeably brightened, too. Immediately, he complimented them both on looking so terrific—indeed, he later noticed several male guests turning for a second glance as he escorted the two sisters into the hotel dining room.

They drank watered-down daiquiris before dinner, followed by beer, which helped to wash down the overcooked, dried-out chicken and the gummy rice they were served. But the mediocre dinner couldn't spoil their fun. Isabela and Teresa sat wide-eyed and entranced as David described life in America, sometimes embellishing his stories with amusing anecdotes. For his part, he was having an equally grand time. Without feminine company since his arrival in Cuba three weeks earlier—save for Marina Alvarez, who didn't count—he was greatly enjoying the attention of the two sisters. He was further pleased when he discovered that they were ardent supporters of the government and devoted admirers of Fidel.

Being the elder, Isabela made herself the political spokesperson for both sisters. She was a primary-school teacher, she related, and her pupils were, for the most part, the sons and daughters of working people. Even though they came from *familias humildes*, she insisted her students were receiving as good an education as anyone else their age in Cuba.

"That's one of the reasons I support Fidel so strongly," she said with unabashed fervor. "Everyone is treated equally. That wasn't true before the revolution, believe me. Even though I was a child, I can remember the airs that the rich would put on. It was really hard for the working class to get ahead, to be treated fairly and decently."

She paused to take another sip of beer. They were on their second round and David thought that both sisters, Teresa especially, were becoming a little tipsy.

"As an American, David, you can't fully appreciate what it was like then," Isabela continued, slurring her words ever so slightly.

"Not even Teresita, here, knows. She was still an infant when the revolution took over." Teresa giggled and nodded her ascent. "We were a pretty big family and our mother had to work as a maid in order for us to scrape by. Until Teresa was born, she would work five, sometimes six days a week for a middle-class family, who didn't have room for a live-in maid."

"This was in Cienfuegos?"

"No, we lived in Havana. Anyway, she washed floors, cleaned bathrooms, polished the furniture, did the laundry and ironing, washed dishes, and prepared meals, including when her employers held a dinner party. On those occasions, she would have to stay until she finished washing the dishes, even if it was a Saturday night. There were times when Teresita, here, almost forgot who her mommy was."

"*No es cierto*, Isabela," Teresa protested. "You know that's not true. I didn't forget her at all. I just missed her a lot when I was a child."

"Well, anyway, she worked for those people for ten or twelve years straight, including through most of her pregnancies—almost to the moment she was to give birth."

"Are you sure you're not exaggerating, Isabela?"

"*Es cierto*, David. Believe me, they exploited her; they treated her like dirt. Sometimes they wouldn't pay her all they owed her. Yet they thought nothing of asking her to do something extra or to work on a Saturday when they were holding a party. She wasn't a human being in their eyes, just a common maid at their beck and call."

"Is she still alive?"

"Yes, thanks to the revolution. She lives with us in Cienfuegos with a small pension from the government, which she wouldn't have received before the revolution. And she has enough to eat with her ration book and she gets good medical care, too."

"Yes, I know," David said, warming to the subject. "Along with education, the government's achievements in public health are one of the major success stories of the revolution. Cuba is the envy of other Third World countries, you know, when it comes to health and education."

"Exactly! And let me tell you, David, I probably owe my life to the revolution because of the medical care I've received. When the doctors in Cienfuegos thought I might have cancer of the liver, they sent me here, to Havana, to undergo more sophisticated tests. Not only that, but everything was paid for—and we were even put up at the Habana Libre to boot!"

"Yes, and take my word for it," Teresa broke in. "Isabela was a nervous wreck, not knowing whether she had cancer as her doctors in Cienfuegos suspected."

"*Sí, pero gracias a tí, Teresita,* I was able to get through this ordeal and now my test results show I'm all right. So, now you can understand, David, why I'm grateful for all that the revolution has done for me and the Cuban people."

"Yes, I can see that," he replied, nodding his head. "And I'll tell you frankly, your story confirms what I've always said about the revolution—that it's a popular revolution because it has the well-being and interests of the Cuban people at heart."

***

After dinner, he insisted on ordering dessert and some Napoleon brandy. The two sisters eagerly accepted the treat. A while later, they devoured a delicious mango ice cream. He was certain it had come from the enormous *Coppelia* ice cream parlor down the block, near the hotel.

"But tell me," he asked casually, deciding to switch the topic of their conversation to politics, certain that Isabela's and Teresa's views would diverge sharply from those of Chucho and Tomás. "All the revolution's achievements notwithstanding, don't you two miss not having more freedom to do what you want? To read different newspapers? To listen to more than just *Radio Rebelde?* To elect leaders from among different political parties?"

"Don't look at me," Teresa exclaimed, laughing as she rolled her eyes, her voice now thick from the brandy. "I don't have any interest in politics whatsoever!"

"And you, Isabela? Surely, you must have some opinions on the matter."

"Yes, I have," she replied eagerly. "To be perfectly frank, politics bore me. I am happy to let Fidel and the Party lead the way. They know far more than I do about political questions. I'm just too busy trying to do a good job teaching school and getting through life. Besides, as Fidel has said many times, when we had so-called elections before the revolution, what did all those *politiqueros* do for our country, for the common people?"

"True enough. On the other hand, you now have to put up with shortages of food, clothing, and other items that were once plentiful. Doesn't that bother you?"

"Of course the shortages are an irritant. That was especially true a few years back when things were really bad. But before the revolution, you have to remember, much of the working class didn't have the money to buy all the things that were available back then. I'm not just talking about imported luxury stuff, either. No, I'm referring to buying a humble house, renting a decent apartment, getting medical care, or buying even basic necessities."

"And now?"

"Now, as I just said, the situation has improved, though we still have to do without lots of things. But that's the price we have to pay for all the advances the revolution has brought us, including restoring our country's dignity, sovereignty, and independence. So you can be sure we don't want to see the old Cuba come back. And that's exactly what would happen if the enemies of the revolution returned." She stopped and looked at him apologetically for a moment before continuing. "You have to realize, David, that because your country is a superpower, you can have elections and all that. But we Cubans can't afford that kind of luxury as long as we are menaced by the Colossus, as José Martí called your country."

David was more than satisfied. He was elated. His instincts had been right about the two sisters. They were genuinely supportive of the regime. Best of all, they were just plain ordinary people, not government or Party officials. Isabela had provided the tonic to offset what he had been hearing since his arrival in Havana, a welcome relief from Chucho's jaded views. She had rekindled his faith in the revolution.

When at last he turned his attention back to his dinner companions, he caught Isabela looking at him. To his surprise, he felt a stirring inside.

***

Later, back in his room, David heard a soft knock and on opening the door found Isabela standing shyly in the hallway, wearing a worn bathrobe and what appeared to be a negligee underneath. She fixed dark, brooding eyes on him, and asked whether he had anything for Teresa, who had come down with an upset stomach. Instinctively, he knew he could have her if he wanted. But first he would attend to

Teresa. As Isabela waited in the hallway, he slipped his thin cotton bathrobe over his shorts and took two Alka Seltzers from his travel bag. He followed Isabela to her room.

He found Teresa in bed, complaining of indigestion. Dropping the tablets into a glass of water, he let the mixture fizz for a moment before offering it to her. She looked at him apprehensively, but he told her to drink it all, assuring her she would soon feel much better. After all, he told her in jest, "I'm not called 'Dr. Diamond' for nothing." Making a face, she drank the bubbly water, finishing it off to the last drop. She closed her eyes and a short time later began to doze off. As he watched her, he felt Isabela's eyes on him. When he was satisfied that Teresa was asleep, he took Isabela by the hand and quietly slipped out the door and returned to his room.

He had no sooner closed the door than she was on him, her small body pressed tightly against his, her lips and tongue hungrily searching his mouth as her fingers dug into his hair. He almost lost his balance, but recovered and moved her onto the bed. Without a word, he began to undress her, kissing her face and neck, then moving his lips down to her small breasts. She reached down to hold him. He had torn off his robe and underwear when he suddenly thought it best to take precautions. As she lay quietly, he searched for the condoms. Back in bed, he was surprised by the passionate intensity of her lovemaking. In the darkness, she did not seem unattractive or inept at pleasing a man. Soon her whole body shook as she reached her climax, once, then twice, before his own orgasm left him gasping. Exhausted, he lay atop her for a long time, her thin legs still wrapped around him in a tight embrace.

They talked quietly afterward of love and life. David was grateful that the dim lighting partially hid her thin body and limbs and softened her slightly pocked face and the small bumps scattered across her chest and breasts. She told him that she had been married at nineteen, just after she had obtained her teaching degree from the pedagogical institute. Then, without warning, four years later, her husband abandoned her. He stole a boat and fled to the United States, where he was given political asylum as a refugee from communism. At the time, she was stunned by his defection. He had seldom talked politics. Not once had he told her that he wanted to leave Cuba. He had written her only one letter after he arrived in Miami—a cruel letter in which he informed her that he no longer considered himself married to her.

As if this was not shattering enough news, she later learned that her husband had been carrying on a long affair with her best friend, a teacher at the same school where she taught. A few months before his defection, the girlfriend had obtained an exit permit to go to the United States, ostensibly to be reunited with her mother and father, who were already living in Miami. Her husband hadn't gone to the United States to escape communism, Isabela complained bitterly; he had fled to be with the woman he really loved, her former friend and colleague. She was totally devastated.

David's heart softened upon hearing the woman's tale of woe, but all he could do was hold her tightly against him and caress her head gently while he tried to soothe her with kind words. His tenderness only made her cry again as she told him how miserable she was knowing no man wanted an abandoned woman like her, who wasn't pretty like her sister. No, she wailed, she was too thin, too plain for Cuban men.

"Hush, Isabela. Don't talk like that," he said softly, placing two fingers gently on her lips. "Please don't ever again sell yourself short. You must realize that how you see yourself is how others will see you."

"What do you mean?" she asked, wiping the tears from her eyes.

"Well, when I first met you yesterday, you looked so down and mournful. But tonight, when I came to your room, I found a lovely, radiant woman. It wasn't just your dress and makeup, either. It was the attractive glow about you which was due to your happiness over the good news you'd received this afternoon. It shone through, turning you into the beautiful woman you really are."

"You really thought I was beautiful tonight, David?"

"Absolutely," he replied in earnest. "Didn't you notice how the men were staring at you when we entered the dining room?"

He knew very well that what he said about her beauty was a stretch, but to have given an honest answer or even an ambivalent or qualified one would have been terribly cruel. She had wanted to hear him say she was beautiful and he felt good telling her so. It wasn't just because he felt sorry for her, either. No, surprising himself, he found that he actually cared for this innocent young woman; he really wanted to help her overcome her low self-esteem—feelings as foreign to him as thinking himself a loser or lousy lover.

They talked some more, then made love again, finally drifting off to sleep, their bodies entwined. He awoke when he felt her stir, but fell back to sleep, thinking that it had been many nights since he had shared a bed with a woman. When he reached to touch her a while later, she was gone.

Awakening late the next morning, he looked down the hallway and saw that the door to Isabela and Teresa's room was standing wide open. He surmised they had checked out early to return to Cienfuegos. Only when he closed his door again did he see the folded note lying on the floor.

"Dear David," it said in neat handwriting. *"I didn't want to wake you, so this note will have to do. I want to thank you for listening to me, for restoring my faith in myself, and above all, for making me feel like a woman again. Isabela."*

***

After showering, he was about to go downstairs for a late breakfast when Philip Taylor called to invite him to dinner on Saturday night. They could watch Fidel's speech on television commemorating the founding of the Committees for the Defense of the Revolution, Philip told him, with just a barely detectable hint of sarcasm in his voice. He accepted the invitation with pleasure.

Later, at breakfast, as he glanced through *Granma*, the official newspaper of the Communist Party, he sensed someone's presence at his table. He looked up, but for a moment was unable to recognize the stranger silhouetted against the glare of the dining room windows. Then he made out the figure of Captain Joaquín Acosta in military attire.

"Well, David, I see you are feasting on one of our famous Cuban breakfasts," the MININT officer said, laughing, as he gestured toward David's cup of coffee, bowl of plain white yogurt, and a roll with some jam beside it. "May I join you?"

"By all means, Joaquín. Sit down. Actually, the coffee is pretty good, although they could do something with this yogurt. Some fresh fruit would also hit the spot. But they don't even have bananas this morning, much less mangoes or papayas—or what you call *fruta de bomba* here in Cuba."

"Ah, yes," Joaquín nodded in agreement. "We've been able to solve the problem of equitable redistribution, but not production. As a result, we have to ration many basic food items."

"You know, Joaquín, that's something I just don't understand. Here it is, fifteen years after the revolution came to power, and Cuba still has shortages and food rationing. And Cuba is not alone. Virtually all socialist revolutions have failed when it comes to raising agricultural production." He stopped short, waiting for the MININT Captain's reaction.

"Yes," Joaquín admitted. "I know what you're driving at. Agriculture has never been something that communist countries can boast about. But one of these days I'm sure our government will get it right and come up with incentives for farmers to produce more." He called to the waiter and ordered coffee.

"Well, enough about agriculture," David said. "What brings you here, if I may ask? I hope it's not me," he added, forcing a laugh.

"No, my American friend, don't worry. I am only here to check on the hotel accommodations for your fellow countrymen."

"My fellow countrymen? Who are they?"

"I guess the news hasn't been announced yet. My government has given permission for nearly thirty American reporters to come here to cover the visit tomorrow by two of your Senators. I expect that they will talk with Fidel tomorrow night after his speech."

"Really? That's very interesting. Who are the Senators?"

"They're from the Foreign Relations Committee. One is a Republican, Jacob Javits; the other a Democrat, Claiborne Pell. Am I right in characterizing them as representing the more progressive circles within their parties?"

"I'd say you're right."

"To us, they seem to be among the few sane voices in your Congress in calling for negotiations to improve relations."

"Yes, but I'll bet that Ford and Kissinger haven't given their blessings to the visit, at least not publicly. But tell me, since we're on the subject, do *you* think anything will come out of their talks with Fidel?"

Joaquín waited for the waiter to finish serving his coffee. David could feel the MININT Captain's dark eyes boring into him.

"I'm in no position to answer that question," Joaquín replied, once the waiter had departed. "But if your government were to abide by the conditions that Fidel has always insisted must be observed, then anything is possible."

"Perhaps, except those are difficult if not impossible terms for Washington to accept . . . "

"Those aren't the only conditions, my friend. Before negotiations can start, your government must first lift the criminal blockade against Cuba. But you and I know that's not going to happen," Joaquín added. "The powerful, reactionary forces in your country will see to that. They've already started, in fact. Senator Goldwater and other reactionaries are already on the warpath, attacking Javits and Pell for coming here."

"That's not surprising," David noted. "I've always maintained that right-wing circles in and out of the U.S. Government are too opposed to the Cuban revolution to permit normal relations with Havana. But how about your government? Does it really want better relations with the United States?"

"Why are you asking me?"

"Well, because earlier this week, when I was talking to some of your Foreign Ministry people, I couldn't tell whether they had any interest in normalization."

"And what precisely did you ask them?" Joaquín inquired, his eyes suddenly alive with interest.

"It wasn't so much a question," David said, noticing the MININT Captain's reaction. "I simply observed that I thought it could be in Cuba's interest to approach the United States, now that Nixon is gone and Ford and Kissinger might be more flexible."

"And how did they reply?" Joaquín asked.

"Like I said, they were either noncommittal or simply repeated what we've just said—that there were too many reactionary forces in the U.S. opposing normalization."

"I see," Joaquín replied, abruptly evincing disinterest. "I guess you'll just have to ask other government and Party officials if you want a more satisfactory answer. Ask your MINREX escort to line up more interviews for you."

"Well, it's no big deal," David replied. "I'm only curious because most Americans don't think Fidel is interested in normalizing relations with Washington because then he would be without the anti-American card that he's used so effectively. That's all."

"*Mira, chico,*" Joaquín said, somewhat impatiently. "Let me give you a short course on Fidel. First of all, as you well know, he is no fool. He's fully aware that normalization would remove the menace of North American imperialism. To my mind, the threat from the United States has served as the single-most-important unifying element for the revolution. It has enabled the Cuban people to define themselves."

"So, are you agreeing with those American observers?"

"Not at all! Washington's recognition of socialist Cuba would be an enormous victory for the revolution and for Fidel personally. But Fidel knows that 'ain't going to happen,' as they say in your country. As you yourself admitted, your government cannot accept his terms for a dialogue among equals. Therefore, the whole question of normalization is purely academic. Given that reality, the only thing left for Fidel to do is to exploit the issue to Cuba's advantage."

"What do you mean?"

"*Es muy sencillo, chico,*" Joaquín confided as he leaned forward. "Really, it's very simple. Fidel is absolutely certain that Washington will not normalize relations with Cuba. But by meeting with important Americans like the industrialist Cyrus Eaton earlier this year, and now two distinguished Senators, Javits and Pell, he shows his willingness to talk, to be reasonable. That way he demonstrates to the whole world that it's not Cuba but rather the U.S. Government that is the obstacle to normalization."

"That sounds awfully Machiavellian, Joaquín. It makes progressive people like myself appear like well-intentioned but naïve dupes in pressing for normalization."

The MININT Captain simply shrugged his shoulders as he gave David the same amused look as in their first encounter at the Italian Embassy.

"Believe me, David," Joaquín replied as he got up to leave. "I have the greatest respect for American progressives like you, especially since you're all trying to promote better relations between our two countries. It's also possible that I was wrong in portraying Fidel's *modus operandi* toward your country the way I did. So, with that in mind, I urge you to continue making your inquiries regarding our foreign policy. Now, if you'll excuse me, I must go."

***

Another surprise was waiting for David when he rendezvoused with Chucho, Tomás, and Roberto later that Friday night. This would be the last time all of them would be together. Roberto was scheduled to depart the next day for three months of specialized medical training in East Germany. He wouldn't be returning until long after David had left Cuba.

All four were sitting in the lobby of the Habana Libre. Chucho and Tomás were trying to decide where they should go for this special occasion, while Roberto appeared completely disinterested in their quandary. Deeply preoccupied, he sat in his chair, leaning forward, his elbows resting on his knees, both hands cupped under his chin, staring intently at David. At first, David simply thought that the young Cuban was upset over his impending departure. Then, as time passed, the thought crossed his mind that perhaps Roberto was an informer who had fingered them all. He grew apprehensive.

Finally, noticing Roberto's odd behavior, Chucho and Tomás asked him what was wrong. But Roberto only shook his head and muttered that nothing was bothering him.

"Hey, I know what's the matter," Tomás said, trying a more jovial approach. "You're upset because you're leaving Saturday morning and you'll miss Fidel's speech. *¿No es cierto?*"

Everyone laughed except Roberto. He kept his eyes fixed on David. An uneasy silence fell over the four of them. David was now all the more certain that his suspicion about Roberto had been right.

"I've been wondering whether David is a State Security agent," Roberto suddenly blurted out, looking David straight in the eye.

"Jesus, I've been wondering the exact same thing about you, Roberto!" David retorted.

Surprised, Roberto's eyes widened in disbelief, but a moment later he seemed relieved by David's remark. He became more animated and entered into the discussion of where they should go. Finally, the three *muchachos* agreed they should start by going to the famous *Coppelia* ice cream parlor. David was all for the idea. He loved the rich ice cream sold at the enormous parlor, but it usually required standing for an hour or two in a line that extended an entire block or more. However, now that the heavy downpour that had drenched the city had just ended, the queue would not be too bad.

As the four of them walked from the hotel, Roberto hung back and casually took David aside, out of earshot of his two friends.

"David," he said quietly. "I want to clear up something because I probably will never see you again. Do you remember our talk in the car the first time we four were together?"

"How could I forget? It was quite an interesting argument."

"Well, I want you to know that I think the same way as Chucho and Tomás. I, too, believe our problem lies with the system, not with individuals. But I couldn't say that in front of them," he said sheepishly, "in case they're ever arrested and questioned by State Security."

"I don't get it," David said, taken aback by Roberto's unexpected admission. "I don't get it," he repeated. "You're confiding in me but not in your closest friends—friends you've known since childhood?"

"Don't you see? I can't confide in them. They would be immediately compromised. For all I know, they might decide to report me to State Security in order to protect themselves."

"I still don't understand . . . " David said, now more puzzled than ever.

"*Mira, chico*, let me explain it this way. I know that they know that if I was ever arrested and I then revealed to State Security that I had expressed counterrevolutionary thoughts to them, they would be in serious trouble for not having reported the conversation to State Security." Roberto paused a second to see whether David was following his train of logic. "So," he went on quickly, "I have to assume that if they want to protect themselves they must immediately denounce me to State Security. That being the case, I can never be entirely open or honest with them."

"But then why me?"

"Look, it's simple. *Me puedo revelar*—I can reveal myself, as we say in Cuba, to you because you're not likely to be arrested. After all, you're an American professor who's been invited here by the government to carry out research. Therefore, you don't have to protect yourself by informing on me."

Dumbfounded, David recalled Joaquín's metaphor of someone peeling an onion. Hard as it was for him to admit what had happened, he had been completely fooled by Roberto's behavior three weeks earlier.

"Please try to understand my position," his companion continued in a hushed, pleading tone. "I grew up in a poor, humble family, but the revolution has enabled me to go to medical school. I have a professional career ahead of me and I'm grateful for that opportunity. Therefore, I will not jeopardize my future even if it means that I must wear *mi cara doble*, my mask, in front of my closest friends."

"But they spoke frankly in front of you," David protested, still unable to comprehend fully all the ramifications of what Roberto had been telling him.

"Yes, that's true, though I don't know why," Roberto replied after a moment's hesitation. "Perhaps they are braver than I am. Or, though I hope this isn't true, maybe one or both of them are informers for State Security and that's why they said what they said—to trap me into saying something that is *contrarevolucionario*. I just don't know, David."

"That's awful, Roberto, not to have trust in your friends."

"*Es cierto*—I know that. But what else can I do except hide behind my *cara doble*? We're all victims of *desconfianza*—mutual suspicion. Like Chucho said that night, it's an insidious fear that prevents most of us from talking frankly to our friends, even to our family members."

***

Later that night, David recalled Professor Peter Vargas at Berkeley relating a similar incident during one of his trips to Cuba. Vargas had been traveling for weeks, sometimes alone, with a MINREX chauffeur he was certain was fully "integrated" into the revolution. Then, at the very end of his visit, he began asking the chauffeur how he really felt about what was happening in Cuba. At first, the chauffeur tried not to answer, but Vargas persisted with assurances that he could talk freely. Finally overcoming his *miedo*, his fear, the man had unburdened himself with a torrent of vehement anti-government sentiment to an astonished Vargas.

David had been openly skeptical of Vargas's story at the time. He went so far as to imply that Vargas had fabricated it since he, David, had never experienced anything like that during his recent trips to Cuba. "*If that was the case, Mr. Diamond*," Vargas had responded scathingly, "*then you were like so many other revolutionary tourists I've met: You were on a head trip to Cuba.*"

David now had to admit that Roberto's confession not only gave credence to Vargas's story, but also supported the latter's assertion about David being on a "head trip" on his previous visits. Looking back on those trips, he would never have made friends with a Chucho,

Tomás, or Roberto—and if he had, they most certainly would never have opened up to him. But this time he was far more open to the people and reality around him, and that change in him was causing him to reconsider many of his assumptions about the revolution. Now he had to wonder whether Isabela had been entirely truthful with him. Had she, like Roberto, been wearing her *cara doble* to mask opinions she had to conceal from her sister as well as from him? He had no way of knowing. Perhaps even she didn't really know.

***

10

The Debate

Dinner at Philip Taylor's home was arranged for eight o'clock. Located in one of the older, once fashionable neighborhoods of the Vedado section of Havana, Philip's house was below Línea, off of Avenida de los Presidentes, not far from the Foreign Ministry. David arrived there by cab, just after eight o'clock.

Surrounded by a large yard and a massive concrete wall, the old two-story home was much grander than David had expected. Set farther back than the neighboring houses, it was a solid-looking structure with weathered concrete walls and a dark tile roof. Even with the shadows of night falling, he could see that the otherwise imposing home had seen better days. With its peeling paint, the house looked run down, neglected. The yard was equally unkempt; trees and shrubs were overgrown; weeds were everywhere.

At first he wondered whether he had the wrong address until he spotted Philip's battered Ford parked in the driveway inside the yard. He opened the gate, climbed the steps to the large, partially enclosed patio at the front of the house, and swung the wrought-iron knocker against the ornately carved wooden door.

***

"By golly, David, you're punctual," Philip announced, smiling as he swung open the heavy door. "You're one of the few here in Cuba who's on *hora inglesa*—English time—as they call it here," he half-laughed, half-snorted. "Come on in."

"Christ, Philip, for a second I thought I was in the wrong place. You've got a mansion here."

"Well, it's not *quite* a mansion," Philip replied defensively as he ushered his guest into the vestibule. "Besides, we share the house with a Chilean couple who have their own separate quarters and a kitchenette. We have the larger half because we have two kids. But I have to admit it's a pretty big house alright. It was originally owned by a relative of President Machado, who was able to hold on to it after the 1930 Revolution."

"Gives you an idea of how well the upper class had it before 1959," David remarked, as they entered the spacious but sparsely furnished living room. It contained a television set and an odd assortment of furniture—an old leather couch, a stuffed chair, a cheap mahogany coffee table, a rather sad-looking floor lamp, and three spindly cane chairs. He surmised that the original furniture, which surely had been far more elegant, had been removed when revolutionary authorities seized the house.

"This actually is one of the more modest homes in the neighborhood," Philip explained. "You should see some of the houses that were constructed immediately before and after the war. Just a few blocks away is a genuine mansion that was owned by José Martí's daughter. But enough about real estate. Come and meet Elena. She's in the kitchen preparing a special treat for us."

Philip's wife was not at all what David had imagined. She was of slight figure, with dark curly hair cut short, an olive complexion, and a pretty enough face. She was older than he had expected, and looked tired and worn down.

Elena greeted him with a forced, almost glum smile, and a limp handshake. He wondered whether his coming to dinner was an unwelcome intrusion. Moments later, Philip introduced him to their two sons. With his dark complexion and hair, the older of the two looked like his mother; David guessed he was fifteen or sixteen years old. The younger boy was ten at most. Because of his fair skin and sandy hair, he bore a striking resemblance to his father.

Philip took David to his spacious, but cluttered study, where he fussed with the ice and poured them each a large glass of scotch. David in the meantime scanned the book titles on the crude, makeshift bookshelves. He was surprised to see that many of the volumes were on politics and political philosophy instead of engineering. There were even three books on contemporary Cuba, two by Theodore Draper, the other by K. S. Karol.

"You have quite a decent political library here, Philip. Several are major classics, including three forbidden books on Cuba."

"Yep. You see, after awhile I decided to get a different perspective from the one I was reading in the official press, especially with respect to the early years of the revolution."

"And you have some classics on political theory, as well."

"That's because I didn't want to remain a narrowly focused engineer all my life. So, I've exposed myself to some of the great thinkers, starting with Machiavelli, Locke, Mills, and, of course, Marx. Just don't quiz me on them, Professor Diamond."

"No need to fear me doing that," David laughed. "I'd first have to bone up on some of their writings myself. By the way, not to change the subject, but have you heard that Senators Javits and Pell are in town? They're supposed to be meeting Fidel sometime tonight."

"Yes, I heard it over *Radio Rebelde* this morning. However, they've picked a bad time to come."

"You really think so?"

"You betcha. Fidel's speeches commemorating the founding of the CDRs are always more militant and anti-American than usual. I hardly think he'll tone it down tonight just for the sake of two American senators. If anything, he'll weigh in even more precisely because they're here."

"You're probably right, in which case Javits and Pell will have to disassociate themselves publicly from whatever Fidel says. I've heard that they're already coming under attack back in the States just for being here," David observed.

They conversed for several minutes more before Elena poked her head into the study to announce that dinner was ready. Philip took David to the small breakfast room adjacent to the kitchen, where Elena had set an assortment of plates, glasses, and cheap cutlery, along with several bottles of beer, on a well-worn dinette. It was then that he realized that Philip had appropriated the original dining room as his study. The dinner Elena served more than made up for their spartan surroundings. It was a classic Cuban meal, one that was commonplace in Miami, but not in Havana because of food rationing. On the table was a *lechón*, a suckling pig, with fried plantains, and lots of black beans and rice—what Cubans traditionally refer to as *Moros y Cristianos*.

"Wow! What a feast," David declared as he eyed the enormous platters on the table. "I haven't seen food like this since I arrived." "Don't tell me you boys eat like this every week," he said in Spanish, turning to the sons who were waiting impatiently for Philip to serve them some slices of *lechón*.

"One of the perks of being a foreign engineer is that I'm in the countryside at least once a week," Philip answered in English, as he cut off a succulent, steaming slab of pork to put on his older son's plate. "So when I'm there," he added with a sly look. "I usually can persuade some farmer to sell me a *lechoncito* under the table, if you know what I mean."

"I get your drift," David replied with a knowing nod.

"And what I can't get," Philip continued in English, "Elena can usually find at the *diplotienda*. That's where embassy types and other foreigners like me can use dollars or some other hard currency to buy what's not available to most Cubans. So for us, at least, life here can be fairly comfortable as it is for the *nomenklatura*."

David found Philip's candor surprising. Then he realized that neither Elena nor the boys spoke or understood much English. In fact, he noticed that most of the dinner conversation was conducted in Spanish except when a political topic came up, at which time Philip would switch into English. He surmised that Philip was deliberately cutting the rest of his family out in order to be more candid with him—and to shield them in the process. Since they were more interested in food than politics, neither the boys nor Elena seemed to mind.

***

Returning to the study after dinner, Philip did as he had promised—he broke out the bottle of *Añejo*, poured both of them large snifters of the aged, dark amber-colored rum, and presented David with a magnificent Cohiba.

"Can you appreciate what you've got there?" Philip asked.

"What do you mean? Of course, it's a Cuban cigar. I can tell by the aroma."

"Yes, but it's not just *any* cigar, my fine friend. It's a Cohiba! Cohibas have only been made here for the past ten years or so. To my mind, they're the best thing the revolution has produced."

"You know, it's funny but until now I've never heard of Cohibas."

"That's because they initially were produced in small quantities. Then, when Fidel discovered them, he limited their distribution to himself and his most favored associates. After production increased, he began handing out Cohibas to visiting foreign dignitaries. Now they're being sold on Cubana de Aviación's international flights and in hard currency shops for foreigners. That's how I get them. I expect someday the government will start marketing them in Europe and Canada."

"So this is Fidel's private label," David said as he put the Cohiba to his nose.

"Yep. Now, before we light up, let me give you a few pointers on how you can tell if you have a fine cigar. As you just pointed out, the aroma is one telltale sign, so is the sound of the cigar."

"The sound?"

"I kid you not. But first, run the Cohiba under your nose and smell it carefully. Notice how it has a fresh, clean smell, but with a cured, faintly sweet aroma to it. Now put it to your ear like this. Then roll it between your fingertips. Do you hear the little crinkly sound that the cigar makes as it turns? Good! That's another sure sign that you've got a fine, well-cured cigar. Now take my little gadget here and slice off a tiny bit of the tip and you're all set. Good. Here are some matches. Light up."

* * *

Slowly, blowing blue smoke between his pursed lips, David savored the Cohiba's aroma and taste. "Whew! You're right—this is some cigar. It's so smooth and rich." He took another long, satisfying draw on the Cohiba and gave Philip an appreciative nod.

"You know," David remarked after a moment of silence, "I was curious about your remark at dinner concerning the *nomenklatura*."

"What about it?"

"Well, you seemed to imply that Cuban political leaders enjoy perks that are not available to ordinary Cubans."

"Of course," Philip responded. "But don't quote me. O.K?" He paused as he took another draw on his Cohiba while David nodded his ascent. "Listen," he continued. "The only leader who insisted that he and his family have the same rations as everyone else was Che Guevara before he left for the Congo and Bolivia. But that was years ago."

"All right. But if that's the case, then the question becomes whether the Cuban leadership today is anywhere near as corrupt and materialistic as during Batista's time or elsewhere in Latin America."

Taking a sip of *Añejo*, Philip took his time before answering. David had the feeling he was trying to decide how candid he could be.

"I would say Cuba's *nomenklatura*—that is, the ranking members of the Party and government—is not venal," Philip said finally, sounding uncharacteristically cautious. "For instance, it certainly hasn't stashed away millions of dollars in foreign bank accounts for purposes of personal enrichment as occurred under the *Auténtico* and Batista governments."

"That's what I've always thought, too."

"On the other hand, that kind of comparison is somewhat misleading."

"How so?"

"Look, it's political power, not wealth that counts in Cuba today. And as you know, that power is monopolized by Fidel, his closest associates, and, of course, the Party—in other words by the new revolutionary elite."

"So, what you're saying is that not all Cubans are equal. It's more like Orwell's *Animal Farm* where some are more equal than others. Right?"

"Of course. The upper ranks of the *nomenklatura*, for example, live in the best housing and drive late-model automobiles from the Soviet bloc. They can shop in special stores. They can go to hotels, resorts, and restaurants that are reserved for diplomats and foreigners. They can also travel abroad. If nothing else, they don't have to queue up for hours in front of a store to get some rationed item as do ordinary Cubans."

Philip looked intently at David as if to fathom his reaction. He took a long draw on his Cohiba, exhaled, and then continued. "Of course, many of the leaders live rather modestly, even austerely. Like Raúl and Vilma, neither of whom is materialistic. Even so, they enjoy a standard of living most Cubans would die for."

David nodded in agreement. "I'm afraid that what Milovan Djilas called a 'new class' in communist Yugoslavia also applies to Cuba."

"Fidel is a perfect example of what I was saying," Philip resumed, evidently reassured by David's observation. "There's no need for him to pocket millions of dollars because Cuba is his for the asking. He has at least one house in every province and a fleet of cars at his disposal. He can eat or get anything he wants, whether it's homegrown or imported. And to top it all off, he has his own personal slush fund . . . "

"Hold on!" David exclaimed, leaning forward in his chair. "That's the first I've ever heard of anything like that! Are you sure?"

"Absolutely. My source is unimpeachable. He says the government provides Fidel with a private account. He uses it to finance his pet projects or to buy something a poor village needs. Or he'll bankroll some guerrilla group in Latin America, or buy Rolexes for his foreign guests and favorite officials, and so forth. It's his to dispense as he sees fit."

Philip paused to take note of the effect of his remarks on his guest. "We're not talking small potatoes, either," he continued in a more confidential tone. "No, the '*Comandante's* reserves,' as they're called, probably amount to several million dollars, but nobody really knows. The funds are totally unaccounted for."

David savored his *Añejo* for a moment. "Christ, that's not good," he observed, shaking his head in disapproval. "It sounds like Fidel has an open-ended account. On the other hand, you could say that at least he's financing some good causes."

"Even if he does, he's acting like the lord of the manor dispensing largesse to his vassals," Philip quickly rejoined. "As far as I'm concerned, it would be a hell of a lot better if he ordered the government to spend the money on projects that really improve people's lives, instead of on things that advance his political agenda."

"What do you mean by that?"

"Just look at how much money is constantly being spent on Third World solidarity meetings, youth conventions, and countless foreign delegations, and the like. These all consume millions of dollars for causes that are purely political, that only satisfy Fidel's craving to occupy center stage."

"O.K., so his ego is wrapped up in it," David replied. "But so what? I give him a lot of credit for championing the Third World's cause. And you know what? I can't think of anyone who has greater moral authority than Fidel in demanding justice and equity for the have-nots of this world. On this issue at least, you've got to admit that he occupies the high moral ground."

"Oh, it's easy for Fidel to take the so-called 'high moral ground' as you call it. But let me tell you from experience that it's a hell of a lot harder to propose practical, real-world solutions for the problems of poverty and underdevelopment. Just look how he's screwed up Cuba's economy."

David didn't answer for a moment. He was surprised by his host's relentless criticism of the Cuban leader. And he was disturbed, too, because he hadn't expected to hear it from an avowed socialist.

"I respect your views, Philip, especially since you've lived here and witnessed things from the ground up. But I think you're forgetting one thing: Many of the policies you consider wasteful or misguided are nevertheless necessary if Cuba is to overcome U.S. efforts to isolate it in the world. I'm sure the government would be investing in more productive activities if it didn't feel so threatened."

"I doubt it," Philip replied, taking a sip of his *Añejo*. For a moment he hesitated, apparently unsure how candid he could be with his guest concerning the politically sensitive topic they were discussing. "Look," he finally added. "Fidel is really not all that concerned with the economic well-being of his people. Believe me, his primary interest is and has always been political power—complete, total, unbridled power for himself—along with his role in history as the world's number one anti-imperialist."

Seeing David shake his head in silent disagreement, Philip became perturbed. "You don't believe me?" he asked, with an inquiring look as he deftly tapped the inch-long white ash on his Cohiba into the ashtray in front of him.

"Oh, I believe you up to a point," David replied, pausing for another sip of *Añejo*. "It's just that, despite all his flaws, I still consider Fidel to be the greatest leader Latin America has produced since Simón Bolívar and José Martí."

Philip drew lazily on his cigar, his gaze following the blue circles of smoke that drifted toward the ceiling. Then fixing David with a steady look, he said, "My friend, don't make the mistake of turning Fidel into someone of mythic proportions. Beneath all that charm you witnessed at the Italian Embassy, and underneath all the high principles he claims to espouse, lies a cunning, ruthless man, and a great dissembler as well. If it were otherwise, he wouldn't be in power today. In fact, I'll wager he'll be around for another twenty-five years, still defiant, still a thorn in the side of your government because he thrives on confrontation with imperialism."

"Perhaps. In any case he'll still be around precisely because he's a great leader."

"What you're forgetting, David, is that charismatic, messianic leaders like Fidel Castro can mesmerize a whole nation and lead it to disaster. Look at the German people's long-running love affair with Hitler."

"Surely you're not comparing Fidel to Hitler?"

"Of course not. My point is simply that leaders like a Fidel or a Hitler have the capacity to move millions of followers even when they're pursuing the wrong path and destroying their country in the process. But let's forget Hitler. I think Fidel and Napoleon Bonaparte are a much better fit except that Fidel is nowhere near being the extraordinary military and political genius that Napoleon was."

"That's an interesting comparison," David conceded. "One that I've never thought of."

"I'm surprised because one only has to look at the similarities between the two. Of course, both were young when they took power and both were idolized by the majority of their countrymen. Also, Fidel is imbued with a sense of destiny, just like Napoleon was, and wields absolute power and micromanages everything as Napoleon did. But perhaps the most important similarity is that Fidel, like Napoleon in his time, preaches equality and fraternity for the popular masses. Yet, like Napoleon, Fidel doesn't believe in liberty."

***

A long respite from conversation settled between them as if by mutual consent they had called for a time-out. Each used the opportunity to take the measure of the other, sip his *Añejo,* and puff on his Cohiba. Philip, for his part, waited expectantly, ready for David to ask him the question. He had gone over it countless times, but not until now had he dared speak his mind.

Finally, David broke the silence. "So I gather you don't think history will absolve Fidel as he claimed it would back in 1953?"

"Depends who writes the history," Philip answered with a laugh.

"I know that, but I'm interested in your own appraisal since you've been living here for thirteen years."

"I'll be candid with you," Philip said, leaning forward to give David a searching look. "That is, provided what I say doesn't get outside this room. Is that understood?"

"Of course. I wasn't born yesterday, Philip."

"Good, because I have a lot to say on the subject." He settled himself comfortably in the upholstered chair. "Look, there's no doubt in my mind that Fidel's greatest accomplishment lies not only in having defied the most powerful nation on earth, but also in having gotten away with it. And on top of that, he's made you Yanks look foolish most of the time. So I expect that historians will undoubtedly say he was brilliant in outmaneuvering your country. And I would agree with them."

Philip stopped to take another sip of *Añejo*, looked steadily at David for a moment, and then continued. "However, the Cuban people have had to pay a heavy price for Fidel's rule—and I'm not just talking about his role in the missile crisis, when Cuba and the world came close to being blown up. I'm not even referring to his economic blunders, either." Again, he paused for dramatic effect. "No," he growled, "What's even more reprehensible is that early on he had the historic opportunity to launch Cuba on the path of democratic socialism, but he didn't even try. Instead, he botched his historic moment—he imposed a totalitarian communist system on Cuba. And history will never absolve him for that terrible, that costly, mistake."

"Except that I think the U.S. had something to do with his turn toward communism."

"Don't interrupt me, David. Remember? You gave me the floor."

"O.K. Go on."

"All right. Another thing that history should judge Fidel harshly on, but probably won't, is that he obliged hundreds of thousands of decent Cubans to flee their country . . . "

"Excuse me for interrupting again, but some were *Batistianos*," David protested. "At least in the beginning. Besides, you know you can't make a social revolution and still retain the support of the bourgeoisie."

"I'm not so sure about either of your two premises," Philip responded as he leaned forward in his chair. "In any case, Fidel made no effort to reassure Cuba's middle class. On the contrary, he incited hate toward those who were labeled 'counterrevolutionaries.' They became *gusanos* and as such they ceased to be human beings. And by sowing mistrust and fear, he's turned Cuban against Cuban to the point of even dividing families. So, Fidel will leave a divisive, totalitarian legacy."

"Anything else on your tally sheet?"

"Yes. He'll obviously leave an enormous void once he's gone. He not only rules like a *caudillo*, but he also micromanages just about everything. That, along with his and the Party's dictatorship, leaves Cubans ill-prepared to govern themselves." Philip sighed as he settled back in his chair. With a twinkle in his eye, he added,

"That about sums up my view—at least for now."

"Whew!" David exclaimed with a shake of his head. "That's a pretty strong indictment."

"That goes without saying. But do *you* agree with it?"

"On some things, yes. But my main complaint with it is that it's too one-sided. You've not taken into account any of Fidel's more positive, lasting accomplishments."

"Give me a for instance?" Philip quipped.

"Well, for one thing, he's instilled national pride and identity where there wasn't any before. He's also made great strides toward creating a more egalitarian society and eliminating racial discrimination. I'm sure you'll agree that those gains help explain why the Cuban government can mobilize the populace behind it to an extent unseen elsewhere in Latin America."

"Except that, based on my own observations over the years, the popular mobilizations you refer to stopped being voluntary a long time ago."

"Are you saying the government coerces people to turn out?" David questioned.

"To a large degree, yes, although it's disguised. You see, the *Comités de Defensa* make certain that everyone in their neighborhoods turn out for Fidel's speech, or for *trabajo voluntario*, or for whatever else the government wants them for. If they don't, and they don't have a valid excuse, then they're in trouble with their *Comités*, who can make life miserable for them, including at their workplace. Their union representatives as well as Party cadres also pressure them to turn out. In any case, one way or the other, there's always some form of coercion going on here."

"I'm sure that's the case," David conceded. "But even so, don't you think the majority of the population supports Fidel?"

Philip pondered the question before answering. "You know, I've asked myself that question a thousand times. But in the absence of free elections, nobody knows. Support could run 60 percent or more, or 30 percent or less. However, there's no way of knowing really because sometimes what appears like solidarity with the government is feigned."

"I've already experienced the phenomena of the *cara doble*," David added somberly. "So you don't have to lecture me on the need for free, competitive elections."

"Good, at least we're in agreement on something," Philip laughed and looked at his watch. "Hey, by golly, we'd better get cracking! We're going to miss hearing what our great leader has to say tonight. Come on, let's go into the living room. Bring your glass and the ashtray."

***

By the time Philip turned on the Russian-made television set in the living room, Fidel was well into his speech. It appeared that hundreds of thousands of CDR militants and other citizens had filled the *Plaza de la Revolución* to listen to their leader. Finished with washing the dishes, Elena came in and sat down to watch the spectacle. But as time passed and the bearded Cuban leader thundered on, she yawned and eventually excused herself. Philip didn't mind. His wife's absence would enable him to talk freely in English, while they finished off the *Añejo* and what was left of their Cohibas.

He was enjoying his repartee with David. He never engaged his Cuban friends in deep political discussions; they either avoided talking about politics or parroted the party line. David was neither inhibited nor dogmatic. Despite his obvious admiration for Fidel and the revolution, the American was more open-minded than most of the foreign visitors Philip had encountered over the years. He waited for the right moment to interrupt Fidel's long-winded speech so as to resume their discussion.

"Well, what did I tell you?" Philip exclaimed a short while later as the crowd's prolonged applause and cries of "*¡Dale duro, Fidel!*"—"Hit them hard, Fidel!"—caused the *líder máximo* to pause during his marathon address. "I told you he would make a tough sounding speech tonight against you Yankees. Hell, he doesn't care if he embarrasses your two Senators and forces them to do some fancy footwork with the press tomorrow."

"You're right about that," David agreed. "But then again Fidel also knows that Javits and Pell aren't in charge of U.S. policy toward Cuba. So it doesn't get him anywhere to butter them up."

"Are you implying that, despite all we've heard tonight and at the Italian Embassy three weeks ago, Fidel is really interested in an accommodation with Washington?"

"I don't know," David said as downed the last of his *Añejo*. "All I can tell you is that when I was in Washington I heard that Havana had sent out feelers about trying to normalize relations."

"Really?" Philip asked, genuinely surprised. "I find that hard to believe."

"Not even if an accommodation would enable Fidel to checkmate the Soviets?"

"Nope. I just don't think Fidel has any interest at all in normalizing relations with your country."

"Well, that's not surprising after the way we've treated him," David replied after a moment's reflection. "First we pushed him into the hands of the Soviet Union, then tried to overthrow him by means of the Bay of Pigs, the embargo, the assassination plots, and so forth."

As a thunderous applause rolled in at the end of another of Fidel's rhetorical flourishes, Philip rose from his chair. "I think we've heard enough," he announced and turned off the TV set. Just as the Maximum Leader was raising his index finger high in the air for dramatic emphasis, his fiery image flickered momentarily before the screen went blank.

***

They had returned to Philip's study. Somewhere in the house Elena's voice could be heard as she shooed the boys to their bedrooms. Two cats hissed and screeched at each other outside the window.

"Do you want some more *Añejo?*" Philip asked as he poured himself more rum. David extended his glass for a refill.

"You know, I don't agree with what you just said about your country pushing Fidel into the hands of the Soviets," Philip said.

"Don't tell me you believe he was a communist all along."

"Not at all. No, what I'm saying is that it was Fidel himself who decided early on to turn to Moscow in order to consolidate his power and assure the survival of his revolution." He paused to sip the rum. "Just as important, Fidel wanted Soviet support so he could become the liberator of Latin America and carry out his anti-imperialist struggle. But here comes the tricky part: To ensure that Moscow wouldn't abandon his new government he had to transform his revolution into a 'socialist' one and become a bona fide Marxist-Leninist."

"You're forgetting one thing, Philip. We gave him no choice once Eisenhower gave the go-ahead to start preparations for the Bay of Pigs operation in March 1960, after which we began cutting Cuba's sugar quota. He had to turn to the Soviets."

"No, no, David. What you don't know is that the clock started running a lot earlier."

"How so?"

Philip took a long draw on his Cohiba before answering. He was savoring his anticipated moment of triumph.

"Two years ago, I learned about some revelations by Aleksandr Alekseev . . . "

"You're referring to the former Soviet Ambassador to Cuba back in the 1960s?"

"Right, except that Alekseev was the KGB's principal Latin American agent when he first arrived in Cuba in the summer of 1959. He came as a Tass correspondent for the purpose of assessing whether the new revolutionary government could survive and become even more anti-imperialist. Anyway, at a gathering at the Soviet Embassy before he returned to Moscow in 1968, Alekseev described his first meeting with Fidel. That meeting was in *October of 1959*, mind you, which was why he was astounded when Fidel began speaking to him in Marxist-Leninist lingo."*

"Wait a minute. Are you now implying that Fidel was a communist after all?"

"Not at all. I'm saying that Fidel was a consummate opportunist intent upon ensuring his power and grand ambitions. So, to win Moscow's backing, he seized on his initial and later meetings with Alekseev to impress upon him that he was genuinely committed to Marxism-Leninism."

"Fidel may simply have been trying to keep all his options open," David countered.

"You're being much too charitable," Philip replied impatiently. "Don't you see? He was already positioning himself with the Soviets. He was already moving toward a socialist revolution, well before relations with the U.S. really took their turn for the worse. Then, starting in the fall of 1959, he deliberately set that deterioration in motion by sharply attacking the United States, while simultaneously moving against the anti-communists in his own July 26 Movement.

---

* Note to reader: Aleksandr Alekseev later recounted his first meeting with Fidel Castro in October 1959 in his article, "Cuba después del triunfo de la revolución," *America Latina* (Moscow), October 1984. A more detailed account of this and subsequent meetings between Alekseev and the Castro leadership can be found in Aleksandr Fursenko and Timothy Naftali, *"One Hell of a Gamble": Khrushchev, Castro, and Kennedy, 1958–1964*, New York, W.W. Norton & Company, 1997.

After that, he used the threat from 'imperialism' to justify his turn to Moscow."

David was silent for a moment, pondering Philip's words.

"I'll admit your theory helps explain why the revolution suddenly took its more radical course," he finally said. "But I still say that Washington was to blame in the end for leaving Cuba with no alternative but to join the Soviet camp."

"David, don't make the same mistake as Castro apologists do. Don't hold the United States responsible for everything that went wrong with the Cuban revolution after 1959."

"Hey, please don't put me in the apologists camp!" David cried out indignantly. "I've criticized the Cuban government many a time both in public as well as in private."

"Good. I'm glad to hear that," Philip replied quietly. "Because most leftists haven't condemned the Castro regime for having become totalitarian even though they attacked Batista's authoritarian regime. And believe me, there's a significant difference between the two."

"As a political scientist I think I know that totalitarian states are a lot more controlling . . . "

"I'm sure you do, but I've lived here and I've experienced the difference," Philip broke in. "I've seen the way the state tries to control most everything, the way Fidel insists on unanimity, the way he tries to remold the Cuban people into something they're not. That's something run-of-the-mill dictators like Batista don't try to do."

"All of which, of course, constitute some of the classic hallmarks of a totalitarian state, whether communist or fascist. So I agree that totalitarianism stifles freedom and crushes the human spirit."

"Exactly," Philip broke in eagerly. "That's why the Left must not be blinded by the conceit of idealism and allow itself to become the accomplice of totalitarianism in Cuba. No, the democratic-Left in the U.S., Canada, and Western Europe must serve as the revolution's conscience if it is to fulfill its moral imperative. The Right can't assume that role. It must come from the Left."

Philip waited for David's response. But David remained silent for several moments, deep in his own thoughts.

"I think that some of us who once made up the New Left have begun to assume a more critical stance toward Cuba," David finally observed.

"Then you must raise your voices more loudly—and less am-biguously—in condemning what's gone wrong with the revolution. Otherwise, the situation here will only get worse in the years ahead if only because there are no internal forces left to constrain Fidel, Raúl, and the Communist Party."

***

They remained silent for a while like two exhausted heavyweight fighters near the end of a bruising boxing match. Seeing that David had finished off what remained of his *Añejo*, Philip moved to pour him some more but was waved away. David wanted to go one more round. He knew he had been losing the debate to Philip—and, along with it, all the assumptions and beliefs that had made him feel so passionately about Cuba, the revolution, and Fidel. He had to fight back.

"Look, I agree in principle with many of your philosophical points. But having said that, I also think the issue is a hell of a lot more complicated than the black-and-white picture you've just drawn. I mean, you've got to put Cuba in historical perspective."

"I know what you are going to say."

"Please, hear me out for a moment," David insisted. "You just can't condemn the Cuban government without taking into account the historical role of U.S. imperialism. You can't ignore how the Cold War mentality of every Republican and Democratic adminis-tration never gave leftist governments a chance in Latin America. Corporate America, and its allies in the Pentagon and CIA, wouldn't allow Washington to do otherwise."

"I think you're the one who is simplifying things when you start to reduce everything to American economic interests."

"Oh, really?" David shot back. "Have you forgotten how the CIA overthrew the Arbenz government in Guatemala in 1954 after United Fruit had some of its properties confiscated? Or how the CIA tried unsuccessfully to do the same to Fidel seven years later after he nationalized a billion dollars in U.S. businesses and properties? And don't you recall," David asked again, this time more pointedly, "that just a little over a year ago, the CIA helped the military overthrow Chile's elected government and murder its president, Salvador Allende, after American copper companies were taken over?"

"David, I am the first to condemn your country for its arrogance, for being the bully on the block. But you're forgetting that once Arbenz, Fidel, and Allende aligned themselves with the communists internally and with the Soviet Union externally, they endangered U.S. strategic interests and left Washington with little alternative but to oppose their governments."

"But that's my point," David insisted. "There *was* an alternative. We could have tried to deal with them and moderate their policies so as to lessen the threat to our so-called 'strategic interests.' But we couldn't because of the multinationals and the Cold War hysteria in the U.S."

"Well, I do agree with you on a couple of points," Philip conceded. "The U.S. was too imperialistic, which is why it didn't try very hard to come to terms with leftist governments."

"Well, at least we agree on some things," David interjected.

"Yes, but I also believe that it wouldn't have made much difference had you moderated your policy, at least not in Fidel's case. He's the kind of leader who thrives on confrontation and conflict; and, if they don't exist, he creates them to advance his interests." Philip paused for a moment as a sly grin came over his face. "By the way," he continued, "perhaps you aren't aware of it, but that pattern of behavior goes all the way back to his childhood."

"Oh, come on, Philip. Surely you're not going to resort to pop psychology."

"Hey, don't pooh-pooh it, my learned friend. Even by his own account, Fidel was very much *el niño malcriado*. He was the misbehaving child who threatened to burn down the family home, threw tantrums, beat up classmates, or used other forms of extortion to get his way. And he's continued pretty much in the same mold as an adult."

"Maybe so," David replied. "But at least he's speaking out against all the injustices committed against Cuba and the Third World."

"Except that his ranting and ravings strike me as an exercise in pure narcissism. I mean, what other leader keeps his countrymen waiting until ten or eleven o'clock at night and then subjects them to a five- or six-hour diatribe? It's pure self-indulgence as well as demagoguery, I'd say."

"Maybe so, but let me return to what I was saying. Whether or not Fidel turned first to the Soviets or was pushed by us into their arms is immaterial. The reason is that sooner or later the ruling circles in the

United States needed to crush the Cuban revolution. Why? Because they feared that, were it to succeed, Cuba would become a beacon for the rest of Latin America. And that's the principal reason why Cuba became a totalitarian state—it had to defend itself."

Philip was silent for a moment. He looked away from David as if to collect his thoughts. Sighing, he turned to his guest.

"David, I'm going to confess something to you," he said, his voice now low and husky. "I once thought like you. But after living here all these years, I've come to the painful conclusion that I was mistaken. The principal reason for Cuba taking the totalitarian path had less to do with U.S. policy than with the fact that radical socialist revolutions invariably carry within them the seeds of an oppressive system."

"And why is that?" David asked, his interest piqued anew. "I really want to know because your point is directly relevant to my book."

"Look, I'm no political theorist, but I believe that to bring about the kind of radical social changes that we progressives favor, a revolutionary government must first accumulate enormous political power as occurred here in Cuba after 1959. Therein lies a paradox, however, because unrestrained power in the hands of the state soon renders society virtually helpless before it." Philip paused and looked away for a moment. "I'm afraid," he concluded, "that this is the inevitable consequence of all socialist revolutions, whether in Cuba, the Soviet Union, or China."

David watched as his host slumped back in his chair as if relieved of some burden. Stroking his bearded chin several times, he became pensive as he went over Philip's theoretical point. Suddenly, he felt weary, disheartened—and it wasn't simply from all the alcohol he had consumed.

"You could be right," David replied at last in a thoughtful tone of voice. "I've sometimes thought about the paradox you've just described. As of yet, I don't have an answer. Perhaps overwhelming, concentrated power in the hands of the state is the price that must be paid for achieving social justice here and in other underdeveloped countries. That's my intellect talking. But in my heart I still hope that socialism can be combined with real political democracy." Expelling a long sigh, he rose from his chair. "This has been a really stimulating discussion and I'm sure we could go on for the rest of the night. But I'm beat. It's getting late. So, let's see if we can find a taxi to take me back to the hotel."

Philip looked up uncomprehendingly before realizing that his guest had ended their debate. "Hell," he said. "You'll have a devil of a time scrounging up a cab at this hour of the night. I'll take you back myself. By golly, I'm not so drunk that I can't drive!"

***

"I don't exactly know how to ask this," David said on their way back to the Habana Libre. "But why do you remain in Cuba if you're so down on the revolution?" Even in the darkness of the car, he could see Philip stiffen and his hands tighten on the steering wheel.

"At first," Philip replied after several moments, "I was still very idealistic just like you. So I was able to justify the tightening up that started in the mid-1960s. Later, when I finally saw what was happening, I hoped that the revolution and Fidel would sooner or later reject the totalitarian path. Then, after realizing that I was being foolish to think that things might change for the better, I had to remain here for family reasons."

Not wanting to pry, David was prepared to drop the matter.

"You probably noticed that Elián, my oldest son, doesn't look like me at all," Philip suddenly volunteered. "He's from Elena's previous marriage. I want to adopt him, but her former husband refuses to give his consent even though he hardly ever sees the boy." Philip stopped momentarily to clear his throat. When he next spoke, his voice was thick. "The problem is that, without my adopting him, Elián can't accompany us if we decide to go to Canada, and it's completely out of the question for us to leave him behind. So we're stuck here."

"The Canadian Embassy can't help you?"

"Hardly. I get the feeling that embassy officials don't view expatriates like me with much sympathy. In any case, I doubt they could be of much help because Elena's former husband has political clout— he's an alternate member of the Central Committee."

Philip stopped talking for a moment as he waited for the car in front of them to make a left turn. "In the meantime," he resumed, "Elián is approaching the time when he must register for military conscription. Once that happens, he won't be able to get out of Cuba until after he's served time in the army. The only way out is adoption. But I'm afraid that's not in the cards unless his father drops dead from a heart attack."

"Christ! You're really in an awful fix. It must be terribly tough on you and Elena."

Philip nodded, after which he fell silent. But when they arrived at the hotel, he suddenly turned and put his hand on David's shoulder.

"I had a lot to drink tonight," Philip said anxiously. "I probably said a lot of things I shouldn't have," he added, looking keenly at David. "But I felt I could trust you. So I hope I was correct in assuming that you'll not tell anyone about what we discussed tonight. Right?"

"Of course," David quickly reassured him, somewhat surprised by the question.

"Good. Otherwise I could be in a heap of trouble. I don't want to be kicked out of Cuba unless I can take my entire family with me. So, mum's the word, O.K.?"

"Hey, you don't have to worry about me keeping my mouth shut," David replied, wanting to put Philip's fears to rest. "I know how much your family means to you. And I'm honored that you felt sufficiently sure about me that we could have the frank discussion we had tonight. So believe me, I'm not about to violate your trust. You can be sure of that."

***

Despite all the liquor he had drunk, David was too churned up to fall asleep. Until his debate with Philip, he could rationalize what was happening to Cuba by placing the blame primarily on U.S. policy, while excusing the regime's own excesses. Also, he hadn't given much thought to Fidel's obsession with his power and destiny, or whether a new class had emerged in Cuban society. But Philip had forced him to confront these issues head-on—he had too much intellectual integrity to dodge them any longer. And now his intellectual odyssey had ended with all his recent doubts and concerns as to where the revolution was headed being greatly intensified.

The debate had also sapped him emotionally, at the gut level, in ways he had never felt before. Together with the revelations by *los muchachos* and Isabela, Philip's dilemma regarding Elián brought home the human costs of the revolution, something he had previously ignored. He realized now that the revolution wasn't simply an abstract social phenomenon to be dissected, analyzed, and written about. To be sure, tens of thousands of Cubans weren't being murdered or imprisoned by the Castro government—Cuba was not a Soviet Union or a detestable Latin American country ruled by a right-wing military regime. Nonetheless, innocent, ordinary citizens in Cuba were being unjustly imprisoned, cowed, or otherwise maimed in more subtle ways by an arbitrary, oppressive system. No longer could he avert his eyes from these countless individual tragedies, the human wreckage left by the revolution—a revolution that until a few weeks ago had stirred so much fire in him.

***

11

Liberation

Marina Alvarez was furious. She had just returned to Havana the previous evening after spending two days in Matanzas province with David Diamond. Having come to detest the *norteamericano* thoroughly, she was looking forward to being away from him for several days. "*Lo merezco*. Yes," she repeated as if trying to convince someone. "I deserve it." But now, Thursday morning, her superior at MINREX instructed her to arrange another excursion for Diamond starting on Monday. The trip had been proposed by Comrade Carlos Salsamendi, assistant to Comrade Carlos Rafael Rodríguez, which meant of course that it had to be acted upon. The new trip would take them through the eastern half of the island, all the way to Santiago de Cuba. She knew she would need the rest of the day and probably Friday as well to set up the trip's logistics and arrange interviews with local officials, if they were to leave by Monday morning.

"*It's going to be another waste of time,*" she thought. "*Just like our visit to Matanzas.*" Diamond had annoyed her no end by his persistent questioning of the Party and government people responsible for the *Poder Popular* experiment. "Fué demasiado agresivo en sus preguntas—*he was too aggressive in his questions. He was never satisfied with the answers the officials gave him.*"

She was deeply perplexed. "*Why was Rodríguez, a ranking member of the Politburo, going out of his way for this particular* norteamericano?" she asked herself. No matter what Captain Acosta said, she could feel it in her bones that Diamond was no friend of the revolution. Now, starting next Monday, she would have to spend another miserable week with him. Just the thought of it intensified the dull, throbbing ache she had been feeling in her abdomen.

***

David had returned from his two-day trip to Matanzas feeling dispirited. His interviews with local *Poder Popular* officials in Matanzas confirmed his worst fears: The government had no intention of permitting genuine participatory democracy at the municipal level. The Communist Party would control each *Poder Popular* in a municipality through the local Party secretary, who would oversee the work of local government officials. The secretary would also approve the candidates running for municipal elections. Additionally, Havana would have sole power to allocate resources, another means of exerting control over the municipal and provincial governments.

"Philip Taylor was certainly right," David ruefully observed. *"The revolution has given the state too much power for democracy to take hold."* There was now no doubt in his mind that after he returned to the States he would have to rewrite at least one chapter of his book, as well as revise its initial thesis. Both tasks would take time. But even more troubling was the fact that they would present him with a daunting theoretical problem to resolve.

Almost as upsetting to him had been Marina's behavior during their trip. She was thoroughly disagreeable. And more controlling than usual. She took it upon herself to interfere repeatedly in his interviews. He realized now that the incident at *El Fanguito* the previous Tuesday morning had presaged what lay in store for him.

***

Distracted by her paperwork, Marina had not been paying attention to where their car was headed when the driver, Juan, took an unexpected detour through *El Fanguito*. Literally the Swamp, *El Fanguito* was a large shantytown within the shadow of the Havana skyline. During the rainy season, it would become a veritable mudhole due to the heavy rains and flooding from a nearby swollen river. Until that morning, David had not known of its existence.

As the big black Cadillac plowed ahead on the dirt road through the squalid community, he stared in disbelief at the countless shacks with their patched roofs and scrap-wood walls. There were ill-clothed children running barefoot in the dirt and mud, rusted cars lying around in heaps, and pools of fetid water still standing from recent rains. He would have expected to encounter the likes of *El Fanguito* in Mexico, Central America, the Dominican Republic, or Haiti, but not in revolutionary Cuba. Certainly not within sight of the capital. He asked the driver to stop so that he could get out and look around. Marina suddenly came alive.

"Juan, you fool, keep going!" she shrieked to the startled driver. "Why did you go this way in the first place?"

"*No había remedio, compañera*," Juan replied, terrified. "There was no alternative, comrade. Didn't you see the road sign? I had to take the detour."

"What is this place, Marina?" David asked, trying to spare Juan from a further tongue-lashing.

"It's called *El Fanguito*," she replied angrily, her flushed face brick red. "And we shouldn't be here!" Then, speaking to the driver in a loud voice, she exclaimed, "How stupid can you be, Juan? You know better than to drive through here with a foreign visitor in the car. And now he wants us to stop so he can take pictures . . . "

"*¡Cálmate, Marina, por Dios!*" David interjected. "Calm down, for God's sake! The driver had no choice but to take the detour."

"He should've alerted me."

"How was he to know you didn't see the sign?" David said. "And if it'll make you feel better, here, take my camera. You hold onto it."

Marina wasn't swayed. She motioned to Juan to keep driving.

"O.K., Marina, if you won't stop the car, at least tell me about this place. Frankly, I'm surprised to see it."

"That's precisely why we shouldn't be here. We've been told that most foreign visitors wouldn't understand why *El Fanguito* exists. They would only remember it as a blemish on the revolution, even though it predates the revolution by many years."

"But if that's the case, why is this place still here?" he asked.

"Because it is an illegal settlement! It is filled with human refuse from all over the island, despite the strenuous efforts of our revolutionary government to relocate the inhabitants, to find them better housing, even jobs, mind you." She stopped, clearly exasperated. "The trouble, you see, is that these are people who don't want to work. They won't even integrate themselves into the revolution despite the fact that the Party has dispatched its best cadres to reeducate them."

"I know what you mean," David remarked, trying to be sympathetic in an effort to calm her down. "We have some of the same social problems with the slums in the United States. So you see, both our countries are victims of capitalism. Right?"

She wasn't mollified. She was still furious at Juan. But David thought he would try one more time.

"Marina," he asked in a conciliatory voice. "Can't we stop just for a few minutes so I can at least talk to some of the people?"

"Absolutely not! This place is not on our itinerary!" she exclaimed, eyeing him suspiciously. "The only thing you need to know is that the revolution inherited this mess. *El Fanguito* in no way represents what the revolution has done in Cuba. Just remember to write that in your book, *Profesor*."

***

When they arrived in Matanzas David found another surprise awaiting him: a gastronomic delight. Having received instructions from Carlos Rafael Rodríguez's office that David be accorded the red carpet treatment, local Party and government officials had organized a luncheon in his honor, attended by some twenty-five or thirty guests. The second-floor meeting room of Party headquarters where the banquet was being held was plain, ordinary. But the feast that was laid out more than compensated for the room's simplicity. Placed on one long table were enormous mounds of boiled shrimp covered with mayonnaise, followed by plates heaped full of sliced ham, turkey, and pork, to be washed down with beer. A dessert of guava slices with cream cheese, accompanied by a shot of Russian vodka, would come at the end.

David felt guilty knowing that the vast majority of ordinary Cubans would never be able to eat a meal like the one spread out before him. Then, Marina made matters worse. Still peeved at Juan for having taken the detour through *El Fanguito*, she banned the driver from the banquet room.

"No es justo, Marina," David told her firmly. "It's only fair that Juan be invited to join us. Ye gads! It's not like there's not enough food."

"You just don't understand," she hissed. "Juan *no pertenece aquí*— he doesn't belong here. Only important Party and government officials have been invited to the banquet. It's been organized especially for you and me on orders from Comrade Rodríguez."

Fed up with her pettiness, David took matters into his own hands. He went directly to his hosts and told them that Juan should be allowed to attend the luncheon. Immediately agreeing with him, they ordered that Juan be fetched from downstairs. At first, the embarrassed driver appeared reluctant to join the guests, but quickly changed his mind once he saw the mountains of food on the banquet table. Marina just glowered at David.

She later struck back. During the interviews David conducted with different local officials over the next day and a half, she repeatedly interjected herself in their conversations. She would take issue with his line of questioning, or stop him from pinning down an official on a particularly telling point.

"Let me do my work, Marina," he would complain, but to no avail.

"Listen, *Profesor*," she replied tersely on one occasion. "My job is to protect the interests of the revolution and the Cuban people."

By the time they returned to Havana on Thursday evening, they were scarcely talking to one another. David's spirits were down, too. What he had seen during the course of their trip was not the revolution that he had been envisaging and touting over these past several years. And Marina had made matters worse by preventing him from undertaking meaningful interviews. For the first time he began seriously to consider cutting short his field trip to Cuba.

***

On Friday afternoon, Marina telephoned to inform him that they would be going on another trip, all the way to Santiago de Cuba, starting Monday morning. He should be ready to go by nine. They would not return to Havana until the following Friday or Saturday.

"Shit!" David exclaimed aloud as he slammed down the receiver. "That's all I need—a six-day trip with that fucking bitch!"

Worse yet, his research schedule would be set back, and valuable time wasted, on what he was certain would be a Cook's tour of the eastern half of the island, most of which he had already seen. The more he thought about the trip, the angrier he became. He stormed out of his room and took the elevator downstairs. He needed some fresh air.

Still seething when he rushed out of the elevator at the ground floor, he nearly collided with a burly man of medium height, wearing the olive-green uniform of the Revolutionary Armed Forces (or FAR). It took him several moments to realize that he knew the stranger, who was now looking at him with an astonished expression. The thick-set man before him, with his broad handsome face, was Lt. Colonel Antonio Martel.

David had met Martel, a distinguished veteran from the guerrilla struggle, five years earlier when touring the island as a correspondent. A Captain in the Revolutionary Armed Forces at the time, Martel was a specialist in logistics. He had been put in charge of one of the largest sugar mills in Camagüey province after Fidel had turned to his brother and the FAR in a vain, belated effort to get the 1970 *zafra* on track. David had interviewed him for an article on how Cuba's sugar harvest had been militarized. Although David had not fraternized with military people before—American or Cuban—he soon discovered that Antonio Martel was anything but the stereotypical army officer.

In the course of their many conversations, he learned that Martel was the son of a white father and *mulata* mother—hence his dusky complexion, broad features, and tight, curly hair. As a teenager, he had been sent by his father to live with his paternal uncle in Miami, where he attended high school and community college. There he had taken courses in business and English, both of which would help him in the administration of the family's small import-export firm. But to his father's disappointment, Martel joined Fidel's Rebel Army in the summer of 1957 following his return to Cuba. Because he excelled in organizing the supply and replenishment of guerrilla units, he was promoted to the rank of lieutenant in the closing months of the guerrilla campaign.

Martel had liked to practice his English on David, which was better than David's Spanish at the time, so conversation flowed easily between them. David found him to be an unpretentious man. He had a heart as big as his torso was thick and, although married at the time, an eye for women. He was intensely nationalistic and devoted to Fidel. Yet, he was also a free, sometimes irreverent thinker, capable of sharp, savvy insights. Early on he confessed to David that he knew much about army logistics, but not a damn thing about grinding and refining sugarcane. With that, David had liked him immediately. The two hit it off, quickly becoming drinking buddies as David extended his stay at the sugar mill to several days.

"David?" Colonel Martel exclaimed as the two men stood between the bank of elevators.

"Antonio! Jesus, you're a welcome sight! Damn, it's good to see you again after five years!"

The Colonel held David's hand in a vise-like grip while with his left hand he squeezed David's shoulder. "What a fantastic coincidence!"

"I know."

"Yes, but think of it, *chico*. If one of the elevators had arrived a few seconds earlier, we would have missed each other and I would never have known you were in Havana. Such is fate." Pausing for a moment, Antonio narrowed his eyes accusingly. "But tell me, why are you in Cuba? And why didn't you let me know that you were here?"

"I've been here for three weeks," David answered, feeling guilty. "I've been trying to research your *Poder Popular* experiment in connection with the book I'm writing. Anyway, I apologize for not contacting you."

"That should've been the first thing you did, *chico*." Antonio said reproachfully.

"I know, but I had no way of reaching you. Besides that, my MINREX guide seems to think that I'm a counterrevolutionary, so I was afraid I'd cause you a problem if I started making inquiries with military authorities."

Antonio regarded David thoughtfully for a moment. Finally, he announced, "O.K. You're forgiven this time. Anyway, it's great to see you again after all these years. You're looking good, too, except that some gray is beginning to pop up in that beard of yours."

"You should talk, Antonio! I notice that not only have you been promoted, but you've also put on a few pounds since I last saw you."

"Would you believe it, *chico*? I was even heavier a few weeks ago. But I'm training rigorously now, running every day, getting lots of exercise, watching what I eat. I've already lost five kilos. If I keep it up, I'll soon have to order new uniforms."

"Well, *no te pongas flaco, chico*, or Cuban women may find you too thin. By the way, are you still married, if I may ask?"

"Funny that you would ask. No, my wife and I were divorced nearly three years ago. Luckily, we had no kids so no harm was done. And how about you? Still a bachelor?"

"I was a married man until a few months ago. Since then, I've separated from my wife. We're divorcing when I get back to L.A. So, to answer your question, for all practical purposes I'm a bachelor again just like you."

"I don't know about you, but I prefer being single. Now I don't feel so guilty if I cause some *muñeca* to lose her virginity." There was a devilish glint in his dark eyes.

"Oh, come on, as if you ever had any pangs of guilt over that!" David laughed. "In fact, I'll bet right now you're here to meet some young foreign lady. Right?"

"No, but I sure wish it were so." A wide grin spread across his handsome face. "Actually, I am here to see a foreigner. Unfortunately," he added, grimacing, "he's hardly my type."

"Too bad, *amigo,*" David replied, laughing. "But, hey, can we get together? I'm free tonight through Sunday. Then I'll be away for five or six days on a tour to Santiago de Cuba that's been arranged by MINREX."

"*Coño,* I'm sorry, but I'm completely tied up with army business over the next few days. We'll have to wait until you get back. Then I can have you out to my *ranchito* for some drinks and lunch or dinner. And a long talk, too. Just like in the old days."

"That would be terrific. Believe me, it really gives me something to look forward to."

"Good. Here's my phone number at home. Call me there between eight and eleven o'clock at night after you get back. We'll set something up. Until then, *ciao,* David. Enjoy your trip."

"I'll try. *Hasta luego, amigo.*"

David and Antonio had been talking inside the marbled alcove between the opposing banks of elevators. Neither noticed the short, wiry man sitting some thirty feet away in the hotel lobby, ostensibly reading his *Granma* newspaper. All the while the stranger had been watching them intently, deftly lowering his newspaper sufficiently to observe the two men without being noticed. He waited until David had turned to go to the downstairs bar before he rose from his chair and followed Lt. Colonel Antonio Martel from the Habana Libre.

* * *

His chance encounter with Antonio was the tonic David needed. His friend personified all that had attracted him to revolutionary Cuba—the infectious openness of its people, their enthusiasm for the revolutionary project, their fervent faith in Fidel and his government. In fact, the mere prospect of seeing his friend again made the thought of his upcoming trip to Santiago de Cuba with Marina more bearable. He was determined to use the weekend to rediscover the Cuba he remembered

Leaving the hotel early Saturday afternoon after a light lunch, he climbed aboard a crowded bus that took him to a beach in Miramar. It was next to what once had been the old Havana Biltmore Yacht and Country Club. The sandy white beach was packed with men, women, and children, some in the water, others playing on the white sand or lying down and lazily soaking up the hot sun.

After finding a spot for his clothes and towel, David dashed into the calm, emerald waters for a refreshing swim—his first in the ocean. The water temperature was just right, not too warm, yet cool enough to be invigorating. Without breaking stroke, he swam straight out from the beach for about a hundred meters before he stopped to tread water. He looked back at the former yacht club with its expansive terrace and row of graceful palm trees. One of the first acts of the new revolutionary government in 1959 had been to seize the club in the name of the people and turn it into a public school. It was once the exclusive preserve of the rich. But not anymore, he observed with satisfaction. Now, it's part of the people's beach.

After returning to shore and drying off, he walked along the water's edge, admiring the teenage girls and women around him. None wore bikinis. By and large, they wore modest, not particularly flattering bathing suits, probably imported from Eastern Europe or, he suspected, made at home. The older women had the full breasts, big hips, and heavy thighs so typical of Caribbean women, but he spied several younger ones in their teens or early twenties, who had the taller, more lithe figures that were more to his liking. Many were natural beauties, with their dark complexion and hair.

Returning to the spot where he had left his clothes, he turned his attention to the people on the beach around him. He could see that most represented a cross section of Cuba's popular classes after fifteen years of revolutionary change. Many seemed to be either young students with their friends from school or workers with their families. Children were everywhere. Mulattos and Afro-Cubans predominated over whites, but skin color didn't seem to matter—"*Another sign the revolution advances*," he told himself. The people around him were playing catch, roughhousing, chatting animatedly. A few were listening to music blaring from portable radios made in the Eastern bloc.

He smiled as he overheard several families or groups arguing and talking boisterously and excitedly as Cubans were often wont to do.

***

He spent his entire Sunday afternoon in the working-class neighborhood of Cayo Hueso, not too far from the colonial section of Old Havana, and still the home of aging cigar makers. More run-down than when he last saw it, Cayo Hueso was populated largely by Afro-Cubans occupying old tenement-style apartments. He was reminded of Watts, except that he felt far safer strolling through Cayo Hueso, despite the fact that he stood out as a white foreigner. There were only a few instances in which he was the object of hard stares by some men loitering in doorways, on steps, or in narrow alleyways. But by-and-large, everyone else observed him with curiosity or greeted him with broad smiles.

He took his time, stopping occasionally to exchange words with some of the neighborhood children. When they found he was an American, they immediately beseeched him for chewing gum and cigarettes. On one occasion, a group of adults surrounded him, engaging him in friendly conversation. Soon they began plying him with questions about what he was doing in Havana and why the United States was so against Cuba. One of them asked him his opinion about Fidel and the revolution.

"I think the revolution has brought great advances to the Cuban people," David responded. "Especially the popular classes, including people of color . . . "

"*Eso sí*," a wizened old black man broke in, nodding his nubby gray head vigorously in agreement. "*Antes de Fidel* y *la revolución*, before Fidel and the revolution, all of us with dark skin suffered discrimination. Often we were treated *como mierda*, like shit!" The old man stopped for a moment to gauge David's reaction and that of the crowd around them. "That's right," he went on. "One had to be white—or nearly white—to get ahead, to get into the rich man's country clubs, even to go to the beaches, many of which were restricted. *Si eras negro*, if you were black, forget it, man!"

"And now, how has it changed for the better?" David asked eagerly.

"It's like night and day," another man volunteered. "Now, we have our own place to live in and our rent is low. Our food rations give us enough to eat. Besides that, our kids go to schools where they get not only their books and school clothes, but also milk and something substantial to eat. And mind you, they get all of that without us having to pay a single *centavo*. And in case we get sick or our kids need to be vaccinated, we go to any of the clinics and hospitals—again all free, mind you—that are run by the government."

"And don't forget," another interjected. *"No hay desempleo*—there's no unemployment—like before. Hell no! We have jobs thanks to the government—but most of all, thanks to Fidel because without him we wouldn't have had the revolution!"

"Es cierto!" several cried out. "That's right!" Others in the small crowd murmured their agreement.

David was elated by the time he left the group. He hadn't forgotten his conversation with Roberto, but he was certain that the *cara doble* didn't apply to the chorus of sentiments he had heard, almost all of it spontaneous. The outpouring by the crowd had to be genuine, unscripted, this time around. He made a mental note to remember to write down his exchange with the people of Cayo Hueso so that he could later incorporate it into his book. It was the rebuttal he had been looking for to offset the criticisms and cynical observations he had been hearing from *los muchacho*s and Philip. It reminded him of the Cuba he had first encountered in the late 1960s.

He recalled the first time he had visited Cayo Hueso in 1969. What had attracted him then as now was the effervescence, the vitality of the place. Although the Afro-Cuban religious cults were frowned upon by the government, he was sure the people continued to consult their Santería priests, while secretly paying tribute to Changó, and the other deities of the three main Afro-Cuban religions, in the sanctity of their homes. No, the government couldn't stamp out the cults, just as it couldn't dampen the magnetic appeal of Afro-Cuban music among the general population, whether black, white, or mulatto. If it were allowed, he was sure, musicians would now be on the streets with their *tumbadoras*, three-feet-tall Afro-Cuban drums, and *claves,* or sticks, beating out a sensual, rhythmic *rumba* or *son-changu.* And at the sound of their vibrant music, the rest of the neighborhood would have come pouring out of the apartments to dance and sing on the sidewalks and streets.

"God Almighty," he said to himself toward the end of his walk. *"Just because Fidel doesn't like dancing doesn't mean the rest of*

*the population shouldn't do it. Christ, the government has so much
support here that it has everything to gain and nothing to lose by
easing up."*

***

David was still in an upbeat mood when Chucho reached him at
the hotel later that evening. Chucho had been wanting to introduce
him to a friend, a promising young Cuban writer and poet, whom he
referred to only as Gustavo, but the meeting had never materialized.
Now, however, the meeting was on for later that night. David wondered whether Gustavo was a pseudonym since Chucho had inti-
mated that his friend had run afoul of the authorities in recent years.

"Gustavo's problem is that he's a misfit, just like so many other
writers and artists nowadays, who refuse to conform to what the government wants in literature," Chucho had explained earlier. "You see,
he's apolitical. The revolution simply doesn't interest him as a writer."

"So, what does he write about?"

"Oh, some of his stories and poems concern the capriciousness of
life. But the majority deal with the individual self and various forms
of human expression, including carnal pleasures."

"He sounds exactly like the kind of writer that Fidel would consider as being 'outside the revolution,'" David had observed.

"That's right. And he pays for it. You see, the fact that he's a good
writer, yet withholds his talent from the revolution by not writing on
accepted themes, infuriates the authorities and the old guard who
dominate the writers' union. That he's also a *maricón* compounds
his problem because Fidel and the authorities despise homosexuals.
They consider them 'social deviants' left over from the decadent
capitalist past. Between you and me, however, I think they find homosexuals a threat to their *machismo*."

Now, as they headed toward their meeting place, Chucho told
David that Gustavo had first been arrested in the late 1960s. Along
with other homosexuals, social delinquents, and political dissidents
who had been caught in one of the mass roundups by the police, he
had been sent to a rehabilitation camp—one of the Military Units to
Aid Production (UMAP) run by the army. Months later, after his
release, he had returned to Havana, but he continued to be watched
and harassed by State Security agents because of his homosexual
associations and libidinous works. They would raid whatever tem-

porary residence he was occupying in search of evidence of his depraved lifestyle and writings. Sometimes they succeeded, after which he would be incarcerated. But recently, he had found ways to keep his writings from the police. Unable to have his short stories and poems published in Cuba, or to find employment in state enterprises, he managed to survive with the help of friends.

***

It was nearly ten o'clock when David and Chucho arrived at Gustavo's dilapidated apartment house on the outskirts of the city. They had taken a circuitous route to avoid being followed. Gustavo's apartment was upstairs, on the third floor. They waited a few minutes, checking to make sure the place wasn't under surveillance, but it was too dark for David to really tell. He had to place his trust in Chucho's eyes and ears. When Chucho thought the coast was clear, they went inside the building and climbed up three flights of stairs.

Chucho knocked softly on the apartment door and whispered his name. A moment later, they were quickly let into a dimly lit room by a thin man with haunted eyes and disheveled black hair. Gustavo was alone. He reminded David of a wild, frightened, cornered animal.

For a while, David wondered why the meeting had been set up, as the agitated, chain-smoking writer was hard to draw out. Most of the first hour was taken up with inconsequential chitchat as they guzzled the beer that David and Chucho had brought with them. It didn't take David long to realize that Gustavo was still uneasy about meeting him. Now and then he would cast wary glances at Chucho as if to ascertain whether the American political scientist conducting research in Cuba could, in fact, be trusted. More than forty-five minutes passed before Gustavo finally decided that he could bring up more sensitive topics.

"What do you think of Heberto Padilla?" he suddenly asked David.

"Well, I can't judge his poetry, but I happened to be here in 1968 when *Verde Olivo* first denounced him," David replied. "I found the whole affair very disturbing, especially since the attack on him was launched by the army's magazine."

"Yes," Gustavo said, looking at David closely. "It turned out to be a bad sign, for Heberto as well as for the rest of us."

"And the worse was yet to come three years later," David added.

"His Stalinist-like public confession, his *mea culpa* for being too bourgeois in his writings, and his attack on fellow writers for also being insufficiently revolutionary, reminded me of the show-trials in Moscow back in the 1930s." Pausing, he felt Gustavo's eyes on him. "I imagine," he continued, "that Padilla's act of contrition, and the government's campaign against 'ideological diversionism,' all had a chilling effect on writers like yourself."

"Of course," Gustavo stated matter-of-factly. "And like you said, Heberto was partly to blame: No matter what kind of mental torture he was under, he didn't do us any favor by siding with the government in accusing Cuban intellectuals of not being revolutionary enough. After that, some of us really had it bad when it came to being persecuted—men like Reinaldo Arenas. Have you heard of him?"

"No, I can't say that I have."

"He's my hero," Gustavo said quietly, almost reverently. "Someday, he'll be recognized by the rest of the world as one of Cuba's greatest contemporary writers and poets. And if not for his literary accomplishments, then he'll be recognized for his bravery."

"Why? What's he done . . . ?"

"Reinaldo *no se rindió*—he never buckled, it's as simple as that," Gustavo answered, with a confirming nod from Chucho. "He didn't cave in like Heberto. He's endured, despite all the hounding, the arrests, the solitary confinements. I don't think I could be as brave as he."

"From what Chucho has told me, you've had to put up with a lot of persecution yourself. And yet, you've kept on writing."

"I've survived, that's all," Gustavo replied modestly with a shrug. Taking a long draw on his cigarette, he cast an inquiring glance at Chucho, who nodded his go-ahead.

"Would you like to read something I've written?" Gustavo asked, pulling a folded piece of paper from beneath his shirt. "It's a short poem."

"Of course. I would be honored."

Poetry wasn't one of David's strengths, least of all poetry written in Spanish. But with some help with the poem's wording and elliptical allusions, he liked the simplicity of Gustavo's "*La vida.*" He also found it innocuous:

Youth, so many eons ago
Time stretched endlessly before
A road, a life, a universe.
Today, I am a speck of dust
Swirling in the cosmos—
And yet,
A road, a life, a universe
Still to be explored,
Still to be fully savored.

"You can't tell me the authorities object to something like this," David asserted.

"You're right," Chucho said. "State Security agents probably wouldn't have done anything to him if they had found this particular poem on him. And that's why he chose to bring it here tonight."

"Chucho is not entirely correct," Gustavo interjected. "You see, even this poem could create a problem for me because everything must be political in Cuba, everything must serve a political purpose. So precisely because my poem is not political, I must have had some political motive in mind by writing it."

"That really sounds Kafkaesque," David observed, shaking his head.

**

They went on talking for another hour. The more David learned about the treatment of homosexual writers, most of whom he had never heard of until then, like Virgilio Piñera, the more disillusioned, the more outraged he became.

Gustavo didn't let up. He seemed to be testing David, trying to determine whether his reaction to all he was divulging was genuine—whether he could in the end be trusted. The *norteamericano,* after all, obviously had to be sympathetic to the revolution, otherwise he wouldn't have been allowed into Cuba by the authorities. Finally, he nodded to Chucho.

"Gustavo has something to ask you," Chucho announced. "It's a favor. But it could prove risky for you. Do you want him to proceed?"

"By all means," David replied, surprised, yet knowing full well that the "favor" spelled trouble. "What do you want me to do?"

"I have prepared a document," Gustavo replied, swallowing nervously. "In it I've recorded, with names, dates, and other identifying details, the kinds of persecution that writers, artists, dissidents, and, of course, homosexuals have suffered at the hands of the authorities." Pausing, he waited to see David's reaction. "I want you to smuggle it out when you leave Cuba," he continued a moment later. "It should be relatively easy since we don't think the authorities will search a foreigner like you. Then, when you arrive in the United States, we want you to give it to Amnesty International, the *New York Times,* the State Department—anyone who will condemn the repression that exists here. Maybe their denunciation will give us some protection."

David was stunned. He could hardly believe what was happening to him. Just a few hours earlier he had been almost ecstatic over what he had experienced in Cayo Hueso. Now, he not only had become witness once again to the dark side of the revolution. He was also being asked to smuggle out an indictment of the Castro regime.

"Christ!" he thought in panic. *"If I'm caught with that document, I could be thrown in jail for who knows how long."* For a moment, he had visions of being interrogated, roughed up by State Security. He remained silent, weighing the danger he would run in trying to smuggle out Gustavo's document.

Chucho and Gustavo watched him with growing apprehension, exchanging worried glances. The seconds passed as they waited for his reply.

"On the other hand," David pondered his dilemma, *"I just can't cop out on this. I just can't walk away from what I've heard tonight, no matter what I would like to think about the revolution."* He thought of what Philip had told him—that the Left couldn't remain silent but was morally bound to criticize the Cuban government when it abused its power.

"O.K.," he answered at last, taking a deep breath. "I'll do it. I just hope for all our sake that I don't get caught. But first, maybe I could take a look at what I'm supposed to smuggle out so that I'll at least have an idea of where I can hide it."

"Gustavo doesn't have the document with him," Chucho explained, shaking his head. "He couldn't take a chance that the police might stop and search him on his way here. Besides, where would you hide it after you returned to the Habana Libre tonight?

No. We'll figure out a way to give it to you on the very morning of your departure."

"That sounds good," David said, relieved that he wasn't in any immediate danger. For the time being, the worst thing he faced was his trip the next morning with Marina Alvarez to Santiago de Cuba.

***

David didn't get back to the hotel until after one o'clock in the morning. Too wound up to sleep, he read for a while. Finally, around two, he dozed off, only to be awakened an hour later by the presence of someone in his room. He opened his eyes to see the silent intruder, a pen flashlight in hand, rifling through the contents of his briefcase, then moving to the dresser. The man slipped his free hand into the top drawer, feeling for something. David's first instinct was to shout, to confront the stranger. But then he realized that the man was not an ordinary thief. No, the intruder was looking for papers or notes that he had written—or, more likely still, for something Gustavo might have given him. He had to be from State Security!

Aware that David had awakened and was watching him, the intruder abruptly stopped his search. Switching off his light, he turned to David and, with his finger to his lips, motioned him to remain silent. Despite the darkness, David could see clearly the man's malicious grin. Suddenly, he bowed in David's direction. An instant later, he vanished through the door.

David was certain that the man had found nothing incriminating. Early into his trip, he had taken the precaution of never writing down his impressions or making notes just in case his hotel room was ever searched. Still, he was shaken. State Security must have spotted him at Gustavo's place. They had then sent someone to search his room for anything the writer might have given him. But more ominously still, the agent's presence was meant to intimidate, to warn him to stay clear of people like Gustavo.

"Why else would that guy grin at me like a Cheshire cat?" David asked himself. *"Why would he exit the room with an elaborate bow? Shit! He wanted me to wake up and see him, that's why!"*

He didn't fall back to sleep until after four in the morning.

***

Later that morning, after he had awakened, he kept thinking about the intruder's visit and what it portended for the future. Of one thing he was certain: He would be watched more closely from now on with respect to the people he was seeing. Still, he was determined to go through with his decision to smuggle out Gustavo's document. But it was clear that all of them would have to take more stringent precautions. However, he had no way of warning Chucho before departing for Santiago de Cuba that morning, and could only hope that Chucho would contact him upon his return as they had planned.

Preoccupied with what had happened since meeting Gustavo, David hadn't noticed that Marina Alvarez failed to turn up at the appointed time to begin their trip. He began to worry that her absence had something to do with State Security. *"Christ!"* he thought. *"This is what it must be like to live in a police state. You're always apprehensive, paranoid even, over anything that appears out of the ordinary."*

Finally, at ten-thirty, a MINREX secretary called to inform him that Marina was ill. Their trip would have to be postponed a day. A driver would be at the hotel at nine o'clock sharp on Tuesday to pick him up. His anxiety eased.

* * *

The following morning, promptly at nine, David spied Juan, the same driver who had chauffeured him and Marina to Matanzas, stroll jauntily into the hotel lobby. Unlike the week before, Juan no longer was wearing a dour expression, but seemed almost elated.

"¿Donde está Marina?" David asked as they walked outside and he saw that the big black Cadillac from MINREX was empty. "Where is Marina?"

"She's recuperating in the hospital. She had to have her appendix taken out."

"¡No me digas! You've got to be kidding me! Are we going alone?"

"No, not at all," Juan answered with a twinkle in his eye. "You're a lucky man! In fact, we're both lucky. Catalina Cruz has replaced Marina. And take my word for it, she's as beautiful to the eye as she is easy to get along with. Come on, get in. We have to go now and pick her up at her apartment on Calle F."

* * *

Catalina had been rushing all morning. The previous day had been a long, hectic one. First, she had had to convince her superior not to cancel Diamond's trip and to allow her to substitute for Marina as the American professor's escort—not an easy task. Her boss had been reluctant to "waste" her, as she put it, on someone as unimportant as an American professor. Then, because they would be starting the trip a day late, she had had to cancel all the arrangements that Marina had made for their first stopover in Santa Clara, and to compress the rest of the trip into the four remaining days. It had taken her the better part of Monday to reschedule all the appointments and hotel reservations that Marina had originally lined up for the trip. She also added in other officials for Diamond to see. Either deliberately or out of carelessness, Marina had left them off the interview list.

Leaving MINREX after seven that evening, Catalina barely made it in time to the cleaners to pick up the dress she wanted to take on her unexpected journey. When finally returning to her apartment in Vedado after nine o'clock, she had only enough energy to warm up the soup she had made the day before. Packing would have to wait.

She rose early Tuesday morning, showered, savored her *café con leche*, and carefully packed her clothes in a medium-size leather suitcase. She had selected her wardrobe with care—a dress, skirt, and blouse for more formal occasions, but mostly high-fashion jeans and tops she had bought at stylish boutiques during her two trips to Mexico and Italy over the past three years. The purchases had been the only nice things she had done for herself following Ernesto's death.

Her commitment to the revolution had not made her any less feminine—nor any less conscious of how good stylish clothes looked on her. That had been something that Ernesto had always appreciated when he was alive. And now, being completely honest with herself, she had to admit that she was looking forward to the trip with Diamond. She wanted to look attractive in a relaxed but not flashy way, as was befitting a trip to the eastern part of the island, most of which was poorer, more rural, and less sophisticated than Havana and its environs.

Why had she found herself attracted to the American? There were many reasons why she shouldn't be. Joaquín didn't have to tell her. Diamond was hardly like Ernesto. Her lover had been selfless to a fault, exuding an inner beauty and nobility that had immediately drawn her to him—qualities that seemed to be missing in the American, at least to some degree. He also appeared to believe himself intellectually superior, a conceit she had never liked in men. Physically, too, she didn't find him all that handsome. Not nearly as good looking as Ernesto, or even some of the foreign diplomats currently posted to Havana. Besides, his hair was too long for her taste. She suspected, too, that his physique lacked the strength and gracefulness that she had found so seductive in her former lover.

Yet there was something about Diamond that did appeal to her. Perhaps it was his eyes. Large, bold, and somewhat imperious, they also conveyed a wounded innocence. There was something honest about him, a streak of personal integrity that she found missing in so many men except for Joaquín and of course Ernesto. Then, too, she sensed that beneath his serious, academic demeanor lay a boyish sense of humor, an impetuousness even, that reminded her somewhat of Ernesto. She found these qualities lacking in most of the stuffy foreign diplomats and Cuban officials she knew. Yes, she concluded, she was attracted to him because he offered the prospect of fun and distraction, however fleeting, from the sadness in her life that only recently had begun to recede.

Having purposefully left her balcony window ajar, she heard the familiar blare of the Cadillac's horn over the noise of the occasional passing traffic. Going to the balcony to make sure, she saw Juan and David Diamond standing beside the car, looking up with grinning faces.

"*¡Apúrate, Catalina, ya estamos listos!* Hurry up, Catalina," David called. "We're ready!"

"Hold your horses!" she laughed, waving at both men. "*Bajo en un minuto.*"

***

12

Foreplay

With its windows rolled down, the MINREX Cadillac roared east out of Havana along the Carretera Central, the island's central highway, which had been constructed nearly forty-five years earlier toward the close of the Machado dictatorship. As the car sped along, the morning's cool air from the open windows continually ruffled Catalina's hair. More than once, David wished he could lean over to brush away the wisps of dark hair fluttering across her smooth complexion.

She was seated beside him in the back seat, dressed in jeans and a sleeveless yellow shirt. The shirt's soft paleness set off her black hair, green eyes, and tawny skin. She looked every bit as stunning as when he had seen her at the Italian Embassy. It took all his self-control not to look at her too long at any one time.

Initially, they made small talk, though she also queried him about his research. He was reluctant to go into much detail, fearing that he might antagonize her by discussing his disapproval of her government's repressive, anti-democratic policies. He mentioned nothing about *los muchachos*, Philip, Gustavo, or the incident in his hotel room.

Later in their conversation, he learned that she had been sent to a Catholic school in Baltimore when she was thirteen to perfect her English and French. But the real reason for going there, Catalina informed him, was because her parents wanted her safely away from the violence between the police and anti-Batista groups that was spilling onto the streets of Havana. In any event, her two years at the school were not happy ones. She had been a rebellious teenager who couldn't abide the nuns' strict discipline. Finally, getting her way with her parents, she had returned to Cuba during the last year of the Batista regime in time to witness the mounting anti-government struggle.

As the morning heated up, she became drowsy, finally dozing off for twenty minutes. David took the opportunity to appreciate her beauty as she rested her head against the car window, her lips slightly parted, her thick, dark, hair softly framing her face. He noticed the small gap in her front teeth, the speck on her cheekbone, and the faint birthmark on her arm, all of which made her less than perfect, yet even more enticing. He noticed, too, how naturally she bore her beauty. He liked that.

***

Their first stopover was Trinidad, a picturesque colonial city on the southern coast of the island. When they arrived in the late afternoon, the sun still shown brightly on the thick white walls and red tile roofs of the old Spanish-style buildings, casting long shadows across the city's narrow cobbled streets. Despite the lateness of the day, Catalina had arranged for David to interview local Party and government officials for over an hour.

Afterward, they drove another thirteen kilometers down a short, narrow peninsula to the Hotel Ancón, where a refreshing sea breeze brought welcome relief from the day's heat. The hotel sat on a strand of sandy white beach facing the Caribbean, whose vibrant aquamarine waters were just turning a darker hue against the early evening sky. David guessed that the hotel was reserved for high Cuban officials and foreign visitors. Sure enough, when he later met Catalina in the hotel's spacious dining room, she told the headwaiter to charge their dinner and drinks to the foreign guest account maintained by MINREX.

Seated at a table in a corner of the dining room, away from most of the other patrons, they had a view of the beach below and the darkening sea beyond. The ambiance couldn't be more romantic, David observed, as they chatted over drinks—a glass of Italian white wine for her and a scotch on the rocks for him.

"May the rest of this trip be as enjoyable as it's been on this first day," he toasted. "And I've no doubt that it will be, Catalina, because you seem to have thought of everything. Besides, just your lovely presence alone ensures our trip's success."

"*Qué caballero eres*," she replied with an air of amusement. "I didn't know you *norteamericanos* could be so chivalrous. But I thank you. We did have a nice day. And if I may say so, your company has helped make it one."

"Well, I see that Cuban women can be complimentary, too!" They laughed at their little bit of repartee as they touched glasses again in a mock toast.

Later, after having exhausted the topic of their day's happenings, their talk turned more personal. She began by casually inquiring whether he was married. He told her the truth—that he and his wife were separated and would file for divorce after his return to Los Angeles.

"I'm sorry to hear that," she replied sympathetically. Having detected a note of sadness in his voice, she asked whether he and his wife had children.

"No, luckily, we don't." Overcome by an unexpected wave of forgotten emotion, he suddenly felt the need to unburden himself. "You see, we were too busy to start a family. My wife went to work for a high-powered law firm after we got married, while I began teaching full time at the university. Along with my classes, I also became very much involved in writing my book. So we were one busy couple."

She listened with interest, watching his face as his story unfolded. To get through the more difficult part, he fortified himself with a long drink of scotch.

"You said you were a busy couple, but I'm curious about one thing. Were you at any time a happily married couple?"

"I thought we were," he replied with a sigh. "We really seemed to be in love. At least, I knew I loved her. So much so, in fact, that I was completely faithful to her, which came as a surprise to most of my friends."

"Why were they surprised?" she asked, giving him a curious look. She was quick to note his hesitation, as if unsure of how much he wanted to reveal about his past.

"Let's just say that I had a reputation for being a bit of a womanizer back in grad school. And that's where the irony begins," he added with bitterness. "After I married Julie, I became the faithful husband, a real straight arrow because I wanted our marriage to work." He avoided looking at her. "You see, my parents were divorced. I didn't want my kids to be torn apart like I was because of a broken home. Anyway, I was sure Julie and I had the kind of marriage I had always dreamed about, but then things started to fall apart." His throat suddenly became constricted. He fell silent. He looked out the window for a moment and reached for his drink.

"What happened?" Catalina asked gently, watching him.

"I still don't exactly know *why* it happened," he said, turning a serious face to her. "All I know is that over a period of two or three months she began drifting away from me. It started with her working late at the office and going on overnight business trips." He cleared his voice. "Anyway, the long and short of it is that she finally confessed that she'd been having an affair for some time with one . . . with one of the senior law partners in her firm."

A long silence fell between them. He asked the waiter for a beer. Catalina had scarcely touched her wine.

"I may be prying in asking this, but are you still in love with her?" she inquired. "Because if you are, perhaps there's a chance of reconciliation after you get back."

"No way!" he replied, shaking his head vigorously. "You have to understand that something snapped inside me when she told me she'd been having an affair. And then, to make matters worse, she even insisted that what she'd done wasn't such a big deal after all. People do it all the time. After that I just wanted out of the marriage." He paused to let his anger recede. "However," he added a moment later, "I have to confess that it took me awhile to get over our breakup."

"I'm sorry that it turned out that way," Catalina responded kindly. "I can imagine how deeply hurt you must have felt. I would never be able to tolerate infidelity in a marriage. It's terrible for a husband or a wife to betray the other."

***

"And you, Catalina, have you ever been married?" David inquired after the waiter brought him his beer.

"No," she replied after a long hesitation.

"That really surprises me. Is it because you just haven't found the right man? Someone you could really fall in love with?"

He caught the pained look on her face before she averted her glance. It was then that he recalled what Philip had mentioned. Though he reproached himself for having asked the question, curiosity was getting the best of him.

"No," she answered after pausing to sip her wine. She looked at him strangely. "I once was deeply in love with a man. We were planning to get married when he was killed."

"I'm sorry. I didn't know." But of course he did know and now he hoped he would learn more of her mysterious lover.

"There's no need for you to be sorry. You had no way of knowing. In fact," she added, almost as an afterthought, "very few people knew about Ernesto and me, before or after his death."

"How long ago did he die?"

Seeing that she was having a hard time maintaining her composure, he suddenly felt guilty. She took another sip of wine as if to buy time.

"Catalina," he said gently, "you don't have to talk about it if it is painful. Please, don't torture yourself."

"No, it's all right. I'm just not accustomed to talking to anyone about Ernesto, except to the person who introduced us and remained our closest friend, and who was like a brother to both of us." She looked down at her almost empty wineglass. "Ernesto died four years ago," she said, her voice wavering slightly. "He died in Nicaragua on an 'internationalist mission,' helping the Sandinistas fight Somoza. The National Guard caught him after he had been wounded. Those monsters tortured him horribly before they finally shot him." Her voice broke and tears welled up in her eyes.

David watched as a glistening teardrop formed in the corner of her eye; finally spilling over, it slid silently down her cheek. He quickly offered her a fresh handkerchief from his pocket. He wanted to comfort her, to reach out and take her free hand, but his gesture would only have called attention to them. So far the few patrons around them appeared unaware of her distress.

"I'll never understand how some men can be so barbaric!" she suddenly exclaimed in a fierce voice. "The National Guardsmen beat Ernesto terribly, breaking his cheekbone and blinding him in his left eye. After that, when he recovered consciousness and still wouldn't reveal the whereabouts of the rebel hideout, they crushed his fingers and then . . . "

She stopped once more to collect herself. " . . . And then those monsters castrated him," she said in a choked voice. "It was so horrible that when a CIA officer arrived and saw what they had done to him, he went berserk and attacked the bastards." Her voice broke off once more. Shaking, she put his rumpled handkerchief to her mouth to stifle the silent sobs within her.

"God, I'm so sorry," David said in a thick voice. "How horrible. How he must have suffered. And how terrible for you." No longer caring whether anyone saw, he took her limp hand in his. "Please don't upset yourself anymore."

***

Several seconds passed before Catalina removed her hand from David's. Then, she carefully spread out his handkerchief on the table and began smoothing out its wrinkles. She folded the handkerchief neatly, all the while focusing on what she was doing. Satisfied with the results of her handiwork, she looked up. Her green eyes were still moist from the tears.

"I won't need this anymore," she said, handing him the handkerchief. Several moments of silence followed, while she composed herself and he waited patiently for her to continue.

"I would've married Ernesto had he lived," she said, some of her fiery resolve returning. "He was the finest, most wonderful human being I've ever known. Intelligent and idealistic, yet he was a man of action. He also had enormous integrity. He was as solid and selfless a person as you could ever find—someone you could always count on."

"From what you say he sounds rather extraordinary."

"He really was. I used to think of him as the embodiment of the revolution because he fit Che's concept of the 'new man' perfectly. And I wasn't the only one. Even our closest friend admitted that he was more like Che's new man than Che himself."

"That's saying a lot. Besides being a revolutionary Che was a pretty extraordinary person himself."

"Of course," she replied quickly. "But Ernesto was a better human being. He was as honest, forthright, and idealistic as Che, but he lacked Che's ruthless fanaticism. Ernesto did not believe that the ends justify the means, as did Che. For instance, he criticized Che for having ordered the execution of all those Batista soldiers after he took command of La Cabaña fortress. Ernesto said Che was wrong because he hadn't given them a fair trial."

"Wow! He said that about Che?"

"Yes. He said that it didn't matter that they were *Batistianos*. A moral issue was at stake. Those men deserved a fair trial. You see, Ernesto was not at all ruthless like Che because he valued human life and justice too much."

"If that was the case, how could he be an internationalist?" David inquired.

"What do you mean? He *was* an internationalist . . . "

"I know, but to paraphrase Lenin, if he wanted to promote revolution, then surely he had to be prepared to break a few eggs to make an omelet," David said by way of explanation.

"Please, don't turn this into an academic exercise!" she snapped, clearly irritated. "Don't you understand? I was trying to tell you about Ernesto, the man, not some abstract theory about revolution."

"Sorry," he said, taken aback by her sharp retort. "That was stupidly flippant of me. Forgive me."

She regarded him closely, weighing the sincerity of his words.

"What I was trying to explain to you was that Ernesto was capable of killing other combatants, but he wanted to spare innocent men, women, and children. He wanted to avoid killing them at all costs," she said, her green eyes still smoldering, her voice still hard. She examined the glass in her hand, swishing around what remained of her wine. David couldn't tell whether she was searching for the right words or had stopped because she didn't want to go on talking anymore. Then she spoke again, this time without the edge in her voice.

"You see, Ernesto always had this enormous contradiction about him. He was the romantic, idealistic revolutionary, yet he hated the thought of having to take a human life, of having to inflict suffering on the innocent to ensure the revolution's triumph. He wasn't at all like Fidel and Che in that respect. Both of them, you know, wanted the Russians to launch their missiles against your country during the October crisis. Ernesto would never even have dreamed of doing that."

David remained silent. She drank the last of her wine.

"What you have to understand," she went on, "is that Ernesto had a mind of his own. As much as he admired Fidel and Che, as much as he respected Raúl, he was also critical of them for having had so many people shot after the revolution triumphed. The *paredón*, the mass executions, he said on more than one occasion, had sullied the revolution." She looked away for an instant, then shaking her head sadly, added, "I've always thought that his lack of guile and ruthlessness contributed to his capture."

The waiter finally arrived with their dinners.

"I think we've done enough serious talking for the night," she said, smiling for the first time since she began talking about Ernesto. "Let's turn to something more cheerful."

"I'll agree to that!" David exclaimed, relieved to eject Ernesto from their presence. "I think we should finish this delicious dinner so . . . . " He hesitated, noting the face she made on tasting the food. "Oh, so you, too, don't think that it's all that delicious?" She shook her head and they both laughed. "Anyway, let's finish up so we can take a walk on the beach. That can't be spoiled by too much over-cooking."

* * *

They walked barefoot for over an hour on the fine white sand of the nearly deserted Playa Ancón as waves lapped quietly on the beach. Only occasionally did they encounter other couples sitting or strolling. After a while, they sat on the warm sand, gazing at the still sea that lay shimmering under the starlit sky. When they resumed talking, David related the incident at *El Fanguito* and how Marina had tried to keep Juan from the luncheon. "That's Marina," Catalina replied as she rolled her eyes in mock disapproval.

Later as they began retracing their steps, she said in a hushed, confidential tone, "David, I don't want you to repeat what I told you back at the hotel to anyone here in Cuba or in the United States."

"Don't worry. I'll never say anything about what you said."

"Good. I'm sure you understand that what I told you involved not only my government's activities, but also my private life. And I don't want my love affair with Ernesto or anything about him to become public knowledge."

"I understand, Catalina. You can rest assured, I'll never betray your trust."

"Thank you. I hoped you would say that."

When they returned to the hotel, he accompanied her upstairs to her room. After she had unlocked the door and turned around to face him, he extended his right hand. She shook it. But then, on impulse, she pulled him closer to her, and lightly brushed his cheek with her lips. "Good night, David, and thank you for being a compassionate listener," she whispered, as she slipped into her room and closed the door.

Her kiss had caught him totally by surprise. He stood outside her room for a moment, wishing he had responded.

***

They left Trinidad before nine o'clock the next morning, passed through Sancti Spíritus to the northeast, and shortly afterward were back on the Carretera Central, reaching Ciego de Avila in time for lunch with local Party and government officials. Back on the road again, there came the long, mind-dulling stretch of highway through the flat grasslands of Camagüey province. Only livestock were to be seen on either side of the road. The ride was hot and dusty, uncomfortably so, except when they ran into an afternoon thunderstorm, which cooled the big black Cadillac for at least twenty minutes before they were out of it and the heat enveloped them again.

David couldn't help but notice that Catalina seemed strangely distant almost from the moment they resumed their journey. Only once had she smiled sleepily at him when she caught him looking at her as she dozed. Other than that one fleeting glance, the closeness they had experienced the previous evening had evaporated. He was puzzled by her aloofness. He wasn't at all convinced that the reason she deliberately avoided any familiarity toward him was because of Juan, their MINREX driver.

They arrived in Camagüey late in the afternoon. Billowing, rose-tinted clouds hovered high over the city, bathing its white colonial buildings in soothing hues of pink. Large clay pots, once used by Camagüey's inhabitants to collect rainwater long ago, now decorated courtyards and city streets as remnants of the past.

After checking into the Gran Hotel and showering, they met for an early dinner at the hotel's restaurant, which still retained the semblance of decadent elegance from pre-revolutionary days. Located on the fifth floor, it offered a good view of the city below. David hoped the setting would brighten Catalina's mood.

He was disappointed. A large banquet hosted for Cuban and foreign agronomists was going on, making the restaurant too noisy, too bright, and too crowded for an intimate conversation. Service was also annoyingly slow even by Cuban communist standards. David tried to make small talk over their drinks, a watery daiquiri for her and a beer for him. Later, they ate their overcooked, dried-out beef steaks mostly in silence. He looked forward to the end of the meal and their departure.

***

Once outside, Catalina reluctantly agreed to a leisurely stroll along Avenida Agramonte and down Independencia to the Parque Ignacio Agramonte. A large equestrian statue of Ignacio Agramonte, Camagüey's most famous hero, who had died fighting for Cuban independence in 1869, commanded the center of the park. Most of the park was dimly illuminated by the reflected lights of the city. The air was heavy with the fragrant scent of the park's lush gardens. A few couples sat here and there on park benches. David found an empty bench, partially hidden by ferns and trees, where he thought they could talk quietly without being readily seen or overheard.

"I think this is much better than the hotel, don't you?" he asked.

She agreed. "It's a lovely park. I've always liked Camagüey. It has a certain charm even though it's a big city."

After a few moments of idle conversation, which seemed to David to be going nowhere, he turned to her and asked, "What's wrong, Catalina? You've been distant the whole day and this evening as well."

"Have I?" she said absentmindedly. "I'm sorry."

"Come on, tell me what's going on in that beautiful head of yours."

She shook her head, which confused him even further as he didn't know whether she was simply shrugging off his compliment or rejecting his invitation to talk. She watched two couples stroll by, following them with her eyes until they had passed out of earshot.

"I guess I . . . I started having second thoughts about our conversation last night," she said aloud, sounding uncharacteristically unsure of herself. "And also about how I said goodnight to you."

"Why?" he asked, unable to comprehend her concern. "Your kiss certainly was innocent enough."

"It wasn't only the kiss. It was also that I confided so many personal things to you, a *norteamericano,* whom I barely know." She pursed her lips before going on. "Don't you see? Not only did I tell you everything about Ernesto and me, which I've never confided to anyone, I also told you how he felt about Fidel, Che, Raúl. I've never done that before. It wasn't right."

"But Catalina," he objected. "I promised you last night that I'd never repeat what you told me. Besides, I told you things about my marriage that were just as personal."

"I know and I was touched that you felt you could confide in me. But that's exactly what's bothering me. We shouldn't be on such personal terms."

"But what's wrong with that? I certainly feel closer to you because of our talk."

"Please, David, let's be realistic! We're in no position to become 'closer' as you put it. You're a *norteamericano*, a guest of my government—and I'm your guide on what's supposed to be an official tour." She fastened her eyes on him. "Don't you see?" Her voice held a plea for understanding. "I'm reproaching myself for having acted so immaturely, so unprofessionally. I shouldn't have let my feelings interfere with my position or my better judgment."

Seeing the way he was looking at her, she paused. Suddenly, she became more concerned than ever.

"I just can't afford to give you the wrong impression," she added quickly. "Or in any way lead you on. Do you understand what I'm trying to tell you?"

"Of course, though I'm not exactly happy about it." In reality, however, he was pleased because she had all but confessed that she had feelings for him, feelings that she couldn't suppress. That meant that it was no longer a childish fantasy on his part that she might become as attracted to him as he was to her. Still, he realized he had to be careful. He mustn't push her. She had to come to terms with her own feelings about him on her own.

***

David shifted the topic of their conversation to politics, thinking that a more intellectual discussion would afford them safer ground. But soon that discussion became more personal and heated than he had anticipated.

Their quarrel began when she queried him about his political activism as a university student. He knew that her question put him at a distinct disadvantage. He could never compete with her martyred lover, not even if he embellished whatever modest exploits he could claim for his youth—something he wouldn't do. And so, he began by simply telling her the truth: He had become radicalized by all the social and political currents that swept through the 1960s, especially by the free speech movement at Berkeley and later by the anti-war movement.

"So, were you one of those students with long hair and beards, smoking marijuana and engaging in . . . uh, what do you call it, 'free love'?" she asked.

"Whoa, there!" he protested. "I'm not sure I want to get into any lurid details about what I used to do when I was a good deal younger and wilder. No, the only thing I'll confess to is that, sure, I used to smoke pot as most college kids still do. For that matter, I'll occasionally smoke a joint, though not very often."

Her eyes flashed an unmistakable look of disapproval.

"I'm sure I was pretty outrageous in the eyes of lots of people," he hastened to add. "But being a young radical, I was opposed to the Establishment, to all forms of authority, to rules and regulations that were idiotic or hypocritical. And as far as I was concerned, smoking a joint was like drinking: If you smoke too much pot, you get stoned; if you drink too much you get drunk. Yet alcohol is legal in California and most states, whereas you can get arrested simply for possessing marijuana. It's ludicrous."

"Say what you like," she declared in a disapproving voice. "But I think that you're being decadent when you smoke marijuana."

"Decadent?" he exclaimed, stung by her reprimand. "At the risk of offending you, I really think you're being way too judgmental."

"Perhaps I *am* judgmental," she replied, having weighed his accusation. "But I can't accept the kind of behavior you describe. Even the reason for your student protesting sounds self-indulgent, frivolous."

"Do you mean to say that your world doesn't allow for people to be frivolous or non-conformists?"

"No, that's not it at all," she said slowly, pensively. "It's just that what you're saying reminds me of the selfish behavior of the bourgeoisie who lived here in Cuba prior to 1959. They didn't care one iota about the less fortunate people in our society. Now, thank goodness, they're in Miami, where they belong."

For a moment, he didn't respond. He thought of Gustavo, wondering whether her puritanical streak had led her to support the government's punishment of deviant writers, of homosexuals, as well. *"That really would spoil everything,"* he thought.

"I suppose that means that you're in favor of your government's

policy toward non-conformist intellectuals or so-called 'social deviants' like homosexuals?" he finally inquired in an innocent-sound-
ing voice.

"What do you mean?" she asked, looking at him inquiringly. He
couldn't decide whether she was scared or simply taken aback by
his question.

"You know," he said. "Like Heberto Padilla's public confession
three years ago. Or your government's hounding and jailing of other
dissident writers and especially homosexuals." He paused, studying
her reaction. "I'll tell you, frankly," he continued, no longer willing
to bite his tongue, "that kind of repression by your government is
really abhorrent to me. It's truly a blight on the revolution."

There was a long silence. Catalina had a strange expression on
her face, as if she were struggling for an answer.

"I, too, find it disturbing," she said finally. "One of the few arguments I ever had with Ernesto was over our government's policy of
arresting homosexuals and punishing writers and artists who weren't
revolutionary enough. You see, Ernesto agreed with Fidel that they
shouldn't be allowed to do anything that was outside the revolution. I didn't agree. I told him," she resumed quietly, looking squarely
at David, "that the revolution was strong enough to accept non-
conformity, whether in literature, the arts, or even sexual expression."

"I'm glad to hear you say that," he replied.

"Don't misunderstand me," she quickly corrected. "I have very
strong opinions, likes and dislikes, when it comes to how people
should behave. I'm not permissive about it. That's why I'm so critical of the Cuban bourgeoisie prior to the revolution." With a toss of
her head, she added, "And that's also why I detest all those amoral
people in your own country whom I've heard about."

"Like who for instance?"

"Like the hippies and baby boomers who are into drugs and sex
orgies. And then there's all the consumerism in your society, which
I find obscene when there's so much poverty, misery, and exploitation in the world."

"Look, even though you and I, for that matter, may not approve
of many of those aspects of American society, you're missing the
bigger picture . . . "

"Don't tell me that you're now going to become the objective
academic in order to defend what's indefensible about your society!" she broke in sarcastically.

"Hey, look," he exclaimed in exasperation. "You'd better get used to the fact that I *am* an academic. Maybe you're not accustomed to it, but I pride myself on trying to be an objective scholar. So, please, accept me for who I am." When she didn't respond to his outburst, he wondered whether the ghost of Ernesto would forever stand between them.

"You're not taking something into account in criticizing American society," he resumed in a calmer tone of voice. "You're forgetting that all the social ferment and lifestyles you dislike among American youth did help advance some progressive causes. Take civil rights, for instance. We still have a long way to go, but at least we've begun to make some headway."

"Well, I'm glad you acknowledge that racism still exists in your country," she interjected. "Believe me, I saw a lot of it when I was in Baltimore."

"Of course, racism exists," he conceded, doing his best to ignore her sarcasm. "However, at least we've made a start in civil-rights legislation. But this is my main point: Despite what you may think about their amoral ways, the baby boomers are the ones who should be applauded. They're the ones who led the struggle against both racial discrimination and the Vietnam War."

He waited for her response as the seconds passed, hoping she was weighing what he had said.

"All right, *Professor* Diamond," she finally replied in a tone that was neither mocking nor conciliatory. "I'll grant that you've made some good points that hadn't occurred to me. And I'll admit, too, that perhaps I was seeing things too much in black and white, probably because I haven't been in your country for over fifteen years."

"Well, I'm glad to hear that. Maybe we're not too far apart after all," he said, relieved. Still wondering why she had seemed so intent on picking an argument with him, he decided this might be a good time to head back toward the hotel before another disagreement ensued. To his surprise, however, she now seemed in no hurry to leave.

* * *

Leaning back against the park bench, stretching her legs, and making herself comfortable, Catalina turned to David and smiled as if she had something mischievous in mind.

"Well, now that we got that settled," she declared, "let's get back to what I asked you about in the first place: What did you do politically in your radical student days? And this time," she added with an impish grin, "I won't inquire into the other extracurricular activities that you engaged in when you were young and 'outrageous,' to quote you."

Though still wary, he told her about his participation in the anti-war marches, how he had campaigned for Senator Eugene McCarthy, and how he had gone to Chicago in 1968 to protest the Democratic Party's nomination of Hubert Humphrey. He related, too, how he had been caught up in the violent street protests after the Chicago police had charged the peaceful marchers. She listened intently as he spoke, waiting until a young couple had leisurely sauntered by before she commented.

"Ernesto used to say that what happened in Chicago helped Nixon defeat Humphrey because American voters reacted to all the turmoil in the streets. Was he right?"

"Yes, except that what happened in Chicago and afterward was a turning point in American politics. You see, Nixon and Kissinger realized that the American people would no longer support the war and that we had to get out. But besides that, Chicago opened the way for needed reforms within the Democratic Party. And sure enough, four years later, the American people finally got a chance to vote for a real progressive—Senator George McGovern, who was committed to pulling out of Vietnam."

"I know. Nevertheless, Nixon was reelected by a large majority."

"True enough. But less than three months later Kissinger signed the Paris Agreement calling for a cease-fire throughout Vietnam, Laos, and Cambodia—and he had to because of the mounting opposition to the war in the United States."

He waited for her to respond. But she remained pensive; she was in no hurry to reply.

"What I've never been able to comprehend," she said finally, turning to him with a quizzical expression, "is how such an anti-war movement could be tolerated when your country was at war."

"But that's how it *should* be, Catalina. We're supposed to have a democracy in the United States."

"Yes, I know." Again she paused reflectively. "But a few months ago I heard a lecture by a visiting Vietnamese official who said that neither the Vietminh nor the Vietnamese army won the war on the battlefields of Vietnam—that, in actuality, the war was won in the United States."

"Of course. But what are you driving at?"

"Simply that if Cuba were involved in a war somewhere, my government would never allow protesters to undermine the morale of our soldiers . . . "

"Catalina!" he interrupted hotly. "Our involvement in the Vietnam War was immoral! It was so completely contrary to everything my country is supposed to stand for. All I can say is, 'thank God that college students and progressive, decent people rose up to stop the war.' Christ! We weren't a Fifth Column, if that's what you're insinuating. We saved American as well as Vietnamese lives."

To his surprise, instead of responding to his outburst, she simply reached out and took his hand.

"Don't get so angry," she said in a soothing voice. "I admire what you and other Americans did. It was the right thing, the moral thing to do. What I was trying to tell you is that I've always been unable to understand how there could be such a strong anti-war movement in a country like yours, which is so imperialistic. It's a contradiction that I simply haven't been able to resolve."

***

He was scarcely listening to what she was telling him. He was only aware that she had slipped her hand into his. As a warm breeze began to rustle the leaves around them and stir the fragrant night air, he wanted to take her in his arms and kiss her. Instead, he looked at her and asked, "Catalina, what are we going to do?"

"What do you mean?"

He knew that what he said next and how he said it could keep alive their budding relationship—or terminate it abruptly.

"I don't know exactly how to say this," he answered slowly, choosing his words carefully. "I know that a while back you said you wanted our relationship to remain strictly professional. But it's obvious that there's something going on between us..."

Even before he had finished she withdrew her hand and sat up straight. Despite the darkness, he could see the disapproving frown, the annoyance in her eyes. He feared his chances were destroyed.

"Please don't spoil things, David," she said firmly. "We've been having such a good time on this trip up to this point, enjoying each other's company, all the good conversation, even when it became argumentative. It's been such a welcome change for me, and now . . . and now you're ruining it."

"Am I ruining it?" he asked after a moment's reflection. "No, I think I'm just being honest with you in stating the obvious—that at the very least we've become close friends. And I hope we'll draw closer still as our trip progresses . . . "

"Please, stop, David."

"But why . . . ?"

"Because you're complicating things, that's why," she retorted. "I've already told you I can't become involved with you. Yet, you continue to persist. You must stop!" She rose from the bench and walked hastily toward the street.

He caught up with her quickly and fell into step beside her. "I'll back off if you tell why you don't want to become involved with me. Is it because of Ernesto?"

Reaching the edge of the park, she stopped to face him, but waited for several people to pass before answering him.

"Ernesto is only part of it," she answered. Frowning, she looked away, as if she would prefer not to go on with the conversation. Then, looking directly into his engulfing blue eyes, she said, "You're right. Something has been going on between us, but it puts me in a dilemma. To be quite honest with you, you're the first man I've found even remotely interesting since Ernesto died. That's obviously why I've allowed our relationship to become more than professional. But it has also become increasingly clear to me that there can be no happy ending if we continue down this path."

He started to reply, but she held up her hand.

"I have to tell you something else. I'm also unsure about you, about whether you're really right for me. You're an American, with a different culture, with a different outlook on life. And you're very different from Ernesto and our mutual friend, who remains the only man I truly respect and trust."

"But don't you see?" David interjected quickly. "The only way I can gain your trust is for you to get to know me better."

"Perhaps. But that could take months, and by then you'll be gone."

"What you're not taking into account, Catalina, is that right now we're spending a lot of time together. By the end of this trip, we'll probably know each other better than most couples do after a month or two of seeing each other off and on." She didn't answer. "I'm not going to be coy with you. I'm very attracted to you. You're not only the most beautiful woman I've ever met, you're also terribly exciting intellectually and . . . "

"David, please!" she objected, putting her fingers to her lips to shush him. "Can't you understand that you're moving too fast right now? Don't you see that there would be all kinds of serious complications if we were to become more intimately involved?"

"I realize there could be problems, but they're not insurmountable."

"No!" she cried out impatiently. "You must listen to me. You're a *norteamericano*, here for only a short time before you leave to resume your life in your country. So you have nothing to lose by your involvement with me." She stopped to let her words sink in. "On the other hand," she continued, "I would be risking my career if I became involved with you. Life here would become impossible for me. I would perhaps even have to leave Cuba. However, I don't want to abandon my country. Besides, even if I should want to, Fidel would never give me permission to leave."

He wondered why she was so certain that Fidel wouldn't let her go. Before he could ask, she walked forward again quickly as if the hotel loomed as a safe haven.

"In the meantime," she said to him, over her shoulder, "I'm sure you don't want to spend the rest of your life here in Cuba. Right? So, no matter how we might feel toward one another, our situation is really impossible."

He felt momentarily defeated by her negativity, but at least she was talking. He refused to give up.

"Of course, there are big obstacles facing us," he said, catching up with her brisk pace. "But you mustn't write a script about all the bad things that might happen . . . "

"I'm not writing a script," she said, stopping short to face him. "I'm simply being realistic."

"Maybe, but you need to listen to your heart, Catalina. You, of all people, should know that after what you've experienced with Ernesto. Would you have given up all the joy, all the happiness you had with him, had you known he would soon die? I don't think so."

She kept on walking, determinedly, without replying. Seeing that no one on the street was close by, he reached out and took her by the arm, obliging her to stop. As she turned toward him, he caught a frightened, confused look in her eyes.

"Catalina," he said, gently holding her arm. "I don't know how all this will turn out. Maybe we'll just remain friends. Or maybe we'll become lovers. If that happens, then we'll have to find solutions to the problems you mentioned. But, in the meantime, please don't close your mind. Please don't hold yourself back on the assumption that the worst is going to happen. Please, listen to what your heart says."

***

13

Introspection

Leaning her body against the closed door, her heart pounding, Catalina heard David's muffled "goodnight." When they reached her hotel room, he had tried to embrace her, but she had avoided his kiss so that his lips only grazed her cheek. Pushing him away, she had retreated to the safety of her room.

Turning on the room's only light, she sank onto the bed. One thing was clear to her: This situation with David Diamond was moving much faster than she had wanted or anticipated.

***

She didn't understand herself. There were times when she felt an attraction to him. Was it simply physical? Not exactly, although after spending time with him she had to admit that he was better looking than she had originally thought. No. The attraction was also partly intellectual, partly political. Without doubt, she had more stimulating conversations with David than she had had with Ernesto. That the American was progressive, yet different from most foreign sympathizers of the revolution, also appealed to her. She could tell from his questioning of local officials regarding the *Poder Popular* that he was skeptical of Cuba's democratic prospects. And he had been forthright with her in condemning the persecution of intellectuals and *maricones*—a major point of disagreement between Ernesto and her.

At the same time, David's criticisms of the revolution's imperfections were from the perspective of the Left. That was an important, an essential point for her. Basically, in terms of his moral core, David was a man of the Left. And his critical stance was not limited to the revolution, as seen by the fact that he condemned his own country's policies toward Vietnam and Cuba.

Something else about him attracted her—his was an injured soul, just like hers. His wife's affair had scarred him, though not to the degree that Ernesto's death had left her forever with a deep wound. Yes, they shared a common bond.

"Besides that," she told herself, *"he's* simpatico *for a* norte-americano."* He was seldom boring. She discovered that he could be amusing, sometimes even in a self-deprecating way as when he had related how, as an undergraduate, he had once bungled a late-night escape from his dorm by accidentally tripping the fire alarm. She appreciated that warm, more human side to his personality. She also liked his seemingly genuine interest in her as a person, in her life story, in what she had to say, even when she disagreed with him. Yes, he treated her with respect—except for tonight when he tried to embrace and kiss her.

There were, of course, aspects of his character that she disliked. He still smoked marijuana, even if, as he said, infrequently. And then there was his permissiveness. He equivocated too much about morality, drugs, and self-indulgence in American society. In that respect, she observed that he was too much the objective academic—unlike Ernesto, who was so passionate and strong about his belief. *"And I need to see that in a man, I need to know where he stands,"* she thought.

The next item in her inventory was David's intellectual superiority, an irritating trait that had surfaced more than once during his discussions with local communist and *Poder Popular* officials, none of whom had his level of education. On such occasions he had assumed the role of the professor that he was, lecturing his Cuban hosts on the topic of democracy. In fact, the only time he had displayed true humility, she recalled, was at the Italian Embassy when Fidel had toyed with him in front of all the guests.

There was a certain irony in that, she observed with a smile, since it had taken Fidel, who himself scarcely knew the meaning of humility, to put David in his place. On the other hand, she doubted that David was as self-centered and uncaring toward women as was Fidel.

She well remembered years earlier when she had received the invitation from the *Comandante* to have dinner with him in one of his Havana apartments. Still an innocent twenty-one-year-old virgin, she wasn't unduly alarmed by the thought of dining alone with Cuba's supreme leader. Only after being mesmerized for two hours by the sheer brilliance and force of his talk on politics, history, and philosophy had she been abruptly disabused of her naïveté. Without warning, the *Comandante* had propositioned her, expecting she would be another easy conquest—one of countless women who had eagerly jumped into bed with him after his rise to power. Fortunately, she had kept her virginity intact, coming away wiser in the ways of the world. After that, the *líder máximo* was not quite the demigod she had imagined him to be.

No. David was not like Fidel, a man capable of loving only himself. But she wondered if David could give fully of himself. Could he love a woman totally and unconditionally? Ernesto had been that way, but there were few men in the world like him. *"And that's the trouble with David,"* she concluded. *"He's too much like other men. Tonight, he came on too strong, too abruptly—just as Fidel had years ago."*

Still, she couldn't deny the surge of excitement that had shot through her when he openly confessed his romantic interest. That wasn't like her. She had always considered herself different from most other women, always keeping her emotions in check. She was not one to be swept up and easily seduced by men—especially not charming Latin men with their honeyed words and, as was often the case, false promises. Such women who succumbed were weak. They were too ready to fall in love with love, without first making certain that their man truly loved them. The majority of men, she had learned, would say anything—including promising eternal love—if that would get a woman into bed with them. Her own father, she had discovered some years back, was that kind of man.

Ernesto was so atypical of Cuban men in that respect, she mused. He never gave her cause to doubt his word. What he said was what he felt, thought, and would do. Joaquín was like that, too. She could trust him, as she had trusted Ernesto. But she was not at all certain about David's motives.

She found him more erudite and sophisticated than Ernesto. She liked that. Still he didn't compare to the many Cuban and Latin men she had known when it came to charm, wit, and playfulness. Latin men could be outrageously flirtatious, yet not offensive; their banter, their way with words could make a woman feel feminine and special. Yes, although David Diamond tried, he lacked some of those qualities because he was so typically American. Ernesto could be serious, but he could also be passionate and romantic. And he had an endearing boyish charm . . .

Sighing, she realized what she was doing. She was comparing David to Ernesto! Even before meeting David, she had told herself it was time to leave Ernesto behind, to get on with her life. Again, as she had done so many times in the past with other men, she admonished herself for measuring David against her late lover. In any case, she wasn't at all sure that David was the man for her—much less that he could ever begin to fill the void in her life.

David's deficiencies aside, she had a more immediate problem to contend with. Their becoming lovers was entirely out of the question. She had listened to the bromides he had offered, ignoring his ignorance or naïveté, as he blithely discounted all the risks they would run, as well as the impossibility of their situation, if they became romantically involved. She knew that Fidel would never allow her to have an affair with a *norteamericano* like David, let alone allow her to leave Cuba with him. As it was, he had been jealous enough of Ernesto when he found out that she was in love with him. But at least Ernesto was part of his precious MININT. Because of that they were protected.

Joaquín had already warned her not to become involved with David. Had it been another man, that warning would have been enough to give her cause for concern.

"Then, why, Catalina," she asked aloud. "Why do you continue to lead David on? Why don't you make it clear to him that your relationship has to remain strictly on a professional plane?" She shook her head. Some kind of crazy chemistry was going on between them, and it wasn't based on the fact that she liked his looks, his politics, his compassion, or whatever other nice qualities he possessed.

It must simply be physical longing on her part she assured herself. Joaquín was right, after all, in commenting that she was drawn to David because she hadn't had a man for these many years. But she rejected that line of reasoning after she thought about it. She hadn't been searching for anything long-term after losing Ernesto; there would not be another man in her life, let alone marriage, at least not for the time being. That was it! Yes, and how perverse! The very fact that an affair with David would be fleeting largely explained why she was attracted to him. Once he was gone—and the initial passion spent—she would get over him, adjust to his absence, and thus escape any further emotional trauma in her life. She now realized that her aggressive, sometimes sarcastic attitude during the evening had been her way of trying to push him away from her—

and her away from him. It was all finally sorted out. Yet she was not about to be hurried into an affair, even if she decided to have one.

***

Sitting propped up in bed, David went over the events of the evening, berating himself for his argumentativeness, his awkward disclosures—and the kiss! Why did he force it?

Examining his feelings, which he wasn't often wont to do, he realized he had never felt this way toward another woman. To be sure, he had lusted after those who were sexy, smart, and great in bed, like Julie and Cindy. But what he felt for Catalina wasn't simply lust, at least not in the primeval sense of the word. His whole being was affected by her—emotionally, intellectually, as well as physically—in ways he still couldn't quite comprehend.

Sometimes it was the throaty way she said his name that would suddenly make his heart skip. Other times it was her tantalizing smile that made him go all wobbly like a smitten schoolboy. Or, then again, it was the gleeful look that would steal over her face, foretelling her girlish delight in something she was about to say or do.

He wanted to believe that it was more than infatuation with her. She had evoked something in him more profound. Was it passion? Definitely! But a passion that was tempered by a growing sense of love and caring.

Of course, he realized she was less than perfect. She could be extremely rigid and judgmental at times, especially when it came to those aspects of American life that she didn't like. And it was clear as hell that she didn't at all approve when he had mentioned that he still occasionally smoked pot. She could also be rather argumentative, and she had a quick temper—qualities he sometimes found irritating but which, upon reflection, added spice to her personality. *"Be truthful,"* he thought, smiling. *"You really liked it when she stood up to you and fired back."*

He was hooked; he knew it. And he was aware also of the daunting obstacles he would face in trying to court her. In the first place, he wasn't at all certain that she really felt anything toward him. Sometimes she seemed to be leading him on only to pull back, which is what she had done earlier in the day, and again this evening. Her ambivalence about him created another problem—time. Only three or four days remained before their return to Havana, when they would go their separate ways. He wasn't at all sure he could woo her in so short a period. Despite her disarming openness, an inner reserve sometimes rose up as an impenetrable barrier between them.

Utterly perplexed, he wondered if she saw something in him that she didn't like. Perhaps she was right in saying that part of the problem was his being a *norteamericano*. But, instinctively, he felt that the problem had less to do with him than with Ernesto. And, if that were the case, *"how in the hell,"* he questioned, *"can I ever compete with a dead man?"*

The more he ruminated, the more he found fault with his behavior. She had told him in the park to slow down, not to get his hopes up. Yet he had gone right ahead and moved too fast, too openly. Besides that, he had been far too dismissive of her fears about the risks that a romantic involvement with him would entail.

"Christ Almighty," he reproached himself. *"I can't go after her like some chick back in L.A. If we were to get caught having an affair, the worst that might happen to me is that I'd get booted out of the country. But her whole life could be ruined."* He would have to exercise caution for her sake, which might mean that he would have to be ready to pull back if it looked like she was in danger.

In that respect, he would have to start thinking seriously what would be in store for them over the long-run if she were to fall in love with him. She was right, of course, in pointing out that he wouldn't want to remain permanently in Cuba. *"Hell, I'd become as cynical and unhappy as Philip Taylor if I had to stay here."* No. Short of her leaving the island to join him, which appeared highly unlikely, the only solution would be for him to return periodically to Cuba on extended visits—provided, of course, that their romance would be condoned by the government. But such an arrangement wouldn't be good either. It would be hard, if not impossible, to maintain a long-distance relationship when it was difficult to travel back and forth to Cuba. And it could place him at the beck and call of the Cuban government, obliging him to tow its political line for fear of being denied a visa. It didn't look good for them. But what else could he do? Quite plainly he was falling in love with her.

***

Catalina slept fitfully that night, waking several times to the sound of the traffic and other street noises. It was after three when she finally slipped into a deep sleep, awakening in a near stupor four hours later to the insistent ringing of her alarm clock. After showering, and taking an unexpected call from local Party headquarters, she went upstairs to the hotel restaurant. David was already waiting at a table by the window. The morning outside was bright and fresh.

He had taken the liberty of ordering coffee and rolls, which arrived a few minutes after she seated herself. She took her time pouring the hot milk into her coffee, stirring in two heaping teaspoons of coarse, unbleached sugar, and took several sips of her *café con leche*, before turning her attention to her companion.

Much to her surprise, David appeared relaxed and cheerful, as if nothing had happened the previous night. She suspected he hoped she would say something encouraging, but she had more immediate matters to discuss.

"I'm afraid I've got bad news," she announced in a business-like tone. "I was just informed by the First Party Secretary that his people are going to be tied up all morning. So we've had to cancel your interview session for this morning. Perhaps we can reschedule the meeting for Saturday afternoon on our way back from Santiago de Cuba, but I wouldn't count on it. I hope this doesn't set you back too much."

He shrugged noncommittally. "Obviously, it would be best if I have an interview from Camagüey since it is Cuba's third largest city," he said. "But if it doesn't work out I guess I'll be all right if I can complete my other interviews."

"I'll do my best to make sure we don't have further cancellations." She looked at her watch. "If we leave before nine o'clock, we should be able to reach Holguín before noon, in plenty of time for your next meeting. The First Party Secretary should be there, along with city government officials. We'll have lunch with all of them afterward. In the end, you'll have more time for questions than you would have had originally."

"That's good," he replied cheerfully. Almost too cheerfully she thought.

"Anyway, we need to leave Holguín by three in order to arrive in Santiago de Cuba around five or five-thirty. The distance is fairly short, but sections of the road are under repair, so we may be slowed down."

"You're the boss, Catalina," he replied. "So you set the pace."

"Your first interview in Santiago de Cuba is scheduled for six," she continued, wondering if there was a double meaning to his remark. "That should give us enough time to check into the hotel first. It's the Casa Grande. It's right in the heart of the city. Though it's an old hotel, it's pleasant and convenient. You can also see the bay from the upper floors."

"Sounds perfect." Again, he was acting too accommodating. She eyed him curiously, trying to discern what he was up to, but she saw only a bright, innocent look on his face.

"Good," she said. "Now, Friday is going to be a busy day. I've scheduled three more meetings with local Party and municipal officials in the morning and late afternoon. In between, there'll be a tour of the Moncada Barracks, which is on the outskirts of the city. Then we'll leave early Saturday morning in order to return to Havana by Sunday afternoon."

"You know, I would just as soon skip the Moncada Barracks. That would give me the opportunity to extend my interview sessions."

"I guess we could do that."

"It would sure make a hell of a lot of sense, Catalina, because I've already seen the Moncada Barracks. Our group was given a complete tour when I first came here in 1968. The guide showed us where Fidel and his men began their attack on July 26, 1953. Then he explained in great detail how the battle raged and why the assault, even though it failed, signaled the start of the revolution. I'll bet I remember enough of the tour to conduct it myself."

"You're probably right," she answered with a hint of a smile on her lips. "We can drop the tour if you need some extra time for your meetings. But let's wait and see."

Watching him toy absentmindedly with his roll, she felt as if they were performing some kind of intricate dance between the sexes. He appeared to be waiting for the right cue before asking her whether she had given more thought to what he had proposed the night before. She decided to take the initiative.

Dropping her business-like tone, she said, "David, I didn't sleep well last night. I was thinking about what you said."

"I didn't sleep well, either," he admitted, looking up from his plate. "But before you go any further, I want to apologize for my boorish behavior. I don't know what came over me." His apology took her by surprise. For an instant she questioned his contrition, but something in his eyes told her it was genuine. She wondered what had caused this sudden change of behavior.

"I accept your apology," she said. "But I have to reiterate that our situation hasn't changed. As I said last night, I need time—much more time."

"I'm aware of that, I really am."

"Good."

"However, I'm also worried that our time together is running out."

"What do you mean?" she asked suspiciously.

"We have only a few more days by ourselves," he explained, his eyes now fixed steadily on hers. "By next Sunday, we'll be back in Havana, where just trying to see each other will really become complicated."

"What you don't seem to understand, David, is that it will *always* be complicated, irrespective of where we are."

"I know that, Catalina. Believe me, I really do."

"So, what's the hurry . . . ?"

"Because this is the perfect opportunity for us to get to know each other without running the kind of risks you're worried about. Right now, we have your government's permission to be with each other. We're traveling together and staying in the same hotel. We're free to have dinner together and talk as we please." Pausing for a moment, he glanced around to be certain no one could overhear him. "And let me tell you one more thing," he continued, lowering his voice to a barely audible whisper. "You may be thinking that I'm trying to get you into bed while we're on this trip. Well, despite what I did last night, let me assure you that's not the case. I have too much respect for you to try that."

She gave him a dubious look before dropping her eyes.

"Believe me, Catalina, the only thing I want right now is for you to get to know me better, after which we'll see what happens. That's all I ask."

If he was sincere, then he really wasn't asking all that much, she thought. She still feared where it all might end. But in reality the shortness of their time together was her ally.

"I know that you want to hurry things, but I won't be rushed. I need time," she said in a firm voice.

"Of course you do. In the meantime, I promise to be on my best behavior during our remaining days together. Honest."

"I'll believe it when I see it," she said, smiling for the first time. Serious again, she added, "Please be careful. You mustn't give Juan or anyone else reason to suspect that something is going on between us."

***

Everything had gone splendidly for David until their arrival in Santiago de Cuba late that afternoon. The long working lunch with Holguín officials had proved to be the best meeting yet of his entire visit, and Catalina had played no small part in its success, charming Party and municipal government officials with her looks and repartee. *"What a difference she makes,"* he thought to himself, after watching her perform. *"Christ! If Marina had been there, the meeting would have turned into a disaster."*

Having departed Holguín in high spirits, he remained true to his word, observing decorum while in her company. As they headed southbound on the Carretera Central, toward Santiago de Cuba and the Caribbean Sea, he amused her with stories of his childhood, sometimes exaggerating or embroidering his antics for humorous effect. Once, after telling a joke in which he was the butt, Catalina had laughed so hard that Juan—who didn't understand much English— glanced in the rearview mirror to see if he could discern what was so funny.

As they neared Santiago de Cuba, Catalina had ordered Juan to stop the car. They had gotten out, David thought, to stretch their legs. Instead, she stood close to him to point out the distant ridge of mountains to the east. It was the Sierra Maestra, where Fidel and his small band of rebels had commenced waging their guerrilla war against the Batista government nearly eighteen years earlier. "That's where the new Cuba was conceived," she told him in an almost reverent voice.

***

They checked into the Casa Grande in time for David's six o'clock interview. Waiting at the hotel desk was a message for Catalina to call her supervisor immediately. She directed David to proceed alone to the interview, which was being held in the Ayuntamicnto, just up the street and on the other side of the Parque Céspedes. He couldn't miss the neoclassical town hall. She would join him later. She never did.

Returning to the Casa Grande after seven, he called her room. Her voice told him immediately that something was wrong. He didn't accept her excuse that she would inform him later what the problem was. He hung up and rushed down the hall to her room. She let him in, but she made a point of leaving the door ajar.

"What's happened?" he demanded.

"I was going to tell you at dinner," she said. "I'm afraid I've got bad news. I've been instructed to return to Havana tomorrow morning by air. The Ministry wants me to escort a French delegation that's arriving on Sunday."

"What? I can't believe this!"

"Well, I'm afraid it's true. I've got to go back. You're to go through with your scheduled meetings tomorrow. You don't really need me there. Then, you can either drive back to Havana with Juan on Saturday or you can take a flight back to the capital, which I can arrange before I leave."

David couldn't think straight. The only thing he knew was that all his hopes and dreams of spending three more intimate evenings with Catalina were now dashed.

"Couldn't you ask your supervisor for at least one more day?" His disappointment was obvious.

"I did. But she was adamant that I must be back by Friday noon to make all the arrangements for the delegation. There was no way I could argue with her."

"Damn! Just when things were going so well."

"David, these things happen, you know. So, please don't act so upset. It's not the end of the world."

But he *was* upset, and even a bit annoyed with her business-like demeanor.

"You don't seem to be too disappointed," he remarked.

"Of course I'm disappointed, but it can't be helped. Besides, I've had more than an hour in which to reconcile myself to the news." She started to the door in a gesture of seeing him out, saying as she went, "Now, what you have to decide is whether you want to drive back to Havana or take a plane Saturday morning."

"I'll take the plane, of course. I don't want to spend two days driving back with Juan if you're not with me," he replied angrily.

"Damn! This just ruins everything!"

"David, come on now," she coaxed. "Don't spoil things." She reached out and touched his arm. "Let's try to have a good time on this last night together, like we did this afternoon after leaving Holguín. You were the charming, amusing David Diamond I was expecting to be with on this trip."

"All right," he relented. "But just answer one question honestly. Are you really disappointed that you're leaving tomorrow?"

She reflected for several moments before answering him. Then, still serious, she raised her eyes and said, "To be totally honest, my head tells me that I should feel relieved because our situation was becoming too complicated." She paused as a mischievous smile formed on her lips, her eyes suddenly gleaming. "But I must confess, that my heart is heavy because I know I will miss you."

***

A half-hour later they walked to the restaurant where Catalina had made dinner reservations. It was located on Calle Aguilera, several blocks from the Casa Grande, near the Plaza de Dolores. Situated upstairs, the establishment was small and intimate, unlike any government-run restaurant David had seen. He suspected that, like the Hotel Ancón in Trinidad, it was for the exclusive use of the *nomenklatura* and foreign dignitaries. If so, Catalina had probably had to exaggerate his importance and pull rank to get them in.

After a round of daiquiris, they were served a superbly cooked grouper with *Moros y Cristianos* and plantains on the side. Their conversation remained as lighthearted as on their drive from Holguín. They left the restaurant shortly before ten o'clock, casually strolling back along Calle Aguilera in the direction of the hotel and the bay beyond.

As she walked close to him, he sometimes felt her brushing against him; whether it was deliberate or inadvertent, David couldn't tell. It was then that the realization hit him full force: They probably would never see each other again after her departure in the morning. He had to talk to her one last time.

Walking past the Casa Grande, they entered the Parque Céspedes. Instead of taking one of the empty park benches, he guided her toward an immense *ceiba* tree, its heavy limbs and leaves casting dark shadows upon the ground. It was a secluded spot. What people were in the park were either sitting on benches or strolling elsewhere.

"Let's stop here for a second. I want to tell you something," David said when they were safely enshrouded beneath the *ceiba*'s foliage. Even in the darkness he could see her questioning glance. "I just want to say that I've enjoyed every minute of our trip together," he began. He gently took her hands in his. "But more importantly, because of you I've looked at myself and I've changed for the better as a result." He paused momentarily, at a loss for appropriate words. "I don't know what else to tell you," he said awkwardly, "except that I'm going to miss you."

"I'll miss you, too," she said simply.

"Catalina?"

"Yes?"

"Would you allow me a good-bye kiss? No one can see us."

Despite the darkness, he could see her eyes widen with alarm. Several seconds passed. Was she weighing his request? She hadn't immediately turned him down—a good sign.

"Don't worry," he said reassuringly. "It will be just a token kiss, to remind you of the good times we've had together."

"All right," she agreed, her lips parting expectantly as she faced him with closed eyes. He kissed her lightly on the mouth. She opened her eyes, surprised, perhaps even disappointed, by the brevity of his kiss. Then he pulled her closer and kissed her again, this time more fully on her still parted lips, which were soft and moist. Her kiss was as sweet as he had imagined it would be. Holding her tightly against him, he could smell her freshly washed hair, her lightly scented body. She didn't attempt to pull away.

Again he kissed her, this time longer and more deeply. For an instant, he thought he felt her body shudder. Then, abruptly, she put her hands on his chest and pushed him away.

"*¡No más, David, por favor!*" she said breathlessly. "That was more than a good-bye kiss! You're shameless, you're a *sinvergüenza* after all!" Her words were scolding, but there was no bite to them. For a second or two she looked undecided. "*Por favor,*" she said at last. "Behave yourself like you promised you would."

"I'm sorry," he replied, gazing longingly at her. "It's just that your leaving tomorrow has changed everything. All of a sudden, I realize that our time together had run out. I needed to kiss you . . . "

She wasn't listening. She had spun around and started back toward the Casa Grande.

***

Within seconds he was beside her, matching her purposeful and rapid stride. She was flustered and refused to look at him as they walked. Her heart was pounding, but not from walking. Desire had welled up inside her the moment his lips touched hers. She was determined not to let him near her room once they reached the hotel.

"O.K., Catalina," she heard him saying. "You're right, I was out of line—again. And again I apologize."

Too angry to accept his apology, she ignored him and kept on walking. "*Are all* norteamericanos *tan atrevidos?*" she wanted to shout. "*Are they all so forward and inconsiderate?*"

"Would you slow down and talk to me? I don't want our trip to end badly. I don't want to be to blame for having ruined our last night together."

"Well, that's exactly what you've done!" she snapped.

"Look, I'm sorry I've upset you," he said, keeping pace with her. "But we just can't end this way, Catalina. Not only will it end our friendship, it will prevent us from ever finding out whether we could have become closer had we had more time . . . " He was frustrated. But at least there were few people on the street to overhear them quarreling. "Please. I want to see you again," he pleaded. "I want to see you after we're back in Havana."

"That's impossible!" she exclaimed, stopping abruptly to look at him. "Unless I'm assigned as your guide again, I won't have an official reason to see you. And I surely won't have an excuse to meet you at the Habana Libre, or anywhere else, for that matter."

"I could come over to your apartment after dark . . . " he ventured.

"Are you insane?" Her eyes flashed in anger. "Don't you realize that people in my neighborhood, my apartment, might see you? Some of the members of the *Comité de Defensa* on my block are real busybodies. They take their responsibilities seriously during their night watch. They're always on the lookout for strangers or any suspicious goings-on in the neighborhood."

"I know, I know. But I would be extremely careful, I promise," he affirmed. "I would make sure I wasn't seen. Believe me, I'd steer clear of your apartment if I thought I was endangering you." Realizing he finally had her attention, he lowered his voice. "But it's not up to me," he added, looking deeply into her eyes. "I'll only come if you give me permission."

She didn't answer. She felt pulled in opposite directions. There was no question she would be relieved if he didn't come. That way there would be no risks, whether immediate or later on, and there would be no further complications. She could go on with her life as before. However, she knew she would be disappointed if she didn't see him again. *"Maybe late at night,"* she conceded, *"he could come to the apartment without being seen."* This indecisiveness was uncharacteristic of her. She hated it.

"It would be madness," she finally told him, shaking her head, but her voice lacked conviction. She avoided looking him in the eye.

He sensed that she was wavering. This was the moment to assure her that he would be careful, but suddenly he was struck by how terrible it would be if something went awry. Her life could be destroyed. He had to be more than careful.

"Catalina," he said quietly. "You can be sure I'll take every possible precaution if I come. I'm the last person in the world who wants to see any harm come to you. Can't you see? I've fallen in love with you."

She was at a loss for words. She was frightened, yet excited by his words.

"Unless you tell me not to, I'll come Saturday night. I'll wait until after ten," he announced. "And I won't even come near your apartment house unless I'm certain that the coast is clear."

***

14

Rendezvous

The more Joaquín talked, the angrier—and more worried—Catalina became. She had rushed back to Havana on Friday, the day before, only to learn that there would be no French delegation for her to escort on Sunday. Her recall had been ordered, her supervisor at the Foreign Ministry had coldly informed her, by MININT Captain Joaquín Acosta, and she couldn't—or wouldn't—tell her anything more. Catalina had then tried to reach Joaquín at his office, and again at his home Friday night and all day Saturday, but to no avail. Now, here he was at her apartment a few minutes before ten on Saturday night, uninvited, seated calmly on her living-room sofa, insisting that what he had done was for her own good.

What Joaquín was now telling her was even worse than the recall. He informed her that, when he learned that she was with Diamond en route to Santiago de Cuba, he had ordered both of them placed under surveillance. The subsequent report that he received from a State Security agent in Camagüey indicated that she had seemed unusually "cordial"—he emphasized the word with a disapproving look—toward the American professor. As a consequence, the next day, he directed her boss at MINREX to recall her to Havana under whatever ruse she wanted to use. She was to get Catalina out of Santiago de Cuba and away from Diamond as quickly as possible.

Catalina felt violated. Her private life had been invaded and exposed. She had been spied upon by a stranger, who had then reported back to Joaquín. Perhaps there was already a file on her in MININT. Then her anger was quickly replaced by anxiety. The more she thought about what Joaquín had done, the more worried she became about all the possible ramifications of the surveillance.

A stream of questions raced through her mind. Why was MININT after David? Was he delving into sensitive matters? Worse yet, was he working for the CIA? Was Joaquín simply going after David because of his loyalty to Ernesto's memory? Or was he simply motivated by his intense dislike for *norteamericanos?* What exactly had his field agents witnessed? Had they seen the long embrace and kiss she and David had shared on their last night together in Santiago de

Cuba? She thanked God that at least she had had the good sense to phone the Habana Libre earlier in the evening, leaving a cryptic but emphatic message telling David not to come. Otherwise, Joaquín would have discovered them together in her apartment.

***

Standing in a darkened entryway across the street from Catalina's apartment, David felt that the Gods were smiling down on him. The threatening black clouds overhead had left the neighborhood shrouded in darkness. The street was deserted. And he hadn't seen anyone from the *Comité de Defensa de la Revolución* making their rounds.

He had left the hotel early, taking a circuitous route, alternating cabs and buses with walking, before finally arriving outside her apartment shortly before ten. He could see that she was home from the shadows that now and then flitted across her lighted, second-story living room. Lights were on in the two ground-floor apartments, indicating that he would have to get past two occupied apartments before going upstairs. The apartment above hers also had its lights on. He thought it less likely that he would encounter anyone coming down at this hour.

He checked his watch again. It was already past ten-fifteen. Seeing that the coast was clear, he casually walked across the street, past the late 1960s Alfa-Romeo that was parked in front of her apartment building. Moments later, he was in the building's poorly lighted hallway. Moving stealthily past the ground-level apartments with their blaring music, he reached the stairway and quickly made his way to the second floor, to the door of Catalina's apartment.

He was about to knock softly when he heard muffled voices from inside. He froze. Although he couldn't make out what was being said, he recognized one of the voices as Catalina's. The other was a lower-pitched voice—a man's voice, for sure. Catalina and the unidentified man appeared to be arguing, but he couldn't understand what they were saying.

On a hunch, he moved down the hallway to the open window at the front of the building. He was in luck. The voices wafted out through the open balcony door of Catalina's apartment. The man's voice sounded familiar. He strained to hear. It was Captain Joaquín

Acosta who was talking! He felt as though he had been punched in the solar plexus.

***

"Catalina," Joaquín said. "It was for your own good."

"Please stop treating me like a child!" she exclaimed. "You had no right to spy on me! And that's exactly what you did when you ordered your men to place David and me under surveillance!"

"*¡Por Dios, niña!* You know that I had every right to do whatever is necessary to safeguard the security of the state."

"*¡No me digas mierda, Joaquín!* Don't give me that shit! You don't have that right, not with me, especially when you won't tell me why I should stay away from him."

"You know I'm not allowed to tell you."

"I don't believe you!" she cried. "No. I think you persist in coming between us out of some misguided sense of loyalty to Ernesto. Or maybe it's because you dislike all *norteamericanos*, no matter where their sympathies lie, whether with the revolution or not!"

"If I were you, I wouldn't be so sure about where his true sympathies lie . . ."

"What do you mean by that?"

"*Chica*, you know I can't divulge anything that involves sensitive intelligence matters. I've already broken the rules by coming here to warn you to drop this David Diamond."

"Is he working for the CIA? At least tell me that. That's the only reason I would immediately do what you ask. But if he's not, then I don't want you to interfere any more in my private life."

"*Niña*, please use your head!" Joaquín exclaimed in exasperation. "If I knew he was working for the CIA, do you think I would be able to tell you?"

Hearing this, David had the sinking sensation that the floor had been snatched from under him. He leaned against the wall a moment to steady himself.

"You can't fool me, Joaquín," Catalina said. "If you were convinced that David was CIA, you would tell me about it one way or the other to protect me. I know you too well."

"Yes, you're right," Joaquín conceded, his voice so low that David was barely able to hear. "I would do everything in my power to make sure that no harm came to you. But you, on the other hand, refuse to listen to me."

There was a long silence. David waited, tensely, aware that he had begun to perspire.

"Don't you understand?" Joaquín continued in a normal tone of voice. "My mere presence here should be enough warning for you to stay clear of Diamond. Don't you realize that if you get involved with him, and he *is* mixed up with the CIA, I won't be able to lift a finger to help you?"

David could hardly believe the conversation he was overhearing. He could only conclude that Rudy García had fouled up—or, even worse, that the CIA officer had deliberately compromised him in order to play some game with the Cubans. In either case, he was screwed. Joaquín was now after him, and Catalina would definitely want no further contact with him.

"I appreciate your concern, Joaquín," Catalina said in a weary, faraway voice. "I really do. But now I think you'd better go. I need to get some rest and think about all this with a clear head."

There was a moment of silence before David heard Joaquín give what sounded like a long sigh of resignation.

"You're right, *niña*," the MININT Captain replied. "I've said all that I had to say. The rest is up to you. So, I'll leave now. But watch yourself. Good night."

Realizing that Joaquín would see him once he stepped into the hallway, David raced back to the stairwell just as Joaquín opened the door. There wasn't enough time for him to go down the stairs and exit the building without being seen or heard, so he bounded silently up the stairs to the third floor, arriving there unseen just before Joaquín began his descent to the street.

His heart pounding from his narrow escape, David flattened himself against the wall and held his breath. A car was starting. The four-cylinder engine was being gunned by the driver. Of course! It was Joaquín in the Alfa-Romeo! He remembered once having read that Fidel had imported the Alfas a few years back to see whether they could replace the aging fleet of Oldsmobiles used for trips around the island. But Fidel and his security detail found them too small and underpowered. Some of the discarded Alfas must have found their way to the MININT car pool.

With relief he heard the Alfa roar off. The rush of adrenaline left him as quickly as it had come, leaving him suddenly drained. He felt ill. He had to think. What should he do? He couldn't remain safely where he was much longer.

***

As soon as Joaquín started down the hallway, Catalina closed the door and leaned heavily against it, partly from exhaustion, partly from relief that he was finally gone. Spying on her! She was furious. But even more she was frightened by his insistence that she distance herself from David Diamond. She tried to reassure herself with the thought that at least Joaquín had not charged David outright with working for the CIA. Still, her involvement with him was far riskier than she had ever imagined.

She had to count her blessings. She had been exceedingly fortu-nate thus far. The trip could have ended in disaster if MININT agents had witnessed their embrace and kiss in the Parque Céspedes. But Joaquín had mentioned only the previous night in Camagüey. For some inexplicable reason she and David had escaped surveillance in Santiago de Cuba. She hoped she had averted an even more disas-trous situation by leaving a warning hours earlier at David's hotel.

She retired to her bedroom and, undressing, slipped into the white silk kimono that Ernesto had given her before he had left for Central America. In the bathroom, she splashed cold water on her face, hop-ing it would clear her head and settle her down.

Returning to the living room she closed the door to the balcony. It was then that she heard the soft tap on her front door. For an instant, she thought Joaquín had returned. Then her heart stopped. She knew who it was.

Opening the door, she saw an ashen-faced David. He burst imme-diately into the living room.

"Jesus!" he exclaimed. "I thought you'd . . . you'd never open the damn door!"

"*Por Dios*, David, what are you doing here?" she exclaimed, clos-ing the door quickly. "Didn't you get my message not to come? You could have been seen!" A hard lump lodged in her throat.

"I don't know anything about a damn message," he replied an-grily. "I left the hotel early. But you needn't worry. No one saw me—not even your buddy, Captain Acosta."

"You were here . . . ?"

"You bet I was! I was here, all right, long enough to hear the two of you discussing me." He looked at her accusingly, his large blue eyes brimming with anger and suspicion.

"What the hell is going on, Catalina?" he demanded. "What's Joaquín to you? I've got a right to know, damn it! From what I heard a few minutes ago it sounds like my whole fucking life is on the line!"

After Joaquín's warning, she should send him away, but she held back. She was determined to learn the truth.

"Before I can tell you anything," she said, lowering her voice, "you've got to tell me whether you're mixed up with the CIA."

"Christ! Don't you know me better than that by now?" His face flushed red with anger. "Do you think that after Guatemala, the Bay of Pigs invasion, and other plots against the revolution, and now after the overthrow and murder of Allende, that I would have anything to do with the CIA? Come on, now!"

"That sounds like a political speech, David—and a well-rehearsed one at that." She saw a look of disbelief cloud his eyes. Obviously, he hadn't expected her biting antagonism. "Do you really think that just because you say something, I'm going to believe you?" she asked in a voice laced with sarcasm. "Well, I have news for you: I'm not one of your gullible, doting American students! You're going to have to prove to me that you're not with the CIA."

"I am *not* a CIA agent. You've got to believe me. I despise what the CIA has done, what it stands for. I'm telling you the truth."

"That's not enough."

"For God's sake, Catalina! There's no way in hell that I can prove that I have no ties to the CIA. You're asking me for the impossible— to prove a negative."

She didn't reply. Her inquiring eyes searched his face for the truth. She was sure his eyes would not lie to her.

"You swear that you have no connection?"

"Absolutely no connection. None whatsoever," he said, but his glance flickered, and with a rush of fear in her chest her doubts returned again.

Moving away from the door, he quickly surveyed the room with its closed balcony door.

"I'm going to tell you something that I've not mentioned to anybody," he said, turning to face her. He paused, clearly uncomfortable with what he was about to say. "A few weeks before coming to Cuba, a man from the Agency contacted me while I was in Washington . . . "

"You met with a CIA agent?" she hissed. Joaquín had been right after all. Whether from fright or repulsion, she shrank back, enlarging the distance between them.

"Please!" he pleaded. "Please, hear me out! At first, I didn't know who he was or what he wanted. He approached me right after I presented a paper at a conference. He said that it was important for us to talk because I might be able to do something that could help restore more normal relations between the United States and Cuba."

"He was from the CIA and he said this?" Confused, her mind couldn't accept what he was telling her. "That makes no sense at all. I mean, why would the CIA ask you for help in restoring relations with Cuba?"

"I know it sounds crazy, but he claimed the U.S. Government was receiving mixed signals from Cuba about the possibility of normalizing relations. He said I could be of help in establishing whether or not the Cuban overtures were serious."

"Oh, David, don't tell me you agreed to cooperate with him even though you knew he was CIA." Her voice caught in her throat again.

"Please, Catalina, you don't understand. At first, I didn't suspect he was a CIA official. He claimed he was from the State Department. He even showed me his State ID. So, thinking that I might be able to serve as a go-between for our two governments, I agreed to meet him the next day. It was only then, after we had rendezvoused at our meeting place that I became convinced he was CIA."

"Why?"

"Because he tried to get me to agree to a debriefing after my return from Cuba. I was to tell him everything I learned in regard to what Cuban leaders were thinking concerning a possible accommodation with the United States."

"In other words," she said slowly, her eyes narrowing, "he was asking you to spy by providing him with intelligence information."

"That's exactly what I told him!" David exclaimed. "When he tried to convince me otherwise, I broke off our conversation." He saw the tense lines of her face relax slightly. There was a chance she believed him. "I walked out on him, Catalina. I told him to go fuck himself! I swear!"

She remained silent, quietly searching his eyes and face for signs that he was lying. She was inclined to believe his story. Somehow, it rang true if only because he needn't have told her about the incident. The more she considered what allegedly had happened, the more convinced she became that he was telling her the truth.

"All right," she finally said, extending her hand in a peace gesture. "I believe you."

He gave a deep sigh of relief. "Thank you," he said, his eyes misting. "Now, please tell me what's going on."

"It's a long story," she added, taking him by the hand and leading him to the sofa.

Sitting, she examined their intertwined hands and it struck her suddenly that her whole life was turning upside down. She felt a renewed fear, aware that she was about to reveal another secret to this *norteamericano* who could yet pose a danger to her, particularly now that he was being watched by Joaquín's men.

* * *

"When we were in Trinidad," she began, her voice low and husky. "I told you about Ernesto and me, but nothing about Joaquín. Until Fidel and a few others in the government learned of our relationship, only our parents knew about it as you'll understand in a moment." She paused to look at him, her normally vibrant green eyes now suddenly serious, somber. "You must promise me that what I tell you will remain a secret."

"I promise, of course," he replied quickly, certain that he knew already what she was about to tell him. "*Either she and Joaquín became lovers after Ernesto died or he's in love with her and that's why the bastard is after me.*"

"Joaquín is my half-brother," she said simply.

"What?" he asked, as if startled out of a stupor.

"Yes, it's true. I didn't find out until eight years ago. My parents—or, more accurately, my father, because he ordered my mother not to say anything—concealed the fact from me. I only learned of it because of my father's rage at Joaquín and at me, also."

"I don't understand. Is Joaquín your mother's son?"

"No. He's my father's illegitimate son." Pausing, she withdrew her hand from his and turned to face him. As she crossed her legs, the corner of her white kimono slipped, revealing part of her thigh. David had difficulty keeping his eyes from straying.

"My father was a successful lawyer here in Havana before the revolution," she continued, oblivious to his distraction. "He was a partner in one of the country's largest *bufetes*—you know, a law firm—that had a roster of wealthy clients. It included members of the Bacardi family and their like. Before joining the *bufete*, my father had had a long affair with a woman. She eventually became pregnant and Joaquín was born out of wedlock."

"Your father didn't want to marry her?"

"No. By the time Joaquín was born, my father had joined the *bufete* and was on his way up. Joaquín's mother was a good woman, a beautiful woman, too. She was an elementary school teacher from a modest middle-class family. She was also a light-skinned *mulata*—but a *mulata*, nevertheless. In my father's eyes, all these factors worked against his marrying Joaquín's mother."

"Your father was ambitious . . . "

"Very much so. He not only wanted to climb the ladder professionally, he also had social aspirations, and marriage to her would have held him back. Besides, he already had his eye on my mother, who came from an established upper-class family. Not only that, her father was also one of the founders of the *bufete*. And so, my father left Joaquín's mother and her new son—his son—and a couple of years later married my mother."

"He abandoned them?"

"Not completely. My father was not entirely without scruples," she said with a shake of her dark head. "After Joaquín was born, his mother continued working and they lived with her parents, who helped raise him. In the meantime, my father sent her money every month, which made life a little easier for both of them. Then, when he became more successful, he increased his payments so that she could rent a small apartment near her parents' home. Later on he paid Joaquín's tuition at a Jesuit preparatory school. He would have paid his way at the University of Havana, too, except that in 1958 Joaquín joined Fidel's guerrillas in the Sierra Maestra. He had just turned eighteen at the time."

"So I take it that Joaquín's mother never married?"

"She never married. As a result, Joaquín never had a father. My father sent them money, but he only saw his son once, and by then

Joaquín was fully grown."

She fell silent. David watched as she drew back the edge of silk to cover her thigh. A sudden, acute sympathy for Joaquín, the man who had become his self-appointed nemesis, stirred within him. It must have been hard on Joaquín growing up an illegitimate child, a bastard like Fidel. The difference was that Fidel's father had not abandoned him. On the contrary, Fidel's widowed father had later married his mother, who had been a maid in the family home, and Fidel grew up with his brothers and sisters. The old man even spoiled him in many ways. Still, it was common knowledge that the young Fidel felt socially ostracized by his illegitimacy.

"I guess Joaquín's childhood and youth must have been really tough," he remarked, giving voice to his thoughts.

"Yes. He never forgave my father. That's why he so despises Cuba's upper class and the United States."

"Sorry, but I don't quite see the connection."

"I'm not a psychologist, but it seems obvious that he hates my father for abandoning him and he also hates *la burguesía*, which my father represented, for having exploited the Cuban people the way it did. In addition to that, he holds the bourgeoisie responsible for not having defended the fatherland against U.S. imperialism. He sees them as accomplices in Cuba's exploitation by the *norteamericanos*."

David shook his head. "Christ! Even personal affairs become laced with the political! And you, Catalina, how did you feel toward your father when you learned about Joaquín?"

He saw the muscles in her face tighten. Having shifted the subject of the conversation from Joaquín to her, he could see that he had touched a nerve.

"This part hurts," she replied, swallowing hard. "When I learned what my father had done, I lost respect for him. Whatever feelings I had left for him were destroyed. It cut me off forever from my family." Tears welled up in her eyes.

David reached for her hand again. "You know, you don't have to go on . . . ,"

"No, no," she responded, shaking her head vigorously. "You might as well hear everything. Otherwise, you won't understand." She withdrew her hand from his again.

***

"Until the revolution came, I had great respect for my father," she began in a hard, cold voice that David hadn't heard before. "Despite his being a successful lawyer, he hated Batista and all the corruption and repression associated with his regime. But from the start, he also considered Fidel, Raúl, Che, and some of the other leaders in the July 26 Movement too radical. Then, for a while after the revolution triumphed there was a honeymoon period. As you know, it lasted only until the summer of 1959. By then, my father was increasingly upset about Fidel and the new revolutionary government. He saw that Cuba was going communist."

"As it turned out, your father was right, although his prophecy was a bit premature."

"Please, let's not discuss the finer points of history," she said in an irritated voice, annoyed at being distracted from her narrative.

"Sorry," David apologized. He settled back to listen to her story.

"The point is that by that time I was already a headstrong girl with my own ideas and I began moving in the opposite direction from my father. I wasn't quite fifteen when Fidel and his *barbudos* marched into Havana at the start of 1959. By the end of the summer I had become almost infatuated . . . " She paused, her eyes aglow with memory, searching for the right word. "Yes, *infatuated* is the word. I was infatuated with the idea of taking part in history. I wanted to be part of a great revolution that was going to purify and rebuild Cuba and improve the lot of its people."

David smiled, sensing that she spoke with the same fervent idealism that had moved her fifteen years earlier.

"Don't laugh, David," she said, catching his smile. "That's the way I was—that's the way I felt along with most Cubans in those early years. Fidel touched all of us. He made us believe in a cause that was larger than ourselves. It was in that spirit that I volunteered to participate in the literacy campaign when I was sixteen, going out into the countryside to teach poor peasants how to read and write."

"You hadn't told me that, Catalina. Good for you!" She barely nodded an acknowledgment.

"My father, of course, was furious," she resumed quickly. "But he couldn't stop me from taking part in the campaign. That was when the breach between us began to widen. It grew as I became more radicalized and his hatred toward the regime increased. Then, in 1962, just before the missile crisis, he sent my mother and my younger sister to the United States."

"And you remained here, with your father?"

"Yes. Because I refused to go to the United States. As I told you, I had been in school there for two years. I had no desire to go back, not even with my mother and sister. History was being made here, not there, and here was where I belonged." She paused for a moment to collect her thoughts. "So, anyway, for the next three and a half years, my father and I lived together at home while I finished school and then went on to study at the university. It was a miserable time for us. We were always at war with one another over the revolution, the sacrifices that everyone was having to make—over life in general."

"And you still hadn't found out about the existence of Joaquín?"

"That's right. I didn't know until 1966, when my father finally went to Joaquín to ask him for a favor. Imagine! My father, who had never bothered to see his illegitimate son for over twenty-five years, suddenly approaches him and has the gall to ask him to pull some strings in his capacity as a MININT officer."

"That's what I call chutzpah. What did he want from Joaquín?"

"My father was making plans to leave Cuba for good. He was going to join my mother and sister in Miami. He asked Joaquín to help him smuggle out some money and jewelry he had stashed away."

"Good Lord! What happened?"

"Joaquín practically threw my father out of his office and told him he was lucky that he didn't have him arrested. My father went home enraged and started drinking. When I arrived he began arguing with me, flying into a tirade over the kind of people that were now running Cuba. He ended up citing Joaquín as a prime example, calling him an ingrate after all he had done for his *bastard* son!"

Her face flushed, she stopped to take a deep breath. Despite the room's poor light, David could see the smoldering anger in her eyes, which now were a vivid green. Then she continued.

"At first, I didn't understand to whom my father was referring during our argument. But at last, as he raved on with bits and pieces of his personal life, the puzzle came together. It dawned on me that I had a half-brother. I was able to get my father to relate some of the details of his earlier affair. We then had a terrible argument when I told him I was ashamed of how he had treated his only son and that I couldn't stay any longer in the same house with him. I left a few days later. I never saw my father again. I haven't communicated with him since he went to Miami eight years ago, although I write and talk to my mother on occasion."

"And Joaquín? How did you finally meet him?"

"I tracked him down soon after the blowup with my father. At first he was suspicious and standoffish. But when he realized how I felt about my father and how angry I was over the terrible thing he had done, he began to warm up. We began seeing each other fairly frequently; after a while we were like brother and sister. He helped me through the hard times and loneliness of getting over the separation from my family. Then one day he introduced me to Ernesto, his closest friend. In fact, Joaquín was more like Ernesto's watchful older brother. We three became very close after that. He was almost as shattered by Ernesto's death as I was."

***

Her story finished, Catalina leaned her head against the back of the sofa and closed her eyes. Her dark hair fell loosely onto her shoulders. In the soft glow of the room's one lamp, her skin was dusky against the white sheen of the kimono. Feeling relaxed for the first time since entering the apartment, David listened to her quiet breathing and let his glance wander over her high cheekbones, her slightly parted lips, her exposed slender throat. He noticed that she wore no makeup. "*God, she's so beautiful,*" he kept saying to himself. Seeing the little creases of weariness at the corners of her eyes, he could tell she was emotionally drained, almost to the point of dozing off. He didn't mind. It gave him the opportunity to trace the roundness of her arms, the curvature of her breasts with appreciative eyes.

When she finally opened her eyes to look at him, he leaned forward and kissed her softly on her lips. She raised her hands as if to resist, but then she took hold of his head and boldly returned his kiss. He felt her warm body beneath the silken kimono pressed against him. They kissed again, this time more deeply. He could feel her yielding. His lips moved down to the cleavage of her breasts as he slipped the kimono off her shoulders. He gasped at her beauty.

"No, no, David! Please don't!" Her cry was a mixture of pleading for him to stop and beseeching him to go on.

"Oh, God, you're so beautiful," he cried, as he buried his face in her soft, fragrant flesh. "I've never wanted any other woman as much as I want you. And I can tell you want me, too, *mi preciosa, mi querida.*"

She murmured and ran her fingers through his hair as he suckled her breasts. "Come," she finally said, pulling his head up and kissing him passionately on the mouth.

"Let's go to bed."

***

Despite their passionate lovemaking, Catalina found he was unable to satisfy her. All his efforts to please her were to no avail. She was too guilt stricken thinking of Ernesto and all the times they made love together. Despite David's efforts, she would only let herself become aroused but not fulfilled by him. Would this always be her destiny? she lamented. Would she be forever in the grip of Ernesto's memory?

"I will make love to you another way," David said tenderly. "Please, darling, let me try."

Pushing him away, she said, "I haven't made love in four years. So I don't think anything you do right now can help." David heard the pain in her voice. "Maybe we can try again in a while," she added. "For now, let's just be still." She lay on her back, her hands clenched at her side, fighting her frustration.

Despite the darkness of the bedroom, David could see the tears that glistened in her eyes as she stared blankly at the ceiling. He was miserable. He didn't know how to dismiss the specter of Ernesto.

Turning at last on her side to face him, she squeezed his hand. "It's all right," she told him and leaned over to kiss him affectionately. "It wasn't your fault."

Later, as they embraced, her hand still clutching his, he began tracing the smooth contour of her leg, hips, and shoulder with the fingers of his free hand. He could feel the warmth and softness of her body against him. They talked with the intimacy that comes only after lovemaking. Strangely enough, he had never felt so close to anyone as he did at that moment. He wanted desperately to please her.

***

They had both dozed off, only to awaken a short time later to the insistent drumming of the long anticipated downpour that was now drenching the neighborhood. Rain splattered noisily through the bedroom's open window, striking the floor tiles. Catalina rose hastily to close the window. The room was partially in shadows.

Back in bed, she examined David, noting that he was hairier than Ernesto, and not nearly as taut and muscular. But that was to be expected. Ernesto was younger, more athletic. He had to keep himself in top physical condition because of his profession. Still, she had to admit that David was more handsome than Ernesto, and his features more refined, although his long, dark locks reminded her too much of American hippies.

Glancing down at his sex organ, now soft and limp, she marveled, as she often had after making love with Ernesto, at how a man's penis could become enlarged and hard. She giggled at her thoughts.

"What are you laughing at?" David asked, eyeing her from his pillow, concerned that she had found his maleness wanting.

"Oh, I'm just being curious," she said, a mischievous lilt in her voice. "Looking at you reminded me of the early times when I made love with Ernesto. Until him I had been a naïve virgin and was just amazed at how a man's penis could grow so large and then afterward shrivel up. I guess I'm still fascinated by the phenomenon."

"Do you want me to explain it to you?"

"No, don't! Any scientific explanation would surely spoil the mystery."

They laughed. She felt fully at ease for the first time that night. She thought it was because of the natural, easy way they talked about his male anatomy. But the real reason, she realized moments later, was that without thinking she had shared with him some of the intimate moments she had had with Ernesto. Suddenly, unexpectedly, a strange feeling came over her. A feeling of lightness and freedom, as if her beloved had released her. *"My darling, my beautiful Ernesto,"* she murmured to herself, her words echoing through her mind. *"You know you'll always be in my heart."*

She felt the warmth of David's skin against hers. She drew him closer to her as if fearful that she might lose him. She nuzzled his neck, then kissed him lightly on the mouth, then again, more deeply. She felt him getting hard and began fondling him. She heard him gasp. She began rubbing his erection against her mound, enjoying both her own mounting excitement and his. As she became moist and more aroused, she felt his hand tighten over her buttocks. He began kissing, almost biting, her mouth in a frenzy of passion.

"Fly with me, *mi preciosa*," she heard him say. "Let yourself go . . . "

She rolled him over so he would be on top of her. Once he had entered her, she pulled him down more deeply inside of her. Wrapping her legs around him, she felt his thrusting as he moved first slowly, rhythmically, and then more rapidly. All sense of time fled as their bodies heaved in unison. The tension and excitement mounted within her until "little explosions," as she once described it to Ernesto, came and she let out a cry.

"I haven't come yet," he told her seconds later, as he rested on his elbows, suspended over her. "Shall we try again for the big one?"

"Oh, yes!" she cried out, catching her breath.

She dug her fingers into his shoulders and began moving her body forcefully with his. He became part of her until she finally felt him shudder and jerk spasmodically. Then she started her climax. This time it was overwhelming in its intensity, as if her whole body and soul had been caught up by some cosmic force. She was unable to stop herself from crying out as he continued thrusting deep inside of her. At last, she felt utterly spent, yet exhilarated.

He lay on top of her, exhausted, his wet body pressed against hers. When he finally lifted himself off, she caught the look of triumph on his face. Laughing, she grabbed his hair in her two hands and began shaking his head from side to side.

"If you keep making love to me like that, David Diamond, you're going to get an even bigger head on those shoulders of yours!"

"What do you mean by that?"

"Well, I haven't told you this before," she said, nuzzling her cheek against his. "But now that we are lovers I can: Sometimes you are the most egotistical man I've ever met."

"What? That's not a very nice thing to say," he protested, grinning. "Especially after I've just finished making fantastic love to you."

"There you go! You just proved my point!" she laughed. "Now, be honest, you know you enjoyed *our* lovemaking every bit as much as I did. Right?"

"Absolutely! I've never experienced anything like it before. It was like we were one and the same. It was indescribable."

Catching the tenderness in his eyes, she pulled his head close and kissed him sweetly.

"Something has happened to me," he confessed. "I've fallen completely, totally, in love with you, *mi querida.* It's a kind of love I've never experienced before. Honest. And it's not just because of our lovemaking tonight, either . . . "

"Shh! Let's not talk yet about love. Let's just enjoy each other for now."

"I'm all for that," he said, kissing her on her lips.

Soon afterward, she turned him on his side and snuggled against his back. She draped her arm over his side and entwined her long legs with his. Soon his breathing slowed and within minutes she knew that he had fallen asleep. She had not felt such contentment since Ernesto was alive. Then she, too, finally drifted off to sleep.

***

David awoke to her leaning over and softly caressing him. The bedroom was still dark. He felt a slight chill in the air from the rain, and glanced at the luminous dial on his watch. It was not yet four-thirty in the morning.

"Why did you wake me up so early?" he complained, sleepily.

"Don't you know?" she asked, as she began to fondle him. "I want you again. I want us to make love one more time before you leave."

"Really? Darling, I'm not sure I'm up to it."

"I know better," she laughed, as she peeked under the sheet.

They became one again in their lovemaking. Only this time, she elected to be on top. Moving her body astride his, she didn't let him go until their passion was sated once more.

"Our lovemaking has been like a three-course meal," she later teased as she lay watching while he finished dressing.

"What do you mean?"

"Why, it's simple," she replied. Her half-smile and gleeful look reminded him of the time at the Italian Embassy when she had introduced him to Fidel. She had something mischievous in mind. "The first time was our appetizer," she went on. "But it wasn't very good because it was undercooked, at least for me. However, the second time was our main entrée. It was superb, absolutely delicious. An extraordinary triumph! And now, we've just eaten our dessert: It was the perfect end to a wonderful repast. What do you think?"

"You're absolutely right." He laughed as he came back to where she was sitting naked on the edge of the bed. Reaching down, he gently took her face between his hands as she looked up at him. "And I'm coming back tonight, *mi amor*, so that we can enjoy another late night feast. I'll be here around ten."

"I won't be able to wait that long!" She wrapped her arms around him, pulling him tightly against her, her chin resting on his chest.

"Nor will I, but we've got to be careful." Pausing, he ran his fingers through her thick, lustrous hair before gently taking her face in his hands again. Gazing deeply into her eyes, he said, "I know you don't want me to tell you this, but I love you."

"You're being impetuous again," she said playfully. "But I won't tell you to stop saying you love me. Now, however, you really have to leave. The sun will be up soon."

She released him and slipped on the kimono she had tossed on the bedroom floor the night before. They embraced and kissed once more. Moments later he was out the front door. She caught a last glimpse of his face before he turned to make his escape down the darkened hallway.

***

The apartment building was silent. No one was stirring. David walked quickly through the shadows of the hallway and down the stairs. When he reached the front entrance, he paused to make sure no one was outside. Seeing that the street was deserted, he walked out and headed for the hotel.

The streets still glistened from the rain. The morning's coolness felt soft and sensual, a good omen, he thought. Although sunrise was some twenty minutes away, he decided to walk all the way to the Habana Libre. No one was within sight. Once he reached Calle 23, he encountered a few persons on their way to work early on this Sunday morning. They paid him no heed.

He was ecstatic. He realized he was totally, helplessly in love. All of a sudden, as he walked through a puddle of water, he had an overwhelming urge to kick up his heels—to sing and dance like the exuberant Gene Kelly in *Singing in the Rain*. He began humming and singing to himself what words he could recall:

I'm singing in the rain,
Just singing in the rain.
What a glorious feeling,
I'm happy again . . .

"You've gone crazy, you son-of-a bitch," he said, laughing to himself.

He sauntered jauntily into the hotel just as dawn was breaking. At the front desk he asked whether there were any calls for him. The sleepy attendant gave him Catalina's earlier message. As he turned and walked toward the bank of elevators, he failed to notice the stranger who had checked his watch when he entered the lobby. The man followed him with small, beady eyes—the same man who had been observing Lt. Colonel Antonio Martel and him before his trip to Santiago de Cuba.

David bid a cheerful *buenos días* to the drowsy elevator operator who whisked him up to his floor. As he unlocked the door to his room, he remembered with a sudden rush all that he had overheard Joaquín Acosta tell Catalina, but he wasn't in the mood to dwell on it. *"I'll deal with him on Monday,"* he thought to himself. *"And somehow clear things up."*

He was determined not to let the MININT Captain spoil his rapture over the night he had just spent with Catalina—nor the all-consuming thought that he would be in her arms again in another sixteen hours.

***

15

Realpolitik

David was awakened by the clamor of the phone. For several seconds he was too groggy to know where he was, what day it was, or whether it was night or day. Then it came to him. It was Sunday morning. It must be Catalina calling. Picking up the phone, he looked at his watch. It was nearly ten o'clock.

"¿*Oigo?*" he uttered, his voice thick with sleep.

"Good morning, David," a booming voice announced at the other end of the line. "Antonio here," the man said in crisp, military fashion.

After a second or two, David realized that it was Lt. Colonel Antonio Martel who was calling. "Oh, Antonio, it's you," he answered, trying to wake up.

"*Pero hombre,*" his friend said apologetically. "You sound like you're still asleep. You must have some *muñeca* with you. I'm sorry as hell to have disturbed you, *chico.*"

"And I'm sorry to disappoint you, Antonio," David answered with a laugh. "Unfortunately there's no one here with me. I only wish there were. Anyway, don't apologize. It's time I got up. What's going on?"

"I'll be getting off duty and driving home in a couple of hours. I thought if you're free I'd swing by the Habana Libre and pick you up. We could have drinks and lunch at the *ranchito,* along with a good talk just like in the old days. What do you say, *amigo?*"

"I think that's a terrific idea. The only thing is, I've got to be back at the hotel no later than eight o'clock."

"That shouldn't be a problem. I can drive you back unless for some reason I have to return to headquarters. But even that would be no big deal. The local bus runs by my place fairly regularly, even on Sundays. It can drop you off close to the Habana Libre."

"Sounds good to me, Antonio. But tell me, are you going to do the cooking?"

"Not to worry, *amigo*, I have a wonderful cook who will prepare lunch for us. I'll call her now to tell her you're coming. I'll be at your hotel around one, so wait for me outside. *Ciao.*"

* * *

241

Still dressed in his khaki fatigues, Antonio drew up to the curb a few minutes after one in his somewhat dilapidated 1959 Chevrolet coupe. David had no sooner settled himself in the passenger seat, when Antonio sized him up and began ribbing him.

"You can't fool me, *amigo*. I know for sure you had a woman last night. I'll bet she's one of those French or Italian girls I've seen in your hotel. Right?"

"You're wrong! Besides, what makes you think I was with a woman last night?"

"*¡Chico!* I've been around men long enough to be able to tell when they've slept with a woman the night before. Sometimes I can see it in the way they walk. But with you, it's easy —it's written all over your face, in your eyes, *hombre!*"

"Oh, come on now," David said sheepishly. In truth, he could hardly keep a smile off his face or his mind off Catalina.

"*¡Coño, es la verdad!* It's plain as day that you're in love." He laughed as he slapped David on the knee. David couldn't help but smile and only halfheartedly shook his head in denial. He was sure he was blushing.

Only later did he realize that the incident involving Gustavo, and Joaquín's suspicions about him, should have put him on guard. But he was too consumed by his thoughts of Catalina and too engrossed in his conversation with Antonio to notice the car that was following them.

It was a gray 1973 Chrysler. Assembled in Argentina, it was one of the new sedans exported by that country to Cuba over Washington's protests. The Chrysler had been trailing them from the time they left the Habana Libre. Three casually dressed men in sports shirts were its occupants. They kept several car lengths behind Antonio's Chevrolet while in traffic. Later, on the open road, they stretched the interval to nearly two kilometers. They seemed to know where Antonio was headed.

Antonio's *ranchito* lay just beyond the western outskirts of Havana, near Arroyo Arenas, an easy drive for him whenever he was stationed at Ciudad Libertad, Cuba's large military complex. When he finally turned into the long graveled driveway, the Chrysler continued past the *ranchito* for a short distance and then turned around, parking some two hundred meters from its entrance. Evidently knowing there would be a long wait, the men had brought *medianoche* sandwiches for their lunch along with lukewarm soda pop to wash them down.

* * *

Comprising one hectare, or just under two and one-half acres of land, and surrounded by royal palms, the *ranchito* consisted of a small, two-bedroom house with detached quarters for the help. Antonio had purchased it for a song in 1960, when its former owner, a petite bourgeois, a small businessman, hurriedly sold it before leaving Cuba. The middle-aged caretaker and his wife chose to remain on the property after working out a mutually satisfactory arrangement with Antonio. Since he was on active duty and frequently moved about, the couple mostly had the place to themselves. As a consequence, they only had to look after the house, cultivate the fruit trees and vegetables, feed the chickens and pigs, and cook for him on those rare occasions when he was home.

After downing their glasses of scotch and soda, David and Antonio sat down to a traditional Cuban meal of savory roast chicken accompanied by *Moros y Cristianos* and fried plantains, topped off by a rich, creamy *flan* for dessert. Thoroughly stuffed and a bit high from the scotch and bottles of Cuban beer they had consumed, they remained outside on the patio where they had eaten. Even in the shade, the warm afternoon left David feeling drowsy. He wished he could nap for a few minutes, but Antonio broke out two Montecristo cigars and soon they were deep in conversation again. But Antonio was no longer interested in discussing Watergate, Detroit automobiles, or Hollywood movies. Instead, he turned serious. He began plying David with questions, seeking his opinion about the changes he had seen in Cuba since 1969.

"Well," David answered guardedly. "Life does seem somewhat easier now."

"Yes, I would agree," Antonio replied. "But that's not what I'm asking about. Don't you find that the revolution has lost something since you were last here?"

"I'm not sure I know what you're driving at."

Antonio took his time explaining as he drew deeply on his cigar, and then watched as the rings of blue smoke rose from his pursed lips. "*Nos estamos sofocando,*" he finally commented, having switched into Spanish as he often did for emphasis.

"You're suffocating? What exactly do you mean by that?"

"*Chico,* I'm surprised at you. Haven't you noticed? Our revolution is losing its originality, its uniqueness, its spontaneity. Cuba is now becoming a replica of the Soviet Union or one of the East European states." He stopped abruptly and looked at David closely. "I can trust you, right, *amigo?*"

"Please, Antonio. You shouldn't have to ask me that question."

"O.K. But just remember," he said sharply, "*tienes que mantener tu boca cerrada*—you've got to keep your mouth shut. And I don't just mean here in Cuba, but back in the United States as well. I won't be revealing any state secrets if I tell you that the DGI is almost as efficient in your country as it is here in Cuba. So don't say anything ever about our conversation. O.K.?"

Recalling Roberto's startling confession of a few weeks earlier out of earshot from Chucho and Tomás, David was quick to nod his assurance. He waited, uncertain of what his friend was about to confide.

"The long and short of it," Antonio resumed in a low, confidential tone, "is that the Soviets have been calling the shots ever since Fidel's fiasco with the 1970 harvest—his *locura*, his crazy scheme, as we call it. We're still not like one of our fraternal East European allies, but it looks like we're headed that way."

"I've heard others say the same thing, Antonio."

"Sure, but neither you nor anyone else has any idea *qué amargo*— bitter is the word in English, no?—this is for *veteranos* like myself. We fought and died for a new Cuba. Now the old communists from the PSP, who didn't do a damn thing against Batista, are moving in with help from the Soviets. They'd like nothing better than to take over the driver's seat. Our only hope right now is that Fidel is aware of what's going on and that he'll rein them in."

"Is that why he's prepared to explore a possible rapprochement with Washington? That way he could escape Soviet domination. No?"

Antonio gave him a quizzical, almost mocking, look. "If you think that, my friend, you don't know Fidel very well. He would never consider turning to the United States, even if it was the only way out of our dilemma."

"But Antonio, the circumstances for Cuba are changing."

"Yes, but Fidel hasn't changed. Don't you remember what he told the accommodationist 'comrades' in the Central Committee back in August 1968—that, no matter how dire the circumstances, Cuba would never approach your government? No. He wouldn't allow it then and he won't allow it now. No way."

"Why, because that would mean he could no longer exploit Cuban nationalism? He would have to swallow his pride?"

"*Mira, chico,* that's only part of it. The more important reason is that Fidel is determined to fulfill his destiny, and he knows that the United States won't allow it. He would have to give up supporting revolutionary movements in Latin America and other parts of the Third World. He would have to give up his struggle with imperialism."

Antonio stopped to admire his cigar before taking another draw. David was thinking he was hearing exactly what Rudy García had wanted him to find out. He waited for his friend to go on.

"But that'll never happen," Antonio said. "Fidel will never compromise with the Empire. Mark my words, he'll never agree to such a quid pro quo with Washington."

"But he's at the end of his rope, Antonio. He's faced with a Hobson's choice: Either he'll have to compromise with Washington to escape Moscow's clutches, or he'll have to submit to the Soviets to remain free of the United States."

Antonio shook his head in disagreement. He looked at David with a knowing, almost cunning smile, but remained silent.

"Well, say something!" David exclaimed. "You just can't shake your head and look at me with that funny grin on your face."

"I can't tell you very much," Antonio replied deliberately, as if trying to heighten his friend's suspense. "But I think I've figured out how Fidel is going to turn the tables on both the Americans and Soviets, and put the old communists in their place in the process."

"That would be like pulling the proverbial rabbit out of a hat."

"Until a while ago, that's what I thought, except for one thing: Fidel is not the kind of man to give up, even when he's cornered. No. My hunch is that he's got something up his sleeve, something that will make Cuba more important to the Soviets. That way he'll regain leverage with them—*leverage* is correct, no? We don't have such a word in Spanish."

"Yes, *leverage* is the right term."

"So, don't you see? Once Cuba has become invaluable to the Soviets, then he's in a position to remain independent, check the old communists at home, and realize his larger world ambitions, all at the same time."

David shook his head in doubt. "That's a pretty tall order, especially when Fidel doesn't have any more cards to play in dealing with the Soviets."

"No, *chico*. I don't think so. You're overlooking one thing: He can find ways to make Cuba more useful militarily for the Soviets."

"Christ!" David exclaimed, unable to hide his concern. "I hope you're not suggesting that Fidel is going to turn Cuba back into a base for Soviet rockets as he did in 1962 . . . "

"No, *chico*," Antonio replied with a laugh. "Don't be alarmed. But just remember that Fidel has always turned to the army at crucial moments to advance his goals—first against Batista, then at the Bay of Pigs and the campaign against counterrevolutionaries, and then later in the 1970 harvest. And I'll tell you something else, which you may not know or fully appreciate." His voice dropped to a hush. "Today, the Revolutionary Armed Forces are larger, more competent, and more professional than ever before."

"So, what are you driving at?" David asked warily.

"Look, *chico*," Antonio answered with a sly glance at David, "I can only tell you that I would bet you my *ranchito* that the FAR will surprise the world by sometime next year. Mark my words."

Normally, David would have been eager to learn more if only to dangle the information in front of Rudy García out of pure spite. But not now. After learning that Joaquín and the MININT suspected him of working for the Agency, he didn't want to know too much. He was about to tell Antonio to drop the whole subject about the FAR when his friend spoke up.

"*Mira, chico, como te dije, no te puedo decir más*—like I said, I can't tell you anything more," Antonio said anxiously, evidently realizing that he'd already divulged more than he intended. "Believe me, even though it's mainly guesswork on my part, Raúl and all the other generals would have my balls if they knew what I've told you. So, as I said before, keep all this to yourself. O.K? Understood, *amigo?*"

***

Just before five, Antonio received an urgent call ordering him back to headquarters. David assured him that it didn't present a problem since he still had plenty of time to return to Havana by bus. A short while later, after giving his friend a strong *abrazo*, he walked up the long driveway, turned left on the main road, and headed toward the bus stop some two hundred meters away.

David welcomed the walk after such a heavy meal and all that beer. He let out a loud belch. The last thing he wanted was to feel bloated and sluggish when in just a few short hours he would be with Catalina. As he walked toward the bus stop, he imagined their coming night together. He would hold her in his arms again, and they would talk of many things or of nothing in particular. Then, they would make rapturous love until dawn.

Lost in his reverie, he paid no attention to the gray Chrysler sedan that passed him slowly and stopped on the road some twenty meters in front of him. Two men got out, one from the passenger side, the other from the back. They stood a few feet apart, waiting for him to approach. His mind still on Catalina and the bliss that lay ahead, David was only dimly aware of their presence.

"¿*Profesor David Diamond?*" the shorter of the two men called out in Spanish.

Startled, David stopped in his tracks. Immediately, he knew who the grim-faced men were, but he refused to be intimidated by them.

"*Sí, yo soy Profesor David Diamond,*" he answered in a strong, defiant voice. "¿*Quiénes son ustedes?*"

"We are from State Security," the shorter man replied curtly in Spanish, flashing his MININT identification card. His cold, beady eyes were fixed on David as if he were some kind of prey. "You're to come with us. Please get into the car."

"Hey, wait a minute!" David protested. "What's this all about? There must be some mistake. You see, MINREX has given me permission to do research here in Cuba. You can even call Captain Joaquín Acosta to verify what I'm telling you."

The two State Security agents weren't impressed. The larger of the two had a menacing scowl on his face. David didn't like the situation. He wished Antonio was with him, but then he realized that his friend wouldn't be able to help since the problem was with State Security. He wracked his mind for something that would persuade the agents to let him go.

"Look here," he declared, deciding that his best defense was to go on the offensive. "Just in case you don't know it, I had the privilege of talking to Fidel a few weeks ago. After that I interviewed Carlos Rafael Rodríguez, who, as you must know, is a member of the Politburo . . . "

"Don't argue," the shorter, wirier of the two men replied brusquely, his patience at an end. "Our orders are to pick you up, and that's what we're doing. Now get into the car!"

He held open the back door for David while the larger man rounded the vehicle to get into the backseat from the street side. David found himself sandwiched between the two men. The short, wiry agent appeared to be in charge; he motioned to the driver to drive on. None of the three men said anything further.

***

David lost track of time as well as his bearings on the drive back to Havana. The shock of being arrested—or was he just being detained for questioning?—and all its consequences had begun to sink in. His first thoughts were of Catalina.

He reproached himself, hoping that she was all right and that Joaquín hadn't taken her in, too, just because she had slept with him. Then the realization struck him that even if she was free, and he was released, he couldn't possibly put her at risk by trying to contact her again. *"Oh, Jesus!"* he thought to himself. *"We'll never see each other again while I'm here in Cuba."*

As the car drove on, he was overwhelmed by a sense of helplessness. And he was scared, too, not only for Catalina but for himself as well. He chided himself for foolishly dropping his guard after overhearing Joaquín's conversation last night. Like a dummy he had never spotted the car or its occupants.

Eventually regaining his sense of direction he became aware that they were no longer headed toward the heart of Havana, toward the Plaza de la Revolución and the headquarters of the Ministry of Interior. Instead, they had veered south onto Avenida Rancho Boyeros. Traffic was light. Only a few buses and trucks. Even fewer cars. They were making good time. After rounding a traffic circle, the Chrysler headed for the Víbora district—toward the dreaded Villa Marista, where State Security detained and interrogated enemies of Cuba's communist state.

David realized his predicament was dire. His passport meant nothing. There was no American embassy to intercede on his behalf. He was in a country where the secret police ruled with impunity, where no "Miranda rights" would be read to him. And no one, not Catalina, not Philip, not Antonio, would dare try to help him. Only Joaquín Acosta could set him free. But the MININT Captain had become his nemesis, the man responsible for having him picked up in the first place. He fought to stem the tide of fear welling up inside of him.

* * *

It seemed to David as though the evening sky was suddenly filled with dark, ominous clouds as they drove into the gated compound. The two State Security agents quickly escorted him through the front door of the building and into a small reception room, where a burly black sergeant sat impassively behind his desk. Two guards, holstered pistols at their sides, flanked the sergeant. The shorter of the two MININT agents said something to the sergeant, then went over to a telephone. David guessed the agent was calling Acosta to tell him that he was being booked.

David surrendered his passport. The sergeant looked at his passport photo and then at David. Satisfied, he thumbed through the passport as if to see what other countries David had visited. At last, he set the passport down next to his typewriter, rolled multiple copies of a form into the machine, and began typing slowly with his index fingers.

As the sergeant pecked away, David glanced around at the room's sparse furnishings. Two chairs and a bench for prisoners or detainees. Dull gray walls adorned with photographs of Fidel, Raúl, and Che. The Cuban flag in one corner. A creaky, old stainless-steel fan in the other corner, its churning blades flaying away at the room's warm, humid air.

Glancing up from his typewriter, the sergeant asked David for his address in Havana and the purpose of his trip to Cuba. He took his fingerprints. Finally completing the form, he signed it, noted the time, and put it in an in-box. Next, he instructed David to hand over his wallet, Seiko watch, and money. After counting the money, he wrote down the make of the watch, and ordered David to undress and change into a pair of sleeveless khaki overalls. He then placed David's personal belongings, including his passport, into a large plastic bag, which he locked inside a file cabinet.

Deprived of his own clothing and dressed in standard-issue prison garb, David felt stripped of his individuality and more helpless than ever. Nevertheless, he decided he'd make one last try. He asked why he was being booked. The sergeant and State Security agents simply ignored him. An instant later, he was escorted from the reception room by the two armed guards. They made their way along a corridor to a narrow circular staircase that led up to the second floor and down to the cellar. One of the guards nudged David forward, down the stairs.

The guard in the cellar checked him in, then unlocked a heavy wooden door with iron braces and pushed him forward past a row of more doors, each with a peephole for viewing the cell inside. Unlocking one of the doors, he shoved David inside, slammed the door shut, and locked it. It was pitch-black inside the cell. David could see nothing. Then light suddenly flooded the cell. It emanated from a blinding lightbulb, encased in a heavy wire cage, hanging from the ceiling.

He was immediately assaulted by a foul stench. Human excrement. He saw the open toilet and wash basin. Both were filthy. He struggled to keep from retching. The cell was no more than eight or nine feet square, with a steel cot bolted to the cement floor. On top of the cot lay a thin, soiled mattress; an even thinner, dirtier blanket lay atop that.

David sat down on the cot and pulled the blanket over him. The cell suddenly seemed very cold. Neither the blanket nor the lightweight overalls offered warmth. He remembered reading somewhere that placing a prisoner in a refrigerated room was one way to break down his resistance. It was probably a technique that State Security had learned from the KGB or the East Germans.

There were writings on the wall: Pitiful pleas from past occupants that they not be forgotten—some perhaps still alive, others long since dead. Crudely scratched into the wall and worn away by time, most were too hard to decipher fully. But one, from Jorge, was easy enough to read: *"Celia, no soy contrarevolucionario. Soy inocente. No te olvides de mí*—Celia, I'm not a counterrevolutionary. I'm innocent. Don't forget me."

He got a hold of himself. He was determined not to break down. His only chance of seeing freedom again—and of preventing Catalina from getting hurt—was to keep his wits about him. *"Come on,"* he urged himself. *"Use your head. Figure out why Joaquín Acosta is holding you. Think of it as a simple exercise, an analytical problem to be solved."*

***

He had only a few facts to work with. First: Joaquín Acosta was after him because he suspected him of being mixed up with the CIA. Second: The MININT Captain was obsessively protective of Catalina, hated *norteamericanos,* and was obviously loyal to Ernesto's memory. Third: Joaquín had not seen him at Catalina's apartment Saturday night. If Joaquín had, there would have been no way he could have stayed with her. Fourth: He hadn't been arrested until immediately after he had said good-bye to Antonio, more than twelve hours after he had left Catalina's apartment. He concentrated on the third and fourth facts. Together, they indicated that his arrest had nothing to do with his stay at Catalina's the night before. That at least was reassuring. Thus far, she had to be in the clear.

Now, his thoughts turned to Antonio. Had Antonio been under surveillance and his place bugged? Did State Security suspect his friend of something? He hardly thought that credible. Antonio was too loyal a revolutionary to draw the attention of State Security. Conclusion: State Security agents hadn't arrested him because they overheard Antonio giving away sensitive state secrets—which, in any event, had not been the case.

A single, logical explanation for his detention remained: His hotel phone had been tapped, probably because he had met with Gustavo a week earlier. Then today, upon learning that he was going to Antonio's place, Joaquín had ordered that he be followed and picked up. But only after he had left the *ranchito.* That way, Antonio would not be involved. He was an officer. His army record, dating back to the guerrilla campaign, was exemplary. Once more David felt relieved. He hadn't implicated a loved one or a friend.

For the first time since he was picked up he felt sure of himself. He had analyzed all the possible reasons for his detention, eliminating those that didn't hold up, so that he wouldn't be blindsided by Joaquín when he was finally interrogated. Yes. He was going to outwit that son-of-a-bitch! And then get out of this hellhole!

Pulling the scant blanket over him for warmth, he closed his eyes to try and sleep. But he was too overwrought. Besides, he couldn't avoid the bright, glaring overhead light. Sleep deprivation was a standard interrogation practice used by police the world over. He knew that. Trouble was, he couldn't stop himself from worrying. He had no idea what was in store for him. All he had been able to do in trying to figure things out was to engage in a rigorous form of guesswork—logical, to be sure, but still guesswork.

A while later, he thought he heard muffled sobbing from one of the neighboring cells. He couldn't be sure. His MININT captors could be playing mind games. He steeled himself for the worst, including screams in the night, and swore he wouldn't cave in. He wouldn't let MININT win the psychological battle. He would think of Catalina, wondering if she knew where he was, praying that Joaquín had spared her.

He remained curled up on the hard steel cot throughout the night, the thin blanket wrapped around him, trying to warm himself. Finally, sleep came to him in the night or perhaps early morning hours. He couldn't tell. He had lost all sense of time.

***

Catalina bathed and washed her hair. After drying and brushing her hair, she dabbed her prized French perfume behind her ears. *"Catalina,"* she admonished, regarding herself in the mirror. *"You're behaving like a frivolous, love-struck girl."* Yet, she couldn't help but smile at the thought. She had made the ultimate sacrifice on behalf of the revolution when she lost Ernesto. Now, she deserved the opportunity to have a man in her life again, however briefly. *"I should be worried about one thing only,"* she told herself, slipping into her white silk kimono. *"And that is that Joaquín does not discover our affair."*

She was impatient. The day had passed far too slowly. Now, with less than two hours remaining before David's arrival, time seemed to stand still. She wished she could move the clock's hands ahead to past ten o'clock, to the very moment she would open the door and see him again. She shook her head as if to diffuse her reverie. *"You have to make yourself busy,"* she told herself. *"Otherwise you'll drive yourself crazy before he gets here."* She went to the living room and picked up the book she had been trying to finish for weeks, but soon realized she was rereading each page.

Just after nine o'clock, the phone rang. Startled, she thought David might be calling to say he would be delayed or couldn't come. She picked up the receiver and heard Joaquín's voice. He sounded strangely official and curt.

"Compañera Cruz," he said. "This is Captain Joaquín Acosta from State Security."

"Yes, *Capitán* Acosta, how can I help you?" she replied in a formal, correct manner. She realized instantly that, in using his official tone, he was warning her that he was recording their phone conversation.

"Since you served as Professor David Diamond's MINREX escort on his trip to Santiago de Cuba this past week," Joaquín declared in a flat, emotionless voice, "I have to inform you that he's been arrested this evening. He is being held by State Security for interrogation. I may need to ask you some questions concerning his behavior during your trip together. So I am instructing you, *Compañera* Cruz, to make certain that you're available over the next few days in case I need further information. Is that completely understood?"

Shaken, she was barely able to assure Joaquín that she would be at his disposal. Hanging up the phone, she felt as though the floor was giving away, the room spinning. She threw herself on the sofa and buried her face in her hands as waves of anguish swept over her. Her worst fears had now been realized—but far sooner than she had ever expected. She didn't understand how in less than twenty-four hours she could go from complete happiness to utter despair.

The only man who had stirred an awakening inside her that she hadn't felt since Ernesto's death, and who had made passionate love to her only the night before, had just been arrested. He was supposed to be with her again that very night. Now she would never see him again. Of that she was certain. Only her half-brother was left. He had been her confidante, her dearest friend, her protector. Now he was her tormentor, the person responsible for her lover's arrest. Desolate, she felt the sobs wrack her body as ten o'clock came and went.

* * *

16

Interrogation

Staggering to the door, David didn't know what hurt most—his groin, the side of his face, or the back of his head. But he did know that he was relieved to see Joaquín Acosta in the room. The irony of the situation hadn't escaped him: He was indebted to the MININT Captain, of all people, for having stopped Lieutenant Torres from roughing him up further. Now, with Joaquín in charge, he hoped the physical abuse was over for the remainder of the interrogation. That was his wish. The truth was that anything could still happen.

***

He had been tired, cold, and hungry when the guard woke him earlier and took him upstairs to the interrogation room. He was disoriented. He had hardly slept due to the overhead light, the hard cot, and the cold cell. Even worse, the guards kept waking him up. They would jerk open the peephole and bang loudly on his door every fifteen or twenty minutes it seemed, though without his watch he couldn't tell how long the intervals really were. Two or three times— it might even have been more since he was too groggy to remember—guards entered his cell and shook him roughly to make sure he was awakened. Once, he awoke from a vivid nightmare in which Catalina was being cruelly interrogated by Joaquín concerning her affair with him—David Diamond, the alleged CIA spy. He had only fallen back to sleep—and even then only for a few minutes—by trying to visualize her dazzling smile, the glint in her eyes when she assumed a mischievous look, and all the other things about her that he had grown to love.

David had no idea what time it was when the beefy MININT guard, with a dark olive complexion and a crew cut, came to take him upstairs to the interrogation room, which formed a three-by-four-meter rectangle. Besides the entry, the room had another door on the opposite wall with a large, flush-mounted mirror next to it. The furniture consisted of a table and two chairs. A tape recorder and a manila envelope were on the table.

David had expected to see Joaquín Acosta. In his stead, a light-skinned mulatto officer stood behind the table. Not as tall and hefty as the guard, he was nonetheless intimidating. The taut fit of his short-sleeve shirt, opened at the neck, revealed a powerful build and muscular arms. Grim-faced, his pale gray-blue eyes alone were menacing. He dismissed the guard, then turned on the tape recorder. He remained standing in front of the table.

"I am Lieutenant José Torres," the officer said in English without smiling. "I am assisting Captain Joaquín Acosta in this investigation. You may sit down."

"Thank you, Lieutenant Torres, but before we go any further I would like to ask why I am being held as if . . . "

"*Profesor* Diamond," Torres cut him off sharply. "Things will go much easier for you if you remember that this is not your classroom. I will ask the questions, you will answer! *¿Me entiendes?*"

"Yes, sir, I understand."

"Good. Now listen carefully. You are to answer truthfully and completely my questions." Torres moved a step closer to David. "Don't try to hide anything or lie," he added, looking down at his prisoner. "Believe me, we already know a great deal about why you're really here, what you've been doing, and whom you've been talking to during your visit." He paused for a second or two, his gray-blue eyes not blinking as he stared deliberately at David. "We know, for example, that you spent several hours with that scum of a writer, Gustavito Durán, before your trip to Santiago de Cuba." He paused again to see the effect of his words on David.

David didn't flinch. He wasn't surprised by the revelation.

"So, you see," Torres continued, this time with a menacing grin, "we just about know everything. That means that 95 percent of the time we can tell immediately whether you're lying or withholding information. And I should warn you, we always get to the last 5 percent during our sessions, except that by then things will have gone badly for you. I'm sure you don't want that to happen, right? So, be sensible and cooperate. O.K., Professor?"

"O.K.," David replied as beads of perspiration began to form on his forehead and in his armpits. He was beginning to feel nauseous, but less from fright than from being famished. In fact, he was surprised at how calm he was.

He studied Lieutenant Torres. The officer was obviously Cuban, yet he spoke English with an unmistakable Jamaican lilt. He suspected that Torres must have had a Cuban father and a Jamaican mother—and it was his mother who had taught him English. *"In any case,"* he observed grimly, *"I'll bet his English pronunciation is the only thing that's lilting about this guy."*

"Professor Diamond, why were you at Lt. Colonel Antonio Martel's home yesterday for nearly five hours?" Torres asked.

"Huh?" David acted surprised, but in actuality he was relieved by the question. It suggested that Joaquín hadn't ordered him picked up to keep him away from Catalina. No. He had been arrested because he had gone to Antonio's place. But now he had to come up with answers that would hold up and satisfy Torres, yet not incriminate his friend.

"Lieutenant Torres," David replied, as Torres sat opposite him at the table, "Lt. Colonel Martel and I are old acquaintances. We haven't seen each other for five years. We ran into each other at the hotel a couple of weeks ago—no, maybe it was ten or eleven days ago. Anyway, yesterday morning he called to invite me out to spend the afternoon at his *ranchito*. That's essentially it, Lieutenant Torres."

"No, man, that's *not essentially it* at all!" Torres exclaimed, inching forward in his chair. "What were the two of you talking about during all those hours when you were at his house?"

"I'm sorry, Lieutenant Torres," David replied, stalling a bit to better formulate his answer. "But we had a lot to drink. So, I really can't recall very much of our conversation, at least not very well." Seeing Torres' growing irritation, he decided to sound more forthcoming. "But let me see. I do recall that we talked about women. And we also talked about what's been going on in the United States—like Watergate and Nixon's resignation, the new car models being offered by Detroit, things like that. I mean, I don't want to sound vague, but it was just general stuff mixed in with lots of small talk . . . "

"Did you and Lt. Colonel Martel discuss Cuba?" Torres interrupted.

David started to feel relieved. Perhaps MININT was simply on a fishing expedition, after all. Maybe Torres was trying to find out whether an army officer, a hero of the guerrilla struggle, had been bad-mouthing the government or the Party. *"Well, I've got news for you, Lieutenant Torres,"* he swore to himself. *"I'm not about to screw Antonio."*

"Why, of course we discussed Cuba," he replied casually. "As a matter of fact, Lt. Colonel Martel asked me whether I thought Cuba had changed compared with my last trip. So I told him what I had observed so far."

"Which was . . . ?"

"Oh, nothing earth shattering. I simply said that life appeared to be improving for the common citizen. He agreed with that assessment." David fell silent.

"Man, is that all?" Torres asked, impatiently.

"I'm not sure I know what else you want from me . . . "

"Look, you son-of-a bitch," Torres replied angrily. "You just admitted that you spent hours with a high-ranking officer in the Cuban army, supposedly a friend you hadn't seen in years. And you expect me to believe that in all that time you didn't talk about politics? About the Cuban government? About Cuba's position toward your country? About Cuba's relationship with the Soviet Union? Or about the Revolutionary Armed Forces?"

David had prepared himself for this line of questioning. He would provide Torres with answers that would put Antonio in a favorable light. Still, he had to be careful. He was about to step into a minefield.

"Well, yes," he began. "Now that you mentioned it, we did talk a bit about Cuba's foreign relations. At one point, for instance, I ventured the opinion that perhaps Fidel might now be more amenable to some kind of quid pro quo with the United States in order to ease Cuba's growing dependence on the Soviet Union."

"And how did Lt. Colonel Martel respond?"

"Why, he shot me down. Said I didn't know Fidel if I thought that. Said Fidel would never reach an accommodation with imperialism if it meant compromising the revolution. Those were almost his exact words."

"Nothing else?"

"Oh, not really," David said, looking Torres squarely in the eye. He was determined not to mention what Antonio had said about the FAR being ready to take on a new mission.

Rising from his chair, Torres moved casually around the table to a position almost directly in front of David. David watched warily as Torres seated himself partially on the table's leading edge, his right thigh slung over the corner. Then, clasping his large hands together in front of him, the officer leaned forward. Noting the unmistakable malice and contempt in Torres' steely eyes, David feared that he had gambled and lost—Torres had caught him lying. He braced himself for the worst.

"Professor Diamond," the MININT Lieutenant said slowly, deliberately, in his Jamaican-accented English. "What did you promise the CIA that you would do during your visit here?"

"Huh?" This time David was caught off guard by the man's question.

"I'll say it again, man: What did you promise the CIA that you would do during your visit here?"

"Lieutenant Torres," David replied steadily, momentarily relieved that now they were no longer talking about his conversation with Antonio. "I didn't promise the CIA a damn thing. Whatever you may think of me, I am not a CIA agent. I'm a university professor. And I'm not cooperating with the CIA in any way."

Torres unclasped his hands and reached casually to turn off the tape recorder. Straightening up, he looked at David seated less than a meter away. For a big man, he suddenly moved with surprising speed and agility. Too late, David saw the open right hand coming. The blow to his face was so powerful that it sent him careening backward, tumbling over his chair, his head slamming against the floor. Dazed, he lay there, spread-eagle. His head hurt from having hit the floor and his face stung as if it were on fire. He had never been hit so hard in his life!

Standing over him, his face contorted, Torres leaned down, grabbed the front of David's shirt and raised him from the floor. "Don't fuck with me, man! Understand? *Mierda de puta*, you were lying to me! I know, 'cause we've got the goods on you right there on the table! And believe me, they show clear as hell that you're working for the CIA!"

Torres' suddenly pushed David down so violently that his head hit the floor again. Momentarily stunned, David couldn't focus his mind on the *goods* Torres was talking about. He was only conscious of the big mulatto officer looming over him. Without warning, Torres reached down and grabbed him by the crotch.

"*Cabrón*," Torres exclaimed as David instinctively fastened a two-fisted grip on the MININT officer's clutching hand. "You lie to me again," the MININT officer warned, squeezing David's testicles, "and I'll make sure you won't ever fuck a woman again!"

"*¡Ya basta, Teniente Torres! ¡Suéltalo!*"

Joaquín Acosta had silently entered the room through the rear door. Being flat on his back, trying to defend himself, David hadn't seen him. Only later, when David was able to think clearly, was he able to put two-and-two together: Joaquín must have been observing the interrogation through the one-way mirror next to the door on the rear wall.

Torres released David, brushed his hands in disgust, and stepped away. He stopped in front of Acosta on his way out, telling him, "*¡Capitán, solamente estaba tratando de suavizar este mentecato para que diga la verdad cuando usted haga las preguntas!*"

Curled up on the floor, his hands clutching his genitals, David was in too much pain to pay attention to what Torres said. The only words he caught were something about " . . . softening up this fool so that he would tell the truth when you asked the questions!" Then, after what seemed like an eternity, the paralyzing pain that had radiated through his lower body began to diminish. He felt fortunate that Torres hadn't grabbed him harder. Feeling nauseous he finally managed to struggle to his feet.

"You don't look too good, Diamond," Joaquín remarked with nary a trace of concern in his voice. "There's a toilet and basin through that door over there. Go clean yourself up." He watched David as he half limped, half staggered toward the rear door. "By the way," he added. "Would you like me to order some coffee and something to eat? You look like you might need both."

"Oh, God, yes," David replied, stopping at the door. "I'm starving. Yes, I'd really appreciate it." Glancing back at Joaquín it dawned on him that the interrogation had been scripted: Torres had been the "bad cop," while Joaquín was the "good cop." Nevertheless, he welcomed the MININT Captain's gesture. Perhaps the worst was over.

***

A cup of hot coffee and two thick pieces of bread awaited David when he returned. Seated at the table, listening to the taped interrogation, Joaquín motioned to him to sit down. David ate like a ravenous animal, chewing chunks of stale bread and washing them down with mouthfuls of *café con leche* sweetened with lots of sugar. He was beginning to feel better.

He searched Joaquín's face for clues, but the MININT Captain remained impassive as he finished listening to the interview taped by Torres. He then erased the tape and switched the player to "Record." At last, he turned his attention to David.

"Are you all right?"

"Yes. I'm O.K. I'll survive."

"Lieutenant Torres sometimes gets carried away. But he's one of our best officers. In your case, he believed you were lying to him. We have evidence, you see, that you were recruited by the CIA before coming to Cuba."

"I don't know what in the hell you're talking about, Joaquín . . . I mean, er, Captain Acosta."

"Are you denying that you were recruited by the CIA?"

"Absolutely!"

"Then, tell me, how do you explain this?" Picking up the manila envelope from the table, Joaquín removed thirty or so large black-and-white glossy photographs. He spread the most incriminating of them neatly on the table so that David could see them.

David was stunned. Displayed before him were photographs of Rudy García and him walking around Washington Circle. No wonder the Cubans thought he was a spy! His predicament was far worse than he had thought.

Suddenly, everything snapped into place. It was obvious that he had been betrayed by Rudy García and set up by the CIA. Either that, or DGI agents had followed him or García to Washington Circle. Whatever the explanation, he now understood why Joaquín had been pursuing him, monitoring his movements, and tapping his hotel phone.

He had to convince Joaquín of his innocence. Trouble was, he couldn't ask him to check with Catalina about the veracity of the story he was about to relate concerning his meeting with Rudy García. "*Hell, no,*" he thought, recalling Roberto's explanation regarding the risks Cubans ran if they withheld incriminating information from State Security. "*I would be getting her in real trouble. I know damn well she hasn't told Joaquín about what I said last Saturday night. No. I've got to leave her completely out of this.*"

***

"Look, Captain Acosta," David began. "I don't know whether it was your agent or some CIA guy who snapped those pictures. I guess it doesn't matter. Either way, the photos make it appear that I'm working for the Agency. But you've got to believe me, in no way am I cooperating with the CIA."

"Diamond," Joaquín snorted, shaking his head. "Your disclaimers aren't enough when we have these pictures of you talking to Rudy García." He gave David a hard, piercing look, the kind of look that David had seen in his nightmare. "Don't pretend that you didn't know that García is the agent in charge of Cuban affairs in the CIA's Operations Directorate," Joaquín continued scornfully. "He runs the Agency's spy network here—or rather what's left of it."

"Look, you've got to believe me," David pleaded. "I didn't know who García was or what he did. Christ, I hadn't even met the man until the day before those pictures were shot. Furthermore, he didn't introduce himself as a CIA officer on either of the two occasions when we met. Believe me, if he had, I would never have talked to him."

"So, why did you meet him?" Joaquín asked, his eyes boring into David.

Shaking his head, David let out a sigh. He rued the day back in August when, against his better judgment, against his instincts, he agreed to meet Rudy García. Had it not been for that ill-fated meeting, he wouldn't have been picked up, he wouldn't have spent the night in a God-forsaken cell instead of with Catalina. Now he had to tell Joaquín everything if he was to clear himself.

"I had presented a talk on Cuba the previous afternoon at the Smithsonian Institution," David explained, a trace of bitterness coloring his voice. "After my talk, García came up and introduced himself as a State Department representative. He said he needed to talk to me about a matter of great importance that could lead to an improvement in U.S.–Cuban relations. Well, I was a bit leery of him, but I have to admit that I was intrigued by what he said." He stopped for a moment to see Joaquín's reaction. The man's face remained expressionless.

"In a nutshell," David went on, "he stroked my ego by hinting that I could play a role in bringing about a breakthrough with Cuba. So, I swallowed the bait. I told him I'd meet him at Washington Circle at eleven o'clock the next morning."

"It was your idea to meet at Washington Circle?"

"Yes. He had suggested meeting me at a restaurant for breakfast, but I didn't like the idea. I thought Washington Circle would at least give me the opportunity to end our meeting and get away if I didn't like what was going on. I was right, except that I never dreamed it would be the perfect place for a photo session of us talking together."

"And what exactly did he talk to you about?"

Realizing that what he said next could be crucial to establishing his innocence, David did not respond immediately. He had to give as full and complete an accounting of the conversation as he could best recall. For all he knew, Joaquín could also have a taped recording of his talk with Rudy García.

"To the best of my recollection, Captain Acosta, Rudy García claimed that the U.S. Government had been receiving mixed signals from the Cuban government concerning a possible rapprochement between Havana and Washington. I then got into a big argument with him by telling him that one could hardly blame Cuba if it sent mixed signals after all that the U.S. Government had done to destroy the revolution. I further told him I believed that there were U.S. Government circles that had no interest whatsoever in exploring the possibility of normalizing relations with Cuba."

"And what did García say to that?"

"He said that I was wrong. He claimed that the real problem was that Ford and Kissinger couldn't risk exploring the possibility of an accommodation unless they were reasonably sure that Fidel was serious."

"So, how did you fit into all of this?"

"Well, we kept on arguing a bit longer . . . "

"Yes, yes," Joaquín said, with an impatient wave of his hand. "But I want to know what he wanted you to do in Cuba."

"Well, he finally asked me to help out my government by keeping my eyes and ears open regarding anything that might have a bearing on the Cuban government's position toward Washington. He was especially interested in what Cuban officials were saying to one another concerning the possibility of rapprochement . . . "

"And you were there at the Italian Embassy when that precise question was asked of Fidel," Joaquín broke in, edging forward in his seat.

"Yes, I was there, but I wasn't the one who asked the question. I asked Fidel another, entirely different hypothetical question that concerned what course the revolution would have taken had U.S. policy been more accommodating in 1959 or 1960. So, you see, I wasn't trying to worm anything out of Fidel concerning exploratory talks with the United States."

"But later, in your interview with Carlos Rafael Rodríguez, you did ask about Cuba's policy toward your country just as García had instructed you to do."

"I'm sorry, Captain Acosta, but Rudy García didn't have a chance to give me instructions about anything. I simply asked the question out of my own curiosity: I just wanted to see if there was anything to García's story. Besides, the question came up only at the end of my interview with Rodríguez."

"All right," Joaquín replied irritably. "I'll look into that. But now get back to your meeting with García."

"Well, let's see. García said I would be debriefed when I returned from Cuba—either in Mexico or the United States. Oh, yes, one more thing. He said that he could be of assistance in securing a Cuban visa for me and in setting up interviews with some high-level Cuban officials."

"You're sure he said that?"

"Absolutely! I remember that part of the conversation because it was then that I accused him of wanting me to be a spy and of him being a CIA agent. Believe me, Captain Acosta, that was the moment when I became convinced that García was with the CIA. And that's when I asked him for his government ID card—see, look, there's the photograph that shows him flashing his ID."

"But it was a State Department ID card, not CIA. Right, Diamond?"

"Yes, but I still suspected that he was CIA. So, moments later, after he kept arguing with me, I told him I would have nothing more to do with him. Then I turned around and ran across to K Street, leaving him alone on Washington Circle. You should have some shots of that . . . "

David rose from his chair to look for a photograph showing him running over to K Street. There was none. He looked quickly through the smaller pile of photos that hadn't been put on display, but again there were no shots of him leaving Rudy García. His heart sank. Joaquín watched him with skepticism.

"And that's the last time you talked with García or saw him?" Joaquín inquired.

"Yes."

"One more thing: Did García say anything more about how he could expedite your Cuban visa? Most importantly, did he mention any names with regard to the interviews he said could be arranged with high-level Cuban officials?"

"No. You see, even if he had been willing to go into more detail, I didn't give him a chance. After I had accused him of working for the CIA, of trying to recruit me as a spy, I left him in a hurry."

"All right." Joaquín rubbed his chin in thought, either mulling over the conversation or uncertain of how next to proceed. For the first time since the interrogation had begun, David felt a stab of hope. He sat again in his chair.

***

"You claim you're not involved with the CIA," Joaquín said, glancing at him. "You also say you're a friend of the revolution. Yet, even before your lengthy visit with Lt. Colonel Martel yesterday afternoon, you were doing things that caught our attention."

"I suppose you're referring to my meeting with a certain writer, a homosexual one at that," David volunteered, knowing full well he wasn't giving anything away.

"Well, well," Joaquín replied sarcastically, a slight smile crossing his lips. "I'm glad to see you're becoming more cooperative. But tell me, why did you and your friend Chucho Ramírez hold that clandestine meeting with Gustavo Durán, a reactionary and a pervert if there ever was one, if you're such a supporter of the revolution? Or didn't you know that he's a man who writes and acts contrary to the most fundamental precepts of the revolution?"

"With all due respect, Captain Acosta," David said slowly and deliberately to emphasize his point. "You must understand that I take my role as an academic seriously. During my visit here, I've tried to see and learn as much as possible. That means I must talk to a wide cross section of people, including those who may be critical of the revolution." He hesitated, unsure of Joaquín's attention. He hoped to keep the interrogation focused on Gustavo, not Antonio. "For what it's worth," he added, "I think Cuba is making a big mistake persecuting intellectuals and artists like Gustavo. In the end, the revolution would be stronger if it were more tolerant."

"What did Gustavo Durán want you to do?" Joaquín asked, ignoring David's comment.

"Nothing," David replied, determined not to reveal anything about the document Gustavo and Chucho had wanted him to smuggle out of the country.

"We'll see," Joaquín said, clearly not believing David. "I'll have Chucho Ramírez picked up and questioned, along with Durán. Then we'll see if your story holds up. But right now, I have more important matters that need to be cleared up."

***

"I want to know more about your meeting yesterday with Lt. Colonel Martel," Joaquín began in a disarmingly friendly tone of voice. "You see, Lt. Colonel Martel is an important army officer, a man entrusted with defending the revolution, and so your talking to him naturally is of interest to us. Who knows? He could have passed on sensitive information that our CIA friend, Rudy García, would obviously like to get his hands on."

"But Captain Acosta," David said in protest. "Lt. Colonel Martel told me nothing of any significance. I mean, it wasn't like he was giving away military secrets or anything."

"Let me be the judge of that!" Joaquín snapped. "Now, what did you and Lt. Colonel Martel discuss yesterday?"

"It's like I told Lieutenant Torres . . . "

"Stop playing games, Diamond!" Joaquín exclaimed, discarding once and for all his chummy demeanor. "I don't want to hear you say again how you talked about women, or automobiles, or Watergate, or about anything else dealing with your country. I want to know exactly what the two of you were talking about concerning *my* country. Am I making myself clear?"

David nodded. *"What in hell are they looking for?"* he asked himself. *"Torres and now Joaquín act as if Antonio told me something I'm not supposed to know about. But it beats the hell out of me as to what it could be. That means anything I say could incriminate Antonio. Jesus!"*

"Before you respond, Diamond," Joaquín said, as if reading David's mind, "I want you to think carefully about anything Lt. Colonel Martel and you discussed—and I mean *anything*—that concerns Cuba's closer ties to the Soviet Union. Is that understood? *¿Me entiendes?"*

"I understand." David swallowed hard, worried more about his friend now than himself. "But I have to tell you that I really feel uncomfortable about this Lt. Colonel Martel is an old acquaintance, a man whom I admire and consider a loyal, committed revolutionary . . . "

"Stop! You don't have to lecture me about Lt. Colonel Martel. I know of his outstanding record. I have no doubts about his loyalty. So, I am not after him, if that's what concerns you. I am interested solely in the conversation the two of you had concerning the issues I just now enumerated."

David realized Joaquín had left him with precious little room to maneuver. He was boxed in. He no longer could equivocate or conceal what Antonio had told him. He could only leave out some details, which could be dangerous because he wasn't sure what Joaquín was looking for.

"All right," he began warily. "It was pretty much like I told Lieutenant Torres. Except that Lt. Colonel Martel appeared upset by the Soviet Union's growing influence over the Cuban government's policies at home and abroad." He paused. *"Christ, I hate this!"* he thought.

"What did he mean exactly?" Joaquín prompted, turning off the tape recorder.

"It's just that he felt that Cuba was following the path of the Soviet Union," David answered. "He complained that Moscow was aiding the old communists in gaining greater power. None of these things, he said, were what he and other members of the Rebel Army had fought for. But he also was hopeful that Fidel would find a way out."

"Did he say how?"

"No, not really. When I told him that perhaps Fidel now appeared to be more receptive to an accommodation with Washington as a way of checkmating Moscow, he said I was a fool to believe that— just like I told Lieutenant Torres." David considered what to reveal next. With the tape recorder now turned off, perhaps he could be a bit more forthright without harming Antonio. "Lt. Colonel Martel said that Fidel's way out was for Cuba to become indispensable to Moscow," he continued. "Once that happened, Fidel would have more leverage with the Soviets and be able to keep the old communists at bay."

"Keep going. I want to know what else was said."

"I disagreed with him. I said I thought Fidel was caught, that he had no more cards to play against the Soviets."

"And how did Lt. Colonel Martel respond? You've been quite helpful so far, Diamond, so don't disappoint me now."

David felt he was finally getting close to pay dirt—which also meant he had to be more careful than ever about what he said. For all he knew, Antonio might have told him something he wasn't supposed to know.

"Well, to tell you the truth," David said, "that's when Lt. Colonel Martel became vague and unclear. He said something to the effect that Fidel could make Cuba militarily more valuable to Moscow. But it wouldn't be like in 1962, when the Soviets put in missiles here."

"So, what did he say Fidel would do?"

"He didn't say anything, really. He only remarked that Fidel had always turned to the Cuban military in periods of crisis, adding that the FAR was ready to take on any new mission that Fidel gave it. After that, he clammed up. He refused to say anything more on the subject."

"I see. Anything more?"

"No, Captain Acosta. I've told you everything. I swear."

Joaquín was silent for a while, a perplexed look on his face. David became alarmed. Had he revealed too much? He didn't think he had, but, in reality, there was no way of knowing whether he had somehow compromised Antonio.

"All right, Diamond, that's it for now," the MININT Captain said, pushing away from the table. "I've got to check some things out about your story. We'll meet again tomorrow. In the meantime, I will continue detaining you here."

David's heart sank. He dreaded the prospect of another night in the basement cell.

"Captain Acosta," he said, getting to his feet. "I'm fully aware that I'm in no position to make this request of you. But I think you now believe that I'm not a CIA plant and that I've been straight with you." He ignored the sudden expression of annoyance that came over Joaquín's face and rushed ahead. "Anyway, is there any chance that I could be held somewhere else? That cell downstairs is really foul."

"You mean to tell me you don't like your accommodations here?" Joaquín asked, with a grim smile. "All right. I'll see if you can be moved somewhere else. It won't quite be deluxe, but it will be an improvement. You'll be able to shower and have some decent food."

"That would be great, Captain Acosta. Believe me, I would really appreciate it."

***

17

Quid Pro Quo

Evening had not yet arrived as Joaquín headed back to Havana, weary after spending more than an hour with Lt. Colonel Martel. After initial protestations and denials, Martel had corroborated virtually all of Diamond's story. How could Martel have been so stupid! Shooting his mouth off with the *norteamericano*.

Still, Joaquín was thankful. He had had the presence of mind during his interrogation of Diamond to turn off the tape recorder just before the *norteamericano* gave potentially incriminating details of his talk with Martel. And he had set up the interview with Martel on the quiet, at a discreet site outside Ciudad Libertad. Otherwise, Martel would have found himself in hot water had Joaquín gone through military counterintelligence. He was glad, too, that he had driven himself rather than having Sergeant Montoya take him to the meeting.

He had taken an immediate liking to Martel, whom he had met briefly years earlier. They had much in common—both serving in Fidel's Rebel Army, willing to do anything for their country, and sharing the same concerns over the rising influence of the Soviets and the old Cuban communists. Martel wouldn't hesitate to sacrifice his life to help the revolution, which was more than Joaquín could say for most of the former PSP types.

It might not be possible, but he hoped he could get Martel off the hook. He simply wouldn't disclose the full extent of his blunder with Diamond. Martel had his patrons among the army brass, especially Division Commander Raúl Díaz Argüelles, who valued his logistical skills. But Joaquín knew that not even Díaz Argüelles could protect Martel from Fidel's or Raúl's fury if either was to learn of the Lt. Colonel's indiscretion. Now, as he drove east, toward Havana, he realized that only he could save Martel. At the moment, however, his first priority was to safeguard the secrecy of Fidel's bold plan. The operation could only succeed if the CIA was kept in the dark in the months ahead. If necessary, even Martel would become expendable to ensure the plan's secrecy.

Martel did not present him with his biggest problem, however. Joaquín could minimize the extent of his indiscretion easily enough.

The more serious problem was that he had to convince his superiors in MININT and, ultimately, Fidel himself, that Diamond knew too much and had to be held incommunicado. That was the tricky part: He would have to conceal part of what Martel had told Diamond, yet reveal enough to require that the *norteamericano* be placed under arrest for as long as necessary. Luckily, the photographs of Diamond's meeting with Rudy García were all he needed for Fidel to approve his house arrest as a suspected CIA spy. If Washington raised a big stink over why Diamond was being held, all the Cuban government had to do was to show the world the incriminating photographs.

"That's still not enough," Joaquín muttered to himself. *"I need to come up with a foolproof scheme. Otherwise, there'll be hell to pay if things start to unravel. ¡Coño! Fidel would probably have me shot if he found out that I had been less than candid about the extent of Martel's conversation with Diamond. And just as bad, that I even tried to play my own game within the government—my second attempt, to be exact, at trying to do something on my own, behind Fidel's back."*

***

It had begun the previous July. Joaquín's elaborate plan to expose the old communists had been approved by his boss, Major José Abrantes, Chief of Staff in MININT. The carefully staged defection of the MINREX Second-Secretary, Manuel Domínguez, would lure the CIA into sending someone into Cuba. At some point, that person would make contact with the old communists to ascertain whether the Cuban government was serious about normalizing relations with Washington. State Security would then show Fidel proof of how the old communists had been scheming behind his back, just like the microfaction had seven years earlier. Except this time, the ex-PSP types were doing it with the *norteamericanos*. He and Abrantes were certain that Fidel would then move against Moscow's minions, who were insinuating themselves into the government.

Later, when he had received the photographs showing Diamond with Rudy García at Washington Circle, he was certain that the American professor was his man. Indeed, when meeting the most influential of the old communists, Carlos Rafael Rodríguez, Diamond had queried him about possible Cuban initiatives toward the United States. But nothing had worked out as planned. Rodríguez had evaded Diamond's question. Later, Diamond's meeting with other ex-PSP types at the Foreign Ministry had also proved inconclusive. No, Joaquín thought with disgust, the only thing that seemed to interest the *norteamericano* was his damn academic research on the *Poder Popular*.

Now, after having interrogated him, he wasn't even sure that Diamond was working for the CIA. So far, his story had held up. First of all, Martel had confirmed that the *norteamericano* had not pressed him regarding the FAR's forthcoming mission. Additionally, during his interrogation, Diamond had claimed that he was the one who had suggested that the meeting with Rudy García be held at Washington Circle. That made sense. An experienced CIA hand like García wouldn't have chosen such a rendezvous site. Furthermore, Diamond had been genuinely alarmed when, after searching through the photographs, he found none that showed him rejecting García as he claimed. *"He's not that skilled of an actor to have feigned the look of panic that I saw in his eyes,"* Joaquín reasoned.

"I wonder if the CIA set Diamond up?" Joaquín suddenly asked aloud. It was certainly conceivable, particularly if the Agency wanted to prevent a possible rapprochement with Cuba. *"Yes,"* he thought to himself. *"That would explain why one of our DGI agents was tipped off about the meeting at Washington Circle. Once we had the photographs, the CIA had to assume that we would arrest Diamond sooner or later. The incident would then prevent Kissinger and the State Department from softening American policy toward Cuba."*

Yet, the more Joaquín mulled it over, the less certain he was that the CIA had deliberately compromised Diamond. If the CIA had tipped off a DGI agent about the meeting, then the plotters would have known that Havana would be able to show the world the incriminating photographs. That meant they would have realized beforehand that there would be no outcry from Washington over Diamond's arrest, and that they instead would have to answer to Kissinger. None of it made any sense. Either something was missing, Joaquín concluded, or Rudy García and the CIA were playing a more devious game than he could ever imagine.

All this speculation was moot, however. What really mattered now was that Diamond had stumbled—maybe unwittingly—onto a piece of critically sensitive information known only to a handful of people in the Cuban government. Even he, Joaquín Acosta, a ranking MININT officer, had only recently learned from Abrantes of Fidel's bold plan to keep the Soviets in check. And now what little Diamond knew could be of enormous value to CIA analysts. *"If they had any brains,"* he told himself, *"the* norteamericanos *will eventually put two and two together, and figure out what Fidel is up to. So that means that Diamond has to remain incommunicado until it's safe to release him."*

He had yet to talk to Catalina. She was the last person who might be able to shed further light on Diamond. No matter how inconsequential, her information could either support or undermine his claim that he was not working for the CIA. Before Joaquín went to his superiors, he had to have all the answers—not only to any lingering questions he might have, but also to all the questions they might conceivably throw at him. He couldn't afford any mistakes. There was too much at stake, including his own career.

***

Joaquín drove straight to Catalina's apartment. Learning earlier that she had reported in sick at work, he called her at home to say that he would be coming over. She had not sounded well on the phone, but he was shocked by her appearance when she opened her door. Her eyes were dull, lifeless, her face pale. He hadn't seen her so wretched since Ernesto's death.

"You look awful, *niña*. What's wrong?"

"You tell me what's wrong!" she said, nearly screaming as she let him in and closed the door behind him. "You called me last evening to tell me that you had ordered David arrested, and now you're asking *me* what's wrong!"

He was not accustomed to seeing his half-sister verging on hysteria. Only once, immediately after Ernesto had died, had she lost control and fallen to pieces. But her behavior then had been understandable; this was not. After all, Diamond had only been taken into custody for questioning—for Cuba's and her own good. She had absolutely no inkling of the high stakes involved.

"Siéntate, mi niña," he commanded, motioning her to the sofa. In

a gentler voice, he said, "I can't explain everything right now. So I'm afraid you'll have to take my word for it when I tell you I had no choice but to order Diamond's detention. Our government had to be protected—and so do you."

"I thought I told you last Saturday night not to interfere any more in my private life . . . "

"Maybe this will come as a surprise to you, Catalina, but I didn't order Diamond to be picked up simply because I dislike him or disapprove of your interest in him." He paused to let his disclosure sink in. "No, *chica,* there's much more at stake here than that. Maybe in a year or so you'll be able to look back and see that I did the right thing."

She didn't respond immediately. She looked at him with uncertainty, trying to determine whether he was Captain Acosta, the State Security officer she had to fear, or Joaquín, the half-brother she could trust.

"Right now I can't accept that you did the right thing," she said finally, shaking her head. "On the contrary, I think you've made a terrible mistake. David is *not* mixed up with the CIA. He's *not* scheming against the revolution. I'm absolutely sure of that."

"You can believe what you want, *niña.* Right now it doesn't make any difference whether or not he's working for the CIA. What matters is that he's in possession of highly sensitive information that we can't allow to get out."

"Surely you're not going to accuse him of stealing secrets about the *Poder Popular!* That's all he seems to be interested in."

"It has nothing to do with the *Poder Popular,*" Joaquín replied. "It's a hell of a lot more serious than that."

"Then at least tell me what he's done." A bit of life came into her eyes as she regarded him with a hopeful glance.

"You know I can't go into details. I can only repeat that he's now in possession of some vitally important information—information that his contacts at the CIA would love to get their hands on. That's all I can tell you."

She sat quietly on the sofa, digesting his words. He could tell she was beginning to soften.

"Is he all right, Joaquín?" she asked at last. "You didn't do anything to him to get him to confess to whatever information you're talking about?"

"No, of course not, *chica.* He's fine," he said, as he began to pace the floor. "He went through a couple of rough moments, but he wasn't harmed physically or psychologically. I don't condone physical or mental torture."

"I'm relieved to hear that," she said with a slight quaver in her voice. Then she grew silent.

***

Joaquín was pacing the length of the small living room. Deep in thought, Catalina was resting her head on the back of the sofa. Only the noise from the street filled the silence between them.

"Joaquín," she said suddenly, urgently. "I don't know exactly how to say this, but there's something important I have to tell you."

"Well, then, say it, *chica.* You know there's no need to tiptoe around things when we talk. Not after all we've been through together."

"Yes. But this is different, so prepare yourself." She paused for a second, watching as he paced. "David was here Saturday night when you were in the apartment . . . "

He stopped and whirled to face her. "He was here?" he asked incredulously.

"Yes. Well, no. I mean he was right outside the apartment in the hallway. He arrived right after you did. He overheard almost everything you and I were saying."

"What the hell was he doing here, Catalina?" he exclaimed, stunned by her revelation. Immediately he understood why his agent had lost track of Diamond last Saturday night. "*That* mentecato *of a* norteamericano," he thought. "*Somehow he was able to shake one of my best men. Maybe he's CIA after all.*" Yet Joaquín was relieved that his agent had lost track of Diamond, otherwise he would have tailed him to Catalina's apartment. This whole affair with Diamond, which he thought he had nearly sorted out, was becoming even more complicated—and increasingly messy. What kind of special charm did this *norteamericano* possess? What had caused a Cuban Lt. Colonel and his own half-sister, both of them intelligent, loyal revolutionaries, to lose their common sense?

"He came to see me," Catalina replied in a subdued voice. "I let him inside."

"I can't believe this! *¿No tienes vergüenza?*" He noted a hint of defiance in her eyes.

"No, I'm not ashamed, not one bit," she said calmly. "But I'm afraid it gets worse, Joaquín. David demanded to know what was going on, so I had to tell him all about you and me. I told him everything." She hesitated, knowing that what she would say next would upset Joaquín. "I told him about our father and what he did," she went on, haltingly. "I told him all about you being my half-brother . . . "

"You had no right!" he broke in angrily. "No right whatsoever to tell this *norteamericano* about my life, what my father did to my mother and me! That's private! No one else knows about it outside the family, except for Ernesto, Fidel, and a few others."

Shaking his head in disbelief, he sank onto the sofa and buried his face in his hands for a moment. He felt her hand touch his shoulder, but he shrugged it off.

"I can't believe what you've done!" he exclaimed, suddenly jumping to his feet, his voice filled with cold fury. "You told this *norteamericano*, this *mentecato*, this idiot who already knows too much for his own good, you told him all about me—the very person who has been watching him! The person who ordered his detention and interrogated him! This is all grotesque! I am surrounded by fools!"

"I'm sorry, Joaquín," she said with regret, her defiance of a minute ago having vanished. "But one thing led to another. In the end I just told him everything because I was certain he wasn't working for the CIA. I had asked him to tell me the truth and he did."

"You expect me to believe he told you the *truth?*"

"But he did, believe me. He told me how he had been approached by some CIA official in Washington before he came here and how he had become angry with the man and turned him down . . . "

"He told you that? That was essential information, important to the security of the revolution. Why didn't you tell me about it immediately?"

"I couldn't, Joaquín. I . . . I didn't have a chance to . . . " She stopped suddenly. He was looking at her suspiciously, waiting for her explanation, his piercing dark eyes filled with disapproval. Trapped, she realized that she now had to tell him everything.

"I let David stay the night," she said, lowering her voice. "And . . . and we made love."

"What?" he cried out in a choked voice. "This gets worse by the minute. Is there anything else?"

"No, Joaquín, that's all," she said weakly. "Besides, I think you've had enough unpleasant surprises for one night."

Too shaken to reply, he sat down again, looking at her with a mixture of anger, reproach, and disappointment. The person he most loved and cherished beyond all else, who was almost as close to him as his mother, not only had betrayed his trust but had gone to bed with this arrogant *norteamericano*—this *comemierda*, this shit-eater of a man. He shook his head in disbelief.

Finally, he roused himself.

"You have no idea how all this complicates things," he said in a dull, expressionless voice. Turning away from her as if he couldn't bear the sight of her, he rested his head against the back of the sofa and closed his eyes.

"You've placed me in a very difficult position as an officer in State Security," he announced. "I should have you arrested for having withheld vital information from me." He fastened cold, angry eyes on her. Their eyes met, then he turned away. "But I can't do that," he said, after a long silence, his voice breaking. "I can't have you arrested." He heaved a deep sigh and grew pensive again. The seconds passed.

***

"Have you any idea what kind of a mess you've created?" Joaquín asked bitterly, turning to look at Catalina. "If your lover spills everything, then Fidel, Raúl, Abrantes, they'll think I didn't arrest you because you're my half-sister. If I'm lenient toward the *norteamericano*, they'll also suspect I did it because of you. And if I treat him harshly, they'll think it's for personal reasons. You've really screwed things up!"

"I'm sorry," she whispered in a contrite voice.

He didn't hear her. He had distanced himself from her. As a State Security officer, he had to put aside their relationship.

"What did Diamond tell you about being approached by the CIA in Washington?" he asked, his voice clipped and impersonal. "This is important, so please tell me exactly everything he said."

Catalina related what David had told her. When she had finished, Joaquín was silent, mentally testing what she had just said against what Diamond had confessed to him that morning. He concentrated on fitting all the pieces of the puzzle together. More than a minute passed before he finally glanced at her.

"Joaquín," she said softly. "I'm really sorry that I betrayed our secret. I truly am . . . "

"I never expected such a betrayal from you," he said coldly. "And you made it all the worse by confiding in a *norteamericano*."

"Again, I can only say I'm sorry . . . and that I hope you can forgive me."

When he didn't respond, she sensed sadly that his forgiveness would be a long time in coming. As after Ernesto's death, a painful breach was once again opening up between them. Still, she would not give up David in order to make amends.

"Joaquín, you must understand one thing: I'm not ashamed of having gone to bed with David. It wasn't something that I did impetuously, without thinking. I gave a great deal of thought to what was happening between us during our trip together. I kept questioning myself, my motives, my feelings. And believe me, I was able to observe David closely. I'm perfectly aware of his defects as well as his good points."

"If you're so aware of his defects, why in the hell did you sleep with him?"

"Is it so hard for you to accept the fact that maybe I just desired him? That I found him physically attractive as well as intellectually stimulating? That I like the fact that he's a man of the Left . . . ?"

"None of that justifies your going to bed with him, especially since you barely know him!" Joaquín broke in, unable to control his anger.

"Of course not," she retorted. "But what you don't realize is that even though the trip lasted only a few days, we were constantly together through miles and miles of travel, always talking for hours. And because of that, I got to know a David Diamond that you've never seen." As she talked, she realized that she was not only trying to explain herself to Joaquín. She was speaking to Ernesto as well.

"Believe me," she continued. "We were constantly conversing about everything. We weren't just talking about his research, either. No, we confided in each other—about our lives, about the failure of his marriage, his wife's adultery, about Ernesto and my love for him. We became extraordinarily close." She stopped as if trying to think of what else to mention. "And of course, we also talked politics. In fact, we even had some heated arguments . . . "

Her voice trailed off. She wanted Joaquín to acknowledge that he understood what she was telling him. She wanted him at least to say something. But he remained silent, his face expressionless, his eyes resting the whole time on the wall across the room.

"So you see," she said, after a moment, "by the time I was recalled to Havana I had come to know him as intimately as one can
under such circumstances. It was obvious to me that he was very
different from Ernesto, that he could never replace Ernesto. And I
discovered some things about him that I didn't particularly like . . . "
She stopped, giving Joaquín an opening, but again he didn't respond. "In some ways, I found him too American, too arrogant at
times. That was especially the case when he was talking to our people
about democracy, about how the *Poder Popular* should work. I also
thought him too permissive, too equivocal, regarding some of the
immoral behavior that goes on in his country. Nevertheless, he was
also very critical of his government's policies toward Vietnam and
Cuba. And I respected him for that."

She stopped again, unsure of what else to say. Joaquín remained
unmoved.

"I don't know what else I can tell you, Joaquín, except that, toward the end of our trip, I knew he was falling in love with me. And
to be honest with you . . . I realized that I was falling in love with
him."

It had taken considerable effort for Joaquín to listen to what
Catalina was saying. Both his emotions and his mind were rejecting
everything she said. Now he no longer could contain himself.

"You can say all you want about your precious *norteamericano*,"
he informed her accusingly. "But the long and short of it is that you
let this *mentecato*, this idiot, into your bed! You let him make love
to you. I can't believe it!"

"No, Joaquín, *we* made love together. And he was to come back
last night, except that you had him arrested." She paused, her green
eyes flashing defiantly. "And I'm not ashamed to tell you," she declared, "that I really wanted him again. I wanted to feel joy once
more. I wanted to feel alive again."

"Don't tell me any more, *niña*. I don't want to hear it!"

* * *

Joaquín's head was throbbing. He had spent much of the night
lying awake, his mind churning over all the implications of Catalina's
revelations about Diamond's visit. He couldn't get over her indiscretion and stupidity. That she had confided their family history to

the *norteamericano* was unforgivable. That she had also slept with him was unconscionable and inexplicable. He had never understood women very well. He had to admit that his half-sister was now among them.

As sleep eluded him, his thoughts would inevitably turn to Diamond—and, as was to be expected, to Rudy García. Whether directly or indirectly, he and the CIA officer seemed destined to cross paths as if their fates were intertwined. *"I wonder if we'll ever meet face-to-face and what I'll say to him,"* Joaquín mused.

Meanwhile, he had to acknowledge that what Diamond told Catalina of his meeting with García was entirely consistent with his subsequent confession during the interrogation. That suggested that Diamond had been telling the truth. Yet, he couldn't exclude the possibility that in both cases the story was a fabrication—a backup contingency that had been devised in advance by the CIA. He had learned from his experience with interrogations that sometimes one couldn't tell whether stories that hadn't deviated from one telling to another were, in fact, true or were fabricated and well rehearsed to ensure consistency. Still, he had to admit that the odds had shifted in favor of Diamond having been truthful on both occasions.

But now it scarcely mattered whether the *norteamericano* was connected to the CIA. What did matter was that he could expose Fidel's forthcoming gambit. If he also talked too much, or if Joaquín himself mishandled the case, then Catalina and Martel would both be endangered. He didn't fall asleep until after two o'clock.

He awoke before dawn, his mind going over how he could best ensure the secrecy of Fidel's plan while also shielding Martel and Catalina. Not until another hour had passed was he able to fall asleep again. Waking up late, he did not arrive at his office until after nine, more than an hour and a half later than usual. But at least now he had the solution to the conundrum that had been perplexing him and refusing him sleep.

He poured himself a cup of coffee, laced it with milk, and ordered that the *norteamericano* be brought to his office. At ten o'clock sharp, as he had instructed, the guard knocked on his door. When David entered, he noted that his hair and beard were disheveled, his shirt and trousers rumpled from sleeping in them.

"So, Professor Diamond, did you find your quarters satisfactory?"

"Much better than the night before, Captain Acosta, although I must say not as comfortable as the Habana Libre."

Joaquín didn't smile. He was in no mood to appreciate humor from the man standing before him. Motioning David to sit down in the chair in front of his desk, he examined him more closely, wondering what attracted Catalina to this tall North American professor other than his superficial good looks and his air of sophistication. Diamond paled in comparison to Ernesto. However, it was to his credit, Joaquín grudgingly conceded, that he had tried to protect his friend Lt. Colonel Martel as much as he could while remaining completely silent about Catalina. Soon, however, the *norteamericano's* character would be put to the test.

***

Without turning on the tape recorder, Joaquín said, "Diamond, for the time being, I'm willing to give you the benefit of the doubt about turning down Rudy García." He saw the look of relief on the American's face. "I also checked out your account of your conversation with Lt. Colonel Martel. He confirms it in all its most important details."

"Well, I'm certainly relieved to hear that."

"I haven't finished," Joaquín said brusquely. "The trouble is that you're now in possession of sensitive information about Cuba's policies."

"Sensitive information? Captain Acosta, I haven't the slightest idea what you're talking about!"

"Please don't interrupt me! You've become a big headache for me! And I don't like how you've behaved . . . " He caught himself. Nevertheless, David gave him a searching, quizzical look.

"Despite what's occurred, I'll try to go easy on you, if I can," Joaquín quickly resumed. "From what I've learned it appears that you're an unwitting victim in all of this. But I still must protect the revolution, irrespective of whatever happens to you. So, pay close attention to what I'm going to propose because your future depends on it."

"I'm all ears, but it already sounds like I have little choice."

"That's right. Anyway, since you're in possession of sensitive information, I can neither release you nor allow you to leave Cuba." Joaquín paused to see that his words had registered. David remained expressionless. "To be more precise," he continued, "I will have to hold you for a year, probably longer."

"Jesus Christ!" David exclaimed. "You can't be serious! Do you realize what this . . . "

"Listen to me," Joaquín broke in, cutting him off abruptly. "One way or another, you're going to be detained in Cuba for twelve or fifteen months, maybe even more. So get used to the idea. Otherwise, it will be that much harder on you." He paused, waiting for his admonishment to sink in. He could see that David was about to protest again, but then thought better of it.

"So listen carefully," Joaquín declared. "I'm going to present you with a proposition because I need your cooperation in order to convince your State Department and world public opinion that we have legitimate grounds for holding you."

"Go on. I'm waiting with baited breath."

"If you cooperate, I'll see to it that you spend your time here in relative comfort under house arrest," Joaquín continued, ignoring David's sarcasm. "However, if you refuse to cooperate, then we'll put you in solitary confinement in one of our miserable cells downstairs or in some other prison like the Combinado del Este. It's up to you."

"What do I have to do to cooperate?" David asked in a quiet voice, seemingly resigned to his fate.

"Simply write and sign a statement that recounts most of what you told me yesterday concerning the CIA's attempt to recruit you. You'll also describe your visit with Lt. Colonel Martel, except you'll omit details of your conversation with him."

"Excuse me, but isn't that going to hurt Antonio, I mean Lt. Colonel Martel?"

"Not the way I am going to work this. In fact, he'll come out a hero for not having told you anything and then for having informed me of your suspicious behavior." He watched his quarry closely. Was Diamond's concern for Martel genuine? Or was it an attempt to find something to bargain with?

"I'll go over a draft with you," Joaquín continued. "Your statement must give sufficient, credible cause for my government to detain you for security reasons. We will hold you on grounds that we need to further investigate your link to the CIA and why you were so interested in talking to Lt. Colonel Martel."

"Do you know what you are asking me to do?" David exclaimed, suddenly cognizant of all the proposal's implications. "You're asking me to commit suicide, that's what! My academic reputation, as well as my reputation on the Left, will be ruined because your allegations of CIA involvement will be supported by my own signed confession! Christ! I'll be screwed!"

"The norteamericano's *true colors are showing,"* Joaquín thought. *"When the chips are down, he can only think of himself."*

"Jesus!" David shook his head in disbelief. "This is like something out of *Darkness at Noon."*

"Professor Diamond," Joaquín retorted contemptuously. "As a student of revolution, you of all people should know that all revolutions require personal sacrifices."

"Very funny," David replied and turned away. When he faced the MININT Captain again, Joaquín caught the gleam in David's eye. He was surprised. It appears that the *norteamericano* was not about to give up.

"What if I don't cooperate?" David asked. "The State Department is going to deny everything you claim about me and the CIA. Therefore holding me is bound to create a big stink and embarrass your government."

"Don't delude yourself!" Joaquín replied with a triumphant look. "You're forgetting that I have the photographs and a tape recording in which you acknowledge your meeting with Rudy García. That portion of the tape is all we need to support our charges that you're working for the CIA. So, in the end, you would be worse off if you don't cooperate."

"You really have me by the balls, don't you?" David finally said in a resigned voice.

"Yes, I would say I do." Joaquín smiled with satisfaction. "Let me also remind you," he added, this time more grimly, "that if you don't cooperate you'll harm Lt. Colonel Martel. You'll also make it much more disagreeable for yourself in prison. And believe me, it will be far worse for you there than it was for you downstairs two nights ago."

* * *

David sat back in his chair, aware that Joaquín was observing him, but too concerned with his predicament to care. His academic reputation would be badly hurt, no doubt, if he signed the confession that Joaquín wanted. But, surprisingly, he was less concerned about that. A confession, after all, could always be recanted or at least explained once he was out of Cuba. No. He was far more worried about Catalina—and about the probability that he would never see her again. House arrest followed by his expulsion from Cuba would make sure of that. The thought of losing her was almost unbearable.

***

Joaquín continued to observe the *norteamericano* in silence. It was clear that Diamond was struggling with his emotions, searching desperately for some way out. "*I was right,*" Joaquín thought. "*The man is incapable of a selfless act. I only wish Catalina could be here to see the real David Diamond.*"

"Let's assume that I do what you want," David said, finally breaking the silence that enveloped the room. "What kind of treatment will I receive while I'm under house arrest?"

"There will be no physical or psychological abuse, I can guarantee that. You can have a radio, possibly a TV, in your quarters. Newspapers from Cuba, like *Granma* and *Juventuo Rebelde*. You'll also have access to books. We're big on education, you know."

"So far, it sounds a hell of a lot better than your damn prisons," David said, ignoring Joaquín's last comment. "But will I be able to receive and send mail? Will I be able to work on my book?"

Joaquín regarded his prisoner with disdain, wondering what else the man might think he was entitled to receive while under house arrest.

"Tell me, Diamond," he said sarcastically. "Do you also want to know whether room service is available?"

"Excuse me, Captain Acosta, but I don't think my requests are unreasonable."

"I'll be the judge of that," Joaquín replied curtly. "All I can tell you is that you'll be able to receive mail, but we'll go through it and censor it if necessary. Of course, we'll do the same with any letters you write." He stopped as if to consider something else. "As to your last question," he resumed, looking hard at David. "I might be able to make it possible for you to continue working on your book, perhaps even get you a typewriter. But you should know that we won't tolerate you writing something that is against the revolution."

"I'm sorry, but I can't give you any assurance that you'll like what I write."

"You're entitled to write what you like," Joaquín broke in. "But don't expect us to accept it." The MININT Captain fixed resolute eyes on him. "That would be *el colmo* for you to write something against the revolution while you're in our custody," he added sarcastically.

Realizing that he had better not press the matter further, David decided to broach a new subject. "Captain Acosta," he began. "I know this may be a bit sensitive, but will you allow me to talk to representatives from either the International Red Cross or the Swiss Embassy?"

"That will be impossible."

"But why? They're both neutral parties."

"You don't seem to understand," Joaquín retorted, clearly irritated. "I'll repeat it again: You will be held incommunicado the entire time that you are under house arrest. No visitors, period! We can't—I can't take any chances with you. I'm already sticking my neck out as it is in setting up this whole arrangement."

It was obvious to Joaquín that the ramifications of a year under house arrest had finally hit the *norteamericano* full force. Noticeably shaken, Diamond suddenly rose from his chair. Grasping the corners of the desk, he leaned forward toward Joaquín, who remained seated.

"God damn it, Joaquín, this isn't fair! You know damn well that I refused to have anything to do with the CIA. They may even have set me up, framed me with those damn photos! And now, even though you know I'm innocent, you're going to hold me for a year or more because of something I apparently stumbled onto—something about which I don't even have a clue!"

The MININT Captain regarded him coldly, unmoved.

***

David slumped again in his chair. As his rage over his own impotence subsided, a deepening sadness took its place. Then he realized that his feelings of sadness and futility were not only over Catalina, whom he would not see again. They stemmed also from still another void in his life—his loss of the revolution.

Suddenly, he hated Joaquín Acosta. It wasn't just because the man across the desk was responsible for his incarceration, for keeping

Catalina beyond his reach. It was also because the MININT Captain represented what was most wrong with the Cuban government—its intolerance of dissent, its repressive, stifling controls over people's lives, and, most of all, its capacity to instill a numbing, paralyzing fear. He had become aware of all these things with *los muchachos*, and then with Gustavo and the incident in his hotel room. But now he himself had become a victim of Cuba's security apparatus. Whatever lingering illusions he had had regarding life in revolutionary Cuba were all but shattered.

Yet, paradoxically, he felt liberated despite his incarceration. He no longer had to wrestle with his conscience, with his intellect, in trying to make Cuba conform to the idealized picture he had been carrying around in his head all these years. He was now free to grasp the reality around him—unlike weeks earlier when he had tried to bend it or avoid it during his long debate with Philip Taylor. He could still see what was good about revolutionary Cuba, but no longer could he rationalize—much less justify—the dark side of the revolution.

Strangely enough, he found himself reconciled to the idea of house arrest. Of course, he hated the thought of being confined for over a year, but at the moment there was nothing he could do about it. Nor could he do anything about what house arrest might do to his career and reputation until after he returned to the States.

What he couldn't accept was losing Catalina. The thought of never seeing her again was tearing at his heart, at his very soul. The indescribable love he had felt for her that Saturday night together made it almost impossible for him to contemplate a life without her. He would do anything to find her, talk to her, be joined with her forever.

David straightened up in his chair. He had to see her one more time, to assure her of his innocence, to convey to her how deeply he loved her.

"I know you said I couldn't have any visitors," he said, looking Joaquín in the eye. "All the same, I would like to request that you make one exception."

"Diamond," Joaquín snapped, his impatience obvious. "Don't even bother to ask! You'll never see Catalina Cruz again while you're here in Cuba. So get that idea out of your mind. Now, here are pencil and paper. Start composing your statement."

***

18

The Debriefing

Rudy García reached the airport terminal with time to spare. The Cubana de Aviación flight from Havana had been delayed by over an hour. But now, at last, he stood unobserved behind the reporters, television cameras, and bright lights encircling David Diamond.

MINREX had notified the State Department via the Swiss Embassy the previous morning that Diamond, after nearly seventeen months of house arrest, would be flown to Mexico City the next day. Rudy barely had had enough time to pack his bag and catch a flight out of National Airport to Houston, and from there to Mexico City. He wanted to be on hand when Diamond arrived in the Mexican capital. Only Diamond could answer the questions that had been nagging him for over a year.

However, the David Diamond who was now nervously occupying center stage was not the man Rudy remembered. This man had aged considerably. He had put on weight. His beard was now more salt and pepper than black. He appeared to be less self-assured than before. And he seemed to have changed in still other ways that Rudy couldn't quite fathom.

Standing deep in the crowd, Rudy strained to hear as Diamond read from a prepared statement. He proclaimed his innocence. His detention and house arrest, he announced, had been prompted by the mistaken belief on the part of Cuban authorities, which was understandable at the time, that he was working for the CIA. Taking into account all the circumstances, he had been treated reasonably well by Cuban authorities. He could not say the same for the U.S. Government, however.

"I have reason to believe that the CIA set me up before I went to Cuba to make the Ministry of Interior suspect that I was working for the Agency," Diamond declared. "A few weeks before I was to leave for Cuba, when I was in Washington for a conference at the Wilson Center, a CIA officer tried to recruit me as a potential intelligence source. I turned him down flat. I therefore categorically deny ever cooperating with the CIA. And that's exactly what I wrote in the statement I prepared and signed for Cuban authorities."

"Professor Diamond," an American correspondent shouted to him. "Were you coerced into signing the confession?"

"No, I was not," Diamond replied after some hesitation. "In the first place, it was *not* a confession. I just wrote down the truth—that I had been approached by a CIA official before I went to Cuba, and that I had refused to cooperate in any way with him or the Agency."

"If that was the case, Professor, why werc you held so long?"

"I really don't know—maybe the Cuban authorities had to check everything out. I really don't know for sure. I have my suspicions, but they're only that. I don't care to go into them. What I can say is that under the circumstances I was treated decently enough, even though spending seventeen months under house arrest was no fun."

"*Profesor* Diamond," a Mexican reporter called out. "Do you think your release was meant to be a signal to Washington that Fidel is ready to improve relations with the Ford Administration now that the Cuban armed forces have emerged victorious in Angola?"

"Gentlemen, I have no way of answering that. As I said, I've been under house arrest. For all practical purposes, I was held virtually incommunicado for the entire seventeen months. My only news sources were the Cuban press and television . . . "

Rudy had heard enough. He wanted to return to the embassy before Diamond arrived there. The one big question he wanted Diamond to answer was why had he told the Cuban authorities about their meeting in Washington Circle? Top government circles in Washington had also been mystified. Why had the Cuban government placed a bona fide left-wing American professor—an apologist for the Castro regime in the eyes of many—under house arrest at the very moment when secret talks were being held on the possibility of normalizing relations between the two countries?*

During the talks, U.S. negotiators had vigorously protested Diamond's detention, asking their Cuban counterparts to release him as a sign of good faith. But the Cuban delegation, which was headed by Ricardo Alarcón, hadn't budged. As a consequence, the secret talks between Washington and Havana, which Kissinger had authorized, and which had commenced shortly after Diamond's arrival in Havana, had almost been derailed. Then, in the third meeting, obviously relishing the moment, Alarcón had sprung the Cuban

* Note to reader: Representatives from the United States and Cuba held four rounds of secret meetings in 1974 and 1975, which stopped after Cuba dispatched combat troops to Angola. See Peter Kornbluh and James G. Blight, "Dialogue with Castro: A Hidden History," *The New York Review of Books*, October 6, 1994.

government's big surprise: Diamond's signed statement describing his meeting with Rudy. From then on, the issue of his detention became moot. But not for Rudy. He needed answers.

***

As the embassy's Ford LTD inched its way through the dense, noisy afternoon traffic, David eyed the yellowish, dirty shroud that hung low over Mexico City. Luckily, the car's air-conditioning system filtered out most of the foul, smog-laden air. He was oblivious to his escort—a young Foreign Service Officer who had met him at the airport terminal and was now seated next to him. He rested his head wearily against the car's back seat and closed his eyes. The press conference had left him drained. Unlike in years past, when he relished fielding questions, he hadn't particularly enjoyed all the attention from the press and media.

During most of his house arrest he had scarcely spoken to anyone. But it was more than just the isolation that had left him unprepared to take on the reporters. He had been uncomfortable when he had had to lie or give evasive answers to their questions. But he had no choice if he was to protect Antonio and, above all, Catalina, from harm. So, he denied that he had been coerced into writing the statement. He minimized the costs of his ordeal. And he pretended that he didn't know exactly why he had been held under house arrest.

After seventeen months of captivity, his arrival in the Mexican capital meant a return to freedom. But it had come at a heavy price. He carried with him the loss he had experienced throughout his entire house arrest. Joaquín Acosta had made good on his promise. He never saw Catalina during his imprisonment.

The first months were the worst. His anguish would return nightly, when all he could do was think and dream about her. His thoughts constantly returned to that Saturday night spent talking and making love. He could still visualize her long slender legs and beautiful naked form, feel her moist lips and the sensuous touch of her smooth skin against his, and even smell the alluring fragrance of her body. Then, as the months passed, the vivid memories began to recede. She appeared still, almost lifeless, as if in a fading black and white photograph. No matter how much he tried to resurrect her, her real self repeatedly eluded him.

Had he been faced with truly sordid prison conditions, he might have had less time to dwell on Catalina and his loss, but his house arrest had been relatively comfortable. He guessed the house was situated somewhere in the Vedado or Miramar district, though he couldn't be certain since he had been taken to it at night in a closed van. He suspected the residence had once belonged to a middle-class family, long gone into exile, because of its heavy, ornately carved mahogany furniture. Its three bedrooms and two baths afforded him some privacy from his guards—always two, day and night. Despite being overgrown with weeds and bushes the large, walled-in backyard afforded him space for exercise and an escape from his sense of confinement. He missed having a swimming pool, though. It would have provided welcome relief from the stifling heat of summer since the house lacked air conditioning.

The food was passable most of the time. Invariably greasy and fattening, it had added, he was certain, ten, possibly fifteen pounds to his once trim build. He was given the Communist Party newspaper, *Granma,* to read daily, also some books he had requested as well as several tomes on Marxism-Leninism that he hadn't asked for. At night he would often watch television with one or both of his guards.

After three months, he was finally given a typewriter. On it, he recorded the impressions and observations he had made during his abbreviated field trip except that he was careful to omit details and names from his experiences. A guard would then collect his typed notes at the end of each day. Usually, they were returned a week or so later, always stamped, but sometimes with pages missing. Often pages came back with notations by a MININT censor noting his sharp disagreement, with a "*¡basura!*" or "*¡tontería!*" penned in the margin. He didn't mind. In rereading what he had written and in reconstructing the missing pages, he was able to commit their essence to memory.

The writing distracted him from the monotony of a day-to-day routine filled with boredom. Under strict orders not to engage in any unnecessary conversation, his guards rarely spoke to him or to each other when he was in their presence. Lacking companionship and intellectual stimulation, he felt the days lingering, scarcely moving at all. The slowly passing weeks and months increasingly sealed him off from the outside world, as did the Communist Party newspaper and government television.

The Cuban media made the world revolve around Fidel and Cuba. The *Comandante's* speeches were reprinted in *Granma* in their entirety or broadcast in full. They presented Cubans with the world according to Fidel. Hardly a day went by without his exhortations, trips throughout the island, and meetings with Party and government officials being duly reported. The progress of the sugar harvest, the increases in selective areas of production, the countless visits by foreign delegations from the Eastern bloc and Third World were extensively covered. The state of preparedness by the Revolutionary Armed Forces the arrangements being made for the First Congress of the Communist Party of Cuba, and other official activities constantly filled the news. After a while, David had the sensation that he was indeed on an isolated island, its inhabitants getting only fleeting, selected glimpses of a larger world that was passing them by.

The media's fixation on Cuba intensified during the last four months of his house arrest. On December 19, 1975, at the First Party Congress, Fidel Castro disclosed that Cuba was "fulfilling an elementary internationalist duty" in having dispatched combat forces to Angola, which earlier that year had received its independence from Portugal. Their mission was to help the Popular Movement for the Liberation of Angola, the MPLA, guarantee that country's full independence from imperialism and apartheid in neighboring South Africa. With that announcement, David finally understood what Lt. Colonel Antonio Martel had been hinting at that fateful Sunday afternoon—and why he was being held incommunicado. The secret operation, begun during the previous summer, had taken Washington completely by surprise. It led to a stunning triumph for the Cuban government as the FAR, with Soviet logistical support, defeated South African forces and eventually installed the Marxist-oriented MPLA in power, thereby extending the Soviet as well as Cuban presence to southern Africa.

When Fidel lifted the veil of secrecy over Cuba's Angolan operation, David had fully expected to be released. After all, there was now a constant stream of news concerning Cuban fighting and the FAR's victories on the Angolan front, rendering whatever Antonio had told him obsolete. But David was wrong. He would remain detained until the end of March 1976.

In the entire seventeen months, he had received only three letters. Two were from Julie, informing him that she was filing for divorce and that she had put all his possessions in storage. The third was from his department chair, assuring him that he would be given additional time in which to obtain tenure following his return to the university. One paragraph in the letter had been blackened out by the censor—presumably a reference to what the U.S. Government was doing to secure his release. Still, he knew from the letter that at least he would have a position waiting for him when he returned. But that was of little consolation. Once he left Cuba, he would be further removed from Catalina. There would be even less hope of ever seeing her again.

Now, as the embassy car slowly wound its way through traffic, his thoughts were of her. How he yearned to see her! To tell her how he hadn't for a moment forgotten her. How she had constantly been on his mind. *"Yes, my love,"* he mused, as if speaking to Catalina. *"Had I been able to put down on paper everything I thought about you while under house arrest, I would now be bringing back reams of typewritten notes with me!"*

***

David's eyes were still closed when he felt the Foreign Service Officer lean forward to say something to the embassy driver. Opening his eyes, he saw that they were approaching Mexico City's Pink Zone, not far from the embassy. Although the FSO hadn't spoken to him since leaving the airport terminal, it was evident that the man had not been pleased with David's comments at the press conference. But David didn't care. His escort's blue eyes and short, sandy hair made him look like a prig—as well as the first WASP he had seen in more than seventeen months.

Noticing that he had opened his eyes, the FSO turned to tell him that the U.S. Government would put him up at the Hotel El Presidente for the night, following his debriefing at the embassy. In the meantime, the FSO said, David could leave his bags in the car. The driver would take him to the hotel after the debriefing. A few minutes later, they passed through the gates of the embassy, and David was quickly escorted into the enormous, solid-looking building—a palpable symbol, he had often thought, of Washington's presence and influence in Mexico.

Even before the FSO had closed the door, David turned to examine the room he had been ushered into, noting immediately that it had no windows. *"Just like the interrogation room at the Villa Marista, except I don't see a one-way mirror,"* he observed. He guessed that the windowless room was meant to hinder electronic eavesdropping from outside the building. Sparsely furnished, it contained a table, a phone, and six high-back, cushioned chairs placed neatly around the rectangular table. *"At least it looks more comfortable than my last interrogation room,"* he thought grimly. He didn't hear the door open.

"Professor Diamond, glad to see you at last. Welcome to Mexico."

David recognized Rudy García's voice. "What the hell! I'm not talking to you!" he roared, whirling around. "God damn you! You really messed up my life, García! Now, get out of my way! I'm getting out of here!"

He bolted for the door. The CIA officer remained rooted in place, blocking the exit.

"Sorry, Professor, but you need to answer a few questions first. So please take a chair and sit down. This shouldn't take long . . . "

Before Rudy finished his sentence David had already thrown his punch. He should have known better. Though shorter, Rudy was powerfully built and in far better physical condition than he was. Besides, David hadn't been in a fistfight since his freshman year in college. But reason fell by the wayside. All the rage that had been accumulating inside him over the past seventeen months—over Rudy García, Joaquín Acosta, Lieutenant Torres, his captivity, and, more than anything else, his separation from Catalina—suddenly erupted. Using the full weight of his body behind his right fist, he aimed the roundhouse haymaker directly at Rudy's square jaw. But to his astonishment, his knockout punch didn't land.

Moving quickly to David's right, Rudy shifted his own body clockwise, deftly parrying David's blow with his left arm. Then, using David's forward motion, he caught hold of David's right wrist with his own right hand and swung David's arm down, using it as a lever, twisting David's wrist behind his back. A split second later, David found himself flung headfirst onto the floor, his face pressing against the rough fibers of the wall-to-wall carpeting. He lay there helpless, his right hand and wrist pinned painfully against his back by Rudy's strong grip.

"Don't try that physical stuff on me, Professor. I could really hurt you. I haven't practiced my Aikido for a while. So calm down."

Rudy waited a moment, resting his bent knee against the small of David's back. "All right," he said. "I am going to release my grip in a second. Then I'll let you up so that we can talk like reasonable men. O.K.?"

David didn't know which hurt more—the physical pain throbbing in his wrist or the humiliation of having his face pushed into the carpet. He felt the pressure of Rudy's weight on him.

"I guess I have no choice, do I?" David said in a muffled voice.

"You O.K.? I didn't mean to hurt you . . . "

"I'll be all right," David snapped, struggling to his feet. He hadn't felt so much anger and impotence since his last session with Joaquín Acosta. But at least here, he'd soon be free. "Let's get this over with, García. I just want out of here so I don't ever have to see you again."

"Understood." Rudy waited for David to sit down, then took one of the chairs opposite him. "First of all," he said, "I want to know why you told Cuban State Security about our meeting in Washington Circle. Jesus, you made a detailed statement that not only compromised you, but it also told them about me and everything that we wanted you to find out."

"What the shit was I supposed to do, huh, García? They had the photos of us walking and talking together!"

"What?" Rudy's jaw dropped. "What are you talking about?"

"I said they had photographs of our meeting," David repeated slowly, deliberately. "I counted at least twenty of them, some showing us when we first met at Washington Circle, then several shots of us talking as we walked, and a couple more of us standing and arguing just before I walked away. When I saw those pictures, I flipped out. I really felt trapped, like I'd never get out of Cuba. That's when I decided to tell Captain Acosta about how you tried to recruit me and how I refused to play your little spy game. That was the only way I could convince him that I was innocent."

David saw the perplexed expression on Rudy's face. Not giving the CIA man the opportunity to respond, he added quickly, "You know, I had a lot of time to think about those incriminating photographs. As a result, I came up with several possible explanations. Do you want to hear them?"

"Yeah, tell me what you think. Frankly, you've taken me completely by surprise. This is the first time I've heard about photographs of us, believe me."

"Perhaps, perhaps not. You see, Mr. García, one scenario is that you and the CIA deliberately set me up. You wanted to create problems between the U.S. and Cuba in order to destroy any possibility of normalized relations. So, let's call that explanation the *set up.*"

He stopped for a moment to let his remarks sink in. Actually, he was savoring the moment. He wanted to prolong it.

"There's another explanation, a more charitable one," he resumed with deliberate sarcasm. "Under this hypothesis, you didn't mean to set me up, but you were careless and didn't see a DGI agent at the Wilson Center. The guy then saw us talking together, after which he tailed you the next day to our meeting at Washington Circle. Or another variation of the same hypothesis is that he placed me under surveillance and followed me to Washington Circle . . . "

David paused momentarily. Having failed so miserably only moments before in a physical assault, he was now enjoying the opportunity to lash out verbally at the CIA officer.

"In either case," he went on quickly, "there was clear incompetence on your part: You failed to spot the DGI agent or agents. And given that Cuba's General Directorate of Intelligence appears to be so much more proficient than your vaunted CIA, I think either variant has considerable plausibility. In either case, you really fucked up."

He saw Rudy García's jaw go rigid as he clenched his teeth. *"Squirm, you son-of-a bitch,"* David said to himself. *"Compared to what I've suffered, you're getting off easy."*

"Despite all the time you've spent thinking about all this," Rudy replied, shaking his head, "you're completely off track about my setting you up. I really wanted you in Cuba helping us. Furthermore, the first variant of your second theory doesn't hold up because I wasn't followed. Whatever else you may think, Professor, I'm not an amateur in this business."

"So far you and your damn scheming haven't proven otherwise."

"Cut that sarcastic crap! O.K.? I'm trying to work this thing out with you. So, I don't need any of your shit."

The two men glared at each other.

In a calmer voice, Rudy said, "Now, the only one of your explanations that begins to have some possible credence is that you were followed. However, I was very careful at your talk at the Wilson Center before I approached you. There were only three or four other people left in the room, and, believe me, none of them were DGI or KGB agents."

"Sorry, García, but all I've heard so far are your denials," David shot back, determined to vent his anger. "On the other hand, I know for a fact that Cuban State Security had the photographs of our meeting, which I paid for dearly. And I hold *you* responsible." He glared at Rudy. "You know, you played me real smart in pretending that I could play a key role in improving relations between Washington and Havana. Shit! Like a sucker, I took the bait, hook, line, and sinker!"

Rudy did not respond immediately. To his disappointment, David wasn't even sure that the CIA officer had been listening very closely. He seemed totally absorbed in his own thoughts. The seconds ticked on.

***

"You know," Rudy said after a minute or so had gone by, "something just occurred to me. Given that State Security must have had those incriminating photos prior to your arrival in Cuba, why did they wait so long to arrest you? From what I heard, you were given the red-carpet treatment by the Cuban government up to the time of your arrest. So why did State Security hold back? Were they waiting to see whom you'd contact? Which leads me to the next question: What were you doing when you got arrested?"

Rudy listened carefully as David recounted how he had spent that last Sunday afternoon with his old friend Lt. Colonel Antonio Martel, and how he was arrested just minutes after leaving Martel's house. His interest was piqued when Diamond related Martel's complaint about the Soviet Union's increasing influence. He was especially intrigued by Martel's vague allusion to how the FAR would soon provide Fidel with the means by which to regain greater autonomy for Cuba.

"Wait, a second," Rudy interjected. "You mentioned earlier that you tried to explain everything to a Captain Acosta. I presume you're referring to Captain Joaquín Acosta. Right?"

"Yes. You've heard of him?"

"You bet. One of State Security's best. You should take that as a compliment. Shows that they were really interested in you. Anyway, back to what happened. After you were arrested, did you tell Acosta what you just told me?"

"Yes. I told him almost everything. Except, I was purposely vague on a couple of things. I didn't want to screw Antonio in case he had been indiscreet with me."

"And Acosta accepted your version?"

"I guess so, because he later checked out my story with Antonio. Anyway, the next morning he demanded that I draw up the statement describing our meeting at Washington Circle and my visit at Antonio's house—except, I was not to identify him by name. I was only to refer to him as an Army Lt. Colonel. I'm certain that Acosta was trying to protect Antonio while making it appear that I had attempted to learn military secrets from him."

"Yes, it would appear that way." Rudy paused as he gave David a funny look. "So now, Professor, do you know why they arrested you and held you so long?"

"Of course. I figured everything out a few months ago. Have you?"

"Yeah," Rudy replied quickly. "From what you've said, it's pretty clear you stumbled onto *Operation Carlotta*. Acosta obviously feared that you were in possession of just enough information to blow Fidel's plans to intervene militarily in Angola if you were debriefed after you got back. But hold on. I just want to be sure about something."

Rudy picked up the secure phone and punched in a long series of numbers. He kept David in his sights while he waited for the call to go through.

"Don, this is Rudy. I'm calling on a secure line from the embassy in Mexico City. I've been talking to Professor David Diamond. That's right. He's told me some interesting things. Anyway, what I want to know is whether the name Lt. Colonel Antonio Martel rings a bell. I think he may have been involved in *Operation Carlotta*. Yeah. O.K., I can wait."

Covering the mouthpiece of the phone, Rudy confided to David, "Don Smith is the best Cuba analyst the Agency has. He's testified before congressional committees several times. He's even briefed a couple of presidents. He's a veritable walking encyclopedia on the Cuban government. Yeah, I am here, Don. Go ahead." Rudy listened for another minute before thanking Don and hanging up.

"Your friend, Lt. Colonel Antonio Martel, was a logistics specialist for Division Commander Raúl Díaz Argüelles. We now know that Díaz Argüelles initially led an advance team of military specialists to Angola at the request of the MPLA. That occurred sometime between late 1974 and early 1975. They were on a secret mission to reconnoiter the situation there. We're now certain that they were assessing not only the MPLA's prospects for taking over the country once the Portuguese pulled out, but also the need for Cuban advisors and combat troops."

"And Antonio was a member of the advance team?"

"Correct."

"That's why he said he was losing weight. He was already getting in shape to go to Angola when I saw him in October."

"Sounds about right. Anyway, after returning to Cuba following the initial mission, Díaz Argüelles and his staff went back to Angola in August 1975. It was then that he became the commander of the Cuban combat forces that were being rapidly deployed there. Without those troops, the MPLA wouldn't have been able to gain control of the country."

"And the U.S. Government didn't know about the operation."

"Not until it was too late. Not only the reconnaissance mission but also all the subsequent planning and execution of *Operation Carlotta* were kept tightly under wraps. I can tell you that I took some flack for not having detected the operation sooner. Still, I've got to hand it to the Cubans for keeping the entire operation secret as long as they did."

"Except that I'm the one who got screwed because of the need for secrecy."

"I'm afraid so," Rudy acknowledged. "Acosta obviously feared that your friend had compromised *Operation Carlotta* in confiding in you as he did. That's why he put you under house arrest and held you incommunicado for so long. He just couldn't afford the risk of exposing an operation that was still in its initial planning stage."

"But why did they keep me under wraps for an additional four months after the operation was disclosed by Fidel last December?"

"An interesting question," Rudy replied. "It may have been simply out of bureaucratic inertia. Or maybe they were trying to protect their assets—the person or persons who set you up. In any case, I don't have a hard answer right now."

"Oh, by the way," Rudy added a moment later. "I forgot to tell you one thing that Don said. Along with Díaz Argüelles, your friend Martel was killed last December when an anti-tank mine exploded under their armored vehicle."

"Oh, shit!" David cried out, visibly shaken by the news. "Poor Antonio. I really liked him. He was such a great guy. No pretense or guile to him, just a plain-spoken man."

Unable to go on, David lapsed into silence. Rudy's mind was already elsewhere.

* * *

"You know, I can't get my mind off those pictures," Rudy said aloud, almost as if he were speaking to himself. "I don't know how the hell a Cuban agent found out about our meeting. And what makes me really mad is that if those photographs hadn't been taken of us, you wouldn't have been placed under close surveillance. You wouldn't have been arrested following your meeting with Lt. Colonel Martel."

"Come on, García, you really don't expect me to believe that you care a hoot that I was locked up by the Cubans, do you?"

"No, you're wrong," Rudy said. "You may not believe it, but I do feel responsible for the fact that somebody set you up. And I'm really sorry, probably more than you can imagine, that you were held under house arrest."

David waited, expecting an apology for the ordeal he had to endure.

"Do you realize how different things would've turned out had you not been arrested?" Rudy asked. "Had I talked to you following your return from Cuba? Christ! We would've learned what Fidel was up to long before *Operation Carlotta* could've gotten off the ground. The course of history could've been changed. We could have denied Fidel his biggest victory since the Bay of Pigs . . . "

"Is your stupid intelligence business the only thing that matters to you?" David broke in, exasperated. "Shit! Because of your silly games I was placed under house arrest for seventeen fucking months! Maybe you don't think that's all that bad in the overall scheme of things, but my life has been wrecked by what's happened to me!"

Rudy was uncomfortable. He had never particularly liked Diamond, but his conscience was bothering him. He let him continue with his tirade.

"Let me explain it to you, García. My professional reputation is in shreds right now. People on the Left, I'm sure, think I've sold out. But I can live with all of that because at least I'll have the opportunity to fight back and clear my name. What's really a hell of a lot more important to me is that because of all of this I've lost the only woman I've ever really loved." Overcome with emotion, he swallowed to keep himself from choking up. "I wasn't allowed to see her the entire time I was under house arrest. And I'm sure I'll never see her again."

Rudy heard the anguish in David's voice and saw his eyes watering. He suddenly felt sorry for him.

"What's her name if I may ask?" Rudy finally inquired, not quite knowing what he could say to console him.

"Her name is Catalina Cruz." Noticing the expression on Rudy's face, he added, "Looks like you might have heard of her."

"To tell you the truth, I've only heard a few things about her," Rudy answered, looking at David with renewed interest. "I know she works for MINREX and that she's quite a looker. I've also heard that she's related somehow to our mutual friend, Captain Acosta."

"How did you know that?" David asked, clearly surprised.

"Ah, despite what you may think, David," Rudy replied, deciding it was time to be on a first-name basis, "the CIA does have some good sources. Anyway, I'd be interested in learning more about your lady friend and how she's related to Acosta, that is if you'd care to fill me in."

"Sorry, but I promised I wouldn't divulge anything about her life. That includes saying anything about her and Joaquín. So, you can forget it, Rudy García."

"O.K., have it your way." The CIA man shrugged. He was glad that the tension between them had finally eased. As he watched David lapse into silence, his thoughts returned to that hot, steamy morning at Washington Circle in late summer, nearly two years earlier.

"Look, David," he said, his tone cordial, "like I said before, I feel largely responsible for how things turned out for you in Cuba. I really am sorry for all that happened." David started to say something, but Rudy stopped him. "I know this won't be of much consolation to you, but I'm going to find out about those photographs, about who set you up, even if it takes me years to do it. That's a promise."

"Thanks, Rudy," David replied with a nod. For the first time since they met, he was starting to change his mind about the CIA officer.

"And one more thing," Rudy added. "I promise to let you know if

I hear anything about Catalina Cruz." He hesitated for a second as if a sudden thought hit him. "Hell, I'll do better than that! If there's ever a chance of you seeing her again and you need my help to make it happen, I'll be there. You can count on that."

***

19

The Boy Scout

It was an uncommonly hot Sunday afternoon in April. Already the usual hordes of tourists were in Washington to witness the cherry blossoms and flowers in bloom. But to Rudy García it seemed that most of the District of Columbia and the surrounding Virginia and Maryland suburbs had decided to escape to the countryside. Other than during the summer months, he could not recall encountering such heavy traffic as he was in on his way to the Chesapeake Bay. He saw that the summer cottages dotting the shoreline were already alive with people, while scores of sailboats were plying the waters of the bay's inlets and coves.

Sitting in his car atop the gently sloping hill, Rudy had a commanding view of the modest cottage below and its surroundings. A sloop was tied up to the dock. A man was working diligently on the deck, oblivious of Rudy's 1967 Volvo. That was what Rudy had hoped for—to arrive unannounced, by surprise. He deliberately had neglected to tell his quarry that he would be coming out this Sunday afternoon.

Over a year had passed since Rudy's encounter with David Diamond in Mexico City. It had not taken him long to figure out who had set Diamond up. But before he could move on his information, his suspect had left the country for an extended period, then retired from the Agency. Rudy, in the meantime, had been sent to Latin America on routine errands as if to do penance for the David Diamond affair. But now all that was behind him. His quarry was where he wanted him. At last he could close in.

Shifting into neutral, he let the Volvo coast the last two hundred yards to the cottage, parking it in the driveway. Before leaving the car, he switched on to "Standby" the two tiny tape recorders that he had taped to his ribs underneath his loose fitting Hawaiian shirt. He walked around the side of the cottage and down the grassy slope to the dock. Lawton Armstrong was on his hands and knees, sanding the boat's wooden deck. Lawton glanced up with a look of surprise at seeing his uninvited guest. Turning off the electric sander, he struggled stiffly to his feet and grabbed a rag to wipe the dust and grime from his hands.

"Why, Rudy, what a pleasant surprise!" Lawton declared in a forced, jovial voice. "When you called earlier this week, I had no idea you'd be coming out today. You should've warned me. That way, my boy, I could've laid out the welcome mat for you." Rudy caught the note of reproach in his voice.

Lawton looked more dissipated than ever. His red face was blotchy not only from the sun but obviously from too much drinking. The bulging stomach on his otherwise slight frame was further evidence that he had indulged himself while in Europe. His white hair was noticeably thinner, more yellowish, and disheveled from the light wind blowing steadily from the east. He was sweating profusely from the exertion of sanding. He appeared short of breath. And he looked nervous.

"Sorry to barge in on you like this, Lawton, but it was such a beautiful Sunday that I decided to head out your way and see if you were in. Hope you don't mind."

"Not at all, my boy," Lawton replied, opening his eyes wide and then blinking them several times as if his William Buckley affectation attested to the sincerity of his welcome. "Glad to see you. Gives me a chance to take a rest from all the sanding I'm doing. After spending nearly a year in Europe, I'm not used to this kind of work. It's really hard on my old knees and especially my back."

"I'm no sailor, but she looks like a swell boat to me," Rudy said as he admired the twenty-four-foot sloop.

"She'll do. Main thing is, I can handle her by myself. Also, the maintenance isn't all that bad. Now, I could sure use a cold beer. How about you?"

They entered the screened-in front porch where Lawton left Rudy while he went inside to fetch the beers. Rudy reached under his shirt to switch on the first tape recorder.

* * *

Lawton reappeared a few minutes later. He handed Rudy one of the two mugs of beer he was carrying, its foam just reaching the rim of the glass. Sitting down, he raised his frothy mug. "Cheers," he said and drank greedily.

"This really hits the spot," Rudy commented as he looked down toward the dock and the cove beyond. "I've got to hand it to you,

Lawton, you sure picked a great place for retirement."

"I enjoy it," Lawton replied. "You might not believe it, but I bought this place for a song twenty-five years ago. It was pretty run-down. That's why it was cheap. Been fixing it up ever since. But I've put most of my money and energy into the boat. I've always loved sailing since I was old enough to take the helm . . . " He paused as if contemplating something. "When you called me the other day," Lawton continued, abruptly changing the subject, "you said you had been put back in charge of Cuban operations. You also said that you wanted to tie up some loose ends regarding the Diamond affair."

"Right."

"I gather, then, that you're here on official business."

"No. This is private, Lawton, just between you and me."

"Really?"

"Yeah. You're the only one who has the answers to what's been bugging me ever since I debriefed Diamond in Mexico City last year."

Lawton stiffened ever so slightly, his pale blue eyes narrowing with suspicion. Quickly raising his mug to gulp down more beer, he avoided Rudy's searching eyes.

"Well, I'll try to help you, Rudy," he said, wiping the froth from his mouth. "But you know, I was only marginally involved with your attempt to recruit Diamond as an asset . . . "

"Lawton, let's cut to the chase real quick," Rudy broke in brusquely. "I know what happened. What I don't know is *why* you did what you did. I'm pretty sure you're not a double-agent working for the DGI, yet you . . . "

"What the hell are you talking about?" Lawton exclaimed in outrage, rising partly out of his chair. "First you accuse me of doing something about which I'm completely in the dark. Then you insinuate that I could be a DGI double-agent—except you don't think so. You'd better explain yourself damn fast or I'll have to ask you to leave. Do I make myself clear?"

"It's real simple," Rudy replied calmly. "After Diamond was arrested, Captain Joaquín Acosta of State Security confronted him with a bunch of photographs showing him meeting me at Washington Circle. No one else besides you knew where our meeting would take place and at what time."

"Rudy, this is all preposterous!"

"Really? Let me refresh your memory. You called me first thing that morning from the Farm. During our conversation, you asked me when and where my meeting with Diamond was going to take place. When I told you it was going to be at Washington Circle, you joked about how Diamond had seen too many English espionage movies. Remember?"

"Of course I remember," Lawton replied in a steady voice. "But none of what you're telling me proves a damn thing. There're any number of possible explanations for what happened."

"Like what?"

"Like, for instance, that you and Diamond might have been spotted by a DGI agent when the two of you first met at his conference. After that, either one of you could've been put under surveillance and followed to the meeting."

"No, Lawton. I know for certain that there was no DGI agent at the conference. I'm also just as certain that neither Diamond nor I were followed." Rudy stopped for a second and looked squarely at Lawton. "And furthermore," he added. "I know you didn't snap those photos yourself. You see, I checked and found that you were at the Farm like you said."

"At least you've got something right," Lawton noted sarcastically. He took another swallow of beer. "Look, Rudy, you're trying my patience, barging in like this and accusing me of setting Diamond up. I think you'd better leave."

"Sorry if I'm not being very polite in view of your hospitality," Rudy cut in. "But I need some answers—and I'll stay here until hell freezes over to get them."

"I'll make sure you're out of here long before then," Lawton declared, his voice laced with sarcasm. He was careful to avoid Rudy's accusatory stare. "All right," he finally conceded, as if resigned to Rudy's inquisition. "Have you considered the possibility that the DGI or, more likely, the KGB intercepted my call to you that morning?"

"No, Lawton, don't you recall? First, you called me on a secure line, remember? Then you made a second call to tip off a DGI agent about our meeting."

"That's getting ridiculous. I've heard enough rubbish, thank you! Please leave at once."

"No," Rudy replied evenly, staring Lawton straight in the eye. "Like I just told you, I'm not leaving until you come clean. I know you phoned your DGI contact. I traced your second call." He watched Lawton's reddened face go slack.

"You did what?" Lawton demanded, his voice cracking. Rudy saw him swallow hard and grip the arms of his chair.

"I simply looked up the records for all the outside phone calls from the Farm and—bingo!—I found that a call was made just after seven o'clock that morning to Washington, D.C. It was made from the same office you used when you phoned me over the secure line just moments before."

"Even if that's true, none of what you say proves a damn thing," Lawton said, regaining his composure.

"I haven't finished. I also traced the number you called. Guess what? It turned out to be a pay phone in Washington, D.C. I don't have to remind you that that's standard procedure in the intelligence business. You had it prearranged so that all you had to do when your DGI contact answered the phone was tell him when and where I was meeting Diamond. Took you less than a minute."

"Rudy, has anyone told you that you have a vivid imagination? Believe me, that's the only way to explain your cockamamie theory." He was shaking his head in mock disbelief.

Even with the late afternoon beginning to bathe the porch in shadows, Rudy could see that Lawton's face had paled. He wore a worried expression. Turning away, he gazed vacantly at the rippling silver waters in the cove beyond.

"You wired, Rudy?" Lawton suddenly asked, turning to him.

"No," Rudy lied, not flinching as he returned Lawton's look. Years of working in the field had taught him how to be cool and convincing when he needed to lie. "As I said," he added, "this is my business, not Agency business."

"I find that hard to believe," Lawton said suspiciously, staring intently at Rudy. "Why haven't you gone to our counterintelligence people with your tale?"

"Simple," Rudy said with a shrug, as if he were confiding in someone. "I couldn't prove that you made that second call. Even if I could, I wouldn't have been able to prove that the person at the pay phone was DGI. So I've decided to confront you directly. Besides, to be honest with you, I also wanted to cover my ass."

"What do you mean?"

"Other than you and me, no one in the U.S. Government knows about the photographs. The Cubans never showed them to our negotiators. So, unless I had proof that you were responsible, I couldn't tell anyone about those pictures. Their immediate supposition would have been that I had screwed up again and now I was trying to blame you for it." Rudy stopped a second to measure the effect of his words, but Lawton's face remained expressionless.

"As it was," Rudy continued, "I was given temporary reassignments while the Agency investigated. Of course, my reputation as a 'cowboy' because of the Managua incident didn't help. So, despite the fact that I was eventually cleared, I decided to keep quiet about the photos."

Evidently relieved, Lawton suddenly stood up. The color having returned to his face, he seemed sure of himself once again. "You want another beer?" he asked. "I am going to get some stronger stuff myself."

"No, thanks, I'm fine. Come to think of it, though, I'll have a glass of water."

As soon as Lawton was inside, Rudy stopped the tape recorder. Rising quietly, he positioned himself out of sight along the wall beside the door. He didn't want to take any chances. He had to be able to take Lawton down quickly in case he returned armed.

***

Lawton returned armed only with a tall glass of scotch and water in one hand, the *Washington Post* tucked under his arm, and a glass of water in his right hand, which he offered to Rudy. As he turned to sit down, Rudy used the opportunity to restart the tape recorder beneath his shirt.

"Let's see if you're as good an intelligence officer as they say you are," Lawton said smugly, unaware he was being recorded. "Right here is a possible motive for doing what you claim I did." He handed the newspaper to Rudy. He took a long gulp of whiskey as he watched Rudy scan the paper.

"You mean this report on the Carter Administration's decision to open up the U.S. Interests Section in Havana next September? I don't get it. What does that have to do with what happened nearly three years ago, in 1974?"

"You're a smart, capable intelligence officer," Lawton said condescendingly. "But, my dear boy, I'm afraid you still have no idea of the big picture."

"Cut the crap, Lawton."

"You know, Rudy, you're just like most of the people in our government. You lack vision. You don't have the ability to think strategically, long-term, like our friend Fidel. Now, there's a man who can think far ahead and plan his moves."

"I'd appreciate it if you'd get to the point," Rudy said impatiently.

"I will, old boy. But in the meantime, don't begrudge me my little moments of triumph."

"Lawton, you seem to think this is a game. Well, let me set you straight: You really bungled it when you told your DGI contact when and where I was to meet Diamond."

"Oh, please, Rudy! Don't be so melodramatic! The worst thing that happened was that your left-wing Jewish professor, that apologist for the Castro government, got his comeuppance—nearly a year and a half of house arrest ordered by the very government that he pimps for. Now, that's sweet justice for you!"

"Is that why you set him up, to get him arrested?"

"I'm not admitting to any such thing, my boy," Lawton replied, a sly smile curling his lips. He took another sip of scotch and water. "But don't you find it extraordinary," he added with a knowing, superior look, "that Kissinger was considering holding secret talks with Havana despite Castro's track record of lies and deception?" Not waiting for Rudy's reply, he said, "Worse yet, despite Cuba's incarceration of Diamond, a bona fide American citizen, the State Department still went ahead with those exploratory talks with the Cuban government—no less than four of them, mind you. It took Fidel's military buildup and intervention in Angola in the summer of 1975 for Kissinger, Eagleberger, and all the others at State to finally realize that they had been had."

"Let me see if I've understood you correctly," Rudy said, setting aside his glass. "You're telling me you deliberately set out to sabotage those talks?"

"Don't you see?" Lawton continued, ignoring Rudy's question. "There are few people in our government who understand Fidel Castro or who are his intellectual match. And to make matters worse, we have a democracy, while he has the luxury of presiding over a dictatorship. So, even though we're the superpower and Cuba is a puny island-nation with only seven or eight million people, we're constantly being outwitted by this megalomaniac."

"So, you thought you had to save us from our own stupidity, from our inability to ever deal effectively with Cuba. Is that it?"

"I'm not answering that, Rudy. But the fact is that Fidel and his regime have been tolerated by no less than six American administrations. Doesn't that make you ashamed? Aren't you outraged by the ineptness of our leaders? We should have finished him off properly when we had the chance, instead of trying to do it on the cheap with the Bay of Pigs invasion . . . "

"Which you tried to prevent by warning Bissel and others that the operation was doomed to failure," Rudy interjected.

"Ah, yes," Lawton said, nodding ruefully. "That famous memo of mine that disappeared into a dark hole after the Bay of Pigs fiasco. You see, my boy, I had committed the worst sin of all: I was proven right when the operation ended in disaster. No one likes to be proven wrong, least of all the powers that be."

Pausing, Lawton took a long gulp of his drink. His eyes narrowed as he peered intently at Rudy.

"You know," he added with bitterness, "that memo should have boosted my career. I was right on target in arguing that Castro was still adored by the majority of Cubans. And I was right again when I insisted that the only way to topple him was to invade Cuba with U.S. forces. Instead, I paid dearly for having been proven right. My career went nowhere after that."

Rudy watched as Lawton swallowed another mouthful of scotch, thinking that Lawton was more of a boozer than he ever imagined.

"Anyway," Lawton resumed, a slight slur to his words, "after the Bay of Pigs, I realized that our politicians and policymakers would never learn from their mistakes. Sure enough, Kennedy relied on half-measures by trying to use the Mafia to kill Castro. But worse than that, he failed to use our overwhelming military power to get rid of the bugger once and for all during the missile crisis."

"Lawton, you're forgetting that if we hadn't given Khrushchev a way out and invaded Cuba instead, we could have ignited World War III."

"Perhaps. On the other hand, had we not allowed Fidel Castro to turn Cuba into a communist state, we would never have had a missile crisis." He stopped and looked at Rudy. "I've said this to myself many a time, and now I'll say it to you," he announced, as if he were about to reveal some priceless words of wisdom. "The sheer incompetence of our leaders in not knowing when and how to use power borders on the criminal."

"You can't say that about Kissinger," Rudy objected.

"Yes, I initially had high hopes for Henry," Lawton conceded after a moment's reflection. "But then he became the architect of détente, giving the Soviets and their proxies a free hand in the Third World. And he compounded his error by authorizing secret exploratory talks with Havana at the very moment Castro was planning his large-scale military intervention in Angola."

"You're forgetting one important detail, Lawton: Neither you nor anyone else knew what Castro was planning. In the meantime, we were receiving signals from Havana indicating an interest in normalizing relations. We had to check the Cubans out."

"No, no, Rudy, don't be such a Boy Scout! Don't you see? It doesn't matter one iota that I was in the dark about Angola along with everybody else. The point is, Castro has never been interested in normalizing relations with us. On the contrary, he's determined to screw us whenever and wherever he can!"

His face flushed with triumph, Lawton stopped his ranting and took the last swig of scotch. He stared bleary-eyed at Rudy for several seconds, trying to ascertain whether his listener had understood the full import of his brilliant insight.

"We'll forever be his enemy, I tell you," Lawton continued. "No matter what we do. He needs to go up against us and play the role of David against Goliath. Without 'imperialism' to do battle with, he would be nothing in Cuba, much less in Latin America or the world."

Lawton suddenly rose from his chair. "You want something else to drink besides water? Another beer, maybe?" he asked.

"No, thanks. I'm fine. I have a two-, maybe three-hour drive ahead of me."

"Suit yourself. I'm getting a refresher." After Lawton had lurched back into the house, Rudy turned off the tape recorder.

***

Taking up his position next to the door, Rudy waited for Lawton's return. He was anxious to put an end to the man's tiresome pontificating; he had to steer him back to the issue of the photographs before his tapes ran out. Finally hearing Lawton fumbling with the door, he switched on the second, backup recorder. His host had returned unarmed.

"Rudy, you've got to admit that we're an ahistorical, apolitical people. We're incapable of learning from the past," Lawton declared as he let himself down heavily into his chair.

"Excuse me, Lawton, but I didn't come all the way out here to discuss political philosophy or history."

"Don't be so impatient, my boy," Lawton replied, drinking his newly replenished scotch. "The point that I started to make is now we've got the naïve Carter people in office. They think they can wean Castro away from Moscow by concluding an agreement with the Cubans to open up Interests Sections in Havana and Washington. I think even you'll agree with me, Rudy, that that's utterly absurd." Rudy remained silent. "And to top it off, the media and all the pundits are talking about the possibility of restoring trade relations, even diplomatic ties, as part of a grand strategy to detach Havana from Moscow. What softheaded rubbish!"

The shadows continued to lengthen across the porch floor as the wind picked up. Lawton contemplated his glass for a moment, then he resumed his monologue.

"Mark my words, Rudy, sooner or later Fidel Castro will send his troops back into Africa now that he has taken Carter's measure. He's got a good thing going, you know. Because of what he accomplished for them in Angola, the Soviets are paying him off big time with huge increases in economic and military assistance. And that's not all. He's now the darling of the Third World for having gone up against the South Africans and apartheid."

Drawing himself up, Lawton paused momentarily for dramatic effect. Looking directly at Rudy, he said, "So, I predict that our friend will find another pretext to intervene somewhere else in Africa. And I'm as certain as I am sitting here that Carter won't do a damn thing."

"You could be right," Rudy conceded, feeling anxious. "Right now, though, I want to know who it was you called about my meeting with Diamond at Washington Circle."

"My boy, you know I'm not going to admit to any such thing,"

Lawton reaffirmed. Though he was bleary-eyed, his voice thick, and his words slurred, Rudy had to admit that Lawton was still his old canny self.

"In fact, just in case you *are* wired," Lawton announced loudly, "I herewith deny that I contacted anybody from the DGI, the KGB, or any other intelligence agency. And furthermore, your phone records don't prove a damn thing." Pleased with himself, Lawton sank back into his chair, a vacant look on his face. He took a long sip of scotch and let out a throaty chuckle.

"You know, Rudy, you haven't changed a bit," he declared. "You're still every bit the Boy Scout, just like seven years ago!" He paused as if losing his train of thought. "But to be honest with you, I admire that sort of thing—honor, loyalty, country, and so forth. Sort of rare these days, don't you think? We just don't see too much of it any-more, eh, Rudy, what with this new generation of anti-war protesters and appeasers. But you're different. A real straight arrow, I can tell. Like I was when I first entered the Clandestine Service."

Lawton's voice trailed off. Either he had lost his train of thought again or he was deep into his own musings.

"Come on, Lawton," Rudy snapped. "I haven't got all evening! Just tell me who you called and why you called."

Lawton shook himself out of his reverie, and looked away toward the distant, shimmering waters, now a dark silver gray as the sun dropped lower in the western sky.

"Christ, but you're obsessed!" he replied with a sigh of resignation. "Well, I guess that's a good quality to have in our business of spycraft. O.K., to satisfy your curiosity, I'll give you a hypothetical answer."

"What do you mean?"

"Simple, my boy. I'm not going to tell you anything that could incriminate me in the event you decide to bring some ridiculous charge against me—or in case you've been lying to me and you're wired. No, I'm going to frame my answer hypothetically, without admitting to its veracity. It'll all be theoretical. Understood?"

***

"You and I know that I would never commit treason," Lawton began. "On the contrary, all my life I've tried to serve my country well—so well, in fact, that it cost me professionally. In the meantime, I became increasingly disturbed—outraged is more like it—by our blunders in Cuba, then in Vietnam, and lately with the Soviets over détente. Yet I've felt absolutely helpless to stop our decline."

Lawton paused to take another drink. Rudy noticed that Lawton's bloodshot eyes held a mixture of cunning and triumph. When he spoke again, it was with a sudden air of bravado.

"So, Rudy, let's suppose that I became all the more upset upon learning that Henry was considering exploratory talks with Havana. Why? Because I was convinced that Castro would get the better of him and our illustrious State Department—as eventually he did. But then you came up with your idea of recruiting Professor Diamond. So, if I was a man wanting to derail those pending talks and the possibility of rapprochement with Castro, this would be my golden opportunity."

"In other words, that's when you began to set things up with your DGI contact."

"Like I said, Rudy, I'm not going to admit anything. No. All of this is hypothetical."

"All right," Rudy broke in irritably. "Go on."

"So, let's just suppose that I knew that a certain Cuban individual, a former intelligence operative whose ass I had once saved, was now residing in Washington. Let's also suppose that I suspected he still had ties to his old comrades in the DGI. By having arranged things with him beforehand, all I had to do was inform him of your meeting with Diamond."

"So that he could photograph us with a telephoto lens," Rudy interrupted, his voice taut. "After which he'd turn the negatives over to the DGI station chief at Cuba's UN Embassy in New York! Right?"

"Sounds logical to me, but of course this is all purely hypothetical."

Rudy felt the anger rising inside him. He had to force himself to remain calm. The incriminating tapes would be enough to destroy Lawton.

"Don't do anything foolish, my boy," Lawton said nervously, sensing Rudy's anger. "Don't even think about doing what you did back in Managua. Besides, you owe me one for having saved your ass over that affair. You really do, you know," Lawton added, staring warily at Rudy.

"Don't worry," Rudy reassured him. "I'm not going to beat the shit out of you. But it's not because I owe you. It's because you're just too damn pathetic a figure." He stared contemptuously at Lawton. For a moment, he feared that the man was too drunk to comprehend what he was about to tell him.

"Just think of it, Lawton," Rudy said in a cutting voice. "You were once a CIA officer who enjoyed wide respect for having tried to stop the Bay of Pigs. But now you're a disgrace to the service. And, believe me, that's how you'll be remembered—as the man who, out of bitterness, out of delusions of grandeur, not only betrayed the trust of a fellow CIA officer, but was also responsible for a major intelligence failure by the Agency."

Seeing Lawton's stupid sneer riled Rudy all the more. He was determined to make Lawton comprehend what he had done. He delivered his accusation slowly, emphatically.

"You see, Lawton, you mucked things up real bad by helping Fidel Castro achieve his biggest victory since the Bay of Pigs. Yes, you of all people!"

"What do you mean?" Lawton asked, trying to clear his besotted brain.

"Listen carefully, you bastard! If it hadn't been for you, we would've learned about Fidel's plans for intervening in Angola from Diamond himself. You want to know why? Diamond was virtually informed about the forthcoming operation by a Lt. Colonel Antonio Martel. Martel later accompanied Division Commander Díaz Argüelles and the rest of his team on their secret mission to Angola. That was seven or eight months *before* we got the first inklings of the Cuban military buildup in and around Angola."

"So, what does that have to do with me?"

"It has everything to do with you, you son-of-a bitch! The pictures your man took alerted Captain Acosta at State Security. He then put Diamond under surveillance the moment he arrived in Havana. As a result, Diamond was detained right after he left Martel's home. And once Acosta learned what Martel had revealed, Diamond was placed under house arrest. The Cubans feared—and rightly so!—that Diamond would blow *Operation Carlotta* if we debriefed him on his return to the States."

Lawton's jaw went slack as Rudy's words sank in. His whole body sagged. An aura of defeat, of hubris gone astray, suddenly enveloped him.

"You screwed up real big-time, you pompous asshole," Rudy declared with finality as he stood up. "But I guess that's not surprising in view of the way you've been boozing it up. Now, I'll leave you to your own misery."

* * *

Rudy had already turned the Volvo around and was halfway up the long driveway when Lawton burst through the front door of his cottage. Half staggering, he was brandishing a Colt .45 semiautomatic. Wildly waving the pistol, he tried to steady himself to aim at the rapidly retreating car. He got off one round, but it went far wide of its intended target. The Volvo disappeared over the crest of the hill.

Once on the main road, Rudy glanced cautiously in his rearview mirror, then checked the two micro tape recorders to make sure they had captured Lawton's incriminating diatribe. Satisfied, he settled in for the long drive back to his apartment in Falls Church.

As he drove on, he wondered whether the evidence on the two tapes would finally erase his reputation as a hothead, a cowboy, a loose cannon—the reputation that had dogged him throughout much of his career, because of what had happened in Managua seven years earlier.

Back then, in 1970, the Deputy Director of Intelligence had appointed Lawton to head a three-man board of inquiry to investigate Rudy's conduct in what became officially known as the "Managua Incident." Lawton had persuaded one of the other members of the board to rule in Rudy's favor. The outcome had not pleased some of the higher-ups at Headquarters. It evidently hurt Lawton's career more than it did Rudy's because the board of inquiry was the last significant assignment that Lawton received before his retirement. To Rudy's way of thinking, this explained Lawton's dissipated condition when he saw him in Bob Watson's office, four years later.

Even though he had been appreciative of Lawton's role in clearing him, Rudy had never felt that he owed the older man anything. Not once had he regretted what he had done in the National Guard compound. Given the same circumstances, he would do it all over again in a flash.

* * *

Nicaragua had been Rudy's second overseas assignment, but he was unprepared for the venality and brutality of the Somoza regime.

In the country less than three weeks, he had been ordered to go to the National Guard compound in Managua to question a young Cuban intelligence officer, Lieutenant Ernesto Padilla, who had earlier infiltrated into Nicaragua, only to be badly wounded and captured during a firefight between National Guardsmen and the Sandinista rebels. When Rudy first interrogated him, the man was woozy from his wounds and medication, but not to the extent that he wasn't able to respond to questions. However, the Cuban would give only his name and rank, steadfastly refusing to say anything more. Rudy decided to hold off further interrogation for a day or two. He left the compound after advising the guardsmen to leave the Cuban officer alone.

The ghastly scene he encountered when he returned to the interrogation room two days later was burned into his memory. Sprawled naked on the table, Lieutenant Ernesto Padilla moaned weakly, his once handsome face almost unrecognizable. He was scarcely alive. One of his eyes had been gouged out; his fingers were smashed to bloody pulps; and he had been emasculated. One of his testicles was still partially dangling from his blood-soaked groin. Staring helplessly at the moaning hulk, Rudy thought he heard Padilla's faint cries for *Catalina*.

The three guardsmen started laughing. The fattest of the three quipped that *Catalina* would find that her Cuban lover was no longer a man.

Later at the hearing, Rudy would recount how he had been overcome by the barbarity of it all. Without thinking, he had exploded into action. He disabled the fat guardsman with a crushing kick to the groin, probably rendering him forever impotent. He caught the second guardsman in the throat, hitting the carotid artery with the knife-like edge of his right hand, causing the man to crumple to the floor. He hovered near death, Rudy was told later. The third guardsman fumbled for his pistol. Before he could get it out of its holster, Rudy had grabbed his arm, twisting and snapping it out of its socket. The man shrieked in pain. The next thing Rudy remembered was the door crashing open as other guardsmen rushed into the room with their weapons drawn. One of the men hit him with the butt of his rifle, knocking him to the floor. He would have been killed as he lay there, except that the guardsmen knew that he was a CIA officer. His captors had to be content only with kicking him several times before they called the American Embassy to come and escort him out of the compound.

His CIA station chief had been furious with him, berating him for having set back the Agency's close relations with the Somoza government. Within forty-eight hours, he was sent back to Langley. Thinking he was washed up at the CIA, Rudy wondered what he would do next. But a month later, much to his surprise, two of the three members at the hearing, with Lawton in the lead, ruled that his behavior had been unfortunate but understandable, given the circumstances and his inexperience. All charges of misconduct were dropped.

After the hearing, Lawton had come up to Rudy and told him that he really hadn't given a damn about what had happened to either the Cuban intelligence officer or the three National Guardsmen. What had concerned him, instead, was Rudy's fate. He hated to see a promising intelligence officer like Rudy punished or forced out of the Agency's Clandestine Service for having attacked three members of Nicaragua's National Guard. They were thugs. They were expendable. Rudy was not.

Initially, Rudy thought that Lawton had been sympathetic to his plight as a young CIA officer. Like Lawton with the Bay of Pigs two decades earlier, Rudy had instinctively done what he thought to be the right thing. Later, when he came to understand the man better, and thus to separate the Lawton Armstrong of whistle-blowing fame from the man that he had begun to detest, he wasn't so sure. Maybe Lawton had been pursuing his own vendetta in exonerating him at the investigative hearing, getting back at those superiors who blocked his promotions in the Directorate of Operations. Now, after his long session with Lawton, he wondered whether the hearing on the Managua incident had been Lawton's first step on the road to betrayal that would eventually lead him to set up David Diamond.

* * *

Rudy had stewed for months over the outcome of his Cuban operation. Castro's biggest triumph since the Bay of Pigs could have been averted had it not been for Lawton's treachery. Now the Cuban dictator was riding high over his success in Angola, thumbing his nose at Washington, all the while becoming Moscow's most privileged client.

"And in this respect I've got to agree with you, Lawton," Rudy said out loud, shaking his head in disgust. "Fidel is sure to intervene somewhere else in the next year or two, but this time it will be with a lot of direct Soviet support. Shit!"

As he drove on, he became calmer, musing that perhaps he remained too much the idealist in wanting to see good triumph over evil. *"I've got to learn to put everything in perspective,"* he told himself. *"I can't make everything turn out right all the time. Maybe, like Lawton said, I'm still too much the 'Boy Scout.'"*

He vowed he would start paying more attention to his personal life. He would return to New Mexico for a needed vacation. The visit, perhaps, would cleanse and restore his soul. He sorely missed his family. Close relatives. Old friends. He hadn't been back home for almost four years. He'd soon turn thirty-five.

At his age, it was high time he found himself a good woman. She didn't have to be glamorous or beautiful. Just someone warm, intelligent, and caring. He remembered how much he envied David Diamond when he confessed to his love affair with Catalina Cruz. Would he ever be as passionate about a woman as Diamond seemed to be? *"She really must be something,"* he said to himself.

***

20

The Reckoning

Joaquín stood nervously in Fidel's office at Communist Party Headquarters, warily watching the *Comandante* as he barked instructions over the phone. Besides Fidel and himself, only an aide and his boss in State Security, Major Abrantes, were present.

The office was like a war room: On one wall was displayed a large map of the Horn of Africa, with colored pins indicating the advance of the ten-thousand-man Cuban expeditionary force into the Ogaden. Under Cuban command, but with a Soviet General and his staff serving as advisors, the FAR's forces had been sent earlier in November 1977 to aid Ethiopia and its Marxist government wrest control of the disputed region from Somalia. As was his nature, Fidel insisted on closely monitoring battlefield developments and issuing his own tactical instructions. But Joaquín knew full well that he had not been summoned to Fidel's office at midnight to discuss Cuba's newest overseas deployment.

When the *líder máximo* finally looked up and saw him, his face darkened and his eyes flashed with suspicion and anger. Joaquín didn't flinch. He had nothing to feel guilty about. He felt only the sadness that had been with him since hearing the bitter news of the previous day.

"So, Captain Acosta," Fidel began, his voice laced with sarcasm, "I suppose you've come to inform me that your half-sister, Catalina Cruz, defected two days ago while on an official mission to Spain." He paused to see Joaquín's reaction. "Or perhaps you're here to explain to me *why* she defected, *why* she betrayed the revolution." Again he paused, his eyes narrowing. Joaquín waited, knowing full well that Fidel wasn't finished.

"Yes. Given that I already know of her betrayal, you would perform a more useful service if you would explain her motives," Fidel continued in the same sarcastic vein. "After all, you're not only her half-brother, you're also supposed to be a Captain in State Security whose duty it is to prevent such things from happening."

"*Comandante*, I have no idea why Catalina has betrayed the fatherland," Joaquín protested, looking Fidel straight in the eye. "We've hardly spoken to each other in the past three years. Believe me, her defection was as much a shock to me when I learned about it yesterday as it is to you, *Comandante*."

Fidel bowed his head momentarily, his beard touching his chest. He gazed at his clasped hands resting on his stomach as if contemplating his response. It was one of his classic, Moses-like poses; Joaquín had seen it on countless occasions. But then, abruptly, he looked up at Joaquín, his dark, burning eyes boring in, ready to catch him in a lie.

"Why is it that sometimes I am the last person in Cuba to learn about some things?" Fidel asked, his voice brimming with anger. "Eh? I ask you, Acosta, why is that so?"

"With all due respect, *Comandante*, I have no idea what you are talking about."

"I'll tell you what it's about!" Fidel exploded, pointing to a paper on his desk. "It's right there in this report to you from one of your men in the field. It's nearly three years old, but I've only learned about it now—about how, when she was in Camagüey, your half-sister was showing a romantic interest in David Diamond, the American she was supposed to be escorting. That's why you had her recalled, right, Acosta?" Fidel paused, but his penetrating black eyes remained fixed on Joaquín. The office was absolutely still. No one dared say anything. "But then," Fidel continued, briefly nodding toward Abrantes, "you didn't even tell your superior here about your half-sister's improper behavior. Perhaps because you already suspected that she had begun her psychological—no, worse yet, her ideological—defection from the fatherland." He stopped abruptly, his fierce eyes fixed on Joaquín. He wasn't expecting Joaquín to reply, at least not yet.

"But the story didn't end there," Fidel went on, his voice dropping almost to a conspiratorial whisper. "No, the end came when Diamond pays a visit to Lt. Colonel Martel. Suddenly this *norteamericano*, with his CIA connections, knew too much. He posed a grave danger not only to *Operation Carlotta* but also to your half-sister. So, you recommended that we hold him incommunicado, but not just for the purpose of ensuring the secrecy of our military operation. No, it was also to protect your precious Catalina!"

Fidel was glaring at him. A lesser man would have shriveled under his withering look. But not Joaquín. He knew he could say nothing in his own defense, if only because most of what Fidel had alleged about his behavior was in fact largely true. Abrantes, meanwhile, remained absolutely mute. Joaquín knew his boss would not step in and try to save his skin. He waited for the ax to fall.

"I hold you responsible for your half-sister's shameful betrayal," Fidel said, barely able to control his rage. "Besides that, I could have you shot for withholding crucial information from me and trying to pull off something behind my back! Do you know that, Acosta?" He looked away for a moment, knowing full well that Joaquín would not reply to his rhetorical question. Seconds passed before he resumed in a calmer voice. "Nonetheless, I'm going to spare you because you're the only one who can bring Catalina back."

Joaquín could only stare uncomprehendingly at Fidel. He didn't quite understand what the *líder máximo* was expecting him to do.

"Yes, Acosta," Fidel went on as if reading Joaquín's mind. "I want you to go to Madrid on the earliest possible flight, find Catalina, and persuade her to come back. Tell her that I promise that nothing will happen to her if she returns. But if she refuses, she will have proven herself to be an enemy of the revolution. I cannot guarantee her safety then. Do you understand? Now get out of here and see to it that you bring her back!"

***

Joaquín was awakened from his deep slumber at six-thirty by the continuous ringing of the phone. He had been unable to fall asleep until well after three in the morning following his meeting with Fidel. When he finally answered, he could tell immediately from the Cuban operator's voice that it was an overseas call. His heart skipped when he heard Catalina's unmistakable voice even though it sounded terribly distant and undulating as it echoed through the underwater sea cable. He sat up in bed, alert, cautious, fearing that Fidel or Abrantes had already ordered that all his incoming and outgoing phone calls be monitored.

"I'm sorry to be disturbing you so early in the morning, Joaquín, but I wanted to reach you before you left for your office."

"Where are you, Catalina?" he broke in, taking care not to use one of the endearing terms like *niña* or *chica* that he had grown accustomed to employing over the years.

"I'm in Madrid," she replied simply, clearly not willing to be more forthcoming. "I can't tell you any more than that. So, *por favor*, Joaquín, don't waste any more time trying to find out where I am. Just listen to me. All right?"

"I'll hear what you have to say in a moment," he answered brusquely, "but first I must tell you that you must come back, Catalina. You've done a terrible thing—to the revolution, to the Fatherland, to Fidel, and, of course, to me personally."

"I can't and I won't come back!" she said, using the same determined voice that she often used when talking with him. But he wasn't about to be deterred.

"Fidel has told me to tell you that nothing will happen to you if you came back. He promised me that. And I believe him," Joaquín added, though he knew he didn't sound terribly convincing. "So, please, reconsider. Otherwise, I'm going to fly to Spain to find you and bring you back."

"Don't bother to come, Joaquín. You'll be wasting your time. Believe me, I've thought about this a great deal and I've made up my mind that I can't live in Cuba any longer."

"But why?"

"That's why I called you, Joaquín. It's been so long since we last saw each other and talked that you couldn't possibly have suspected that I would ask for political asylum the moment I had the opportunity."

Her voice began to fade in and out, but it had been clear enough when she vouched for the fact that he had known nothing about her planned defection. He was thankful that she was taking care to protect him in the event their talk was being recorded.

"You see," she said, her voice once again coming in loud and clear, "I can no longer believe either in the revolution or in Fidel. No, our noble cause—our quest for social justice, for a new, independent nation—was replaced years ago by Fidel's obsession with power and total control."

"You're talking *tonterías,* Catalina!" he said angrily, fearful that her heresy would forever make it impossible for her to come back.

"No, Joaquín, I see it all clearly now—a consistent pattern that for me began first with Ernesto's death, then David's imprisonment and the dispatch of Cuban soldiers to Angola, and now more soldiers to Ethiopia. They all became victims of Fidel's grand ambitions. And not just them. All their loved ones have also been sacrificed before the altar of power politics and personal ambition."

"No, Catalina, you're wrong," he broke in angrily. "Whatever the sacrifices, they've all been committed on behalf of internationalism. They've all been to advance the noble cause of socialism in Cuba, Latin America, Africa, and the rest of the Third World!"

For several seconds he heard nothing—only a long silence at the other end, interrupted by the intermittent crackling and static of the telephone line.

"I was afraid you'd say something like that," Catalina said. He could not be sure whether her comment was genuine or she said it to protect him. "Anyway, *mi querido* Joaquín, I see that we remain terribly far apart, ideologically, politically, and now geographically. For those reasons I fear I'll never see you again." She paused momentarily. "That makes my heart ache," she continued in a distraught voice, "because I love you. Please take good care of yourself."

Before he could respond, he heard the phone go dead at the other end, followed an instant later by a suspicious clicking on the line. His phone had been tapped.

* * *

Later that morning, as he knew he had to, Joaquín reported the gist of his conversation with Catalina to Abrantes. His boss remained impassive, noncommittal. He only reaffirmed Fidel's order to bring his half-sister back from Madrid as quickly as possible.

"That could turn out to be an almost impossible task, even if I'm able to locate her whereabouts," Joaquín complained.

"That's why Fidel has ordered that you be assisted by *el lobo*— he's already in Madrid and in touch with our embassy."

"You mean the Basque assassin for ETA?" Joaquín cried out with alarm, his face draining of color. "I don't understand. Why does Fidel want *el asesino* in on this? Or is this your idea?" Joaquín looked with suspicion at Abrantes, but his superior remained taciturn and only shrugged his shoulders.

"Look! Even if you won't tell me whose idea this is, I don't see why we can't use our own people from the DGI instead of an assassin from ETA," Joaquín said.

"*Mira, chico,*" Abrantes responded testily. "I don't presume to know everything that goes on in Fidel's mind, but he probably figures that *el lobo* is as familiar with Madrid as you are with Havana. Maybe, too, he'd rather have an outsider with no known links to the Cuban government helping you rather than assign one of our intelligence agents. Or maybe," he added darkly, "it's because he's not sure you're up to the task and he wants to make certain that your half-sister returns to the Fatherland where she belongs." Abrantes caught Joaquín's concerned look. "You know as well as I do," he added grimly, "that Fidel doesn't take kindly to those who abandon the revolution."

***

Although he had wanted to sleep in late on Saturday morning, David woke up early, restless and anxious. He had put in long hours over the past ten days grading papers and painstakingly going over the galley proofs of his book. He had felt a great sense of accomplishment when he returned the corrected proofs to the publisher. It wasn't simply because his book comparing Cuba with other socialist revolutions would soon be published. He had every reason to believe that it would be well received in scholarly circles; two anonymous reviewers had had nothing but praise for the manuscript. But now he was left with little to do over the Christmas vacation. Unaccustomed to having idle time, he wondered whether he should try to get away on a trip somewhere.

As was usually the case when he awoke in the morning, his first thoughts were of Catalina. He had not heard from her in months. Their correspondence had always been intermittent. Most recently it had depended on her being able to smuggle out her letters through the diplomatic pouch of the Spanish Embassy. But then her last letter had warned him that her contact at the embassy was returning to Spain. She would have to find another secure way to get letters to him. Still, it had been an inordinately long time since she had last written. He was becoming increasingly worried.

He remembered the joy he felt the day he received her first letter a year after his return to Los Angeles. Philip Taylor had smuggled it out when he finally managed to take his entire family out of Cuba in April 1977. David had opened the letter with trepidation, not knowing what to expect. But his hopes had soared upon reading the letter:

Mi querido *David,*

Forgive me for not writing sooner, but it was impossible. I had to be extremely careful not to commit another "indiscretion" that would be seen by some as an act against the revolution. But at last I can write with the hope that this letter finds you and that you are well and safe. Most of all, I pray that your bruised and battered soul has had time to heal after what Joaquín and my government did to you.

I write these words in great sorrow. I fear that I shall never see you again. I cannot leave Cuba, and you, my dearest, are forever barred from returning here and to me. Hence, I write with anguish in my heart—anguish because we were cruelly and unexpectedly torn from one another after one brief moment of bliss. Anguish over the long house arrest that you had to endure. Anguish because of what Joaquín did to us.

And now I write to you with yet another pain in my heart because of my growing estrangement from a revolution that I once believed in so fervently. I no longer can. I can accept all the material sacrifices we've had to endure for more than eighteen years. But I cannot accept the sacrifices in human life required to pursue Cuba's so-called internationalist missions in Africa and elsewhere. Nor can I condone the oppressiveness of a political system that stifles the human spirit and turns Cubans against Cubans. I do not know where my journey of rediscovery will end, but take it I must if I am ever to become a whole person again.

However, do not worry for my sake. I am still at MINREX, wearing my own "cara doble" as I have now come to realize most of we Cubans must do to survive. I hope that perhaps someday I can again travel abroad or be posted to one of our embassies in Europe or Latin America. If that happens, then we may be able to see each other again—that is, if you haven't fallen in love with someone else by then. In the meantime, if you want, write to me in care of Philip; he will see if he can send the letter in his government's diplomatic pouch. I send you my love forever.

Your Catalina

He penned a long, loving letter, which he sent through Philip and the Canadian Embassy. Not too long afterward, that avenue was closed to them. Catalina then used someone in the Spanish Embassy, but they were able to exchange only a few more letters before her contact there departed. Her last letter reaffirmed her longing for him as well as her disenchantment with the revolution. That letter had arrived in October. It was now the second week in December.

He was still in bed when the phone rang at seven-thirty.

"Hi, Professor. Hope I didn't wake you up. It's Rudy García here. I'm calling from Langley."

Hearing Rudy's unmistakable voice, David hoped the CIA officer was calling him with news about Catalina. They hadn't talked in several months.

"It's O.K., Rudy. You didn't wake me, but how come you're calling so early on a Saturday morning? Is something up?"

"Yeah, but first tell me, has your lady friend called you?"

"Do you mean Catalina?" David asked cautiously, his hopes beginning to rise.

"Of course. I can tell you don't know the news. It's now been confirmed: Catalina Cruz defected in Madrid two days ago."

"Oh, my God! Are you sure?" David bolted upright in bed, his heart beating rapidly.

"Absolutely. I was hoping she might've called you by now, but I guess she hasn't. Right?" David's mind was racing with the news and assessing all its implications. "Look, David," Rudy went on, his tone now sharp, business-like. "If she calls you, try to find out where she's hiding out. If she can't tell you over the phone, then see if you can at least arrange a meeting place in the next day or two. In any case, call me—but not at my office since I'll be leaving soon. Here's my unlisted home number. Are you ready?"

Hurriedly reaching for a pencil and paper, David hardly had time to think about what the CIA officer had in mind.

"Now, listen," Rudy said. "Whether or not Catalina calls, you've got to catch the first flight to Madrid. I'll meet you there. You're going to need my help, even if she calls you in L.A. and tells you where she's hiding out."

"I don't quite understand, Rudy," David interjected. "Why would I need your help if she calls and tells me where she is?"

"Trust me, David, you *are* going to need my help. So once you know your travel arrangements and where you'll be staying in Madrid, call me at home with the information. If I'm not there, just leave a message on my answering machine. That way I can meet you in Madrid after you arrive."

"Why are you doing this, Rudy?"

There was a momentary silence at the other end before Rudy spoke again.

"Just say I owe you one for all the shit you put up with back in Havana. I'll tell you more after we meet up. In the meantime, be sure to call me if she tries to reach you. So long and good luck, David."

***

For a while, David didn't dare tie up his phone to make his travel arrangements for fear Catalina would be trying to reach him. But after an hour of fruitless waiting, he picked up the phone and, working as fast as he could, booked himself on a red-eye to Miami and then on Iberia's morning flight to Madrid. Next, he made an overseas call to the Hotel Emperador, where he reserved a room. Then he left all the information on Rudy's answering machine. He had been on the phone for less than forty minutes.

He made himself coffee and breakfast, then packed. By mid-afternoon, Catalina still hadn't called. When the phone finally rang, he grabbed the receiver before the second ring.

"Hello," he said, barely able to control the excitement in his voice.

"Is that you, David?" Philip Taylor inquired.

"Philip? Why are you calling me? Have you heard anything from Catalina?"

"Slow down, lover boy," Philip said kiddingly. "No, I haven't heard from Catalina, but I just learned that she defected in Madrid a couple of days ago. Apparently you already know that. Right?"

"Yes. I heard about it early this morning. When you called I thought it might be her. Look, Philip, I'm sorry but I really can't talk much longer in case she's trying to reach me. I'm already set to go to Madrid tonight to find her. I'm sorry for being so terse, but I've got to get off the phone."

"Hey, no problem. I understand. But just in case she calls me, I'll tell her that you're going to Madrid. Do you already know where you're staying?"

"Hotel Emperador."

"O.K. Good luck."

"Thanks. I'll need it."

David could only hope that he would be as fortunate as Philip

Taylor had been when the Canadian expatriate finally managed to take his wife and their two sons to Toronto. They had left at the beginning of April, some six months before a new Cuban expeditionary force had been dispatched to fight in the Ogaden that following November. Had their departure from Cuba been delayed, Elián, the older of the two boys, most certainly would've had to report for compulsory military service. Even if the teenager hadn't been sent to the Horn of Africa, the rest of his family would have had to remain in Havana until his tour of duty was completed.

Evening came and went without a call from Catalina. With each passing hour, David became more concerned. Had something happened? Had Cuban intelligence found her? Were they holding her against her will? Had she changed her mind about him? He wouldn't know the answers until he found her. At ten o'clock, thinking she might call after he left, he changed the outgoing message on his answering machine to tell her when he would be arriving in Madrid and where he would be staying. Then he took a cab to LAX for the first leg of his flight to Spain.

* * *

It was already dark when David arrived at his hotel, jet-lagged from his long flight, but too wrought up to sleep. He took a quick shower, shaved, and lay down on the bed to await Rudy's call. He had just begun to doze off when the phone rang.

"Meet me on the sidewalk at the hotel entrance in fifteen minutes," Rudy said tersely. "I'll be driving a light blue Ford sedan. I know where she is."

David finished dressing and ran a quick comb through his hair. Seeing himself in the mirror, he wondered whether Catalina would notice his graying temples and salt-and-pepper beard, along with the fine lines that had now begun to encircle his eyes. But he didn't have time to dwell on how much older he looked. The phone was ringing again.

"Hello?" he answered cautiously.

"David?"

"Catalina?" he cried out. "You got my message? Are you downstairs?"

"No," she answered quickly. "I'm at the house of some friends. I couldn't reach you at your house; I had incorrectly copied your number. But I've found you at last, *mi querido*, thanks to Philip Taylor. He told me where you were staying."

"Good old Philip! But now I'll come and get you. Just give me your address. I've got a friend who's waiting for me downstairs with his car. God, Catalina." Tears of joy began to well up in his eyes. "It's been so long."

"I know," she replied, her voice choked with emotion.

Minutes later, armed with her address, he rushed out of the hotel lobby and onto the Gran Vía where he spotted the blue Ford, with Rudy at the wheel, already at curbside. Leaping into the front seat, he informed Rudy of Catalina's call to tell him where she was. Rudy nodded his agreement upon seeing the address. Soon they were weaving their way through Madrid's Sunday night traffic.

"How did you find out where she's hiding?" David inquired.

"It took some doing," Rudy replied. "I don't know whether she told you, but she's staying at a house belonging to a Spanish diplomat."

"Really? I would think that might create some problems for the Spanish government."

"Yeah. I don't think the government is too happy about it. Anyway, the story is that she struck up a friendship with Ambassador Fernández and his wife when he was First-Secretary at the Spanish Embassy in Havana. She became particularly close to the wife, so the first thing she did was to call her when she defected. It was the wife who took her in. There was nothing the Ambassador could do about it. He was confronted with a *fait accompli*."

"She's so lucky the way it turned out."

"You can say that again. Of course, the Spanish government wants to keep her whereabouts under wraps. It doesn't want to have any problems with the Cubans. But I have to hand it to our embassy people. They kept digging until they finally learned where she's at."

"Well, I appreciate all you've done, Rudy. But why are you going to all this trouble to help me out? I mean, I never thought of you as being much of a romantic."

Rudy chuckled, "Oh, don't be too sure about that. But anyway, like I once told you, I felt badly over your house arrest in Havana. And now I feel even more responsible because I know who framed you."

"I think you'd better fill me in," David said.

Rudy glanced at David and then quickly briefed him on how Lawton Armstrong had set him up. As David listened to Rudy's tale of intrigue gone afoul, all the old, smoldering anger rose to the surface again, only this time it was directed at Armstrong.

"So, after you got the goods on him, what happened? Is the asshole behind bars?" David asked.

"No," Rudy replied grimly. "He's dead. Just when the Inspector General's office was about to start its formal inquiry, Lawton killed himself while driving one night. He was drunk and ran into a tree. As far as I'm concerned, the bastard got what he deserved."

But David no longer was interested in Armstrong. He could only think about Catalina.

"I think you also should know that I have another reason for being here," Rudy suddenly announced, interrupting David's thoughts.

"What's that?"

"We've learned that your friend, Joaquín Acosta, has come to Madrid to take Catalina back to Cuba. I want to meet the guy. Maybe I can turn him so that he'll work for us."

"Oh, shit!" David cried out.

*　*　*

Having left her modest wardrobe in the hotel when she defected, Catalina put on the clothes the Ambassador's wife had lent her, after which she applied a little lipstick and brushed her hair. Her streak of feminine vanity had not deserted her; she very much wanted to look good for David. More than three years had passed since she last saw him. Though she was still a striking woman, the mirror told her she wasn't quite the stunning beauty she once was. The passage of years, coupled with the tragedies in her life, had left her face drawn, her green eyes less vivid, and her raven hair less lustrous. She hoped David wouldn't notice—or, if he did, that he wouldn't care because of his love for her. And she was confident of his love. Not only had he repeatedly affirmed it in the four letters he had written, but also it was further attested to by his coming to Madrid in search of her.

She was glad that her hosts were out for the evening. Better yet, the housekeeper and cook had the day off and they wouldn't return until the next morning. She wondered about the friend David was bringing with him. She hoped he wouldn't be staying too long. As it was, she and David were likely to have but a short time together before the Ambassador and his wife returned.

She heard the buzzer go off and rushed downstairs to open the front door.

***

David and Rudy located the handsome two-story house on Antonio Rodríguez Villa without trouble. Save for a few parked cars, the darkened street was empty. The upstairs lights were on in the house; a few moments later, additional lights were turned on downstairs. Before Rudy could say anything, David was out of the car and had run up the front steps to push the buzzer at the front door. Nothing happened. He buzzed again. By this time Rudy was at his side. Finally, the intercom clicked on.

"*¿Quién es?*"

"It's me, Catalina," David exclaimed impatiently, waiting for her to unlock the heavy wooden door. Seconds passed without anything happening. The only sound was a muffled movement from inside the house. David and Rudy exchanged glances. Were the Ambassador and his wife scurrying upstairs to allow them privacy?

At last, Catalina unlocked the door that opened into the darkened vestibule. So overjoyed was he at seeing her that David didn't notice the apprehensive, almost frightened expression on her face, much less suspect that something might be amiss.

"Come in," she said stiffly.

He quickly entered the vestibule, followed by Rudy. Turning to embrace Catalina, he froze when he saw Joaquín Acosta lurking in the shadows behind the door.

"What the hell?" David exclaimed. He stole a glance at Rudy to see if he had noted Joaquín's presence. But Rudy's eyes were fastened on the far end of the vestibule—on a stranger holding a Walther PPK semiautomatic pistol fitted with a silencer.

***

"Well, Professor David Diamond, so we meet again after all," Joaquín declared as if greeting an old friend. "We've been expecting you, though I didn't anticipate you would arrive here so soon."

"I'm sorry, David," Catalina cried out. "I thought it was you when I first heard the buzzer and opened the door."

"You don't have to apologize to him, *niña*. Your lover here led us to you."

"That's bullshit, Joaquín!"

"No, my friend. You conveniently left a message on your answering machine saying that you were going to Madrid and would be staying at the Emperador. So all we had to do was intercept Catalina's call to your room and wait for her to tell you where she was hiding." Joaquín smiled triumphantly. "After that it was simply a matter of getting here first."

"I'm sorry, Catalina," David said, his hungry eyes devouring the sight of her. "I made a stupid mistake. But when you didn't call, I decided I'd better let you know I was coming."

"Who's your friend, here?" Joaquín suddenly demanded to know, motioning toward Rudy.

Taking his gaze off *el lobo* and the gun, Rudy turned to Joaquín, allowing the latter to see his face more fully in the faint light of the vestibule.

"Though we haven't actually met," Rudy said evenly, "we do know each other, Captain Acosta. We're both in the same business. You probably have my picture on file."

"Ah, ha!" Joaquín exclaimed, his eyes suddenly bright with recognition. "So at last I get to meet the famous Rudy García." He turned to Catalina. "Do you know who your lover's friend is, Catalina?" Catalina was silent.

"No, of course you don't. Well, let me tell you. *Señor* García is in charge of the CIA's spy activities in Cuba. In fact, he's the man who recruited your precious *norteamericano* here to collect sensitive information on our government. And collect he did." Joaquín paused. He seemed to be relishing the moment. "You see, Catalina, right after spending the night with you, your lover found out about *Operation Carlotta*. That's why I had no alternative but to pick him up immediately and commit him to house arrest. So now, do you finally understand why I had to protect the revolution? That I wasn't just trying to protect you from your lover?"

Catalina appeared crestfallen as she stared at Joaquín. For his part, not understanding what Joaquín had been saying in English, *el lobo* simply kept his gun leveled at Rudy, all the while fingering its trigger, his lips drawn cruelly.

"Joaquín," David said heatedly. "You know damn well that I wasn't spying on your government, that I turned Rudy down. Tell him, Rudy!" he added, turning to the CIA officer, who had been keeping the gunman in his sights.

Rudy shifted his gaze to the MININT officer. "David refused to work with us. In fact, he practically ran away from me when I broached the subject. The photos your agent took of us should've shown you that," Rudy added pointedly. Catalina was now looking at him intently, keenly attuned to his story. "What I didn't know at the time was that David had been set up by one of our own people to be the fall guy in his private little game of intrigue. It was Lawton Armstrong—you've heard of him, I'm sure. As I found out later, Armstrong notified your agent where I would be meeting David so that he could take pictures of us. You see, Armstrong wanted you to believe that David was working for us."

"Excuse me," Joaquín interrupted. "But why would Armstrong want to do that?"

"The son-of-a-bitch wanted to create an incident that would prevent any reconciliation between your government and mine," Rudy replied with bitterness. Joaquín looked uneasy. "You know damn well what I'm saying is true, Joaquín." He had deliberately called the MININT officer by his first name, a small gesture by which to reach out and try to bring him around.

Rudy now turned to the woman. It was obvious why Diamond was infatuated with her. She had a beautiful, classic face, made all the more striking by her green eyes and long, black hair.

"And that's why I'm here helping David," he said, directing his comment to Catalina. "I felt I was partly to blame for his arrest in Cuba. I wanted to make it up to him."

Catalina looked in bewilderment first at Rudy, then at Joaquín, and finally at David, searching their faces for clues to the veracity of Rudy's account and, with it, David's innocence. At last she reached for David's hand. Looking intently at her half-brother, she announced her verdict.

"I'm sorry, Joaquín," she said firmly, "but I have to believe Mr. García. Everything he's said coincides with what David told me the night before he was arrested. I believe him and I believe David." She fastened her eyes on her half-brother and said, "I won't be tricked into going back to Cuba."

Joaquín shook his head in reproach. A moment later he ordered them all out of the vestibule and into the adjoining living room.

***

They had been in the cavernous room for some time, surrounded by fine furniture and some exquisite pieces of Spanish modern artwork on the walls. But nobody noticed. They were at an impasse. Nearly thirty minutes of arguing and cajoling on Joaquín's part had failed to shake Catalina's determination not to return to Cuba. Except for him, she told her half-brother, there was nothing left for her to go back to. She no longer could believe in her government, in Fidel, in the revolution. And no matter what assurances Fidel had given, she feared something would happen to her if she returned. Deep down, Joaquín feared that she could be right.

Making matters worse for Joaquín was her warning that the owners of the house—an Ambassador and his wife as he was surprised to learn—would be returning at any moment. They had gone to an evening function, she informed him, and it was already past ten o'clock. That news alarmed Joaquín. He had been advised at the Cuban Embassy not to take a weapon with him in case he was stopped by Spanish authorities. In the event of an emergency, any need for a gun would be met by the Basque. But now, since Joaquín was unarmed, he might not be able to prevent *el lobo* from killing the Spanish diplomat—and most likely the others as well. Fortunately, the Basque was still in the dark. Joaquín had taken the precaution of making sure they all spoke in English, which *el lobo* did not understand.

"Give it up, Joaquín, before things get out of control," Rudy announced impatiently. "You know Catalina won't go back with you. In the meantime, there's going to be hell to pay when Ambassador Fernández returns and finds you here. And, to top it all off, your gun-toting partner has an itchy trigger-finger. I have the distinct feeling that he's got a mind of his own. He's not going to listen to you."

Joaquín had to admit that Rudy García was right. But he didn't know how he could get out of his terrible predicament—a predicament created by Fidel when he ordered him to bring back his half-sister with the help of *el lobo*. For all he knew, the ETA assassin had been given separate, secret orders to seize Catalina by force or even kill her if he, Joaquín, couldn't persuade her to return. And if the Ambassador and his wife were killed as well, a major international ruckus would ensue, something that Fidel neither had anticipated nor would want to happen.

***

Rudy, David, and Catalina had been made to stand in a loose semicircle facing *el lobo* and Joaquín. Rudy was closest to the gunman, who kept his Walther semiautomatic pistol trained on him. Rudy suspected that the MININT Captain was unarmed. It didn't much matter. All things considered, he would be awfully lucky if he could take down the gunman before the man got a shot off.

Rudy sized up the thin, scruffy-looking gunman. By his looks and accent, it was obvious that he was neither Cuban nor Spanish. He looked vaguely familiar. Then, from the deep recesses of his memory, Rudy recalled a series of photographs in one of the classified reports he had received on European and Middle Eastern terrorists going in and out of Cuba.

"That's who the guy is!" Rudy said to himself. He was one of ETA's shooters wanted for the assassination of several Spanish officials. Suddenly Rudy understood why Joaquín insisted on speaking in English and not Spanish. *"He wants to keep the guy clueless as long as possible because he knows that he can't control him. Holy shit! We're in even bigger trouble than I thought!"*

Rudy felt perspiration creep down the back of his neck. Now he understood why Joaquín had insisted that they remain standing in a semicircle instead of ordering them to sit down. With Rudy and David strategically placed, the assassin might not be able to get off more than one shot before one of them jumped him. Rudy's glance flickered from the gunman to the MININT officer. He caught Joaquín's eye. In that instant he knew he had read the situation correctly—he had been right about what Joaquín hoped would happen.

"¿Qué dice la mujer?" the gunman suddenly inquired of Joaquín. The Basque's patience had finally run out. *"¿Es que no quiere regresar a Cuba contigo?"*

The moment both Rudy and Joaquín had been dreading had arrived. The ETA man had guessed that Catalina was not going back to Cuba. Rudy waited for Joaquín to make the first move, knowing that the MININT officer would have to distract the gunman, otherwise the ETA assassin would shoot Catalina first and then Rudy.

"Let's not become impatient, *chico*," Joaquín answered in Spanish as he tried to stall for time. "She's acting like a lot of temperamental women do when they can't make up their minds. But I've always been able to reason with her. It just takes time."

"No!" the gunman roared. He swung his gun toward Catalina.

***

Even before the tension had escalated and *el lobo* had turned, David knew that Catalina would be shot, and probably the rest of them as well, unless somehow Joaquín stopped the gunman. But already Joaquín did not appear to be in control. Maybe he didn't have a weapon of his own. In any case, the gunman apparently couldn't understand what Catalina was saying, but he was becoming visibly more agitated by the unmistakable tone of defiance in her voice. The man's sinister, almost wild eyes were nervously shifting back and forth between Rudy and her. David read the concern in Rudy's face. Then, as he watched, unnoticed by the gunman, Rudy shifted his weight ever so slightly forward, almost imperceptibly, onto the balls of his feet. He was coiled to strike.

David knew what he had to do. It was what Ernesto would have done had he been alive. What Joaquín would do. He was not in the least frightened, unlike when Lieutenant Torres had knocked him down and stood looming over him. Fear had been near to choking him then. Yet now, even though he was in far more danger, he felt prepared—most of all, determined to do whatever he could to not lose Catalina again. Though he could feel the rush of adrenaline, he was surprisingly calm.

He waited, watching, poised to move. When the gunman abruptly turned his pistol on Catalina, he saw Rudy spring forward, but it was clear that the CIA officer would not reach him before he fired.

***

For Catalina, it was like viewing a movie sequence shot in slow motion. She watched in horror as the gunman, only a few paces from her, suddenly trained his gun on her. Rudy García sprang in a desperate attempt to reach *el lobo* before he pulled the trigger, but she knew Rudy would be too late. Then, just before the gunman fired, David bounded in front of her, almost knocking her down. The bullet meant for her smashed into him, spinning him halfway around as he cried out. The deflected bullet had missed her head only by inches, though she wouldn't realize that until later. It took all of her strength to stay on her feet, bracing herself against the dead weight of David's falling body.

She watched as the assassin turned immediately to shoot Rudy, who was hurtling toward him. Just before he pulled the trigger again, Joaquín sprang on him from behind, grabbing his shooting arm and forcing the gun upward. The Walther went off with a muffled pop, the shot going wild. A split second later, Rudy seized the gunman's shooting wrist with his left hand, keeping the gun pointed upward. Then he uncoiled the full force of his powerful body behind his free right hand, jamming the heel of his open palm upward into the assassin's nose. *El lobo* emitted a terrible scream as the splintered fragments of nasal bones penetrated deep into his brain. He crumpled to the floor, his body twitching convulsively as he lay dying.

Catalina gasped at the sight of blood splattered everywhere—on the dead man, all over Rudy and Joaquín, and on her hosts' pale Oriental rug and hardwood floor. For a fleeting instant she felt faint but quickly recovered. David hadn't lost consciousness, but he lay slumped on the floor. She could see that he was losing blood from the bullet wound in his shoulder. Kneeling, she cradled his head, assuring him that he would be fine, telling him that she loved him. She feared he was on the verge of going into shock. He mustered a weak smile, joking in a faint voice that he hoped he wouldn't have to get shot each time for her to say those words.

"*No seas tonto,*" she replied with tears in her eyes. She sent Rudy to get towels from the downstairs bathroom as her half-brother knelt at her side to take a better look at David's wound.

"You'll be all right, David," Joaquín said, with a reassuring nod to Catalina. "It looks like the bullet went clean through your shoulder. Lucky for you it wasn't a larger caliber." He applied his handkerchief to the wound. "But you did a brave thing, *amigo*, jumping in front of her like that. It saved her life," he added in a voice heavy with emotion.

"Did you know he planned to kill me?" Catalina asked, looking at Joaquín accusingly.

"*Niña*, how could you even think that? I was ordered by Fidel to fetch you back, not to kill you."

"Then why did you bring that horrible man with his gun? You must have known . . . "

"Yes, I suspected something was up," Joaquín admitted. "But I couldn't do anything about it. Abrantes informed me at the last minute about *el lobo*, here." He nodded toward the body lying on the floor. "He was to meet me here in Madrid, supposedly to ensure the success of the mission. I really don't know whether it was Abrantes' or Fidel's idea."

"It had to be Fidel's!" Catalina exclaimed vehemently. "At the very least, he had to give Abrantes the go-ahead. You know as well as I do that no one does anything in Cuba without Fidel's permission."

***

Rudy was at her side with towels in hand. He and Joaquín pulled David up to a sitting position so that they could stanch the blood flowing from the entry and exit sides of his wound. Then they braced him against the wall so that he remained sitting up. Color began to return slowly to his face.

"Well, I'll be damned," David declared in a surprisingly strong voice as he eyed the two men. "I never expected to see the CIA and Cuban State Security working together!"

Rudy and Catalina laughed at his wisecrack. Joaquín only smiled uncomfortably.

"Stay with us, Joaquín," Catalina suddenly proposed, laying her hand on his arm. "You can't go back to Cuba after what's happened here tonight."

"No, *niña*, you know that's impossible." Joaquín shook his head. "I must go back. You know I can never betray the revolution." He was aware that his words inferred her betrayal.

"*¡No seas tonto*, Joaquín!" she exclaimed. "Don't you see that the revolution is dead? It was dead even before Ernesto died. Except none of us would admit it back then. Six years ago we could still hope that our beautiful dream would someday, somehow, become reality. But no. The reality is that the revolution died years ago, just like Ernesto!"

She regarded him with sadness in her eyes, knowing full well that what she said was painful to him, especially to hear it from her.

"Believe me," she went on sympathetically, "it was hard for me to admit what was happening to our beloved Cuba over these past several years. But in the end I couldn't remain blind to what Fidel was doing and has done. Now it's time for you to open your eyes, too, to see that he long ago ceased being the 'Fidel' who promised us a new, better Cuba, and that instead he's become 'Castro' the *caudillo*."

Seeing that Joaquín was unmoved by her words, that his eyes were burning with resolve, she withdrew her hand from his sleeve. Her eyes had turned a more vivid green; anger smoldered in their depths. A moment before her voice had been soft, entreating, but no longer. David and Rudy both watched in fascination at the change in her, wondering how Joaquín would respond.

"Don't you see?" Catalina cried with renewed vehemence, annoyed at his stubbornness. "After all the tyranny and venality we experienced in the past, we now have two dictatorships—one Fidel, the other the Communist Party. And you, Joaquín, you know deep in your heart that I'm right—that Cuba deserves better."

"I don't care what you say, what you believe now," Joaquín answered, unmoved. "I will not change my mind. I can't. I remain a revolutionary no matter what."

He locked eyes with her for a long moment, then reverting to the role of the MININT Captain in charge, he directed her to phone for an ambulance.

* * *

As Catalina disappeared into another room to make the phone call, Rudy took the opportunity to draw Joaquín aside.

"I think you know you're in deep trouble right now," Rudy said quietly. Joaquín nodded in agreement. "Besides an ambulance, we're going to have to call the police. That means there'll be lots of questions. So, I've got a proposition for you."

"Go ahead," the MININT Captain replied, eyeing Rudy suspiciously.

"I can get you out of this mess if you'll come over to our side."

Joaquín drew back as if Rudy had struck him a physical blow. "Forget it, Rudy García," he replied. "Don't try to turn me," he added with contempt. "Like I told Catalina, I wouldn't betray the revolution even if I knew that Fidel planned to have me shot when I got back. So cease and desist. You are wasting your time."

"All right." Rudy shrugged. "Have it your way."

***

Joaquín turned away, but Rudy, having second thoughts, was suddenly at his back.

"You know damn well you've got to get out of here before the ambulance and police arrive," he declared. "The Ambassador and his wife will be coming back any minute, too."

"Look, it's obvious that I should leave as soon as possible," Joaquín retorted sarcastically. "But there's still a problem to be solved. What will the three of you tell the police, the Ambassador, about what's happened here tonight?"

"A good question," Rudy replied, sizing up his opponent. "You and I are professionals, and we both are trained to tidy up loose details. So here's how I propose we can do it: If you leave now, before anyone arrives, no one in the Spanish government will ever know you were here. That way, you and your government will be in the clear. And that should satisfy Fidel and hopefully get you off the hook for not having returned with Catalina."

Joaquín nodded in tacit agreement. "That's fine, but what will you tell the police?" he asked.

"That's easy. We'll just tell them that your gunman broke into the house with the intention of killing the Ambassador—which makes sense since the guy is a wanted ETA assassin. Then David and I struggled with him and David got shot. But I was able to kill the bastard." Pausing, he fixed Joaquín with a steady look. "It's virtually foolproof," he added.

"It's a good plan," Joaquín agreed.

Striding over to Catalina, who was on her knees at David's side, Joaquín took her by the hand and drew her to her feet. "I'm afraid this is good-bye, *niña*," he said in a husky voice. "Maybe this time forever." He stopped to rein in his emotions. "First Ernesto died and now you'll be gone," he said, shaking his head. "I shall miss you, *chica*." He planted a kiss on her wet cheek. They embraced for several seconds.

"As for you," Joaquín said, looking down at David as he extended his hand. "I'm sorry about the bullet. And I must also confess that I misjudged you back in Cuba. You're a good man. Even if you are a *norteamericano*," he added with a wink. "I know you'll take good care of Catalina."

"You bet I will. Good-bye, Joaquín."

"After what's happened tonight," Joaquín remarked, addressing both Catalina and David, "you can both rest assured that the Cuban government won't come after you again. I'll make certain of that. Now I've got to get out of here. Rudy will explain everything."

"Good-bye, Joaquín," Catalina whispered, tears in her eyes. "I will pray that nothing happens to you on your return to Cuba. You know Fidel doesn't like to lose."

"Don't worry, *niña,* I can handle Fidel."

***

Rudy accompanied the MININT officer to the front door.

"Before you go, I've got to ask you a question."

"What's that?"

"You saved my life a little while ago. Why? That guy would have shot me if you hadn't jumped him."

"Well, for one thing, I knew that he would try to kill Catalina again," Joaquín said. "Besides, I also 'owed you one,' as they say in your country."

"You owed me one? How so?"

Joaquín stopped at the front door and turned to the CIA officer. "Do you remember when you were stationed in Managua?" he asked, in a somber tone. "You interrogated a Cuban intelligence officer captured by the Somocistas. Do you remember Ernesto Padilla?"

"Of course."

"Well, Ernesto Padilla was Catalina's fiancé and my dearest friend. So there was no way I was going to let *el lobo* kill you after what you did to those three guardsmen in Managua, those animals, who tortured him to death. No." For the first time all evening, Joaquín smiled. "You were our avenging angel. You were our only consolation that those bastards got what they deserved." He stopped abruptly and averted his gaze for a moment as if he were pondering a thought.

Rudy waited for Joaquín to go on, hoping that he might be reconsidering his offer to become a double-agent, but when the MININT Captain looked again at Rudy, the smile was gone from his face.

"I've now squared accounts with you," Joaquín said, his shoulders squared, his head held high. "So we're back to zero, my friend."

"What do you mean by that?"

"Simply that we're both free now to resume our previous roles as mortal adversaries," he replied, a knowing grin curling his lips.

"I guess you're right," Rudy answered, smiling. "But even so, I hope the Gods will look kindly on you when you return home, Joaquín. You'll need them, you know. You're going to have a hell of a lot of explaining to do—even more than I will when I get back to Langley. Believe me, your job will be ten times tougher than mine because you're going to have to deal with Fidel."

Author's Note

As a scholar and policy analyst, I have written scores of books, monographs, and articles on Cuba for over thirty-five years. I visited the island three times—in 1959, 1967, and 1968—before the government of Fidel Castro made me persona non grata and denied me further visas. My background and experiences as an observer of the Cuban scene are reflected in this work of fiction.

Because this is a novel, most of its principal characters—Joaquín Acosta, Lawton Armstrong, Catalina Cruz, David Diamond, Manuel Domínguez, Rudy García, Gustavo Durán, Sheila Frankel, Antonio Martel, José Torres, Don Smith, and Peter Vargas—are fictionalized composites of people I have known at one time or another in this country or Cuba. Philip Taylor, Marina Alvarez, and *los muchachos* (Chucho, Roberto, and Tomás) are pseudonyms for persons I had dealings with in Cuba in 1967 and 1968. Although I did not meet Fidel Castro on those trips, I've studied his political personality closely for years. I had two meetings with Carlos Rafael Rodríguez in his office in 1967 and 1968, and later met his assistant, Carlos Salsamendi, at conferences in Germany and Spain in 1983 and 1986. Rodríguez died in 1997.

The historical setting of the novel is true: The Castro brothers did hold several meetings with Aleksandr Alekseev in 1959. A CIA officer did try to find an American academic going to Cuba to test whether the Cuban probes in 1974 were genuine. Washington and Havana did hold secret talks in 1974–75. According to a defector, Division Commander Raúl Díaz Argüelles did lead a reconnaissance and planning team to Angola in early 1975. Cuba did mount a large-scale intervention in Angola in 1975–76. Division Commander Díaz Argüelles did die because of a mine explosion. And Cuba did deploy another 12,000 troops to Ethiopia in late 1977.

I personally experienced several situations that I've described in this novel during my 1967 or 1968 visits to Cuba. Among them were the detour into *El Fanguito*, Marina's scolding of the driver because of the incident, the sumptuous luncheon that local officials hosted for David, Marina's attempt to exclude the driver from the lunch, David's late-night discussion in the car with Chucho, Tomás, and Roberto, the party that all four attended, Roberto's subsequent confession to David the last night they were together, and the MINREX chauffer's surprise revelation to Professor Vargas. Still, I've cut most of the plot and related scenes from an imaginary cloth as is true of any work of fiction.